"Readers looking for a good historical mystery/romance or a historical with a little more kink will enjoy *The Duke Who Knew Too Much*." -*Smart Bitches, Trashy Books*

"This was an incredibly steamy, emotional and all consuming read that I could read again and again." -Candace, *Goodreads* on *Regarding the Duke*

"I've now read each of Grace Callaway's books and loved them—which is exceptional. Gabriel and Thea from this book were two of the best characters I read this year. Both had their difficulties and it was charming to see how they overcame them together, even though it wasn't always easy for them. This is my favorite book of 2015." -*Romantic Historical Reviews* on *M is for Marquess*

"I LOVED this book! It took me back to a Johanna Lindsey novel. What a fantastic idea to turn the Regency genre on its head and do an 'underworld' take on it. Talk about original!" -Judge on *The Duke Identity*, winner of the Daphne du Maurier Award for Excellence in Mystery & Suspense

"I'm still ugly crying AF!! I am so in love with Adam and Gabby. This was the perfect blend of romance, steamy sex, and intrigue…My heart hurt for all the things Adam went through…and I cheered for Gabby as she emerged from her safe shell." -*Estela Reads Romance* on *Regarding the Duke*

"Callaway is a talented writer and as skilled at creating a vivid sense of the Regency period as she is at writing some of the best, most sensual love scenes I've read in a long while. For readers who crave sexy, exciting Regency romance with a fresh plot and intriguing characters, I would highly recommend *Her Protector's Pleasure*." -*Night Owl Reviews*

"Wick and Bea bring out the best in each other and I love how their relationship progressed in an organic way. Their love story is both incredibly steamy and heartfelt (the best of both worlds!)...I really enjoyed the mystery arc, which actually took a surprising turn that I didn't see coming. Unlike most historical romances that I read this year, Callaway crafts an interesting and engaging mystery that actually holds my interest." -*Romance Library* on *The Duke Redemption*

"Grace Callaway's book is the first in her 'Heart of Enquiry' series, and this excellent brew of romance and intrigue and emotion is also *Stevereads* best Romance novel of 2015."-*The Duke Who Knew Too Much* named the #1 Best Romance of 2015 by *Stevereads*

"Wow! Five star fairy tale of a book! Best book of the series. That's saying something because these books are always fantastic. This book checked off so many boxes on my catnip list: grumpy, brooding hero; poor, but sweet heroine; mystery to solve (something that makes Grace's books standout from the rest); HOT!!" -Nancy, *Goodreads* on *The Return of the Duke*

"Grace Callaway writes the way Loretta Chase would if she got kind of dark and VERY naughty." –Nicole, *Goodreads*

ALSO BY GRACE CALLAWAY

LADY CHARLOTTE'S SOCIETY OF ANGELS

Olivia and the Masked Duke (Spring 2021)

GAME OF DUKES

The Duke Identity

Enter the Duke

Regarding the Duke

The Duke Redemption

The Return of the Duke

HEART OF ENQUIRY

The Widow Vanishes (Prequel Novella)

The Duke Who Knew Too Much

M is for Marquess

The Lady Who Came in from the Cold

The Viscount Always Knocks Twice

Never Say Never to an Earl

The Gentleman Who Loved Me

MAYHEM IN MAYFAIR

Her Husband's Harlot

Her Wanton Wager

Her Protector's Pleasure

Her Prodigal Passion

Abigail Jones

The Return of the Duke © Grace Callaway, 2020.

Print ISBN: 978-1-939537-46-1

All rights reserved. Without limiting the rights under copyright reserved above, no part of this publication may be reproduced, stored in or introduced into a retrieval system, or transmitted, in any form, or by any means (electronic, mechanical, photocopying, recording, or otherwise) without the prior written permission of the copyright owner.

This is a work of fiction. Names, characters, places, brands, media, and incidents are either the product of the author's imagination or are used fictitiously.

∼

Cover Design Credit: Erin Cameron-Hill/ EDH Graphics

Cover Image Credit: Period Images

The Return of the Duke

Game of Dukes

Grace Callaway

If you have ever wondered if you are special...
you are.

PROLOGUE

DARKNESS FELL AS FANCY SHERIDAN WALKED, LOST IN HER thoughts. The daughter of a travelling tinker, she made her home on the open road. At present, the forest silver-plated by the moon was her room, the canopy of stars her ceiling, and the gravel-strewn path her carpet. She breathed in the crisp night air and tried to let go of her churning tension.

As part of a tinkering family, she was used to doing odd jobs to make ends meet. She'd inherited a plethora of skills from her da and dear departed ma. Tonight, she had found work in the kitchens of the village inn, and while scrubbing pots wasn't her favorite pastime, she would have done the task with her usual verve...if the cook hadn't accosted her.

Fancy, my arse. I know your kind. Tinkers ain't no be'er than gypsies. The cook had cornered her in the larder, his greasy spittle scalding her cheek. *Meet me behind the inn after you're done wif the pots, and if you give me a nice ride up Cupid's alley, then I'll give you the lefto'er mutton to feed your beggarly kin.*

She swiped a hand over her burning cheek, kicking up dust with her worn half-boots. How she *wished* she could have thought of some scathing retort to put him in his place. Instead, she'd been paralyzed by his menacing nearness and insulting offer.

Ma's voice had rung in her head. *Keep your 'ead down around settled folk, me girl. If there's trouble, wait for an opportunity—and run.*

Fancy had fled the instant she'd collected her meager pay from the innkeep. Her brother Godfrey, who'd also found work at the inn, was supposed to walk back with her to the cottage, but he got caught up dallying with one of the barmaids. Fancy had decided to journey back alone rather than wait for him and risk another encounter with the cook.

Humiliation and anger flared even though she was no stranger to this sort of treatment. At two-and-twenty, she had dealt with her share of blackguards who assumed she was easy pickings because she belonged to a travelling clan. Like Romany nomads, tinkers were oft treated with suspicion and hostility by settled folk. She'd developed a thick skin when it came to society's prejudices, yet this latest degradation pierced her to the quick.

You know why it 'urts. Her throat swelled. *Because it's a reminder o' your station in life. And why you'll ne'er be good enough for the Duke o' Knighton.*

Reaching into the pocket of her patched skirts, Fancy closed her fingers around the button she kept as close as a secret. She knew it by touch: the carved ridges of the crest, the smooth circumference, the heft of precious metal. Like its owner, the button was the genuine article...and far too fine for the likes of her.

As she trudged along the wooded path, she couldn't get Severin Knight, the Duke of Knighton, out of her head. She saw his rough-hewn handsomeness, his cool grey gaze. His eyes reminded her of the sky during a storm, hazy and opaque, with flashes of emotion that jolted her with tingly awareness. He was tall, muscular, and breathtakingly elegant, a study in refinement from the top of his dark head to the champagne shine of his boots.

More importantly, Knighton was a true nobleman, in action as well as in name. One could tell a lot about a man by how he treated others and, despite their differences in rank, His Grace treated her with courtesy and respect. His attention caused her pulse to race and her knees to wobble like a custard tart fresh out of the oven.

Unfortunately, Fancy didn't have the same effect on him. While he was polite, he was here on a single-minded quest. He'd arrived five days ago to court her bosom chum, Bea.

Bea was Lady Beatrice Wodehouse. Although she was a duke's sister, she lived as a reclusive spinster due to an accident that had scarred her cheek. When Fancy's father had sought work on Bea's estate five years ago, she and Bea had become instant friends, and the Sheridans had made Camden Manor, Bea's Staffordshire estate, a stop on their yearly migration.

Knighton needed a duchess, and Fancy understood why he saw her friend as a sterling candidate. Scar or no scar, Bea was beautiful, with innate poise and aristocratic manners. Unfortunately for Knighton, Bea was currently being pursued by another gentleman, railway industrialist Wickham Murray, and Fancy could tell her friend was falling for the dashing Scot.

Which left Knighton out in the cold...and as far beyond Fancy's reach as the glittering stars.

For how could a tinker's daughter hope to win the heart of a duke?

Although Fancy had the soul of a dreamer, she also had both feet planted on the ground. She had seen enough of the world to know the way it worked. Only in the safety of her imagination could she weave her faerie tale ending. There, she could dream of a prince with stormy eyes falling madly in love with her. He would give her a kiss that would make the earth tremble and the oceans roar. Then he would sweep her off to a castle in the clouds, where they would live happily ever after.

In reality, she would be lucky to find some halfway decent

fellow who respected her. Who saw her as more than a broodmare for his offspring and helpmate for the chores. Who might look at poor, ordinary Fancy Sheridan and see something...special.

A snapping twig punctured her reverie, her fantasy prince disappearing in a puff. She spun around, had an instant to glimpse a looming, hooded form. She felt a stab of terror, then something slammed into the side of her head. Pain exploded at her temple as she tumbled to the ground.

An instant later, she felt nothing at all.

I

FIVE DAYS EARLIER

Riding up the manicured drive toward Camden Manor, Severin Knight reflected upon the irony that he was fulfilling an old dream. As a boy growing up in a London rookery, he had fantasized about becoming a gentleman. Those dreams had helped him to endure the cold, hunger, and other assorted miseries of poverty. At age fifteen, he'd been hired on as a stable boy by the noble Viscount Hammond, giving him a glimpse into what a life of money and privilege entailed.

The Hammonds were never cold or hungry. A fire burned in every hearth of their spacious residence, and they ate their meals in courses, never finishing the abundant dishes. They spoke in cultured tones and didn't fight or worry about anything. While they each had their own private chambers, they never had to be alone if they didn't wish to be. They had servants, guests, and each other. They existed in a realm of calm and harmony.

Watching through a window, Severin had seen a portrait of perfection. The Hammonds' joy was painted in lavish strokes, the gilded frame of wealth separating them from the outside world. Everything about the family was beautiful...most of all Imogen.

The thirteen-year-old girl with the strawberry blonde curls had captured Severin's adolescent heart from the moment he'd pushed her out of the path of an oncoming carriage. Her grateful papa had rewarded Severin with employment, but it had been Imogen who'd given him the resolve to better himself.

Because of her, he'd worked to pull himself out of the gutter. To amass the necessary wealth to live in her world. To become a gentleman worthy of her hand in marriage.

He supposed accomplishing two out of the three goals wasn't bad.

He had lifted himself out of poverty, initially by working as a guard-for-hire, then investing his profits into manufacturing. He now owned factories in Spitalfields and beyond, employing hundreds of workers in the silk-weaving trade. His influence in Spitalfields was such that men and women of the neighborhood came to him when they needed help. Having been in their positions (and, frankly, worse ones), he did what he could. He loaned money, settled disputes, and saw that justice was served in his territory.

He had become a leader in his community, earning a seat at the table with other men of influence in London's underworld. These men were called "dukes" for they were indeed considered nobility amongst the lower classes. Severin, in particular, was known as the Duke of Silk, a nod to his business interests and his smooth, collected manner.

Then a year ago, he'd made a startling discovery: not only was he a duke of the underworld, he was a *bona fide* duke. A team of solicitors had tracked Severin down and brought him to see Arthur Huntingdon, the dying Duke of Knighton...and the father Severin had never met.

Severin's *maman* had kept his true origins a secret, all the way to her bitter end in Bedlam. On his deathbed, Arthur Huntingdon had explained that she'd done so in order to protect Severin. Knowing the sacrifices she'd made, how much she'd suffered because of his sire's perfidy, had made Severin want to refuse the damned title.

A wiser part of him resisted the urge to cut off his nose to spite his face. It was too late to save his *maman*, but it wasn't too late to claim what was rightfully his. There was a delicious irony, after all, in bringing about what his mother's in-laws had done everything in their power to prevent. His Huntingdon grandparents would be turning in their graves to know that the son of a seamstress was now the holder of their illustrious titles and estates. That his blood would run in the veins of any future Knightons he chose to beget.

The inheritance hadn't come off without a hitch, of course. He'd had to fight some distant cousin in the courts to prove that he was, indeed, the legitimate heir to the duchy. It had taken close to a year, but thanks to the help of an unexpected ally—his father's older sister, Lady Esther, Countess of Brambley—he'd secured the title last month. According to his sire's will, he'd inherited something else as well: the guardianship of four half-siblings in their teens, his father's bastards by two different mistresses, both deceased.

Severin did not wish to be responsible for four young humans. He was a busy man; he had factories, territorial skirmishes, and diversified investments to manage. Furthermore, he had no clue what he was supposed to do with his father's unruly by-blows. What did he know about having a family?

For some infernal reason, however, he couldn't bring himself to abandon them. His father had kept his siblings on a property in France, and when Severin had arrived, their situation had been disgraceful. He'd turned to his Aunt Esther, but on this matter she was less helpful.

Your half-siblings are animals, she'd said succinctly. *I am far too old to manage a menagerie. You need someone with the energy and connections to launch them into Society. Moreover, you are thirty years old and ought to be thinking about your future issue—an heir and a spare, at minimum. In short, Knighton, what you require is a wife.*

She had advised him to start shopping for a duchess. Given that the Season was over, pickings would be slim, but there were still suitable candidates to be found in London. Severin, however, had neither the time nor the inclination to browse for a wife he wanted because that ship had sailed. Five years ago, Imogen had wed the Earl of Cardiff.

Which circled Severin back to the irony of the situation: now that he was rich, titled, and a catch for any lady, the only one he wanted was out of his reach.

Hence, he'd made this foray into Staffordshire. If he couldn't have the woman he wanted, he would make do with one who met the basic requirements. As it happened, the Duke of Hadleigh, a gentleman for whom Severin had done favors in the past, had mentioned that he had a sister who would make an ideal Duchess of Knighton.

According to Hadleigh, his sister Lady Beatrice Wodehouse was beautiful, sensible, and the ripe age of four-and-twenty. Because of an accident that had left her scarred, Lady Beatrice led a cloistered life at Camden Manor, an estate she ran on her own. Severin did not give a farthing about the scar. What he cared about was that Lady Beatrice sounded level-headed and mature, the sort of woman who would welcome the marriage of convenience he had to offer.

Arriving at the manor, Severin saw that it was well-maintained, surrounded by graceful oaks tinged copper by autumn's approach. The property spoke well of its mistress's management abilities, and Lord knew he needed someone who would keep a firm rein on his siblings. The ivy-covered house had an elegant design, wings flanking the main building, sparkling pedimented windows adorning the structure.

Nothing was out of place...except perhaps for the girl arguing with the donkey.

The petite female and beast were blocking the front steps. The former stood with her back to Severin, her thick, glossy plaits of chestnut hair reaching her waist. She was scolding a grey donkey, which was sprawled on the gravel at the base of the stone steps, obstructing the entryway to the manor.

"You can't just plant yourself there pell-mell, Bertrand," she lectured the beast. "'Ow are folk supposed to enter the 'ouse? Get up."

The donkey gave her a bored look, its black-tipped tail swishing idly.

"You 'eard me." The girl planted her small hands on her hips. "Move along *now*."

The beast stretched out and laid its head on the bottom step.

"You ain't the only one who's tired, Bertrand. But we've supplies that need to be delivered to the fields," she went on. "Seeing as 'ow you're the beast o' burden, you're supposed to be 'auling that cart yonder instead o' *me* trying to 'aul *you* off the blooming steps."

The donkey lifted its head, looked at her, and yawned.

"Sweet Jaysus," she exclaimed. "Stop being such an *ass*."

A muffled sound escaped Severin, startling him. He could not recall the last time he'd laughed. The female whirled to face him, delivering another dose of surprise. Because of her braids and short stature, he had underestimated her age. She was no girl but a woman.

A rather pretty one.

Her heart-shaped face was dominated by large, doe-brown eyes, her thick lashes fanning rapidly as she stared back at him. Her skin was sun-kissed, her cheeks tinted a charming rose. She had delicate features...except for her lips which were lush and plump, the color of crushed berries. Just above the left side of her mouth was a tiny beauty mark, nature's way of punctuating temptation.

Beneath her serviceable brown frock, her bosom was full and high, her waist narrow enough for him to span with his hands. The fullness of her patched skirts hid her lower shape, but he would wager his factories that she was nicely rounded, with hips that would cradle a man as he plowed her. He became aware of a tightening in his own lower regions, the faint hum of lust in his veins.

Devil take it, he thought with a frown. *What is the matter with me?*

He did not make a habit of ogling women. He found it particularly distasteful when men took advantage of servants like this young female, who had a right to go about her duties without harassment. The fact that he'd entertained debauched thoughts about her was unacceptable and, frankly, baffling. He prided himself on self-discipline, his ability to keep his baser emotions and urges in check. This quality had allowed him to transform himself from a guttersnipe to a gentleman in the truest sense of the word.

Yet this female stirred his most primal depths. He'd never seen a mouth as carnal as hers...as kissable. He chalked up his reaction to the fact that it had been years since he'd experienced the sweetness of lips against his own. That was no excuse, however.

He dismounted, using the time to get himself in check.

"Beg pardon, miss," he said with a nod. "I have come to pay my addresses to your mistress."

The woman blinked at him. "I don't 'ave a mistress, sir."

"You are not in employ here?"

"I 'elp Bea when she needs me..." She furrowed her brow as if she were having trouble finding words. "But I ain't 'er servant."

"Whatever the case, I wish to go inside." He eyed the donkey, now lightly snoring upon the steps. "Would you kindly get your beast to move?"

"I tried," she said, sighing. "Bertrand doesn't listen to anyone but my da."

"If you don't mind, I will have a go."

"Are you certain?" She ran a dubious gaze over his clothes. Today his valet had dressed him in a charcoal frock coat, silver cravat, and Prussian blue waistcoat, his buff trousers tucking neatly into his polished boots. "When Bertrand gets angry, things can turn messy."

"I can manage a donkey." Having spent years mucking stables, he knew how to handle obstinate four-legged creatures. "The key is letting them know who is the master. Let me fetch something first."

As he went to retrieve his secret weapon from his saddle bag, she said haltingly, "You're not going to...'urt Bertrand, are you? 'E's got a sensitive nature—"

"Ease your mind. I'll not hurt the beast."

He returned, finding her obvious relief oddly endearing. She was a tender-hearted thing if she cared about the troublesome ass. He couldn't resist teasing her a little.

"I won't need to use a whip, you see. Beasts sense and obey my natural authority."

Her relief turned to skepticism. "Really."

"Stand back and see for yourself." Once she moved aside, he crouched next to the donkey. In his most ducal voice, he said, "I am your master, Bertrand, and you will do as I command. Arise, donkey."

Bertrand sniffed, his ears flickering. His expression went from bored to slightly less bored. As Severin rose, the donkey followed suit. Hearing the servant girl's astonished gasp, he hid a smile and lured the donkey away from the manor steps to the shade of a nearby tree.

"You *did* it." The female followed them, her brown eyes shining with admiration.

"Did you doubt my abilities?" he asked in mock affront.

She bit her lip then nodded.

Her honesty was so enchanting that he asked, "What is your name?"

"Fancy Sheridan," she said shyly.

The name suited her. Simple yet lovely, with a light-hearted ring to it.

"And you, sir?"

"Severin Knight," he replied.

It was the name his *maman* had given him, true enough. He could have used his title. Yet being a duke was still new to him... and he wanted to prolong this unexpected moment of fun and freedom.

"It's not that I didn't trust in your abilities," Miss Sheridan said earnestly. "But other than my da, I 'aven't met any master o' beasts—"

"The gent's going to be a master o' an *angry* beast if 'e doesn't give Bertrand whate'er 'e 'as in 'is coat pocket," a new voice announced.

Severin turned to see the arrival of a wiry, grey-bearded man. The fellow looked like an elf from a children's story, his twinkling blue eyes peering out from behind a pair of wire-rimmed spectacles which sat crookedly on his nose. He wore a turquoise velvet smoking jacket and a plaid waistcoat lined with mismatched buttons. His cap sported colorful and clashing patches.

"Take me word for it," he said to Severin. "A donkey be an excellent judge o' character and, if you pass muster, you'll ne'er 'ave a truer friend. To stay in Bertrand's good graces, I suggest you live up to your end o' the bargain."

Knowing the jig was up, Severin removed the *fruit glacés* he'd hidden in his pocket, holding them out to Bertrand. The donkey swiped up the treats with its tongue, munching contentedly—as well it should. Those candied cherries came from a renowned confectionary in Paris, and they'd cost Severin an arm and a leg.

"Why, you're no master o' beasts," the female said indignantly. "You're a master o' *bribes*."

Severin tried to look penitent. At the very least, he managed not to laugh.

"I beg your pardon, Miss Sheridan." He bowed. "I could not resist."

"Be you wanting something 'ere at Camden Manor, sir?" the bearded fellow asked.

"This is Mr. Knight, Da," Miss Sheridan said. "'E's looking for Bea."

"Milton Sheridan, of the tinkering Sheridans, at your service." Her father kept his bespectacled gaze on Severin. "Be you wanting Miss Bea for a particular reason?"

Sheridan's trade explained the odd attire, but Knight found the tinker's suspicious manner odd.

"I have an introduction from her brother," he said shortly.

"Ah. You be a friend o' 'er family then." Seeming reassured, Sheridan went on, "She's in the fields, sir. 'Er barn caught fire last night, and she be there supervising the clean-up."

A product of London's slums, Severin had learned to trust his instincts for they'd saved him more than once. Something about the tinker's guarded manner and the way he spoke of the barn fire stirred Severin's nape. The last thing Severin needed was more complications. He should turn around, head back to London. He could take his aunt's advice: do the pretty with eligible ladies until he found a wife to provide him with an heir and a spare before they both went their merry ways.

Severin was aware of Fancy Sheridan staring at him. For some reason, the look in her velvety eyes stirred the ashes of an old dream...one that he knew couldn't be resurrected. He had given his heart to Imogen, and although she loved him back, she'd been forced to marry another.

Our love is rare, Knight. Like a flower I once saw at an exhibition. Imogen's melodious voice floated through his head. *The Queen of the Night blooms but once in a lifetime.*

He felt a familiar, bittersweet pang. He'd had his chance at love and come to Staffordshire for a different purpose entirely. While happiness would not be his, he could still have the satisfaction of doing his duty. Of fulfilling the destiny that was the result of his *maman*'s sacrifice and that others had tried to steal from him.

He squared his shoulders. "Please direct me to Lady Beatrice."

2

LATER THAT AFTERNOON, FANCY AND HER FAMILY RETURNED TO the cottage where they stayed during their visits to Camden Manor. Bea always reserved the largest cottage for them, and Fancy had the rare luxury of her own bedchamber. The snug bungalow also boasted an indoor bathing room, and after a day spent cleaning up after the barn fire, Fancy was in sore need of a bath.

As she filled the copper tub with buckets of heated water, her mind whirled. So much had happened in a single day. First and foremost, there was the danger facing her bosom chum. According to Bea, clues found at the barn suggested that the fire had been no accident. For weeks now, Bea had been receiving threatening unsigned notes, warning her to leave her land. The list of potential culprits was long: plenty of men coveted Bea's land and didn't approve of an independent woman managing her own affairs.

Fancy was determined to help her friend in whatever ways she could. She'd asked Da and her brothers to check the locks on Bea's property. Between Fancy's odd jobs in the village, she kept an eye on Bea, and she wasn't the only one doing so. Wickham

Murray, a dashing railway industrialist, had taken a clearly protective stance with Bea as well.

When Mr. Murray had first arrived, Fancy hadn't known what to make of him. A charming Adonis, he'd come to buy the estate that Bea had no intention of selling. Yet, day by day, Fancy had witnessed the conflict between the pair turn into a passionate romance. While Bea called herself a "realist" who didn't take stock in love, Fancy was a dreamer who believed in faerie tale endings. Her intuition told her that Bea had found her Prince Charming.

Today, Fancy had had the wild thought that she'd found her own prince as well.

Disrobing, she stepped into the tub, the thought of Severin Knight warming her as much as the steaming water. Sweet Jaysus, the fellow was a looker.

"Handsome" was too paltry a description for Mr. Knight. With his dark hair, cool grey eyes, and rugged features, he affected Fancy down to the fibers of her being. She'd never responded to a man that way before. She had *felt* his gaze in the racing of her pulse, the leashed power of his brawny form in the throbbing of her blood. His deep voice had scattered goose pimples over her skin.

What she'd felt had been more than physical attraction, however. She was usually shy and awkward around strangers... especially toffs like him. Her ma had taught her that it was best to keep her head down around rich settled folk, and she'd learned not to attract undue attention. Yet Mr. Knight had treated her with courtesy, offering to help her with Bertrand. And the way he'd managed the willful donkey had been brilliant and humane... albeit a tad crafty.

Mr. Knight, she'd observed, wasn't the kind of man who wore his emotions on his finely tailored sleeve. Unlike her brothers—who also enjoyed playing tricks on her—he was subtler in his reactions. A smile had lit his grey eyes, even though his mouth had retained its rather stern line. For some reason, the hint of boyish delight in such an austere and elegant gentleman had made her heart thump with longing.

Sighing, she let herself enjoy the soak before soaping and rinsing. Donning an old flannel robe, she returned to her room to dress for supper. Bea had invited her and Da to the manor, and the other guests that evening would include Mr. Murray and Mr. Knight who, as it turned out, knew each other.

Mr. Murray had been with Bea at the barn, and he and Mr. Knight had seemed equally surprised to see the other. Fancy had gleaned that the men had had business dealings in London, the air between them crackling with male competition. Learning that Mr. Knight had come to pay respects to Bea—apparently he was a friend of Bea's brother, the Duke of Hadleigh—Mr. Murray had seemed none too pleased.

Supper should be interesting, Fancy thought wryly.

She opened the wardrobe, pondering her choices. Not that there was much to ponder: she had two dresses, and the one she'd worn earlier in the fields needed a good sponging. Which left the putty-colored frock as her other option, unless...

She crossed over to her travelling trunk. The enormous battered case held all her earthly belongings. Opening it, she took out the tissue-wrapped dress lying on top.

She'd made the dress for herself, using a bolt of pink silk Bea had given her for a birthday present. She'd copied the latest fashion, giving the dress a modern silhouette with a long, fitted waist and full skirts. Since she hadn't had enough ribbon for trimming, she'd used some leftover silk thread in white and pink to embroider tiny blossoms along the neckline and hem.

At the time, she'd argued with herself over the pointless extravagance: when, after all, would she have reason to wear such a gown? A wise woman would sell the dress, use the money for something more practical. Fancy had kept it, and now she knew why.

She would wear it during her supper with Severin Knight.

Beneath her worn robe, Fancy's heart fluttered. She knew she was a dreamer...but what did it hurt to dream? As Ma had oft said, *Ain't nothing wrong with sticking your 'ead in the clouds from time to time, me girl...as long as you also keep both feet on the ground.*

Ma had been a wonderful storyteller, and her tales of romantic adventure had fueled Fancy's imagination as well as her inquisitive mind. In the story of the girl in the cinders, for instance, why was the slipper made of glass, a material every tinker knew was notoriously difficult to mend? What if it broke? Glass also did not stretch; what if the poor girl's feet swelled after standing all day sweeping ashes, and the slipper didn't fit her? How unfair would *that* be?

Ma would just laugh and say, *That's why these be faerie tales, me girl, and not stories o' everyday living.*

Nonetheless, Fancy took heart in her ma's stories, whimsy and pragmatism waging a cheerful war within her. During the long trips with her family or whilst doing chores, she would dream about how she would meet her own prince. She'd never guessed that the meeting would take place over a grumpy donkey.

Da had brought Bertrand back from a fair a few months ago. Since Da had had a collection of silver spoons to barter, Fancy had been excited at what he might bring back.

A donkey brings good luck, he'd declared when she and her brothers groaned at Bertrand's arrival. *Mark me words, children: ain't nothin' more important than luck.*

Fancy could have listed several more important things. New wheels for the wagon, for example. Or shoes for her fifteen-year-old brother Tommy, whose toes were poking out of an oft-mended hole at the end. Or candles to relieve the long, dark nights in the family caravan...

"Fancy!" Her eldest brother Oliver's shout came from another room. Like all of her kin, he had a hawker's booming voice, and it carried through the cottage. "'Ave you seen me neckerchief?"

"In the drawer next to your shirts," she called back.

She heard the opening and slamming of drawers, followed by, "Found it, petal!"

O' course you did. She shook her head with fond exasperation. *That's where I put it after I washed it, didn't I?*

"Fancy!" Tommy stuck his head into the room. Her youngest brother had the gangly build of an adolescent, his brown curls flopping over his brow and brushing the collar of his shirt.

She added giving him a trim to her mental list of tasks. "Yes, dear?"

"I'm 'ungry," he announced. "What 'appened to the jam tarts?"

"Liam," she said succinctly.

"Did you eat me tarts, Liam?" Tommy yelled.

Her second youngest brother, a slightly larger version of Tommy, sauntered by.

"Time and tide wait for no man, lad," Liam said.

Fancy was not fooled by Liam's philosophical tone. Or the casual way he ruffled their youngest sibling's hair. Both actions were designed to rile Tommy who, of course, took the bait.

"It weren't no time nor tide that took me tarts but your great greedy gut!" Tommy said, scowling. "I *told* you I be saving those last tarts Fancy made for me tea."

"What're you going to do 'bout it, eh?" Liam taunted.

The next instant the lads were brawling and bouncing off the walls. Since this was a regular occurrence, Fancy simply closed the door. She was grateful that there *was* a door to close. When her family was on the road, all of them confined in the wagon, her brothers were like lampreys trapped in a barrel, constantly tangled up and thrashing against one another.

She'd just donned her unmentionables when her father's voice filtered into the room.

"Fancy, do you 'ave a moment?"

"Coming, Da." Throwing her robe back on, she went to let him in.

Da was already dressed for supper, wearing his best jacket and waistcoat, both of which Fancy had altered to fit his short, wiry frame. His hair and beard shone silver from a recent wash, and a perfect, fragrant gardenia—she had no idea where he'd found it—graced his buttonhole. His blue eyes twinkled at her from behind his wire-rimmed spectacles.

Some folk saw her father as naught more than an eccentric beggar; to Fancy, he was the dearest person in the world. He was a man with big ideas and an even bigger heart. Two and twenty years ago, he'd discovered an infant in a field and brought her home to his wife. Although the pair were struggling to feed themselves, they'd kept the babe and raised her as if she were their own.

Fancy had been so loved by Milton and Annie Sheridan that she oft forgot that she didn't share their blood. But even she had to admit that Da could be generous to a fault. He'd give the shirt off his back if he thought another needed it more. When Ma had been alive, she'd kept a rein on him. After her passing two years ago, the reins had been passed to Fancy. She wished she had half her mother's deftness and grace when it came to managing Da and the boys.

"Why ain't you changed yet, me girl?" Da asked. "Miss Bea be expecting us in an 'our."

"I was interrupted by the lads..." Fancy trailed off as her father stopped by her bed, examining the pink dress. "I'll, um, be ready soon."

"This be the frock you're wearing?" Da turned to her, his blue gaze sharp. Although a dreamer by nature, he was also shrewd, especially when it came to his children. "Thought you be saving it for a special occasion."

"I was." Heat climbed up Fancy's cheeks. "I thought Bea's party might, um, be the occasion to wear it. Since she'll be 'aving guests from London."

"Looking to impress one guest in particular?"

She bit her lip, too embarrassed to admit the truth.

Da gave her another long look. "That toff ain't for you, petal. 'Aven't I always told you 'is kind and ours don't mix?"

He had. Time and again, he'd drilled it into her that those who travelled and those who didn't belonged to different worlds. One could do business with settled folk, be friendly with them, but in the end the two worlds were like oil and water.

"Yes, Da," she said. "I just thought since Bea..."

"Miss Bea is a fine friend to you and us Sheridans. But that don't mean she understands our world...or that we understand 'ers. Take this arson business." Da shook his head grimly. "It's all on account o' 'er land. As if anybody 'ad the right to possess the earth and sky the good Lord made for all o' us."

Since Fancy had heard this refrain all her life, she knew he wasn't expecting a reply.

"Now I've seen the way you be looking at this Knight fellow," Da said. "'E's grand to be sure, but 'e ain't for you. Gents like 'im care only for their money and estates, and they marry their own kind, who can bring 'em more o' the same."

"I know," she said quietly. "Don't fret, Da. I've got my 'ead on my shoulders. I know no gentleman would look twice at me."

"That ain't the point, and it also ain't true." Da took her hand in a callused grip, giving her a brief squeeze. "You be a fine woman, Fancy, with a worthy set o' skills and a tender 'eart. Any man be lucky to make you 'is wife. And you've 'ad no lack o' suitors. Three fine fellows asked me permission to court you...and you turned 'em down."

Because all those men wanted was a wife to travel with them and do the chores, she thought glumly. *To 'elp with the tinkering.*

"Those men weren't right for me," she said.

Da raised his brows. "Not even young Sam Taylor?"

The Taylors were another tinkering clan and close friends of the Sheridans. Sam, the eldest son, was a couple years older than Fancy. Although handsome and nice, he wasn't what she longed for: a prince. By prince, she didn't mean a man of wealth or rank, but one with a noble heart. One who would love her the way heroes loved their heroines in faerie tales, with an all-consuming passion. She yearned for the devotion she'd seen between her parents, who'd loved each other through thick and thin, health and sickness...and even beyond.

Since Ma's passing, Fancy had overheard her father talk to his wife as if she were still there.

Annie, me girl, he'd say. *You wouldn't believe what I brung back from the market today.*

Her parents' love outlived death, and *that* was the kind of love she wanted.

"Sam ain't right for me," she said quietly.

"'Ow will you know when the right man comes along?" Da asked. "You ain't getting any younger, petal. Your ma, God rest 'er soul, was seventeen when I married 'er. Amongst our kind, you're getting long in the tooth."

What if I don't want to marry amongst our kind? Guilt followed on the heels of the thought, one that she'd been having more and more often. To her secret shame, she'd grown tired of moving around. Of packing and unpacking. Of bartering her skills to strangers to earn her keep.

That was why, in her dreams, her prince carried her off to a castle, which didn't have to be an *actual* castle. What would she do with all those rooms...and could you imagine the cleaning? She shuddered. A cozy cottage would suit her better. She would settle there, in a place that she could call her own, and use her skills to take care of the people she loved.

Yet she couldn't share this dream with her da for fear of hurting him. He was set in his travelling ways and wouldn't understand. She didn't want to appear ungrateful for the wonderful life he'd given her. Even worse, she thought with an anxious pang, he might think that she didn't fully belong...that the foundling he and ma had raised wasn't a true Sheridan after all.

"Maybe I won't marry, Da." She managed a light tone. "I'll stay with you forever."

"The winds o' change are blowing, me Fancy," he said gently. "I feel it in me bones that you'll be leaving us soon. I just pray that the lucky chap who wins your 'eart is deserving o' you."

At her father's solemn words, a shiver ghosted over Fancy's nape.

The moment was broken by the slamming of the front door, the squeal of cupboards being opened and closed. Her brother Godfrey's voice boomed from the kitchen.

"Can't a man get a decent bite after a day's work?" he bellowed. "Where're Fancy's tarts?"

"You and your tarts," Oliver's voice retorted. This was a sly reference to the fact that Godfrey, who was a year older than Fancy, was the skirt-chaser of the family.

"Liam ate all the tarts!" Tommy shouted.

"Bleedin' tattler," Liam returned.

More thudding and swearing ensued.

Da patted her on the cheek. "All right, me girl. I'd best go settle the lads and let you get dressed." He unpinned the gardenia from his lapel, pressing it into her palm. "To go with your pink frock."

"You think I should wear the dress?" Fancy said in surprise.

"Ain't no reason to waste something so pretty. But wear it for yourself, me Fancy. Wear it knowing that you made that dress with your own two 'ands, that you're as grand as anyone at that supper table tonight, which is to say...wear it with pride."

Bemused, Fancy watched her father leave. She raised the gardenia to her nose, its sweet perfume stirring the romantic notions of her heart.

Notions, she told herself firmly, that she would be wise to keep under wraps.

3

Things were not going as planned, Severin brooded that evening.

He was the first to arrive and sipping on an aperitif in Lady Beatrice Wodehouse's well-appointed drawing room. As he waited for his hostess to make an entrance, he contemplated abandoning his plan. Not because he didn't find his duchess candidate pleasing: Lady Beatrice was all that her brother had claimed her to be. During his brief meeting with the lady as she'd managed the aftermath of the fire, Severin had found her competent and sensible. She was lovely too, her scar adding to the uniqueness of her pale blonde hair and violet eyes.

In fact, Lady Beatrice was fashioned from a similar mold as Imogen, being tall, willowy, and fair. Women like that never lacked for male attention, so Severin ought not to have been surprised to find another suitor sniffing after Lady Beatrice. The fact that his competition was Wickham Murray, however, was irksome.

Severin knew Murray, both being self-made industrialists who had deep roots in the London underworld. Murray's moniker was The Iron Duke since he was a partner in Great London National

Railway, along with Adam Garrity and Harry Kent, two other powerful underclass men with whom Severin was acquainted.

In general, Severin respected Murray and his partners. At least, he wouldn't make the mistake of underestimating any of them when it came to negotiating a deal. He'd heard through the grapevine that Great London National Railway was in trouble, shareholders starting to revolt because of some delay in laying down track...as it happened, in Staffordshire.

It couldn't be a coincidence that Murray was here now. If Severin had to guess, the Scot was after Lady Beatrice's land. He took a sip of the bitter liqueur, wondering if she and Murray were lovers.

Murray was a rake whose prowess with females was the stuff of legend. Severin wouldn't put it past the too-charming Scot to use seduction to get what he wanted. After all, he'd seen the bastard in action before. He'd once faced Murray over a table at an exclusive gaming hell and lightened the other's pockets by a thousand pounds. Murray had retaliated by luring Sally, Severin's then-mistress, into his own bed.

Severin had enjoyed a mutually beneficial arrangement with Sally, an obliging female who never confused sexual pleasure with intimacy. All she had wanted was a generous stipend and the lease on a cottage, which he'd been glad to provide in exchange for her professional services. It had been damned inconvenient to find her replacement. More to the point, Murray's past actions showed that he had no compunction about using a female as a pawn in his games. Severin wondered how much Lady Beatrice knew of Murray's past dealings...and his present motives.

Regardless, Murray was an unforeseen obstacle, and Severin wasn't looking for complications. That was why he'd come to Staffordshire: to find an aristocratic spinster who would jump at his offer of a marriage of convenience. Now that he'd met Lady Beatrice, he didn't think she had any interest in jumping for him or anyone.

Did he want to go through with his plan to offer for her? After their brief exchange, he wasn't sure of his odds, and he wasn't keen on taking on a losing proposition. On the other hand, he had an ace up his sleeve: he had not revealed his title. Murray had greeted him as Severin Knight—the news of his inheritance was only now spreading through London—and Severin hadn't corrected him...yet.

As a businessman, Severin knew how to bide his time, play to his advantage. Surely his title would make Lady Beatrice look favorably upon his suit. He didn't have time for an extended courtship. By now, his siblings had probably torn apart his new Mayfair mansion brick by brick, sending Aunt Esther running for the hills.

As he contemplated his conundrum, awareness stirred his nape. He turned and saw Fancy Sheridan entering on her papa's arm. Her eyes met his across the room; she smiled shyly.

His blood heated with startling swiftness, probably because it had been simmering since their meeting earlier today. He didn't know what it was about the chit that made him itch with lust. Although pretty, she was not his usual preference. In truth, Lady Beatrice was more his feminine ideal, yet he felt no physical pull, no crazed desire to get to know his potential duchess between the sheets.

Fancy Sheridan, however? He burned to know her in the biblical sense.

Get your mind out of the gutter, he told himself in disgust. *You need a duchess, not some toothsome tinker's daughter.*

He steeled himself as the Sheridans approached. Fancy—*Miss Sheridan*, he corrected himself—looked the part of a genteel young lady this eve. Instead of plaits, her glossy brown tresses were bound in a topknot, baring the slender curve of her neck. She wore a simple pink gown that flattered her petite and curvy form. The off-the-shoulder cut displayed her smooth, sun-kissed skin and the rounded tops of her bosom. She had a gardenia pinned to her bodice, right between her breasts, and he had an urge to bury his nose in that fragrant, shadowed crevice—

Bloody hell, man. Rein it in.

"Good evening, Mr. Knight," Milton Sheridan said.

"Sir." Severin inclined his head. "Miss Sheridan, may I say how lovely you look?"

The nicety rolled off his tongue. It was the sort of thing a gentleman would say to any female, even if she resembled a mythical Gorgon. The women he knew would think nothing of it; indeed, Imogen had been the first to train him in the art of courtesy.

Even though he had been her family's servant, one who still reeked of the stews, she'd snuck out to the stables to give him lessons, teaching him his letters and how to speak and act like a gentleman.

It is considered ill-bred for a gentleman to show excessive emotion, she had explained. *Feelings should be expressed only in private...and even then, only the pleasant ones. That is how men and animals are different: men have the self-discipline to curb their baser instincts.*

He had absorbed Imogen's lessons, hoarding the time he spent with the angelic daughter of the house like precious coal to get himself through wintry reality. By that time, his *maman* had been in Bedlam, doing worse with each visit, and there'd been naught he could do about it. Thanks to Imogen, his only friend, he'd learned to curb his helplessness and rage, to channel them into something more useful than brawling in the streets like an animal.

"You think so?" Miss Sheridan's soft words brought him back.

From any other female, the question would be coy. A prelude to flirtation. Seeing the insecurity in her richly fringed eyes, Severin knew that wasn't her intention.

"The gown suits you well, Miss Sheridan," he said.

"Thank you. I made it myself," she said earnestly.

Her artlessness disarmed him. He couldn't think of another female in his acquaintance who would admit to such a thing. It was clear that Miss Sheridan not only lacked social polish, she didn't even know what it was. Yet something about the way she looked at him, with wonder and vulnerability, tugged at his gut.

It was the sort of look that Imogen had given him. After he saved her from the runaway carriage, she had considered him her champion. *My Knight,* she'd called him. She'd told him fantastical stories of chivalrous knights who'd battled dragons to save their fair princesses. That Imogen had found him, a brutish rookery lad, worthy of being her gallant had filled him with pride.

"How talented you are, Miss Sheridan," he said politely.

"Me Fancy be full o' talents, Your Grace," Sheridan said with unmistakable pride. "She washes dishes quicker than anybody I know, bakes pastry so light it could float on air, and being me daughter, there's nothing she can't fix."

Miss Sheridan blushed, either embarrassed at her father's bragging or at the fact that the skills he listed qualified her to be a remarkable servant. Either way, Severin took pity on her.

"Actually," he said, "I know there is one thing Miss Sheridan can't do."

Sheridan's eyes narrowed behind his spectacles. "And what would that be?"

"She cannot convince a donkey to move," Severin said gravely.

Miss Sheridan's lips tipped up and, by Jove, she had a beguiling smile.

"That is because I'm not a cheat," she said primly.

"Bribery isn't cheating," he countered. "It is a legitimate strategy to achieve one's end."

"To achieve one's end...or to move a donkey's end?"

Her quip surprised a smile from him. Although she needed polish, she didn't lack for wit. Or for charm: the sparkle in her brown eyes was rather delightful.

"Both," he admitted.

Their banter was interrupted by the arrival of Lady Beatrice, who was every inch a duchess in a sweeping gown of blue taffeta.

By her side was Murray, whose eyes narrowed upon Severin. At the unmistakable look of challenge, Severin's hackles rose.

Backing down had never won him anything. He'd come all this way to get a wife...and he couldn't let himself be distracted. He would honor his *maman* and her suffering by excelling in his role as the Duke of Knighton. He would do right by his estate, make his siblings respectable, and sire future generations of Knightons. To accomplish these goals, he needed the right woman by his side.

He bowed to Miss Sheridan. "Please excuse me."

She lowered her gaze. "O' course..."

Her voice trailed behind him as he headed toward Lady Beatrice to play his winning card.

4

Two days later, Fancy perched on the bank of the stream, a fishing pole in hand. It was late afternoon, and she'd already caught a pair of fat brown trout, their spotted scales gleaming in the basket on the grass beside her. She hoped to catch a few more fish to feed her brothers' voracious appetites.

She'd taken off her half-boots and dangled her feet above the water. Now and again, a few cool droplets danced off the river stones, tickling her bare toes. She breathed in the perfume of the outdoors: sunbaked moss, balsam of trees, the mineral richness of the muddy shores. Around her, colorful leaves rustled in their last dance before fall.

Slowly, she relaxed. Her burdens gave way to the singing crickets, rush of the water, and softness of the grass beneath her. In the arms of Mother Earth, she could breathe easier and see the crux of her troubles.

She was developing a dangerous infatuation with Severin Knight. Severin Knight who, as a wealthy, elegant gentleman, was already too far above her. As the Duke of Knighton, he existed on a different plane altogether.

He had revealed his noble title at supper two nights ago and the reason for his visit: he was seeking an aristocratic lady to be his duchess. Knighton's announcement had hit the supper table like a Roman candle. Mr. Murray had exploded with rage, calling Knighton out to the garden. Bea had gone out with them and filled Fancy in on what happened afterward.

Mr. Murray had told Knighton to leave, and being an independent woman, Bea hadn't liked that. She had instead invited Knighton to stay at Camden Manor since he was a friend of her brother. Yesterday, he'd made explicit to Bea what he was offering her: a marriage of convenience. Apparently his newly inherited duchy had come with four illegitimate half-siblings, and he needed a duchess to guide them...and to provide him with heirs.

He offered me a 'partnership,' Bea had wryly told Fancy in private. *One in which he and I would respect each other and work toward shared goals without sentiment being involved. I turned him down.*

Fancy knew that, not long ago, Bea might have accepted such a proposition, but Mr. Murray had changed Bea's views on what a relationship could be. Bea was falling in love with the handsome Scot, who clearly returned her feelings.

This meant that Knighton's suit was bound for failure. Not that it mattered where Fancy was concerned. After all, a duke wasn't going to fall for a tinker's daughter.

Sighing, Fancy gave her pole a testing tug: it was slack and lifeless, much like her hopes.

Obsessing o'er Severin Knight is stupid, she scolded herself. *Worse than stupid, it's selfish. You ought to be thinking o' Bea's welfare and not some unattainable cove.*

Since the arson, Bea, with Mr. Murray's assistance, had started investigating suspects. The task wasn't simple since all of Bea's potential enemies were powerful men. Fancy had helped where she could, listening to her friend, asking her brothers to keep their eyes and ears open for any threats.

In fact, she'd landed a job in the kitchens of the village inn tomorrow night, and she planned to listen for gossip about Bea there. Years ago, Bea had made the decision to give shelter to those deemed outcasts by society. Her tenants included fallen women and those with physical and other differences, and some of the locals wanted her tenants gone.

But who would go so far as to set fire to Bea's property?

"*That* is what you ought to be concerning yourself with," she muttered to herself. "The safety o' your bosom chum."

As if in agreement, the tip of her fishing rod gave a little jerk.

A fish...but it was a cautious one. It gave teasing, indecisive nips at the bait.

"That's it," she said under her breath. "Don't you want to take a nice bite o' that juicy worm?"

She held the pole as still as she could, but the line went limp. As her hopes began to dwindle, the line burst into life, the powerful yank nearly pulling her off the bank. She jumped up, digging her bare heels into the grass, holding onto the rod with all her might. The fish broke the surface in a gleaming arc...blooming hell, it was the biggest trout she'd ever seen!

Its power matched its size. As she tried to land it, it fought back, thrashing angrily, drenching her with powerful sprays. Droplets dripped into her eyes, but she tightened her grip on the pole. As she and the fish battled on, the ground beneath her feet grew slick and muddy. Inch by inch, she was slipping toward the edge of the bank, but she refused to let go. She pulled, her arms straining, her feet sliding toward the river.

A strong arm hooked her around her waist. "Steady there, I have you."

She jerked in shock, her back colliding with the very hard form of the Duke of Knighton. His bulging muscles caged her and prevented her from falling into the river. He took over the rod, his hand dwarfing hers. The fish continued to whip against the water, but it was only a matter of time before Knighton emerged victorious.

He landed the giant trout, its majestic body flip-flopping

against the bank, splattering water and mud everywhere. Coming to her senses, Fancy pushed at the duke's arm, and he released her immediately. She went to grab her wooden club, ending the fish's suffering with a firm thwack.

Panting, she looked up at the duke.

He was staring at her, his expression inscrutable.

All at once, she registered her bedraggled state. She was soaked, her dress a wet clinging mess. Damp tendrils had escaped her braids and hung in her eyes. And, Sweet Jaysus, she was holding a bludgeon covered in fish scales.

Springing up, she set aside the club and tried to put herself to rights.

"If I may." Knighton undid the carved gold buttons of his charcoal frock coat and moved toward her. Before she could register his intent, he draped the garment over her shoulders.

"Oh, no." She was horrified that she would damage the coat. "I'm dripping wet, and your coat is much too fine—"

"Take it, Miss Sheridan. I insist. I won't have you catching cold."

"I 'aven't been sick a day in my life," she protested. "We Sheridans 'ave sturdy constitutions."

"Nonetheless, you are soaked through and shivering," he said gently.

She realized that he was right. And his jacket was seductively warm, the wool smelling of...him. Of a mix of expensive spice, leather, and male that made her heart speed up whenever she caught a whiff. Goose pimples prickled her skin, the tips of her breasts stiffening beneath her wet bodice.

She clutched the lapels together over her bosom. "I'm obliged to you. I'll clean your coat before returning it."

"No need. My valet will take care of it," he said.

He flicked a few droplets off his waistcoat, which was woven out of tobacco brown silk and had a subtle striped pattern. Without his frock coat, his brawny virility was even more apparent: the heavy width of his shoulders and chest, tapering down to his lean torso and hips. His water-splotched buff trousers clung to the ridges of his thighs and calves before tucking into his tall boots.

He rolled up his wet shirtsleeves, revealing corded forearms dusted with dark hair. His hat lay on the bank where it must have fallen during the battle with the fish. A breeze stirred the thick, precisely clipped layers of his hair and the edges of his bronze silk cravat.

Beneath his sheath of elegance, she glimpsed a dangerous edge to his masculinity. An animal sensuality lying behind his ducal restraint. With his raw power, he could have been a blacksmith or a prize fighter.

If only 'e were something other than a duke, she thought glumly. *Then 'e wouldn't be so far out o' my reach.*

His gaze swept the length of her, and her cheeks burned. Of course he would find her disheveled and in her most-mended dress, which she'd been meaning to dye since it had faded to a nondescript beige. It still bore the ash stains from the barn fire since she'd decided to wear it on her fishing expedition before washing it. She looked down past her dirty skirts to her bare toes curling in the grass. If one could spontaneously combust from shame, the ashes that were once Fancy Sheridan would be floating away on the breeze.

"Do you, er, fish often, Miss Sheridan?"

His inquiry broke the awkward silence.

"Yes, sir—I mean, Your Grace." Desperately, she tried to think of something else to say. "It's for my family's supper."

His gaze flicked to the basket of trout. "That's quite a catch you have."

"My brothers 'ave 'earty appetites. They're 'ungrier than a pack o' dogs. I 'ave four o' them."

"Dogs?"

She blinked. "Brothers."

"Ah." He paused, then cleared his throat. "I am glad to run into you today, Miss Sheridan."

"You are?" she said in surprise.

"I have been hoping for a chance to get better acquainted."

Foolish hope sparked in her chest. "You want to get acquainted...with me?"

He nodded, the sunlight picking out glints of coffee-brown in his black hair. "I am a stranger here, Miss Sheridan, and could use a friend. An ally."

Understanding snuffed out her giddiness. As a daughter of a tinker, she knew when someone was bartering with her. There was only one thing she had that the Duke of Knighton wanted, only one reason why he would wish for her to be his ally.

"You want me to 'elp you with Bea," she said flatly.

The flicker of his thick lashes conveyed his surprise at her directness. Did he think she was stupid just because she didn't come from his class? Hurt pinpricked her heart. In the stories she wove, her prince always saw through her ordinary façade, sensing something special beneath. And he didn't try to use her to win her friend's hand.

See? she told herself. *You're just infatuated with 'im. You don't really know 'im.*

"I appreciate your candor, Miss Sheridan," Knighton said smoothly. "And your loyalty to Lady Beatrice. Because you are a good friend, I am certain you want what is best for her."

"And you think you are what is best for Bea?" she asked.

"I'm offering her one of the highest titles in the land, along with the fortune and privileges that go with it," he said with a confidence she wished she didn't find so appealing. "And, unlike my rival, I've been honest and clear about my expectations for marriage."

Fancy wanted to hear him state his terms. "What are they?"

"I need a wife with the pedigree and fortitude to introduce my four adolescent half-siblings, who were born on the wrong side of the blanket, into polite society. They are unruly and require guidance."

"Why can't you manage them yourself?" To her, he seemed like the kind of man who could manage anything.

His lashes flickered—his version, she suspected, of a startled look.

"Because they do not know me," he said. "I'm more or less a stranger to them, someone who appeared on their doorstep after their father died. I took them from their home in France to live in London with me, and they haven't...adjusted."

"Maybe they need time." She thought of all the places she and her brothers had lived. By now, she was used to constant upheaval, but when she'd been younger, it had taken her time to settle in a place. Time and the security of her parents' love.

"I do not have the time or the experience to deal with a family," he said curtly. "That job is better delegated to a wife."

"What do you mean you don't 'ave experience with a family?" She tilted her head. "What about the one you grew up in?"

Something raw flashed in his eyes before he schooled his expression.

"That is beside the point," he said dismissively. "As a busy man, I wish to have a wife to oversee the domestic sphere. What I'm offering her in return is more than a fair exchange."

"What are you offering...other than money and status, I mean?"

"Other than money and status?" He arched his dark brows. "My dear Miss Sheridan, what else would a lady want from a marriage?"

She couldn't bring herself to say it aloud. Was too afraid of giving herself away.

"Ah, I see." His mouth formed a tight line. "This is about love, is it?"

Now that he'd brought up the topic, she wasn't about to back down.

She lifted her chin. "Bea deserves a husband who loves 'er. She deserves every 'appiness."

"If you want your friend to be happy, Miss Sheridan, then do not wish love upon her."

Taken aback by his bleak statement, she said, "But love...it's the key to 'appiness. Love is *everything*."

"As someone who is older, who has seen more of the world, I must disabuse you of your romantic notions." His flat words sent a chill through her. "Love might seem wonderful, but it is far more likely to lead to pain than joy."

"Did someone 'urt you?" she asked without thinking.

There it was, that flash in his gaze. Catching a better glimpse this time, she saw pain...mingled with sadness.

His mask of composure slid back into place. "It would be ill-bred of me to discuss intimate matters with you, Miss Sheridan."

"I'm sorry." She bit her lip, questions whirling in her head. "I didn't mean to pry."

"I would not fault you for your innocence." He clasped his hands behind his back. "Take it from me, a gentleman who has more experience of the world, love is unreliable. Money and social position are far less risky propositions."

She didn't know why he expressed such cynicism, but she couldn't agree with it.

"I ain't inexperienced, Your Grace," she said with quiet pride. She thought of her many travels, the people she'd met who'd been devoted to one another, the love between her own mother and father. "I know what love is, and I've seen more o' the world than you know."

He looked briefly astonished, his eyelids lifting a fraction.

"I see." He made a clearing sound in his throat. "Be that as it may, my proposal to Lady Beatrice is solid and real, a true foundation for a marital union. Unlike Murray, I will not stoop to seduction and false promises."

She frowned. "Why do you think Mr. Murray's promises are false?"

"Because I know Murray. He is a rake."

Fancy didn't doubt that Mr. Murray, with his looks and charm, had all the makings of a rake. But even rakes could fall in love. And her intuition told her that Mr. Murray truly cared for Bea and vice versa.

"People can change," she averred.

"Certainly, like a leopard can change its spots." A muscle stood out along Knighton's jaw. "I'm not making any headway with you, am I? You won't support my suit because I won't promise to love Lady Beatrice."

"That's not why," she said honestly. "I won't support it because I think Mr. Murray *is* falling in love with Bea and she with 'im."

"We'll see about that." Knighton donned his hat and gave her a stiff nod. "Good day to you, Miss Sheridan."

"Good day, Your Grace..." she began.

He was already walking away. Surrounded by his jacket and lingering scent, she looked after him, wondering who had broken his heart. And she didn't know if it was her tinkering or womanly instincts that made her yearn to mend it.

5

THE FOLLOWING NIGHT, SEVERIN LAY WITH HIS HANDS BEHIND his head in one of Lady Beatrice's guest chambers. The late summer heat wasn't relieved by the open window, so he slept in the buff, a sheet draped over his lower half. He stared up into the canopy of the tester bed. It was the wee hours, yet sleep evaded him, probably because of his looming failure.

The encounter with Fancy Sheridan yesterday had spurred him to take control of his courtship. He'd spoken with Lady Beatrice earlier today, again pressing his suit and pointing out his opponent's weaknesses. He'd made a tactical error. His attempt to open her eyes to the kind of man Wickham Murray was had provoked her ire. She'd told him in no uncertain terms that she would not marry him.

Severin knew a losing proposition when he saw one. Clearly, Murray had won the lady's heart, which seemed to rule over her head. Pity that. If she'd been more clear-eyed and less emotional, she could have been exactly what Severin was looking for.

Now there was no point in staying. Severin would leave on the morrow and head back to London. He would take his Aunt Esther's advice and make a foray into the Marriage Mart. Hell, if he let her, his aunt would be happy to choose the next Duchess of Knighton for him. While he wasn't certain Aunt Esther had his happiness in mind—it was difficult to know if the prickly widow held any affection for him—he knew that she valued the family name.

Severin ought to be making a list of suitable duchess candidates. Mapping out contingency plans. Instead, his thoughts were occupied by Fancy Sheridan.

By how soft and pleasingly rounded she'd felt tucked up against him as he'd landed her catch. By the scent of her, some unique mix of sunshine, wildflowers, and woman. Most of all, by her blatant admission that she was no virgin.

I ain't inexperienced, Your Grace. She'd said it without shame. *I know what love is, and I've seen more o' the world than you know.*

Just how experienced *was* this lusty tinker's daughter? How many men had she tumbled in the hay with? Heat flooded Severin's groin, and his cock rose, butting against the sheet.

An errant fantasy fogged up his brain. At another place and time, she might have been a welcome diversion. A breath of fresh air amidst the suffocating demands of his life. He imagined setting her up in a cottage outside the city, his own little country escape. She would greet him at the door, wearing a sweet smile on her lips...and nothing else.

Animal need clawed at him. He reached beneath the sheet, fisting his erection. He stroked his distended flesh, imagining Fancy gripping him the way she'd gripped the fishing rod, with pure feminine determination. He saw her smiling at him, with that disarming warmth of hers, and his lust took an errant turn into some deeper, darker corner of need.

He steered it back, concentrating on her ripe, raspberry lips. That teasing beauty mark.

Seed leaked into his gliding fist as he pictured her naked on her knees in front of him. Had she sucked a prick before? If not, it would be his pleasure to teach her. He would break in her pretty mouth with tender care, easing his shaft in inch by inch. Since this was a fantasy, he imagined her taking all of him which, given his size, was something not even his most experienced mistress had managed to do.

His chest heaved, his fist moving faster. Once she got him hard and wet, he would have a taste of her. He wondered if she would be shy about having her cunny licked, if any of her lovers had been skilled in the art of gamahuche. He'd only done it to two women, both of them longer-term mistresses, and he'd enjoyed how wild it had made them.

Would Fancy go up in flames when he ate her pussy?

He groaned softly, deciding that she *would*. After she came in his mouth, he would have her mount him. It wasn't his favorite position, but he wanted to see her expressive eyes as she took his cock into her body. As her pink petals spread around his glistening shaft and she sank down on him, all the way to the thick base. Gripping her lush hips, he would wrench her up and down his prick while her firm, rounded tits bounced for his viewing pleasure.

Would her nipples be as red as her lips? Would she pant his name while he suckled them? Would she beg him to kiss her, to take that lush mouth of hers as she rode him? He slid his fingers into her chestnut locks, crushing her lips to his, tasting her sweetness…

His climax surged. He gritted his teeth against a shout as he shot his seed into his fist. Chest heaving, he lay back against the pillows, sated yet empty. A familiar feeling.

After the affair with Imogen—and, on occasion, during—he'd had bedpartners. He had needs, after all, and the impersonal rutting had nothing to do with the purity of what he felt for her. Imogen had never required his physical fidelity, only that he be her champion. But he had made her a promise, one he'd been faithful to: she was the only woman he had kissed. Several weeks after her marriage, Imogen had found him at his offices in Spitalfields. It had been their first meeting since she failed to show up the night they were supposed to elope.

Forgive me, Severin. I could not dishonor my family. I had to go through with marrying Cardiff, even though I don't love him. Her cornflower blue eyes had shimmered. *Please promise you won't forget me. Please say I will always have a piece of your heart.*

Unable to help himself, he'd gathered her in his arms and kissed her, tasting her tears.

I will never forget you, my darling, he'd vowed, stroking a strawberry blonde tendril from her temple. *My love is yours until the day I die. And my last kiss will be with you.*

Her tearful joy had filled him with bittersweet pride. In that moment, he had finally shed his guttersnipe roots and felt like a true gentleman. While he couldn't save his lady from an unhappy marriage, he would be her worthy and loyal knight.

That had been five years ago, and he had kept his promise. He hadn't kissed any of his lovers. Hadn't missed it, in truth. Kissing evoked intimacy, and he was done with that. With the pain and unfulfilled promise of it. While Fancy Sheridan thought that love brought happiness, he knew from personal experience that she was wrong. One could not rely on love. At any given moment, love could pull the rug from under one's feet.

The chit might have had a tup or two, he reasoned. *But she has no idea how naïve she is.*

That he found himself fantasizing about her was troublesome. More troublesome still was the fact that he'd frigged himself whilst thinking about *kissing* her. While Miss Sheridan's sexual experience might qualify her to be a potential lover—his code of honor would not permit him to tup an innocent—he knew that she was not mistress material. She couldn't separate her feelings from fucking, for one thing. She was too naïve, too romantic...and too damned nosy.

He thought of the questions she had asked him on the riverbank. About why he couldn't manage his siblings. And about his experience of his own family. She'd caught him off-guard because no one had asked him such personal questions before.

Not even Imogen. For years, she had been the only one in his corner, and she didn't like to speak of unpleasant things. And Severin's life had been unpleasant. There'd been no polite way of sharing that his *maman* had whored for their survival. That she'd drowned her miseries in blue ruin. That she'd become mad from the drinking, lost control of herself, and he'd failed to save her from living out the rest of her life like an animal in Bedlam.

Thus, he had never told Imogen any of it, and she hadn't asked. Yet Fancy Sheridan, whom he'd known for precisely four days, wanted to dig into his darkest corners? The old scar on his chest tautened in warning.

He needed to stay away from her. Far. Away.

Shifting onto his side, he tried to find sleep. To his disgust, he couldn't stop thinking about the tinker's daughter. He wondered if he would see her before he left...if he would ever see her again. Either option left him feeling unsettled. He mulled over the strange lightness he felt in her presence. Her endearing candor and odd mix of shrewdness and innocence. Her sensual mouth and pretty tits...

He must have drifted off for noises yanked him from the murky depths of a dream. Years of living in the stews had trained him to wake fully, and he sat up, alert. It was still dark, not yet dawn.

Urgent voices and footsteps sounded in the corridor.

His neck prickling, he got out of bed, pulling on his dressing gown. He opened the door and stopped a maid who was racing by. The lamp she held illuminated the worried lines of her face, the disheveled strands slipping from beneath her cap.

"What is going on?" he asked.

She bobbed a hasty curtsy. "Pardon the disturbance, Your Grace. But it's the mistress's friend, Miss Sheridan," she said in a shaking voice. "She was working in the village last night, and 'er pa says she never came 'ome."

~

Fancy opened her eyes. Her vision was blurry, shapes wavering in and out. She tried to move—and white-hot pain forked through her head. Waves of agony washed over her, nausea pushing up her throat. She tried to breathe, realizing with burgeoning panic that she'd been gagged, a thick piece of cloth secured around her mouth. A rope bound her to a tree.

Eyes stinging, she inhaled through her nose until the pain subsided. She blearily took in the trees and brush around her. She knew these woods...an isolated stretch that straddled Bea's and the neighboring squire's estates. The memory plowed into her: she'd been walking home, thinking about Knighton when someone had attacked her. Her left temple pulsed where she'd been struck. After that, she had no memory of how she'd arrived here, what had happened in the time she'd been unconscious.

Terrifying possibilities flooded her. She was no sheltered miss; travelling daughters were raised with cautionary tales of what could happen to a girl if she wandered off alone. Fancy's gaze swept downward, a muffled sob of relief escaping when she saw she was fully clothed, still wearing the dress of the night before. She forced herself to do a mental check of herself nonetheless.

The throbbing pain at her left temple. The gag wedged in her mouth. The chafing at her wrists where the rope bound her to the bark. She made herself take inventory of more private parts, and relief seared her eyes when she felt no new or odd sensations there, no feeling of...violation.

A shudder passed through her. *Thank you, Lord.*

But her travails weren't over yet. She was trapped in the forest...and who knew what her assailant intended? Had he tied her here, with the intention of returning? Was her attacker even a man? She could not recall any identifying details of her assailant, only a sense of looming menace.

Worry about that later. For now, try to get out o' here.

She struggled with the bonds; they were knotted and wouldn't budge. She tried wriggling her hands free but only succeeding in scraping her wrists further. Her legs were equally immobilized. Next, she bent her head, trying to get at the rope over her chest with her teeth. Maybe she could gnaw her way through...but she couldn't reach.

She tried calling for help, her shouts diminished by the gag.

Panting and lightheaded, she paused to catch her breath. As she did, thoughts swarmed her.

Am I to die alone in the woods? Surely Da and the boys will be looking for me, but 'ow will they know to look 'ere? Is my life going to end this way, in fear...and disappointment?

Severin Knight flashed in her mind's eye. Stupid to think of him at a time like this. In fact, if she hadn't been so blooming distracted by him last night, then maybe she would have heard her assailant's approach. Maybe she wouldn't be in this predicament if she didn't have her head in the clouds, dreaming of a prince who didn't even believe in love. Dreaming of a faerie tale ending that would never be hers because she wasn't a princess but plain ordinary Fancy Sheridan.

A tinker's daughter who just wanted to live.

Please, God, let me survive this, she bargained desperately. *I promise to give up my silly dreams. I promise to be grateful for whate'er you intend for me, to be content with my lot in life.*

A breeze brushed her cheek. A distant rustling raised the hairs on her skin.

Was the attacker returning? Was it a wild beast? Or someone who could help her?

"'Elp! Someone 'elp!" she shouted desperately into the gag. "I'm over 'ere!"

She yelled until her throat was raw, until her voice faded into hoarse, animal sounds. Still, no one came. Her face wet with tears, she slumped against the tree. The pounding at her temple spread to the rest of her head, blackness flickering at the edges of her vision.

"Miss Sheridan, I've got you."

Her head was tipped back, and she stared up woozily...at Severin Knight? He wasn't his usual impeccable self. His head was bare, his black hair disheveled, his jaw shadowed with a night beard. His eyes weren't remote as they scanned her face; they were stormy, emotion flashing like lightning.

He finished freeing her from her bonds and held her by the shoulders, his grip gentle but firm.

"Are you all right?" he asked tersely.

The relief was overwhelming, her answer emerging as a sob. "I think so..."

"You are safe now, sweeting." He swept her up in his arms, against his thundering heart. "I won't let anything happen to you."

She clung to his words and his strength as he carried her out of the woods.

6

"We must put an end to this," Wickham Murray declared as he paced in front of the fire.

Severin shared the sentiment, yet he contained himself, remaining seated in a wingchair while the Scot prowled in front of him. They were in an upstairs parlor of Lady Beatrice's manor, and the other occupant was Fancy's father. Milton Sheridan sat on a nearby divan, his bearded face ashen and blank.

Poor bastard's in shock, Severin thought grimly.

At the moment, a physician was examining Miss Sheridan, Lady Beatrice staying with her friend. Severin knew the question that would haunt any father when his daughter was abducted, beaten, and found in the woods. The doctor would undoubtedly give them an assessment soon. The tension that pervaded the room was that of men who can do nothing but wait.

"Whoever is behind this will pay for what they did," Murray said, raking a hand through his disheveled bronze hair.

Severin gripped the arms of his chair. Again, he didn't disagree. He flashed back to how he had discovered Miss Sheridan: slumped against a tree, trussed like the trophy of some sick hunt. His heart had punched his ribs when he saw her bloodied temple, the purplish swelling, the paleness of her lips. Then she had raised her head, and icy rage had flooded his veins at the terror in her brown eyes. And on her face…

Her bloody assailant had painted a curving red line over her right cheek. A grotesque parody of Lady Beatrice's scar. In the carriage, Severin had wiped away the ghastly mark on the pretense of drying Miss Sheridan's tears. In her state, the last thing she'd needed was more of a shock. Yet the crude marking, along with a note pinned to her skirts, had revealed the motive of the assault:

Friends of the Bitch Beware.

Fancy had been targeted because she was Lady Beatrice's bosom chum. Whoever was trying to scare Lady Beatrice into selling her land hadn't hesitated to make the tinker's daughter into collateral damage…and Severin wanted to rip whoever the bastard was from limb to limb.

How dare someone hurt a woman as sweet and vulnerable as Fancy Sheridan? His fingertips dug into the leather, the chair's frame creaking. *What if I hadn't found her? What happened before I got there?*

Helpless anger roared over him. He couldn't let himself think of the possibilities. Had to concentrate on the fact that she seemed unhurt. He inhaled, trying to gain control of himself. Trying to block out unbidden memories of another time, his mother's bruises and tears.

His chest burned. He'd failed his *maman* because he'd been a boy. Now he was a man, and he was no longer powerless.

"What progress have you made with identifying Lady Beatrice's enemies?" he demanded.

Murray continued pacing. "We've interrogated most of the obvious culprits behind the barn fire: the neighboring squire who is after her land, the village rector who wants her and her tenants gone, and the factory owners who want to transport their goods over her property. All the men have motive, yet we have no proof of anyone's wrongdoing. I will not rest until I find and stop the villain behind this," he vowed grimly.

Severin did not doubt the Scotsman. It was clear to him now that Lady Beatrice and Wickham Murray had sunk their hooks equally into one another. Which boded well for Lady Beatrice's safety...but what about Miss Sheridan? Who would look after her?

Clenching his jaw, Severin glanced at her father. The tinker was incapable of hurting a fly, let alone protecting his daughter from a murderous foe. Miss Sheridan's brothers were no better: it had been her damned brother Godfrey's job to walk home with her, but instead he'd chosen to dally with a barmaid. He had chosen a tup...over his sister's welfare.

During the search for her, Godfrey had been stricken with guilt. That hadn't appeased Severin for the bastard deserved to feel like shite. If he represented the protection available to Fancy, then she was a sitting duck.

Severin flashed to her tender worry that he might hurt her donkey, the endearing way she'd called him the Master of Bribes. The way she'd bantered with him and asked meddlesome questions. He saw her on the riverbank, refusing to let go of that deuced fish because she wanted to feed her family supper. He heard her loyal defense of her friend's happiness and her spirited rebuttal to his views on love...a tinker's daughter telling a duke what was what.

And Severin knew he could not allow her to come to harm.

"Until the villain is captured, it is not safe for the women to remain here," he said.

"I am of the same mind." Murray braced his hands on his hips, his hazel gaze meeting Severin's. "London?"

It was the obvious choice, for both men had resources there.

"Aye," Severin agreed. "As soon as possible."

Murray nodded, sprawling into the adjacent wingchair.

"Beatrice will not want to abandon her estate," he muttered.

"Convince her," Severin said.

The Scot shot him a wry look. "In case it has escaped your notice, she is a lady whose opinion is not easily swayed once she has made up her mind."

He *had* noticed. In truth, he, himself, preferred females who were possessed of a less obstinate nature. While Lady Beatrice's steel backbone would have been a boon where his siblings were concerned, it was not a quality he sought in a mate. He liked females with a softer touch.

He lifted his brows. "As your intentions toward our hostess appear to be honorable, you might as well get used to changing her mind. I don't envy you, Murray."

"Don't you?" The other's voice was bland, his gaze wary.

"Not a whit." In fact, Severin suspected he had dodged a bullet. "I wish the two of you well."

Murray gave a slow nod. "I appreciate it, Knighton. And I'm obliged for your willingness to help Beatrice."

It wasn't just the lady that Severin was concerned about, but that was none of Murray's business. He lifted his chin in return; that was all that was needed to acknowledge that the two were on the same page. As dukes of the London underworld, they shared a moral code. An eye for an eye, yes, but innocents—women and children, in particular—were to be protected.

The door opened, and the men rose as Lady Beatrice swept in. She looked haggard, shadows smudged beneath her eyes.

Apprehension tautened Severin's chest. *How is Fancy?*

"Fancy's asleep now." Lady Beatrice motioned them to sit, joining the tinker on the divan. "The physician said that rest is good for her. He did a thorough examination, and the bruise on the temple and chafing at her wrists were the only injuries he found. He said no permanent damage was done and that she ought to be right as rain after a few days."

A breath left Severin, one he hadn't realized he'd been holding. No permanent damage, only the superficial injuries. *Thank God.*

"Who would do such a thing to me Fancy?" Sheridan spoke up, his bespectacled gaze bewildered. "She's a good girl, never done 'arm to a fly."

"Fancy didn't do anything to deserve this," Lady Beatrice said. "It's my fault."

"The fault is not yours," Severin and Murray said as one.

"O' course this ain't your fault, Miss Bea," Sheridan added gruffly. "You've always been a friend to us Sheridans and Fancy especially. If I know me daughter—and I do, seeing as I raised 'er since she was a babe—she would not be wanting you to feel responsible for the actions o' the bastard who did this, pardon my plain speaking. She'd be telling you to concentrate on 'ow to keep yourself safe from this sneaky coward."

"Sheridan is correct," Severin said, leaning forward in his chair. "We must plan for your safety, Lady Beatrice, and the safety of Miss Sheridan."

"Knighton and I have a plan," Murray cut in.

"What sort of a plan?" Lady Beatrice asked warily.

Murray faced her. The Scot inhaled deeply before presenting the plan for London. Having bargained with Murray in the past, Severin noted with faint amusement that the famed negotiator showed signs of nerves. Murray was talking quickly; the more Lady Beatrice's eyes narrowed, the more words spilled out of his mouth. As if he hoped to lecture her into submission.

Yes, I definitely dodged a bullet, Severin thought.

"What do you think of the plan?" Murray concluded.

Severin grimaced at the strategic misstep. Never invite an opponent's opinion...unless you were certain it aligned with yours.

Murray obviously realized his mistake, his shoulders tensing for rebuttal.

Lady Beatrice raised her brows. "When do we leave?"

Severin was relieved at her compliance. He would be able to keep Fancy safe. He would provide escort to London and protection to the women until Lady Beatrice's nemesis was stopped.

After that, he would wash his hands of the affair and redouble his efforts to find a wife.

As Murray ironed out the details with his lady, Severin glanced at the tinker. Milton Sheridan had been sitting quietly, not participating in the discussion about London, and now his forehead was wrinkled. Was the man confused about the plan?

"Mr. Sheridan," Severin said to get the tinker's attention. "How long will it take for you and your family to prepare for London?"

"We be travelling folk, Your Grace. Not long."

Hearing the other's hesitation, Severin asked, "Is there a problem?"

"Not sure as yet," Sheridan muttered as he rose. "I'll be looking in on me Fancy now."

Not liking the feeling in his gut, Severin got to his feet. "Allow me to join you and pay my respects to Miss Sheridan."

7

Run, a voice whispered in her head. *Run...but you can't hide from me.*

Fancy's lungs burned, her muscles straining as she dashed through the forest of darkness. She had to get away. She ran into a barrier, the impact jarring her. She swept her hands desperately over the surface, trying to find a way out...

"Fancy, dear, wake up."

She opened her eyes. Heart hammering, she saw with confusion that she was standing at a door, her hand rattling the knob. Bea was beside her.

"You were sleepwalking," Bea said in low, soothing tones. "It was a bad dream."

The memory of the attack pounced, smothering Fancy in terror. Panic clawed at her insides, whispering in her ear, *Run. Hide.*

"You're safe," Bea murmured. "It's over now. Let's get you back into bed."

Numbly, Fancy let her friend guide her. She climbed into bed, and as Bea wiped her cheeks with a handkerchief, she felt wetness on her skin. Had she been crying? She tried to take calming breaths, waiting for the fear to subside. For the quaking to leave her limbs.

Bea ran a hand through her white-gold hair, which fell loosely over her voluminous lawn nightgown. She had stayed with Fancy these past two nights, sleeping in a cot set up nearby. Fancy had a lifelong habit of sleepwalking, especially during times of turmoil. When she was a girl, her ma had had to keep an eye out for her nighttime travels. Her best friend knew this and had kept a faithful vigil over her.

"Thank you." She wetted her dry lips, blinking in the dim light. "What time is it?"

"Nearly dawn." Bea propped some pillows behind her, lifting a glass to her lips. "Take some water, dear. Drink slowly."

Fancy took cautious sips. The cool liquid soothed the parched tissues of her throat. Gradually, the tide of panic began to recede.

"I feel better," she said.

"I'm glad, but you mustn't rush things." Bea set down the glass, sitting in the chair beside the bed. "You've been through an ordeal."

Seeing the tired circles beneath her friend's eyes, Fancy said softly, "So 'ave you. You don't 'ave to stay with me. I'm fine now."

"You are not fine, my dear. No one would be after what you endured." Bea's voice had an uncharacteristic wobble. "I'm so sorry, Fancy."

Bea had been apologizing since yesterday, when Fancy had surfaced from the dose of laudanum the physician had given her. Fancy's brother Godfrey had been weighed down by guilt as well, although she'd done her best to reassure everyone that no one was at fault except for her attacker.

"It ain't your fault some bastard conked me on the 'ead." Fancy tried to make her words light, to chase away the shadows in her chum's lavender gaze. "Serves me right for walking 'ome by myself."

The wooded path flashed in her mind's eye. Her throat clenched.

Will the open road e'er feel safe again?

"If it isn't my fault, then it is most *definitely* not yours." Bea's gaze shifted to her left temple. "How's your head?"

Gingerly, Fancy touched the bump. The swelling had gone down, leaving in its wake a tender ache. "Better. I no longer feel dizzy."

"Do you think you could sleep some more?"

Thinking of the shadows that awaited in her dreams, she shook her head.

"Me neither." Bea gave her an assessing look. "Do you feel up to talking?"

Fancy nodded. "About what?"

"The Duke of Knighton."

Severin Knight...her literal knight in shining armor. The relief she had felt when he'd appeared washed over her now. She remembered the security of his brawny arms as he carried her to safety, his heart drumming beneath her ear. She was indebted to him—owed him her very life. When he'd paid her a brief visit yesterday in Da's presence, she had tried to express her gratitude.

Say no more, Miss Sheridan, for you owe me nothing, he'd said firmly. *It was my honor to be of assistance. My only regret is that I could not prevent this atrocity.*

He'd worn his usual austere expression. Yet she'd glimpsed the lingering thunderclouds in his eyes, and awareness had flashed through her. Beneath his controlled façade, he was roiling with emotion. Because of her?

But then he'd bowed, saying he didn't want to interfere with her rest, and left. Had she imagined his turmoil? Even if she hadn't, he was a protective, honorable man who would be riled up if any woman had been beaten and kidnapped. His reaction might not be specific to her.

"What is going on between the two of you?" Bea asked.

With sudden clarity, Fancy remembered the bargain she had made just before her rescue. She'd promised God that she would give up her foolish dreams if He allowed her to live. She recalled the breeze that had caressed her cheek and then Knighton had appeared.

God had kept His end of the deal; she had to keep hers.

She twisted the coverlet between her fingers, mumbling, "There ain't nothing between us."

"Dearest, I know you too well." Bea's voice was gentle. "You like him, don't you?"

She bit her lip. "Is it obvious?"

"Only to those who know you well." Notches of worry formed between Bea's brows. "Fancy, I'm not sure Knighton is right for you—"

"I know." Because she *did* know. "'E's a duke, and I'm a tinker's girl. 'E's rich and powerful, and my only assets are what I can do with my own two 'ands. 'E's an elegant gent...and I can barely read and write, except for what you've been teaching me. I know 'e's far too good for the likes o' me," she concluded earnestly, "but you ain't got to worry. I got my 'ead on straight now."

Bea frowned. "First of all, he is *not* too good for you. You're capable, beautiful, and kind. You have more class and grace in the tip of your finger than many so-called ladies could hope to possess. Trust me, I speak from experience. After my accident, those girls who were supposed to be my friends turned their backs on me. But you have been true and loyal; through thick and thin, I've counted on you, and you've never let me down."

Fancy's eyes welled. "I ne'er will, Bea. You're my best friend."

"It is because I am your best friend that I must caution you against Knighton." Reaching over, Bea gave her hand a gentle squeeze. "Not because you are not good enough for him, but because I don't trust his intentions where you're concerned."

"'E doesn't 'ave any intentions toward me." With a watery

sigh, she recalled their exchange on the riverbank. "'E wouldn't even notice me if I weren't your friend."

"You're wrong. I've seen the way Knighton looks at you. He wants you, Fancy."

A shiver danced up her spine. "You think so?"

"Yes," Bea said solemnly. "But not in the way you deserve. Since I've refused his offer, he will have to look for a duchess elsewhere. I do not doubt that he will, as he seems like a man wedded to his goals, no pun intended. But while he is searching for his aristocratic bride—and even after he weds her—he will be open to other sorts of relationships. That is what gentlemen of the *ton* do. They marry for duty and find their pleasure elsewhere."

"You think Knighton would want me to be 'is...lightskirt?" Pain clutched her heart. Along with another feeling...a shameful, wanton curiosity.

What would it be like to be in Knighton's bed?

"I'm saying I want you to be careful." Bea squeezed her hand again before letting go. "You see the good in people, you always have. You're trusting and optimistic, and I don't want you to get hurt by a man like Severin Knight. I won't deny that his austerity is its own brand of charm. But beneath that, I suspect he's quite coldblooded."

"'E wants nothing to do with love," Fancy agreed unthinkingly.

Bea's brows shot ceilingward. "The two of you have discussed the topic?"

"In passing." Cheeks warm, she confided, "I think someone 'urt 'im in the past, and that's why 'e's afraid o' love now."

"Dash it, this is *precisely* why you must be careful around him. You're already making excuses for the fellow, bleeding over his 'wounded' heart." Bea shook her head. "Have you considered that perhaps he simply doesn't have one?"

Fancy thought of Knighton's boyish trick with Bertrand, how he'd saved her from falling into the river and given her his jacket. She recalled the pain in his eyes when he'd said that love was a risk. And his stark look when he'd talked about not knowing how to manage his siblings and how...alone he'd seemed.

"'E does 'ave a heart," she said with certainty. "'E's shown me courtesy time and again during 'is visit. And 'e stayed to search for me when 'e could've left."

Bea pulled a breath through her nose. "A fact for which I will remain forever grateful. But that doesn't mean I trust him with your well-being. I've discussed the matter with Wick, however, and he thinks it would be better for us to have Knighton's protection for the trip to London."

Yesterday, Bea had informed Fancy of the plan to go to London for shelter. There, they would also follow up on clues about the attacker that Bea and Mr. Murray had found. Fancy felt twin twinges of anticipation and anxiety: despite all her travels, London was one place she'd never been. Da refused to take the family there, saying that the city was too dangerous and no place for a Sheridan.

Yet in two days' time, escorted by Mr. Murray and Knighton, Fancy and her family would be departing with Bea for that mysterious metropolis shrouded in fog. She could not shake the feeling that an adventure was about to begin.

"Despite their bad blood, Wick claims that Knighton is a man of honor," Bea continued.

"What 'appened between them?" Fancy asked curiously.

"Wick hasn't been forthcoming about it...other than to say that Knighton was the loser. Men." Bea rolled her eyes. "When it comes to competition, they behave like children."

"Ain't that the truth." Having grown up with brothers, Fancy knew this for a fact. "Did Mr. Murray tell you anything else about the duke?"

"He said that Knighton came from the stews and has a rags-to-riches story. Prior to inheriting an actual duchy—Wick hasn't the faintest how Knighton pulled that one off—Knighton was already known as one of the 'dukes' of the London underclass because of his success in Spitalfields. He owns multiple fabric manufactories. His particular moniker is the 'Duke of Silk,' due to his trade, obviously, but also his smoothness of manner. Wick says Knighton is known for his stoicism, refinement, and for keeping his cards close."

Fancy absorbed the information. She'd sensed that beneath Severin Knight's noble bearing was a ruthless strength of will. Although breathtakingly elegant, he'd never seemed like a man born with a silver spoon in his mouth. Knowing that he'd built his empire by the sweat of his own brow fueled her admiration of him.

"That explains a lot," she murmured.

"Knowing all that, will you promise to be careful around Knighton?" Bea pressed.

Hesitating, she said, "I promise."

In truth, she doubted she needed to be careful. Bea, being a loyal friend, was overestimating Fancy's effect on Knighton. Why would a duke be interested in a tinker's daughter who argued with donkeys and fought losing battles with fish?

If Knighton showed concern for her, it was because of his nature. He might have been hurt by love in the past, but he still had a noble heart. That was why he had stayed to rescue her and volunteered to provide escort to London.

"That puts my mind at ease, dear," Bea said.

"I ain't the only one we 'ave to worry about." It was Fancy's turn to reach out, to take her friend's hand. "'Ow are things with Mr. Murray?"

Bea looked nonplussed. "They're rather, well..."

"Spit it out."

"Splendid." Bea's features pinkened. "Wick is everything I never thought to find."

"I'm glad," Fancy said warmly.

"Things are far from settled between us. We still have to

apprehend the villain behind the attacks." Bea's brow pleated. "And iron out the issue of the railway and my land."

"But you're 'appy now."

"Well, yes. I suppose I am."

"Then enjoy it, dear." Fancy smiled. "No one deserves it more."

~

As the day of departure approached, Severin felt increasingly on edge.

He'd had the unsettled feeling since Lady Beatrice had agreed to the London plan. In his experience, the warp and weft of life was never without wrinkles. Call him cynical, but when things seemed to be going too smoothly, he knew he was about to hit a snag. His history had taught him this.

At age fifteen, he had hauled a girl out of the path of a runaway carriage, only to be struck down himself by Cupid's Arrow. He'd lost his heart that day to Imogen and had it crushed when she'd married another man ten years later.

At age eighteen, he had quit the Hammonds to work as a guard-for-hire. He'd proven good at the job and saved up enough money to finally get his *maman* out of the madhouse. He'd paid a mad-doctor to certify her sane, found an attendant who could look after her while he was at work. When he'd told her that during his last visit to see her, his mother's grey eyes had lit up with rare joy and lucidity. When he'd arrived to take her from Bedlam the next day, an attendant had broken the news: she'd died during the night.

This year, his life had taken perhaps the most unexpected turn of all. He'd inherited a duchy and the guardianship of four siblings. Two of whom hated his guts for trying to curb their wild ways and the other two, well, he hadn't a clue what to do with thirteen-year-old twins. Yet he couldn't leave the four to fend for themselves; he knew what that was like and wouldn't wish it on anyone.

In short, life was not easy. If it seemed to be, then trouble was just around the corner.

Thus, Severin was not surprised when Milton Sheridan strode into the drawing room, where he, Lady Beatrice, and Murray were discussing the plans for departure. Severin rose, the hairs on his nape prickling. Even the tinker's mishmash of an outfit—an appalling mix of puce, saffron, and rust—did not detract from the resolute set of his features. Milton Sheridan looked gravely determined, and that did not bode well.

"We won't be going to London with you, Miss Bea," Sheridan announced.

Lady Beatrice's cup rattled into her saucer. "Why not?"

"Sheridans ain't city folk," he said. "We do be'er in open fields, with the sky above our 'eads."

"But it's not safe here," she protested. "After what happened to Fancy—"

"It's precisely what 'appened to me girl that has me mind made up. We be moving on, Miss Beatrice. The road's our true 'ome and where we be the safest. We travelling folk know places that others don't and, what's more, we be looking out for one another."

It was clear to Severin that the bloody tinker had made his mind up. Gone was the fellow's usual good cheer; everything from his posture to his tone said that he would not be moved. *Goddamnit.* The pressure in Severin's veins rose; he wanted to throttle some sense into the man. Didn't Sheridan realize the danger to which he would be exposing his daughter? Did he really think that he and his ragtag comrades could protect Fancy from harm?

When Severin had paid her a brief visit, his chest had clenched at her fragility. She'd looked so small and vulnerable amidst the mounded pillows, her thick locks streaming over her shoulders, her big brown eyes dwarfed by the purplish lump at her temple. And her fear...by Jove, it had shown in every delicate line of her face.

She was terrified, and she needed protection.

Try as he might, he couldn't shake off the need to give it to her. Logically, he knew it was a bad idea. He had a wife to find, siblings to corral, estates and businesses to run. More to the point, Fancy was a temptation he could ill afford. She was not suitable to be his wife or his mistress...hell, she was like no female he had ever known.

He'd rationalized accompanying her and the others to London; he was headed back in that direction anyway. Sheridan's new plan, however, was far less convenient. To protect Fancy, Severin would have to take off for parts unknown and for God only knew how long.

"But Fancy's not fully recovered." Lady Beatrice went over to Sheridan, as if her proximity would persuade him. "She needs to be looked after."

Sheridan's reply was a stony stare.

"Allow me to offer my escort." *God's teeth, tell me I didn't just say that.*

Severin felt the heat of stares turned upon him.

"You?" Lady Beatrice's voice rose in astonishment.

The words kept rolling off his tongue. "My carriage will offer Miss Sheridan the comfort she needs during her recovery. I will stay with her and her family until they are safely out of harm's reach. You have my word."

Sheridan looked him up and down. "The travelling life ain't suited for toffs."

"I'll manage." The cove had no idea of Severin's origins. Growing up in the rookery, he had eked out a living that would make the tinker's life seem majestic by comparison. "Miss Sheridan's safety must come first."

Lady Beatrice looked as if she might say something, but Murray cut her off.

"It's a good idea," the Scot said. "Sheridan, if you must travel alone—"

"I must," the tinker insisted.

"Then accept His Grace's escort. If danger befalls you, Knighton is a man you would want by your side." Murray flicked his gaze to Severin then back to the tinker. "Trust me on this."

Severin wasn't sure what to make of the Scot's praise. He supposed he could return the compliment...but he decided against it. The other's head was swelled enough as it was. It was best not to encourage sentiment. Next thing you knew, he and Murray might end up friends.

"You may join us, Your Grace," Sheridan said with clear reluctance. "But mind you, we be keepin' a pace and won't be stopping for nobody."

"I shall endeavor to keep up," Severin said wryly.

"We'll leave bright and early tomorrow. Mind you be ready." Wagging a finger at Severin as if he were a misbehaving puppy, Sheridan departed.

"Thank you, Knighton." Murray approached and clapped him on the shoulder. "This is generous of you."

Lady Beatrice arched her brows. "Quite generous."

"Think nothing of it." Severin kept his tone nonchalant.

His mind whirled. *What the devil have I done?*

8

On the day of departure, Fancy and her bosom chum exchanged tearful goodbyes. She clung to Bea, every fiber of her balking at deserting her friend in a time of need. What if the villain launched another attack? Fancy might not be worth much when it came to fighting, but she had a strong pair of lungs and could scream bloody murder as loud as anyone.

She had mounted that argument over and again to no avail. Da could be as stubborn as Bertrand when he made his mind up. Nothing she said could sway him from his plan that the Sheridans should go their own way.

"Don't blame your father, dear," Bea said now, as if reading her mind. "He wants what is best for you. Indeed, his decision might be the right one."

"'Ow can you say that?" Fancy swiped the back of her hand over her eyes. She'd never been a watering pot, but since the attack, she'd found herself perilously close to tears over naught. "I would be an extra pair o' eyes and ears. You don't know when the bastard might strike again—"

"Wick and his men will look out for me."

Her friend's confidence quieted Fancy's protests more than

any arguments could have. For Bea had never been a trusting sort, especially when it came to men. Yet now she exchanged a look with Mr. Murray, standing at a discreet distance by his waiting carriage. Some unspoken message passed between them. And Fancy realized the truth that her friend had not yet put into words.

Bea 'as fallen in love, she thought in wonder. *And Mr. Murray loves 'er back.*

Bea was glowing in a primrose carriage dress, her lavender eyes sparkling, her white-gold hair bound proudly back and no longer hiding her scar or her beauty from the world. Love had transformed her, prepared her for any hardships ahead. She had Mr. Murray to depend upon now, and he could offer more protection than a tinker's daughter ever could.

Gladness and a poignant ache filled Fancy's heart.

"You're in good 'ands," she said with a smile.

"So are you." Bea leaned closer. "But, my dear, don't forget your promise to me. While Wick says Knighton is honorable, you must remain on guard. If he tries to take advantage of you—"

"'E won't," Fancy said tremulously. "But I won't forget my promise."

Bea touched her forehead briefly to Fancy's "Take care, my dear. I shall miss you."

"You be careful, too." Fancy's smile wobbled. "Until we meet again."

They hugged and then Bea was gone.

Fancy wiped away a few errant tears, then went to help her da and brothers finish packing up the wagon. They were loading the last travelling cases when a conveyance pulled up the circular drive. Her eyes widened. The time she'd been in Knighton's carriage when he rescued her, she hadn't been in a frame of mind to notice its splendor. The enormous black coach, led by half a dozen bays with glossy manes, was like something out of a faerie tale. Its lacquered sides and spotless windows, framed by fringed velvet curtains, were dazzling.

The carriage pulled to a stop in front of her.

Her brother Liam ambled over and said in fervent tones, "Gor, pinch me, Fancy, for I must be dreamin'. *This* be our ride?"

"Yes," she said, equally awestruck.

While Da had accepted the duke's offer to accompany them to Northumberland, where there was a secluded campground known only to tinkers, he had decreed that it wasn't right for Fancy to travel alone with Knighton. Her brothers had drawn straws; Liam, who'd chosen the shortest, was to be her chaperone. He'd endured ribbing from the other lads who'd lifted their pinkies at him, calling him a bona fide nob since he would be travelling in a lord's fussy carriage rather than a tinker's good, solid caravan.

Liam was getting the last laugh, however, for their brothers now watched on with open-mouthed expressions as the driver opened the door to the sleek coach, letting down the steps. From what Fancy could see, the interior was upholstered in midnight velvet and outfitted with fixtures of polished brass.

Then the Duke of Knighton emerged, and she lost track of the carriage altogether. He gleamed from the top of his hat to the toe of his boots. His strapping form was clad in shades of dark blue and grey, his jaw freshly shaven above his cravat of maize silk.

Sweet Jaysus, 'e's 'andsome, her heart sighed.

He bowed and held out a gloved hand. "Ready, Miss Sheridan?"

"Yes, Your Grace." Her heart thumping, she placed her hand in his.

His fingers engulfed hers, his masculine heat seeping through the barrier of black leather. He handed her up into the carriage, and Liam bounded in next, letting out a whoop of excitement as he took in the spacious and modern cabin. The facing benches were wide enough to fit four people apiece, with plenty of leg room.

Sprawling next to her, Liam opened the wicker hamper on the floor.

"Gor, get an eyeful o' all 'em victuals," Liam exclaimed.

"Mind your manners." Fancy shot an anxious look beyond him, where Knighton was conferring with Da. "You don't want 'Is Grace to think you're a beggarly sort, do you?"

"This meat pie be nearly as good as yours."

Her gaze flew back to Liam, who was munching away on a golden pastry.

"Put that *back*," she said in a hushed tone. "You can't 'elp yourself to whate'er you like."

"That's what it's 'ere for, ain't it?" Liam took another large bite. "Besides, what would 'Is Nibs do with a 'alf-eaten pie?"

"Well, just don't eat anything else."

"The 'ell I won't." Her brother looked at her as if she'd lost her mind. "There be a bloody feast in front o' me and no Tommy, Godfrey, or Oliver to fight me for it. But since you be me sister and the one who 'itched us this fine ride, I'll share the goods with you if you ask nicely."

"I don't want—"

Fancy caught herself as Knighton returned. He took the opposite bench, the cabin seeming to shrink in his presence. It wasn't just his size; his virile male aura seemed to fill any space he occupied. His expensive scent curled in her nostrils, causing her heart to thrum like a hummingbird's wings.

"Are you both comfortable?" he inquired. "Do you require anything before we depart?"

His tone was neutral, no hint of sarcasm or condescension. Yet Fancy's gaze strayed to the open picnic basket, then to Liam's greasy fingers. Then to the crumbs clinging to the corner of her brother's mouth.

Knighton must think we're a pair o' ill-bred bumpkins, she thought miserably.

She knotted her fingers in the worn folds of her skirts. "No... that is, thank you, Your Grace."

"Actually, guv, would you 'ave anything to wash down this fine pie with?" Liam asked. "I'm feelin' a might parched."

She cringed at her brother's boldness.

Knighton showed no sign of derision. He merely reached to the side of the cabin, opening a leather-covered compartment perfectly designed to look like part of the wall. He reached inside and pulled out a corked bottle. Even more marvelous was the fog of condensation clinging to the bottle: there must be *ice* in that compartment, an unheard of luxury.

"Gor, will you take a look at that?" Liam cried. "If that ain't the cleverest contraption I e'er saw, and I be a tinker's son!"

"I had the carriage maker design it specifically," Knighton said.

Removing glasses from another hidden compartment, he passed them to Liam and Fancy. He popped the cork and poured out the effervescent gold liquid.

Excitement shone in Liam's brown eyes. "Be that *champagne*?"

"From a vineyard I own in France," the duke replied.

"Gor, I ain't tried champagne before," Liam chortled.

Fancy shot her brother an annoyed look. Did he have to wave their lack of sophistication as if it were a blooming flag?

"I've 'ad champagne before," she rushed to say. "At Bea's."

"I hope you both enjoy this vintage." Knighton filled his own glass and raised it. "To a safe journey ahead."

As the carriage glided off, Fancy took a tentative sip. The beverage was crisp and delightfully cold. Bubbles tickled her nose, lively flavors dancing upon her tongue.

"Do you like it?" Knighton's gaze met hers.

She nodded. "It tastes a bit like figs and 'oney. And currant buns, maybe."

The duke's brows shot up. Blushing, she realized how silly she must have sounded comparing expensive champagne to an ordinary morning bun.

"I don't taste currant buns, but it does quench a man's thirst." Liam drained his glass. "'Ow 'bout a topper, guv?"

As Knighton refilled her brother's glass, he said, "You have a refined palate, Miss Sheridan."

She blinked. "I do?"

"Fig, orange blossom honey, and *pain aux raisins*. Those were the champagne's notes as described by the vintner himself."

"Really?" She furrowed her brow. "What's a *pan o' rays ann*?"

The stern line of his mouth twitched. "A *pain aux raisins* is a pastry. The French version of the currant bun which, in my opinion, is more delectable. Then again, I prefer French cuisine to English fare."

Intrigued, she asked, "'Ow come you know so much about the French?"

Knighton paused to pour more champagne into the emptied glass Liam held out.

"Have a care, lad," he cautioned. "Champagne can go to the head."

Liam gulped down the contents. "We Sheridans can 'old our spirits."

"Suit yourself." The duke handed him the bottle.

With champagne in one hand and a sandwich he'd ransacked from the basket in the other, Liam was as happy as a pig in mud.

"As to your question, Miss Sheridan." Knighton returned his attention to her. "My mother was French. Her ancestors several generations back were Huguenots. Fleeing religious persecution in their native country, they ended up in London."

"Is your given name French? I've 'eard plenty o' names in my travels but never that one."

"Yes, *Severin* has French roots. It means 'serious.'" His expression was wry. "I have been told it suits me."

It did, in some respects.

"Except around donkeys," she said.

Surprise and a hint of amusement lightened his eyes. "*Touché*, Miss Sheridan."

Pleased at his response, she sipped her beverage. "Do you speak French?"

"*Oui.*"

She would take that as a yes. She studied his impassive features, her head filled with questions about his unusual past. According to Bea, he'd come from the London slums, which was a strange place for a duke's son to grow up.

"'Ow did your parents meet?" she asked.

His lashes fleetingly veiled his gaze. "That is a long story."

The champagne must have lent her courage, for she said, "We 'ave a long road ahead o' us."

"The tale is tedious, and I make it a habit not to bore young ladies," he said rather smoothly. "I would rather learn about you, Miss Sheridan."

"Me?" She couldn't help but snort. "My life ain't interesting at all."

As if in agreement, her brother let out a snore. He'd fallen asleep, his head leaning against the padded leather, a beatific smile upon his face.

"It would be interesting to me as I've never met a tinker's daughter before," Knighton said.

"You don't 'ave to watch grass grow to know it ain't a thrilling prospect," she returned.

At the smile that lit his gaze, her breath lodged. She knew then and there that she could get addicted to that look on him. To the way his mouth retained its firm edge, yet faint crinkles appeared around his eyes, silver glinting in the dark grey pupils.

"You underestimate your own charms, Miss Sheridan," he murmured.

She knew that he was just being polite. A man like him

doubtlessly had London's most beautiful ladies throwing themselves at him. Yet here he was stuck in a carriage with her, a girl with a big purplish bump on her head and a brother whose snoring could wake the dead.

Gathering up her courage, she said, "You don't 'ave to say that, Your Grace. I'm already grateful for all you've done. I'm in your debt for rescuing me. Now you've gone out o' your way to escort me when a man like you must 'ave more important things to do—"

"Your wellbeing is of the utmost importance," he said.

"Why? I'm no one special," she blurted. "And Bea 'as already decided on Mr. Murray—"

His brows lowered into a foreboding line. "You think I am escorting you to impress Lady Beatrice?"

"You did ask me to be your, um, ally," she said uncertainly.

"Let me make myself clear: my concern for your welfare is not for anyone's sake but your own." His jaw tautened. "I have not been a gentleman if that is what I have led you to believe."

"You've been a perfect gentleman," she protested. "Kind and gallant—"

"I cannot claim to be either of those things. I can assure you, however, that you are safe with me. I will protect you, Miss Sheridan, have no doubt of it."

His speech, delivered in cool, dispassionate tones, affected her the way a fervently uttered sonnet would. Her heart pounded giddily. Despite her promise to turn over a new leaf and let go of her silly fantasies, her infatuation was getting worse. The prince of her dreams was close enough to reach over and touch...yet he was forever out of her reach.

Fancy slipped her hand into the skirt of her pocket. With mingled guilt and furtive delight, she caressed the button she had snipped from the jacket he'd lent her that day on the riverbank. She'd rationalized her small theft by telling herself that his valet surely had a spare. For her, this would be the only part of

Knighton she would ever have. A keepsake that she would treasure all her life.

"Deny it if you must, but you're a true 'ero in my eyes," she said with quavering emotion.

The intensity of his gaze gathered like a storm. His nostrils flared slightly.

"I am no hero, Miss Sheridan," he averred, "but I would like to ask you a favor."

What favor could I possibly do for 'im?

"Yes?" she asked.

"I would like for us to start anew. If you could find it in your heart to forget my fumbling words on the riverbank, I should like for us to be friends."

Friends. With Severin Knight. It wasn't her faerie tale dream, but it was more than she'd thought possible. His offer cemented her belief that he was a decent man and not the seducer Bea feared he might be.

If I think o' 'im as a friend, Fancy said to herself, *then maybe I'll stop thinking o' 'im in other ways. Ways that a tinker's daughter should never think o' a duke.*

"I'd like that, Your Grace," she said shyly.

"In that case, let us do away with formality. Call me Knight." He sat back, his gaze steady.

"If I'm to call you Knight,"—her tongue curled around his name, the intimacy causing her tummy to flutter—"then you ought to call me Fancy."

"Fancy." His eyes held a faint smile. "That wasn't so difficult, was it?"

"No, it wasn't." She meant to smile back, but to her mortification, she yawned.

"You must be fatigued," he said gently.

Since the attack, she hadn't slept well. She'd been plagued by terrifying dreams. As a result, she *was* tired, the dull ache at her temple making the rest of her head feel as heavy as an iron pot.

"I think I could use a nap," she admitted.

"You are safe with me. I'll keep watch. Rest now, Fancy."

Lulled by the warmth in his grey eyes and the smooth motion of the carriage, she closed her eyes and slipped into a healing sleep.

9

"We be almost there, guv!" Tommy, the youngest Sheridan, exclaimed as he looked out the window at the passing wooded landscape. "Ain't no camping spot sweeter than this one in all o' Cumberland, I reckon."

Severin nodded and cast a meaningful glance at Fancy, who was dozing. Getting the message, Tommy piped down, although he kept his nose pressed against the glass like an eager pup. Having travelled with the Sheridans for five days now, Severin was used to the exuberant ways of Fancy's kin. Liam had bragged about the amenities to be found in Severin's carriage, and since then the other brothers had jockeyed for the position of riding with Fancy.

To Severin's surprise, he found himself liking the lads who had a cheerfully adaptable approach to life. They didn't seem to be bothered by sleeping in a different place each night, be it in an abandoned hayloft, on the narrow bunks in their family's wagon, or beneath the stars. Oliver, the eldest brother, had informed Severin that they were skipping some of their usual stops in order to get distance from Staffordshire. Apparently, the family typically made stops to do patchwork and other chores for a number of farmers. In return, they would be offered hospitality, and Oliver bemoaned missing out on Farmwife Jenkins' baking in particular.

Severin couldn't help but be impressed by the vast number of skills the Sheridans possessed. The tinkers he'd come across in London had specialized in mending and hawking tin. Around the campfire last night, Milton Sheridan had told him country tinkers were different.

"Aye, me da taught me tinwork, as 'is da did before 'im. But tinkering ain't limited to that." Milton had taken a puff from his pipe, letting out a wreath of smoke that hung in the firelight. "The travelling life is about bein' free as God meant us to be. Free from the shackles o' society and 'aving the skills to stay that way."

"The skills," Severin learned, included everything from horse trading to picking crops to cleaning chimneys. Indeed, the Sheridan boys had made a game of it last night. They each had to list an ability they possessed in turn, with no repeating, and the last brother to name a new skill would be the winner.

That had been Godfrey, with his contribution of "candle-making."

To which Oliver had replied, "Let's not forget skirt-chasing, eh, the only thing Godfrey be *actually* good at."

Godfrey had launched himself at Oliver. Which had led to the other lads jumping in with joyful whoops. Fancy had watched on, shaking her head in fond exasperation.

Watching her sleep now, her lashes dark fans against her cheeks, Severin felt an unwelcome stirring of possessiveness. She looked so damned feminine and small curled up in a corner, her braided head resting against the velvet squabs. Her bruise had faded to a yellowish color, and she'd lost some of the jumpiness she'd had right after the attack. Still, Severin took care not to startle her.

He had also observed that she seemed different from the rest of the family. Physically, she was more delicate, although she could have taken after her mama whom Severin understood had died in recent years. In her manner, Fancy seemed quieter than her kin, more apt to observe her family's shenanigans than jump in.

She'd grown more comfortable with him during their journey. He saw more of her wit and sense of humor. She was easy to talk to...perhaps too easy. Although he wasn't one for chitchat, he found himself answering her questions about his work, what it was like to live in London. He spoke a little about his aunt and siblings, and she never pushed, seeming to understand his desire for privacy. She emanated a natural, unaffected warmth that both drew him and made him wary.

For a woman who'd claimed to be experienced in the ways of the world, she had an uncanny air of innocence about her. Maybe it was just her eyes. Those doe-like orbs radiated purity: an untainted spirit. At any rate, what business was it of his how worldly she was? She could have slept with one man or a hundred, and it would still be none of his business.

Then why do you get hard looking at her? his inner voice accused. *Why do you burn to know what she tastes like...all over?*

His intensifying fantasies about Fancy were proof positive that he needed to get her to safety and himself back to London. Before the journey, he had written his man of business and his aunt, letting them know of his delayed return. According to Milton Sheridan, the remaining trip to Northumberland would take under a week. Surely Severin could put a leash on his lustful impulses until then. Once he saw Fancy safely settled at the tinkers' camping ground, he would leave.

The coach arrived at a clearing. In the distance, Severin saw a dilapidated stone farmhouse, the decaying fencing and fallow fields conveying that it hadn't been inhabited for some time. The Sheridans' wagon had rolled to a stop in front of the house, next to a similar wagon painted bright yellow and green.

"Gor, that looks to be the *Taylors'* caravan," Tommy said excitedly.

From the grin on the adolescent's face, Severin assumed this was a good thing.

"Friends of yours?" he inquired.

"Aye, the Taylors be friends o' me da's and 'is da's before that. We usually cross paths with 'em, but I weren't thinkin' it'd be 'ere at the farm'ouse," Tommy said. "This'll be grand! There be a field out back, perfect for kickin' a ball. The Taylors 'ave five lads. If Fancy'll play, we can go family against family!"

Yawning, Fancy sat up and rubbed her eyes. "Play...what?"

"Kickball," Tommy said eagerly. "The Taylors be 'ere!"

Severin frowned. "Your sister is recovering from an injury."

"Ne'er mind, then." Tommy eyed him. "You'll play in 'er stead, won't you, guv?"

"I will not," Severin said.

"Then we'll take 'em four on five." Tommy slid Fancy a sly look. "I wager Sam'll go easy on us, seein' as 'e's sweet on Fancy."

Seeing the roses bloom in Fancy's cheeks, Severin asked, "Who is Sam?"

"The Taylor's oldest boy. 'E's a rippin' fellow. I thought 'e might end up as me brother-in-law, but there's still time yet." With a mischievous grin at his sister, Tommy opened the door, bounding out before the wheels had completely stopped. He ran toward the group of males milling in front of the farmhouse, shouting, "Taylors, oi! Good to see you!"

Severin looked at Fancy, brows raised.

"Pay Tommy no mind," she muttered. "We'd best, um, join everyone."

She bolted from the carriage before he could help her.

Severin alighted, prowling behind her. A strapping blond man dressed in a loose shirt and chamois breeches stepped into her path. The fellow was nearly of a height with Severin, with legs like tree trunks and a ruggedly handsome face that probably made milkmaids swoon.

Severin narrowed his eyes as the fellow grabbed Fancy by the waist, lifting her in a circle.

"Sam Taylor, put me down at once!" She sounded out of breath.

"Put the lady down." Severin's voice was not breathless. "Now."

Taylor pivoted, his brow creasing. "Who the devil are you?"

"The man you will answer to if you do not release Miss Sheridan at once," Severin said.

Taylor's gaze slitted.

"Let go o' me, you oaf." Fancy freed herself. "This is the Duke o' Knighton. 'E's been escorting us."

"A duke, is 'e?" Taylor looked Severin up and down, his expression unimpressed. "Where did you find the toff? And what do you need an escort for?"

"It's a long story..." she began.

"And there'll be plenty o' time to be tellin' it after we've settled in." Milton Sheridan came over, his tone genial. "Fancy, why don't you 'elp Mrs. Taylor in the kitchen? She's got 'er mind set on preparing a feast to celebrate us all bein' together."

"Yes, Da." With a relieved look, she darted off toward the farmhouse.

"I'll see if Ma needs anythin' brung in." Taylor set off after her in a determined stride.

"Sam and me Fancy 'ave known each other all their lives," Milton said. "They fit together, don't they, Your Grace?"

Severin watched as Taylor reached Fancy's side. The blond fellow fell in step with her, and she blushed prettily at something he said. Looking at the fresh young pair, surrounded by their loving families, Severin was once again an outsider peering in on happiness.

"Yes," he said flatly. "They do."

At dusk, Fancy went searching for Knight with a plate in hand.

He wasn't with the group eating in the kitchen, nor was he sitting around the fire with Oliver, Godfrey, and some of the Taylor boys. She skirted around her family's wagon when she saw Sam leaning against it, having an earnest conversation with Da.

Sweet Jaysus, she hoped that Sam wasn't bringing up marriage again. She thought she had put the matter to rest in the spring, and she didn't want any unpleasantness marring the relationship between his family and hers. It had been awkward enough in the kitchen with Mrs. Taylor. While she and the redheaded matron prepared supper, the good lady had dropped broad hints about how she wished to see her son settled with a woman from another travelling clan.

As much as Fancy hated disappointing Mrs. Taylor and her own family, she didn't have those kinds of feelings toward Sam. And she couldn't control the yearnings of her heart, foolish as they might be, any more than she could the sun from rising.

Fancy approached Knight's coach. The driver, who was happily digging into his own dish of Mrs. Taylor's excellent cooking, said that the duke had gone to the pond. Fancy declined his offer to escort her there. She'd been stopping at this abandoned farmhouse since she was a girl, and she knew her way around.

The pond was situated just beyond the clearing behind the house. She passed by the logs the lads had used as makeshift goal posts for their game of kickball, her aproned skirts whispering over the trampled grass. As she passed through a small copse of trees, her heart sped up, her hands growing clammy against the plate, but the boisterous voices of her family and friends carried on the breeze, reassuring her that she was safe.

At the pond, she spotted Knight by the water's edge. He'd set his hat and jacket on the ground, and he had a foot propped on a boulder. He looked solitary, not just because he was by himself. There was a remoteness to his gaze as he studied the sunset-painted water, as if he wanted to discern some secret beneath the rippling surface.

At her approach, he turned. In that unguarded moment, she saw a maelstrom of emotion in his eyes: pain and...longing brighter than the sun's dying rays.

What is 'e thinking about? she wondered. *Or, more precisely...who?*

He straightened, his gaze shuttering. "Good evening, Fancy."

"I'm sorry to disturb you," she said hesitantly. "But you weren't at supper, and I thought you might like something to eat."

His gaze fell to the tin plate she held out.

He took it from her with a quiet, "Thank you."

"You're welcome." With a smile, she handed him the wooden utensils she'd tucked into her apron pocket. "Mrs. Taylor's known for 'er 'otpot, and there won't be much left once the boys are done."

At his stoic nod, she paused. Since the start of the journey, when he'd requested that they be friends, she'd felt increasingly at ease in his company. Spending hours in a coach together had a way of doing that. Yet now she felt her shyness returning; clearly, he didn't want her to be there.

"I'll, um, leave you to enjoy your meal in peace," she said.

"No, stay." He seemed to come to himself. "I would enjoy the company."

"You've 'ad plenty o' that this week," she said with a touch of humor. "I've been told we Sheridans are an acquired taste. It would be understandable if you're wanting time alone."

"Your brothers are a boisterous lot." He gave her an amused look and then did the most gallant thing: with his free hand, he spread his jacket over the grass like a picnic blanket, gesturing for her to sit. "Please. Stay with me so that I do not have to sup alone."

Sensing that his request was genuine, she acquiesced, and the two of them sat side by side in companionable silence. He dug into the stew, which was the result of a group effort. Mr. Taylor had done work for a butcher in a nearby village, bringing home a leg of mutton. Mrs. Taylor had chopped up the meat, braising it with chunks of onions and carrots. Since Da had fixed up the farmhouse brick oven, Fancy had sliced potatoes thinly, laying them on top of the stew along with dollops of butter and baked it. The result was a golden-brown crust, the rich filling bubbling beneath.

"This is delicious," Knight said.

"I'm glad you like it." To distract herself from his nearness, she wrapped her arms around her raised knees, looking out over the water as dusk spilled vivid pink and orange over the surface. "It's beautiful out 'ere, isn't it?"

"Indeed." He cocked his head; in this light, his dark hair had a violet sheen. "I don't think I've heard so many crickets before."

She couldn't help but grin. "Those ain't crickets."

"They aren't?"

"No, those are courting toads." She peered at him curiously. "You 'aven't been in the country much, 'ave you?"

"I inherited a country seat, which I have yet to visit." He paused to eat from the plate balanced on his lap. "Work keeps me in London."

"You 'ave to keep an eye on your factories?" she asked.

He nodded. "Among other things."

"What other things?"

He took a bite, swallowing before he answered. "Weavers are a contentious lot, not that I blame them. Taxes and modernization are eroding their livelihood. I have my hands full trying to convince them that, since they can't fight industrialization, they must join it. I have a new weaving machine I plan to introduce, but I have to do it in such a way that the workers will accept it and not walk out or go rioting in the streets."

"That sounds taxing," she quipped.

"Never jest about taxes to a weaver, Fancy." His mouth curved faintly. "Now it's not just work that occupies my time, but also the responsibilities that come with the title. Management of the estates, investments...and my half-siblings."

In his brief mentions of his kin, she'd gathered that they were a handful.

"They can't be as 'ard to manage as mine," she said teasingly.

"Don't be so certain." His glance was wry. "In addition to brothers, I have a sister who is a hardened flirt and another who fancies herself a revolutionary."

Fancy stared at him. "'Ow did they become that way?"

"It's not their fault, I suppose." His eyes darkened. "While my sire took care of them materially, he provided no other guidance. When their mothers died, he brought them to live with him in his chateau in the south of France. I went there to fetch them. Cecily and Jonas, sixteen and seventeen respectively, had their own wing and carried on however they pleased. I lost track of how many drunken rakes and trollops I passed on the way to find Jonas's room. Cecily I couldn't find at all since she was out gallivanting with some fortune hunter."

"Sweet Jaysus," Fancy said, blinking.

"The thirteen-year-old twins, Toby and Eleanor, lived in a separate wing. They were put under the care of a governess who seemed more like a prison warden. The children were practically chained to the schoolroom and had little contact with the outside world."

"But your sire—"

"Was too busy seeing to his own pleasures to pay his bastards any mind."

Fancy stared at Knight's harsh profile. "Then you're a *prince* to care for them. To look after your brothers and sisters when no one 'as before."

"I am merely doing my duty," he said curtly.

The more she got to know him, the less she believed that that was his only motivation. He had a caring, noble heart even if, for some reason, he refused to admit it.

"Enough about me." He set his empty plate down with undue care. "Tell me about you and Sam Taylor."

Heat pulsed in her cheeks at the sudden change in topic.

"There...there ain't much to tell," she stammered.

"Your brother Tommy disagrees."

"Tommy 'as a mouth like a tap," she said darkly. "'E doesn't know when to turn 'imself off."

"He's not the only one with an opinion about you and Taylor." Knight lifted his brows. "I heard your father and Mrs. Taylor talking about how grandchildren could connect your families."

Why does Knight care about my relationship with Sam? Could 'e be... jealous? Or is 'e just showing the concern that any friend would?

"It doesn't matter what they say. I turned Sam down in the spring," she admitted. "'E's a good decent fellow, but I think o' 'im like one o' my brothers."

"He doesn't think of you in the same fashion."

It wasn't a question but a statement of fact.

"Because 'e doesn't know me, not truly," she said earnestly. "If 'e did, 'e would know that I'd make 'im a terrible wife."

"You couldn't be a terrible wife if you tried." As her heart soared, he frowned. "That is, for the right man—a man who shares your background—you have all the skills to recommend you. Your father is quite proud of your accomplishments."

"Sure, I can cook, sew, clean. But what if I want to be more than a good tinker's wife?" She blew glumly at a strand of hair that had escaped its plait. "What if I want more than to travel in endless circles bartering my skills?"

He studied her. For a tense second, she feared he might gainsay her. And she didn't want to know what that would feel like, to have her dreams mocked by the man who starred in them.

"You are different from your family," he said.

The quiet statement didn't feel like judgement. A part of her considered sharing the truth: the reason she was different from her kin was because she was not a Sheridan by blood. Yet her ng friendship with Knight already had a vast social chasm to bridge. She wasn't ready to put even more distance between them by admitting that she was a foundling.

An unwanted babe who'd been abandoned in the fields.

"I'm a Sheridan in the ways that count." That was no lie.

"All right, Miss Fancy Sheridan." He looked into her eyes. "If you don't want to be a good tinker's wife, what *do* you want?"

His husky question teased over her skin like a feather. Goose pimples prickled, her nipples rising into hard, tight buds. Mesmerized by his intent gaze, she swayed toward him...and gave him the truth.

"I want a faerie tale," she whispered. "I want a prince who thinks I'm a princess even though I'm ordinary. I want 'im to love me with all 'is 'eart because I'll love him just as madly. I want to settle in one place with 'im and 'ave a family, one we would nurture and love together. That's what I want."

Knight's eyes darkened, his pupils edging out the light. His gaze dropped to her lips, and she saw his nostrils quiver. Below the granite ledge of his jaw, his throat worked above the loosened knot of his cravat. A magnetic force pulsed between them, his head lowering toward hers, her own tilting up...

He drew back sharply. "You would be better off with Taylor."

"B-beg pardon?" she said, startled.

"He seems like a reliable sort," Knight said brusquely. "And a constant one, if he's still waiting on you despite being turned down. Take it from me, Fancy: it's better not to gamble on love."

Looking into his eyes, she felt as if she'd run headlong into a steel wall. His features were hard and impenetrable, all hints of desire gone.

"Love ain't a gamble," she whispered.

He rose abruptly and offered her his hand. "I had better escort you back before the others wonder where you've gone."

Ignoring his help, she got on her own two feet. "I can find my way back, Your Grace."

Pride allowed her to hide the pain of her shattered hopes. Hopes that she'd been foolish to have in the first place and even more foolish to share. She walked stiffly back to the farmhouse, willing herself not to run or cry, wishing she wasn't so blooming aware of Knight's presence behind her.

10

THAT NIGHT, FANCY HAD TROUBLE FINDING SLEEP. SHE AND Mrs. Taylor shared the single bedchamber in the farmhouse, but she couldn't blame the good matron's snoring for her restlessness. As she listened to her roommate's deep slumber, she tossed and turned on her own straw pallet because she could not stop thinking about Knight.

Did I imagine that near-kiss moment between us? Why is 'e so jaded about love? What 'appened to 'im in the past?

At dawn, she rose with a surge of unexpected energy and decided to put it to good use in the kitchen. Between what the Taylors had brought and the food supplies that Bea had insisted the Sheridans take with them, Fancy had plenty to work with. She made a hearty breakfast of eggs, potatoes, and stewed beans, even doing a bit of baking.

The Taylors and her family exclaimed over the food. She waited for Knight to emerge, and when he didn't by mid-morning, she decided to go to him. She didn't want to break the fragile filaments of friendship that the last week had woven between them. After this journey ended, they would part ways, and she wanted their memories of each other to be good.

She found Knight at his carriage, sitting at a table while his valet poured his tea. He stood when she approached. She didn't know how his valet did it, but Knight looked as if he'd risen from a night in a palace rather than camped out in the middle of a field. His cravat had a crisp knot, and he was wearing the charcoal-grey jacket he'd once lent her. She cast a surreptitious glance at his left sleeve; sure enough, his valet had replaced the gold button that, at this very moment, was snug in the pocket of her skirts.

"Good morning, Fancy," Knight said pleasantly.

His tone held no hint that anything unusual had happened between them the night before. And perhaps nothing had. Perhaps that moment had been a product of her imagination and hopeless yearning.

Count yourself lucky, she told herself. *'E ain't 'olding your rude departure last night against you. Follow 'is lead and keep everything friendly-like.*

She set the plate on the table. "I made breakfast and thought you might be wanting some."

"Thank you," he said politely.

Reaching into her apron pocket, she removed a napkin-wrapped bundle and held it out to him.

"What's this?" he asked.

"Open it, and you'll see."

He unfolded the rough napkin to reveal the stack of three golden pastries shaped like disks. The slashes she'd made in the buttery tops showed off the dark and moist currant-filled interior.

When he looked up, there was a smile in his eyes. "You baked Eccles cakes?"

"Or, as we Sheridans like to call them, *squashed fly cakes*," she said with a grin.

His brows rose, a silent question.

"When Tommy was small, Liam told 'im that Eccles cakes were filled with ground-up flies. For years, the rest o' the family wondered why Tommy refused to eat them."

Knight's lips twitched. "And Liam, out of the goodness of his heart, volunteered to eat Tommy's share?"

"Clearly, you know my brothers," Fancy said. "Anyway, the cakes are for your tea, but I brought you some now in case my brothers got to them first."

Instead of waiting for tea, Knight lifted a pastry to his mouth. His white teeth sank into the cake, buttery flakes drifting to the ground. He chewed, swallowed, and took another bite. She watched in surprise as he finished the pastries in rapid succession.

"You like Eccles cakes, I take?" she said, bemused.

He wiped his mouth with the napkin.

"I like sweets in general," he admitted. "And your delectable Eccles cakes in particular."

At the compliment, her tummy turned as gooey as the filling of the cakes when she'd pulled them from the oven.

"I'll make more," she offered breathlessly.

He shook his head, the smile still lurking in his eyes. "Trying to fatten me up, are you?"

She stared at his long, hard, virile physique. "You couldn't be anything but perfect."

Blooming 'ell...please tell me I didn't say that aloud.

The crease between his dark brows told her that she had.

"I mean, um, you being tall, you 'ave room to spread it around." Cheeks on fire, she floundered on. "Unlike me. Being short, um, everything shows."

Room to spread it around? Everything shows? A swirling vortex of embarrassment engulfed her. *Sweet Jaysus, could I embarrass myself anymore?*

"Fancy." His voice, gentle yet firm, anchored her. "Thank you for the cakes and breakfast. Before you came, I was about to look for you."

Breathe in, breathe out. You can't die from 'umiliation.

"You were?" she managed.

"Yes. I wanted to tell you that I'm leaving tomorrow."

"Leaving?" she echoed stupidly.

He gave a brisk nod. "I spoke with the Taylors this morning. Since your father informed them of what happened at Lady Beatrice's estate, they are anxious for your wellbeing. They've decided to accompany you to Northumberland and stay as long as necessary. Mr. Taylor said that he and his boys will keep a lookout for any troublemakers. Between them and your own kin, you'll have a veritable army looking after you."

She blinked, trying to take in the words. What they meant.

"So you're going." Her throat clogged. "Just...like that?"

His eyes were unreadable. "It is best that I go. For both of us. You have the Taylors now...and Sam, in particular, gave me his word that he wouldn't let anything happen to you. As for me, I have neglected my affairs for too long and must return to London."

What did you think 'e would do, you nitwit? Stay forever? Propose and carry you off to a castle in the clouds?

She didn't know why it hurt so much. He was only departing a few days earlier than planned. It was better to make a clean break of it, she told herself numbly. For both of them to go on their separate ways as God intended. He was a duke who needed to find himself a duchess in London.

She was a tinker's daughter...who was going to live out the rest of her life alone.

Because, in her heart, no one could ever measure up to Knight. Not ever.

"O' course you must go," she forced herself to say. "You've stayed too long already."

"Fancy...I wouldn't go, if I thought you were not safe. But you're in good hands," he began.

"I understand." She fixed her lips into a smile. "And in case I forget to say it—thank you, Knight. For everything."

After a pause, he said quietly, "It was my pleasure and my honor."

"I'd best go find Da. 'E feels a storm coming on and wants to fix up the barn for Bertrand and the 'orses. I promised to 'elp 'im."

Knight gave a nod.

Shoulders straight, acutely aware of Knight's gaze upon her, she walked away from him and back to the world where she belonged.

~

Half past midnight, Severin left the makeshift sleeping quarters of his coach with a lamp in hand. It was clear that he would not find sleep that night, and he would rather take a walk than toss and turn on the squabs. As Milton Sheridan had forecasted, a storm was nearing: the air was humid and heavy, the moon playing peekaboo behind drifting clouds. Animals and insects rustled with anticipation.

Severin walked on. As he strode past the Sheridan caravan and past the dark farmhouse where Fancy slept, he told himself that he was doing the right thing.

You have to leave. Before you do something you'll both regret.

Yesterday, he'd come too damned close to kissing her.

He didn't know what it was about Fancy Sheridan, why she roused his basest instincts. A part of himself that he kept locked away, reserved for the females who would welcome his carnal attentions. Yet what he felt toward Fancy wasn't just pure lust, either.

He...liked her. Liked talking to her and being her friend.

It wasn't the intense adoration he felt for Imogen. Imogen held his heart and always would. Fancy, however, made him smile...and had a hold on a different part of him altogether.

His cock ached. His bollocks felt full to bursting. He hadn't been this randy since he was a green lad, and it confused him. Before Fancy, women had fallen into two categories: those he fucked and Imogen. Fancy, with her warm sensuality and innocent dreams, was neither. Despite her sexual experience, she wasn't the sort of woman he could tup and leave; she was too sweet, too trusting. At the same time, she possessed none of the qualities that would make her a suitable Duchess of Knighton.

Frustration drove him on to the clearing behind the house, the first drops of rain landing. They felt cool and invigorating, and he wasn't ready to turn back. For once, he wasn't ready to do the sensible thing. He continued past the meadow toward the pond even as the winds began to gather, his lantern flickering.

Speckled with moisture, he stared out over the dark water. There was primal beauty in the swaying trees, the rippling waves, the teasing flash of the moon through the clouds like a lady's ankle through her skirts. He breathed in, the scent a world away from the London alleyways of his youth. Here, it didn't smell of rubbish and human misery, mixed with the rancid tang of the Thames. Nor did it smell of rarefied London, the burning beeswax, flowers, and perfumes. Here, the fragrance was of the earth, forest, and water...of freedom.

An errant thought entered his mind. When had he last felt free?

He couldn't recall it; maybe he never had.

As far back as he could remember, there had always been some pressing thing that he had to do. Taking care of his *maman* after the drink ruined her, stealing and fighting in the streets to survive. Then he'd met Imogen and the Hammonds, and new ambitions had taken root in him.

He had no longer wanted to live like a beast. He'd wanted to be rich, cultivated, different than what he was. For Imogen, he'd worked to transform himself into a gentleman.

Although he'd lost her, his ambitions drove him on. Even now, when he was a lord of the realm, he felt that restless dissatisfaction prowling inside him.

When will it stop? When will I feel, if not happy, then at peace?

A flash of white distracted him from the rare moment of introspection. He squinted at the object moving on the other side of the pond. What was it? It didn't look like a forest animal. Was it...a woman? In a nightgown?

Bloody hell, he thought with a jolt. *What is Fancy doing out here—in her nightclothes?*

The obvious reason pierced his skull like a metal spike. Was she about to meet with a lover? Had her demurring about Sam Taylor been false? Or had he, Severin, pushed her into the other man's arms with his foolish, *stupid* praise of Taylor's reliability and constancy?

Heart hammering, Severin watched as Fancy disappeared into the thick forest beyond the pond. She was moving as quickly as a doe, like one who knew her path.

To Taylor? Was Taylor waiting for her in some cozy hideaway?

An internal war raged inside Severin, pitting reason against instinct.

Should I leave her be? What business is it of mine if she and Taylor are lovers?

But it isn't safe for her to be out here alone.

She won't be alone for long if Taylor's waiting for her—

But, damnit, she's mine to protect...

Mine.

Cursing, he sprinted after her.

∼

He didn't catch up to her until they were deep in the woods. She was walking at a rapid pace, heedless of the blustery winds.

"Fancy. Stop, it's me," Severin called. "What is the matter?"

When she didn't respond, he grabbed hold of her arms, turning her around. Her eyes were wide and unfocused.

"Let me go," she growled.

A memory punched him. Of his *maman,* during one of those

episodes that had led to her custody in Bedlam. The unrecognizable light in her eyes as she'd looked straight at him—and brought down the knife...

He caged his demons. Fancy wasn't mad. Something else was going on.

"Fancy, I need you to look at me." He gave her a gentle shake. "Tell me who I am."

She blinked. Seemed to snap out of her strange state. "Knight?"

Relief flooded him. "Yes, sweeting."

"Why...why did you wake me up?" She looked confused. "What are you doing in my room?"

"You are not in your room," he said warily. "You're in the forest."

"The forest?" Seeming dazed, she looked around her. "What am I doing 'ere?"

"You were walking. At such a quick clip that I thought you knew where you were going."

"I...must 'ave been wandering in my sleep. I do that sometimes."

Understanding dawned. "You sleepwalk?"

"Yes, since I was a girl..."

She blinked as a droplet landed on her cheek, followed by another. She looked at him, her eyes huge and luminous in the moonlight, her hair free and waving down to her waist. Despite her befuddled state, she looked like a friendly wood faerie, the kind that in children's stories led lost men to safety.

"It is starting to storm." Knight stripped off his jacket, putting it around her shoulders as droplets began to pelt them. "We're too far away from the farmhouse. I saw a place where we can wait out the rain. Come with me?"

He held out his hand. She took it, her small hand curling in his. Together, they ran to find shelter.

11

Fancy awoke with a start. After a disorienting moment, she remembered where she was.

In the hollowed base of an old tree...with Knight. He'd taken her here after waking her from an episode of sleepwalking. Knight was sitting up and she leaning against him. They'd been waiting out the rain and must have dozed off.

Knight had an arm around her, the warmth of his body insulating her from the chill. His chest rose and fell beneath her cheek, his scent curling in her nostrils. In this cozy den, the rain a hypnotic drumbeat in the background, she felt as if she were in a dream. Suspended in a bubble free of time and earthly constraints.

She raised her head, studying him. The watery pre-dawn light that filtered through the opening limned his strong features. Fascinated, she saw that he had a night beard. The dark scruff added to his dangerous virility and framed his beautiful stern mouth. Longing pierced her, a sweet and urgent ache. He was her hero, and he had once again come to her aid.

She lifted her hand, tracing a finger lightly along his prickly jaw.

His eyes opened, and she found herself staring into fathomless depths. She could have pulled her hand away, but instead she curved her palm around his jaw, feeling the taut leap of muscle. The moment trembled between them.

"I cannot offer you anything." His voice was deep, strained. "Nothing beyond the moment."

She knew that, of course. If the choice was between a moment with him or none at all, then she'd already made her choice. Although she was a novice to bodily desire, she felt no shame or fear over it. She trusted her heart to guide her. And it told her that making love with Knight was right, the most natural thing in the world.

"Then let's make the most o' the moment," she whispered.

A primal sound came from him. Then he hauled her onto his lap.

His kisses fell hungrily upon her forehead, her cheeks, and she shuddered not from cold but from yearning. From the molten need that spread from her core and bubbled through her veins. She was hot as a flame, feverish with a lifetime of wanting.

Of waiting for him, her prince...her Knight.

When he captured her earlobe between his teeth, she gasped at the foreign sensation. He drew her sensitive lobe into his mouth, suckling and tonguing. Her woman's place fluttered and dampened, and she squirmed in his lap. Through her nightdress, she felt the unmistakable proof of his arousal, his thick, hard manhood wedged against her bottom.

She felt dizzy with need. Mad with it. With her longing for this man.

As his lips descended to her throat, she threaded her fingers in his hair. The scrape of his bristle against her skin, the rough silk of his hair between her fingers was an indescribable delight. He lowered her to the bed of moss, pushing his jacket off her shoulders, his hands curving around her breasts. She moaned his name as he thumbed the stiff tips through her nightgown.

"You like that," he said huskily.

It wasn't a question, yet she panted, "Yes. Oh yes."

In the dimness, his eyes had a feral glint. "What about this?"

He lowered his head, and she moaned as he suckled her through the fabric. The worn material was no defense against his hot, licking kiss. The mind-melting swirl of his tongue. He sucked on her nipple, and the sensation reached deep into her center, drawing forth her intimate dew. Her inner muscles quivered, clutching on emptiness. She'd never felt anything like this, this heady desperation, as if she would fly out of her skin.

"Do you want more, Fancy?" he said.

This time it was a question. She felt it in the stillness of his frame and steadiness of his gaze. The choice was hers.

"I need you, Knight," she whispered. "Whate'er you'll give me."

Hunger flared in his eyes. A heartbeat later, she felt him pushing up her nightgown. Her breath became tattered as his hand roamed up her calf, past her knee to rest possessively upon her bare thigh. When his thumb traced the crease of her leg, she whimpered.

"So impatient," he admonished.

She knew he was teasing, yet for some reason his stern tone made her squirm even more.

"Touch me, *please*," she pleaded.

"Like this?" He slid a finger through her intimate folds.

"Yes," she gasped.

"What a soft, sweet pussy you have," he murmured. "Made for petting."

In her travels, she'd overheard men speaking about bodily parts and the sexual act, those conversations always seeming crude. Yet hearing her elegant duke engage in naughty talk inflamed her, as did his masterful caressing between her legs. She felt a flash of worry about how damp she'd gotten there, but his growling response reassured her.

"I love how wet you are." His tone was low, guttural. "How ripe for the taking."

His touch travelled upward, finding a hidden peak. He rubbed in slick, mind-robbing circles. She moaned at the exquisite pleasure.

"Christ, that's a pretty sound," he said thickly. "I want to hear you moan for me, Fancy."

Her heart stuttered as he pushed a long, thick finger into her.

"*Knight.*" She couldn't help but gasp at the fullness.

"Devil and damn...you're tight."

She didn't have time to make sense of why he sounded surprised because in the next instant he began moving his finger. The sensation was...indescribable. She moaned as he sheathed his digit deeper and deeper, her body clutching onto what he gave her. At the same time, he kept rubbing her secret bud, tightening the coil in her belly. When he stirred her wetness, something in her sprung free. She cried out as she catapulted into bliss.

"God, you're sweet," he rasped. "I can't wait to be inside you."

He shifted, wrestling with his clothes. Then he came atop her. Even with pleasure buzzing through her veins, she tensed as he aligned their bodies. His private part nudged hers, and her breath hitched with sudden panic: his manhood felt *huge*, built proportionally to the rest of him. When the blunt tip pushed at her entrance, she stiffened.

"Relax, sweeting, I'll be gentle," he said raggedly. "I won't hurt you."

Seeing the desperate need in his eyes, balanced by the determined clench of his jaw, she knew that he spoke the truth. That he wouldn't lose control with her. That despite his power and size, she was safe with him.

"I know," she whispered. "I trust you."

Because she did.

Fancy's sweetness edged Severin's lust into combustible territory.

He was harder than he could remember ever being, his cock weeping with eagerness as he notched himself to Fancy's pussy. Despite his mind-obliterating desire, he advanced slowly. He would cut off his own arm before hurting her and, knowing his own size, he'd taken care to prepare her. She was dripping for him, her slick dew easing his way inside. Still, her sheath was snugger than he expected, the pleasure pulling harsh breaths from his lungs. Inch by inch, he pushed into her pulsing heat.

He gazed down at her. "How does that feel?"

"Um...full?" She ran her tongue over her plump lips, and her gaze widened when his cock twitched inside her. "You're big."

"But you can take me, can't you, sweeting? Tell me you want me."

"I want you, Knight," she said softly.

"Good because I need to move, Fancy. You feel too bloody fine."

He took her tremulous smile as permission. He withdrew a little, the wet suck of her passage sizzling up his spine. He pressed his hips in, and her body yielded more. He couldn't stop himself from taking what she offered, from sinking his cock deeper and deeper into her giving softness. When he felt her pussy kiss his stones, a jagged breath left him. He ground his hips, and she mewled like a kitten.

Hunger took over then. He pushed back her thighs, canting her cunny up for his taking. At this new angle, his shaft grazed against her pearl, and his balls pulsed at her clenching response. He plowed her harder, burying himself in her tight pussy, the reality of Fancy better than his hottest fantasy. She held him, her hips pillowing his hard thrusts, her hands weaving through his hair. Then she began to spend again, her convulsions massaging his plunging prick.

The climax surged over him, so potent that he almost didn't pull out in time. He wrenched himself free and fisted his turgid flesh. He jerked himself once, twice, shuddering as he shot his seed onto her thighs.

Panting, he hung over her, his mind hazy with pleasure. He couldn't gather his breath, let alone his senses. She smiled at him and laced her fingers around his neck. Suddenly, she surged upward, her lips aimed at his, and panic flooded him.

He backed away from her. "I cannot."

She blinked, looking confused. "What...what do you mean?"

"I cannot kiss you," he said hoarsely.

She sat up fully. "Why not?"

"Because I..." He trailed off as voices filtered into the hollow.

"Fancy! Where be you?"

Her eyes widened. "It's my family," she said in an urgent hush.

She tried to extricate herself from him and put herself to rights, but Severin knew it was too late. Seconds later, her brother Godfrey stuck his head through the tree's opening.

"Fancy, thank God! We be looking...*Knighton?*" In a blink, Godfrey's disbelief morphed into rage, and he bellowed, "What the bleeding 'ell are you doing with me sister?"

∼

Later that morning, Severin found himself seated across the table from Milton Sheridan. They were in the main room of the tinker's caravan, the décor conveying the multiple uses of the space. A small iron stove occupied one corner, surrounded by various cooking utensils suspended from pegs. Stacked against another wall were baskets of assorted goods. On the wall directly behind the tinker hung the tools of his trade.

Severin didn't think it was a coincidence that he found himself facing not only the father of the woman he'd compromised but a wall of dangerous instruments as well. A saw with glinting teeth swayed with subtle menace next to a pickaxe and hammer. A collection of knives was lined up on the narrow worktable beneath.

He clenched his jaw, balling his hands beneath the table. He accepted full responsibility for what he'd done and, consequently, for what he now had to do. Anger at himself roiled in his belly.

What the bloody hell was I thinking?

He hadn't been using his head...not the one above his shoulders at any rate. The beast in him had taken over. Hence, the present unthinkable situation. He was going to have to marry Fancy Sheridan. A tinker's daughter who possessed none of the qualities that he required in a bride. She was a sweet creature, yes, but one who had no pedigree or connections, who was likely going to be eaten alive by his half-siblings, and who had a greater chance of sprouting wings and learning to fly than being accepted by the *ton*.

As bad as all that was, another reality was worse: he had taken Fancy's virginity.

Shame scalded his gut. At the time, he didn't even know that he'd deflowered her. Yes, she had been exquisitely tight...but he'd chalked it up to his size and her petite frame. And she hadn't screamed in pain or reacted however virgins were supposed to act. Having never been with one, he had no clue how a chaste female would react to her first tup.

It was only when he had gone back to his carriage and put himself to rights that he'd noticed the blood on his cock. Fancy's blood. Then her tightness, the innocence he'd always sensed in her, had made sudden sense. The realization that he'd taken her maidenhead on the forest ground, rutted her like an animal, had hit him like a ton of proverbial bricks.

Guilt and self-recrimination had crushed him. He'd ruined her, taken something from her that could never be restored. And for what—sexual gratification?

Memories rose in his brain. Fancy laid out in the mossy hollow like a sensual wood nymph. Her dazed eyes and sweet cries as he'd stroked her to orgasm, the incandescent pleasure of being inside her, of being lost in passion together. That was the worst of it. As wrong as it was, as stupid and destructive as his choice had been, the truth was...he didn't regret it.

"I ain't going to mince words with you, Your Grace."

Milton Sheridan's declaration returned Severin to the moment of reckoning. He was unsurprised to see the anger darkening the tinker's usually genial countenance. Fancy's brothers, too, had looked at him as if they would like to beat him to a pulp. He didn't blame them. Hell, there was no one angrier than he was at what he'd done.

"I wouldn't expect you to," he said curtly. "There is no excuse for my behavior."

"You be hitting the nail on the 'ead." Sheridan glowered, the mismatched buttons on his violet jacket quivering with the strength of his feelings. "Me Fancy doesn't deserve to be mistreated by the likes o' you."

"You're right. She doesn't."

She deserves so much more than me. Remembering how she had tried to kiss him, he flinched. He had taken her virginity but hadn't even given her a kiss. This was precisely why he'd tried to stay away from her: he'd known from the start that he couldn't give her what she wanted.

He was no prince, and his heart belonged to another.

"She says you ain't to blame—that the fault be 'ers. But I know me Fancy, and she be a good girl. Until you came along with your London ways and corrupted 'er," Sheridan snarled.

"The fault is mine," Severin said flatly. "I'm willing to take full responsibility."

"There be only one solution to this mess."

"I agree," he clipped out.

"You'll leave at once. And you won't bother me Fancy again."

It took Severin an instant to register what the tinker was saying.

"You want me to *leave* Fancy?" he said incredulously.

"I don't want you near 'er again," Milton retorted. "And if I, or one o' me sons, catch you sniffing after 'er, then there'll be no guaranteeing the consequences."

He cast a pointed look at the tools behind him.

Severin shook his head. "I'm not leaving Fancy."

The idea was preposterous.

"The devil you're not." Milton shot up, his palms slamming onto the table. "Ain't it enough that you've ruined me girl? She may be nothing more than a tinker's daughter to you, but to us, she be a gift. E'er since that day I found 'er in the fields, she be a part o' this family. And the 'eart o' it, since me Annie died. I won't 'ave you tearing out our 'eart."

"You found Fancy in the fields?" Severin frowned; Fancy had never mentioned that she was a foundling. "She's not your blood?"

"She be me girl, but we don't know who gave birth to 'er... and we don't be caring one way or another." Sheridan's lips curled in disdain. "But you can't say the same, can you, Your Grace?"

Although Severin kept his expression neutral, he cringed inwardly at the implication that he was a snob. If it were up to him, if he had no responsibility to anyone but himself, then he wouldn't give a damn about Fancy's origins. But it wasn't just him. He had a title and siblings to think of.

Not that it mattered. After what he'd done to Fancy, he would never abandon her. And he...didn't want to, he realized. The idea of never seeing her again was even more unthinkable than marrying her. It didn't feel the same as losing Imogen, true, but he was a different man now.

The memory of his last meeting with Imogen, before he'd left to court Lady Beatrice, surfaced.

If only you had come into the title years ago. Imogen's heartbreaking sadness had enhanced her angelic beauty. *How different things could have been. I could have been your duchess...and my children would have been yours, not Cardiff's. He has never loved me, you know. Perhaps because he's always known my heart belonged to someone else.*

Severin ignored the familiar pang in his chest. The past was decided, but his future was not. And he saw with sudden clarity that he'd made his choice the moment he'd gone after Fancy in the rain.

She was his to protect. *His.*

The attraction he felt for her wasn't wise or right or convenient. It just *was*. And even though it wasn't the pure love he had for Imogen, he would find some way to translate the passion between him and Fancy into a version of happiness. She deserved that much from him.

"Fancy can no more change her origins than I can mine," he said stiffly. "Given what has transpired, there is only one honorable way out of this mess. She and I must wed."

Milton paled, then snapped, "Out o' the question."

Well, this has to be a first. A duke being turned down by a tinker.

He lifted his brows. "Most men would aspire to have their daughter be a duchess."

"I ain't most men, and me Fancy ain't suited for that sort o' life. She be a good girl, free and untainted. London would ruin 'er."

Severin's irritation faded as he saw the darkening of Milton's pupils, the panic written across the weathered features. What was the tinker afraid of? That Severin would mistreat Fancy?

"If by *ruin*, you mean that she will live in a mansion in Mayfair, then I suppose that is true," Severin said coolly. "She will also have a generous allowance in addition to gowns, jewels, and amenities befitting a duchess."

"Those be *things*." Milton looked disgusted, as if the luxuries that Severin had to offer were worth less than dirt.

The irony wasn't lost upon Severin that for years he'd fought for wealth believing that it would win him the woman of his dreams. It hadn't been enough with Imogen. Now that he had riches and was a damned *duke*, it still wasn't enough, this time for the daughter of a peddler.

When will I bloody be enough? a voice inside him raged.

"Things can't make me girl 'appy," the tinker went on in derisive tones. "If you think that material goods be what she needs, then it be for certain that you'll be making 'er miserable."

Fancy's voice whispered in his head, *I want a faerie tale.*

A band tightened around Severin's chest. Her father was right: he couldn't give her what she wanted. He was determined, however, to give her an honorable alternative, and for that he needed to speak with her.

"There is one way to solve this," he said with steely resolve. "Let me talk to Fancy. You have my word that I will be honest with her. She will know what it is that I offer. Let the choice be hers. If she wants me to go, then I will go. But upon my honor, you will not be rid of me otherwise."

12

Nervous butterflies swarmed Fancy as she awaited Knight in the farmhouse kitchen. Her father was stationed just outside and had insisted that the door remain open during the meeting. Even though she had protested that nothing would happen—and that none of this was Knight's fault—her father would not budge.

"The fellow says 'e won't leave unless 'e speaks to you first," Da had said in a stern tone that she'd not heard from him before. "It'll be up to you to put things in order. 'Is world and ours don't mix, Fancy, and London be no place for you. A fortnight ago 'e was courting Miss Beatrice because 'e needs a lady to be 'is duchess. The only reason 'e's offering for you is because o' obligation—and you deserve more than that. You set 'im free, you 'ear?"

Biting her lip, she'd nodded. Though her heart ached, she knew her father was right. Before Knight had made love to her, he'd been clear that he couldn't offer for her. That he couldn't give her anything beyond the pleasure of the moment...and she'd agreed to it. She would not renege on her side of the bargain, would never trap Knight into a marriage he didn't want.

Knight entered, and his presence momentarily sucked the

thoughts from her head, the air from her lungs. Longing pervaded her as she took in his elegance, the shifting power of his form as he prowled toward her. Her senses tingled with memory: the tender-rough scrape of his bristle against her skin, the silky slide of his hair between her fingers, the heated drag of his mouth. She tasted his delicious, masculine flavor... Suddenly, she remembered how he'd pushed her away.

I cannot kiss you, he'd said.

She didn't understand why, after everything else they'd done. Was she...not good enough to kiss? Bea *had* warned her that a gentleman like Knight might only be after a quick tumble. The idea that he would think so little of her wrenched her heart. All the more reason to get this over with. She tried to compose herself as he came to stand next to her by the table.

Stupidly, she wished she had worn something nicer than her faded work dress. But putting on her pink gown would signal a desperation that her pride wouldn't permit. He, of course, looked flawless in a dove grey frock coat and waistcoat with a subtle damask pattern. His jaw was smooth against his crisp cravat, his expensive scent a poignant reminder of what they'd shared, and how far above her he was.

"How are you, Fancy?" he asked.

His concerned tone brought a heated prickle to her eyes. Yearning thumped in her heart.

Don't shilly-shally, she told herself. *Get this over with as quickly as you can.*

"None the worse for the wear, Your Grace," she said.

"Your Grace?" He studied her, then murmured, "After last night... We are back to that?"

"Nothing 'as changed since last night," she forced herself to say.

"I disagree, Fancy. Everything has changed."

Not fooled by his mild tone, she forged on, "We agreed before we...did what we did that it would be for the pleasure o' the moment only. The moment is over, and you needn't feel an obligation to make it more than it was."

His gaze hooded. "We were discovered, Fancy. By your family and the Taylors. Your reputation is at stake."

"My family isn't going to disown me." She managed a dismissive wave. "And the Taylors are like family and won't be wagging their tongues. No one'll know beyond them."

"I will know." Lines bracketed Knight's mouth. "Do you think me so lacking in honor that I would not do what is right, what any gentleman ought to do?"

She tamped down her longing. "We made a bargain, you and me. I aim to keep my part o' it."

"There was no bargain." His jaw muscle flexed. "I was a scoundrel for taking advantage of you in your vulnerable state."

"You were honest about what you were offering," she insisted.

"On the contrary, I was lying to you and myself. You are an unmarried miss, and I am a gentleman. For us, there would always be consequences."

"It's not as if I'm a lady—"

"Don't." The hot flash in his eyes, like bottled lightning, cut her off. "Don't ever say that you are less than anyone, Fancy, because you are not."

Squaring her shoulders, she said, "You don't know everything about me. I am a foundling—"

"I know. Your father told me," he clarified at her look of surprise. "Regardless of your origins, you deserve respect, and I was a bastard for implying otherwise with my foolish actions."

"That doesn't change the fact that I ain't right for you," she said, her voice thick with emotion. "Not two weeks ago, you wanted Bea because she's a lady. You never even noticed me."

"I noticed."

His eyes were still heated, but now in a different way. And the memories of their passion came rushing back, weakening her knees and her resolve. But she couldn't let herself weaken; she had to end what never should have begun.

"You...you didn't want to kiss me," she blurted.

She didn't mean for it to sound like an accusation. He bit out an oath, the vehemence of it surprising her. For an instant, she glimpsed beneath his veneer of ruthless restraint: a hot-blooded man stared back at her with hunger and strange torment.

"It is not a question of wanting." His voice had a guttural edge.

Why else wouldn't he kiss her? She drew herself up. "You needn't make excuses. I know that I'm not the sort o' female you want for a wife."

"Damnit, Fancy. This isn't about you; it is about me and my situation." He exhaled. "There are things I need to tell you so that you fully understand what I'm offering you."

"You don't 'ave to offer me anything."

"Christ, are you always this stubborn?" He dragged a hand through his hair, a gesture of male frustration that she hadn't seen from him before. "Will you do me the courtesy of listening to what I have to say? What I have never told anyone else?"

Curiosity punctured her shield of pride. Stiffly, she nodded.

"Thank you." His gaze lowered briefly before meeting hers. "The reason I didn't kiss you was because of a promise I made years ago. To a lady. I gave her my vow not to kiss anyone else."

A sudden throbbing filled Fancy's ears. She remembered the bright yearning in his eyes that instant she'd caught him unawares staring over the pond.

"Who...who is she?" she asked in a scratchy voice.

"Her name is Imogen Hammond. I met her when I was fifteen and she was thirteen," he said gruffly. "Well, not met exactly—I pushed her out of the path of a runaway carriage. Her family was grateful, and her father hired me on. As the stable boy I did not socialize with the family, but Imogen was kind to me. She would sneak out to see me...and eventually we fell in love."

Fancy felt disoriented, as if she were awakening from an episode of sleepwalking. Far from being a cynic about love, Knight did indeed have a romantic story. One in which the part of the princess was played by Imogen Hammond. Even the lady's name was beautiful.

With dread and anticipation, Fancy asked, "What 'appened?"

"Nothing at first. I knew that her papa would never allow her to wed the stable boy. So I set out to better myself and earn my fortune. I quit the Hammonds and found work as a guard-for-hire. Easy money if you're willing to risk your neck." Knight shrugged, as if it meant nothing that he'd risked his life to win the woman of his dreams.

It ought to have been difficult for Fancy to imagine the duke in front of her working as a bodyguard. Yet she'd always sensed his primal power, which came not from wealth or position but from a deeper essence. The background he'd shared explained much: he was a man who'd literally fought for his success.

"A couple of years into that line of work, I saved a client's life," he went on in the same matter-of-fact manner. "The client, James Hessard, owned a number of manufactories, and he repaid me by offering me a job as his right-hand man. Hessard mentored me in the trade, and I eventually became a partner. When he retired, I bought him out and expanded the business. By the time I was five-and-twenty, I was a rich man, but it wasn't enough. Imogen wed someone else."

"Who?" Fancy asked even though it wasn't any of her business.

"The Earl of Cardiff," he said tonelessly.

"I'm sorry, Knight."

"You have no reason to be. Imogen was a dutiful daughter who could not disobey her family's wishes. She's been married five years now; she and Cardiff have two children."

Despite Knight's neutral tone, there was a faraway look in his gaze. Empathy and yearning fell like pinpricks upon Fancy's heart. He *was* as steadfast and loyal as any knight of old. For five years,

Imogen had been married to another, and Knight still saved his kisses for her and her alone.

Fancy remembered what he'd said about love being a gamble, how it was better not to take the risk. Now she understood why he believed this to be true: he *had* taken the risk, and his heart had been smashed to smithereens.

"Do you...still love her?" Fancy said haltingly.

"Is it love? I no longer know. At times, what I feel for her seems like a habit I cannot break." His smile held no mirth. "None of that matters. Imogen is wed, and she would never betray her husband, nor would I want her to. But I gave her my promise as a gentleman not to kiss another, and I have kept it."

Fancy's chest wrenched at the terrible beauty of his vow.

"You're an honorable man," she whispered.

"Not where you are concerned." He inhaled, then asked, "Why didn't you tell me that you were a virgin?"

Startled by the question, she said, "I, um, didn't think you needed to be told."

"Well, I did. If I had known, I..." He frowned and went on abruptly, "That day, by the stream. You told me you were experienced. You said, *I know what love is.*"

"I remember," she said, thinking back. "We were talking about love, and you were being...well, you expressed a cynical view o' it. When I disagreed, you said it was because I didn't 'ave enough experience o' the world. And I replied that I was experienced because I am. I've been travelling all my life, seen more o' the world than most women my age, I reckon."

"That is what you meant by being experienced. That you'd gone on the *road?*"

"Aye," she said, puzzled by his incredulous tone. "And I said I know what love is because I *do*. My da and ma were devoted to each other. And so are Mr. and Mrs. Taylor and plenty o' other folks I know. What else could I 'ave possibly meant?"

Knight regarded her in stony silence.

It dawned upon her. *Why didn't you tell me you were a virgin?* The only reason he would ask such a question would be if he thought she *wasn't* chaste.

"You thought that I...I'd been with others?" she asked in a painful whisper.

His gaze brooding, he gave a slow nod.

Hurt rose within her, bringing a flood of memories. All the people who had looked down upon her because she was a tinker's daughter. The men who'd tried to take advantage because they'd assumed she had no morals or pride. The nasty assumptions folks made about her and her kin.

Over the years, she'd built walls to block out the pain. But now those very walls—her treasured dreams—were turning against her. She'd steeled herself to accept that there was no future with her prince, no faerie tale ending. She could even bear the pain of knowing that he loved another, if only because it spoke of his devoted heart.

She was *not* prepared for him to think so shabbily of her.

To think that she was...a trollop.

Bea was right, she realized numbly. *He only wanted one thing from me. What happened wasn't magical, it was* cheap.

"Fancy, I'm sorry. Please don't cry."

His jagged words sliced through her daze of pain. She hadn't realized that she was crying. Mortified, she turned away from him, wiping her apron over her eyes, catching the tears she couldn't stop.

"Just go," she said in muffled tones.

"I am not leaving you." Suddenly, he was behind her, turning her around, his arms surrounding her tightly. "God, I'm such a bastard."

His gruff admission unraveled her. She pounded at the cage of his strength, venting her anger at him. He didn't stop her and didn't let her go. He just held her until she stopped fighting and wept. For her broken dreams and lost innocence. She cried, soaking his waistcoat, his hand stroking soothingly over her back. Finally, all she had left were shuddering breaths.

Then Knight spoke, his voice deep and gravelly beneath her ear.

"I cannot apologize enough for what I believed," he said. "Growing up a poor and fatherless urchin in the rookery, I, of all people, know what it is like to be judged for one's origins. How unfair and hurtful it feels. I have no excuse for doing that to you."

In her present state, there were few things he could have said to reach her.

Just then, he'd said them.

His exquisite understanding of her pain was almost as astonishing as what he had revealed about himself. During their journey together, they had discussed varied topics, from his work to his siblings, but the one thing he'd avoided talking about was his own origins. He'd said next to nothing about his mother or his childhood.

She raised her head from his chest. "You grew up poor and fatherless?"

"I didn't know the identity of my father until a year ago," he said steadily. "My *maman* wouldn't talk about it, just told me that he'd died before I was born. I suspected I was a bastard. She worked as a seamstress, barely earning enough for us to survive. I stole, fought, did whatever I could to help put food on our table. She died when I was twenty, and for all the time I knew her, she never had an easy life."

Fancy didn't know what to say. Even though she knew he had a rags-to-riches story, she hadn't realized that his rags were, well, *actually* rags.

He took out a handkerchief, drying her tears as he went on, "Last year, I was summoned to the deathbed of Arthur Huntingdon, the Duke of Knighton. For reasons too lengthy to get into now, he told me that he'd abandoned my mother, but they had been legally wed. Which meant that I was his legitimate issue and sole heir."

"That must 'ave been shocking," Fancy said, wide-eyed.

"To say the least." He cupped her cheek in his big hand. She knew she ought to pull away, but she was mesmerized by his warm and smoky gaze. "I'm telling you my history because I want you to understand that I have never thought you were beneath me in any way. If anything, you are too good and sweet for a man like me. You deserve a fellow who can give you all of his heart, and I cannot do that. But I have other things to offer, if you'll do me the honor of listening to my proposal."

His thumb brushed briefly along her cheekbone before he let her go. He waited silently, his hands clasping behind his back, his manner watchful.

Tell 'im to leave, the voice of reason said. *Don't let 'im 'urt you again.*

Alas, her heart had never been sensible.

"What are you offering?" she asked.

He let go of a breath that she hadn't realized that he was holding. The fact that he obviously cared about her response lowered her defenses a smidgen more.

"I am not a prince, but I do have a castle," he said intently. "Several, actually, if run-of-the-mill mansions count. If not, there are a pair of chateaux in France we could visit any time you want. You said you wanted a place to settle, and I can give you that."

'E remembers, she thought wonderingly. *'E paid attention to the details o' my foolish dream.*

"I can also give you a family in the form of four half-siblings and an aunt. I must warn you however: when you meet them, you will likely wish to give them back."

His wry humor caught her off-guard, and she gave a watery chuckle.

"They can't be as bad as all that," she said.

"They are worse. But if you want to take them on, they're yours."

As she mulled over that, he cleared his throat. "They are, of course, not the only family I could give you. That I would wish to give you, if you were my wife."

Her pulse skipped at the heated look in his grey eyes.

"I want you, Fancy," he said huskily. "While desire is not the same as love, I still say it is the more reliable of the two. And what I feel for you is not just physical attraction. I like you."

He wants me. He likes me.

Thrill tip-toed up her spine; she halted it.

"What do you like about me?" she asked cautiously.

"I like that you are easy to talk to. That you're caring and loyal to your family and friends. I like that you're honest and practical, that you're not one of those milk-fed misses prone to bouts of silliness."

She blinked at the readiness of his reply. She had no idea that he thought these things about her. And there was more.

"I like that you care about cantankerous donkeys, that you don't back down to fish bigger than you are." A smile lurked in his eyes. "I like that you're constantly getting into trouble so that I can come to your rescue."

"I don't constantly get into trouble," she protested.

He raised his brows.

Sighing, she amended, "Although, o' late, it 'as been finding me."

"It is a fortunate thing that you have me around," he said and chucked her under the chin.

The casual, affectionate gesture was the nail in the coffin of her resistance. Although Knight didn't promise her love, it seemed that he could give her the other parts of her dream. That he wanted to.

Maybe he was right. Maybe love wasn't as important as she thought it was. Maybe passion and friendship *were* dependable bricks with which to build a marriage. As she tested letting go of some of her old expectations, she found there was one she couldn't relinquish.

"What about Imogen?" she forced herself to ask.

"She will have no bearing on our marriage." His expression was grave. "I give you my promise to be a good and faithful husband. I won't lie to you, and I ask that you return the courtesy. The fact that we can comfortably discuss Imogen is a good sign, I daresay, of the honesty that is possible between us. Of our ability to communicate and work together as a team."

He was so convincing, even when she knew their path wouldn't be easy. In truth, she didn't know what lay ahead. Yet if she had any talent, it was this: she was good at adapting and making the best of what she had. Rarely in her life had she been given anything whole or perfect. Right now, she had a handsome duke who desired and liked her, who wanted to give her a home and a family.

How much more could she ask for?

"Say you will be mine, Fancy," he coaxed. "Say you'll build a future with me."

"I will." She released a breath. "On one condition."

She was an optimist, but she wasn't stupid. She learned from her past mistakes. If she was to venture into uncertain territory, she would take measures to protect herself.

The softness left his eyes, his mouth taking on an oddly cynical bent. "Name your terms."

Since there was no delicate way to put it, she said in a rush, "I don't want you to kiss me."

She didn't think Knight could be taken aback, but his slackened jaw suggested it was possible.

"May I ask why not?" he asked with obvious care.

"Because you don't want to," she said frankly. "And I don't want to be kissed unless you mean it." *Unless you love me.* "I 'ave my pride too, Knight."

"I never doubted that." He cleared his throat. "What about... other marital activities?"

Her cheeks flamed, but she said steadily, "As you said, we desire one another, and there is nothing dishonest in acting on those feelings. I want to be a true wife to you, Knight."

"I am glad to hear it," he said softly. "Because I mean to be a true husband to you."

He cradled her jaw, leaning in. When his lips brushed tenderly against her forehead, she trembled. And prayed that she had made the right choice.

13

Two mornings later, Severin awaited Fancy in the blacksmith's shop in Gretna Green.

Although the place hadn't been used as a smithy in probably decades, the low-ceilinged room still bore the faint scent of smoke and heated minerals. The whitewashed walls and bouquets of local flora signaled the room's current use as a wedding venue. Severin maintained an aura of calmness as the blacksmith "priest," a Mr. Clewis, puttered impatiently by the anvil over which the marriages were conducted. Twice, Clewis had asked when the bride-to-be would arrive as he had several weddings scheduled for the day.

Severin had shut the man up with coin. Yet he couldn't stem his own unease that Fancy might not show. What were the odds that he would be stood up not once, but twice for an elopement?

Granted, things hadn't gotten this far with Imogen: they'd never left London, for she'd failed to show up at their appointed meeting place. He'd planned to take her here, to Gretna Green, a village just past the border of Scotland that was famous for its trade in expedient marriages. As Scotland's marriage laws were less restrictive than English ones, Gretna had become a favorite destination for English elopements. Blacksmiths could legally carry out the ceremonies, officiating what were popularly known as "anvil weddings."

Severin and the Sheridans had arrived yesterday in the late afternoon. Although Severin wasn't eloping with Fancy, he did want to bind her legally to him as soon as possible. He'd booked an appointment at the blacksmith shop for ten o'clock sharp this morning, and Fancy was a quarter hour late. He wondered darkly if her father was behind her absence.

Sheridan had insisted that Fancy spend the night in the family wagon rather than at the inn where Severin had booked out an entire floor of rooms. For reasons that Severin frankly could not fathom, the tinker remained staunchly opposed to the union. Severin was prepared to take whatever steps necessary to gain the man's acquiescence, if not approval, but Fancy had precluded his interference.

"Leave Da to me," she'd said firmly. "I'll see you at the blacksmith's tomorrow."

Despite her delicate looks and sweet manner, his bride-to-be had a determined streak to her personality. Severin was glad for it: she would need that obstinacy when they had to face his family and the *ton* back in London.

If he succeeded in claiming her as his duchess, that was.

Faced with the potential of Fancy leaving him at the altar—or anvil, as it were—Severin felt his remaining ambivalence about marrying her vanish. Whether she was suitable or not, he wanted her to be his wife, damnit.

He thought back to the condition Fancy had placed on their marriage, the only thing she had asked of him, and an odd spasm hit his chest. At the time, he'd thought that she was going to negotiate for something of material value. It would have been within her rights to ask for jewels, a quarterly allowance, and the like. His past lovers had bargained with him for such things, and he had been generous.

Yet Fancy had stunned him by asking for the opposite. By telling him that she didn't want anything that he didn't freely give. It struck him now that Fancy was the only woman who'd ever made him feel that he was…enough, just as he was.

Before the madness had claimed his *maman*, she had loved him. He thought, with a sharp twinge of the old scar, that she'd loved him even when the illness took away her control. She'd sacrificed everything for their survival. When he was old enough to realize what she was doing, he'd begged her not to do it. He'd offered to steal—to do anything—rather than have her earn their keep in an alleyway.

You are not big or strong enough to do a man's work, mon chou. She'd brushed her worn fingertips across his brow. *If you want to make your maman happy, then be better than what the streets have taught you to be. Don't be like those animals you run with, oui?*

He had tried to be a man, tried to take care of her, but he'd failed.

Then he'd met Imogen, and she'd needed him to be something he wasn't…or hadn't been, at the time. Now that he *was* a duke, it was too late. He couldn't turn back time, even for her.

But Fancy…he felt he had a chance to do right by her. Somehow she had forgiven him for his disgraceful assumptions and the callous way he'd taken her virginity. She hadn't flinched when he'd told her those unsavory facts about his past, although he'd taken care not to share the worst of it, the memories he himself kept locked away.

The important thing was that Fancy seemed to want him, even knowing that he was incapable of giving her his heart. Or even kisses. Her honesty and generosity made him burn to lay claim on her.

Where in blazes is she? he thought with roiling impatience.

He balled his hands. He knew where the Sheridans were camping. If need be, he would go there, fetch his bride, fight off any of her kinfolk who got in his way.

As he turned toward the door, it opened, and Fancy rushed inside.

She was pink-cheeked and a bit disheveled. A shiny lock of chestnut hair had escaped her simple topknot studded with fresh flowers. She wore one of her usual frocks, one that was an indiscriminate beige color and discreetly patched at the hem.

She was the most beautiful sight he'd ever seen.

She hurried up to him, obviously out of breath. "I'm sorry to keep you waiting. I 'ad an accident."

"Accident?" His relief at her appearance gave way to concern. "Are you all right?"

"Nothing is 'urt but my pride." She gave him a sheepish smile. "I planned to wear my best dress, the pink one. I 'ad it on, was ready to go, but Bertrand refused to get moving. I should 'ave let Da 'andle it, but I was in such a rush, I 'opped down and started to lecture the beast. Bertrand doesn't like to be lectured and, the next thing you know, the blooming ass kicked *mud* at me."

Severin's lips quivered. Fancy's story was so uniquely *her*. He couldn't imagine another bride having a spat with a donkey—and losing—on her wedding day, nor one that looked so adorably woeful.

She sighed, looking down at herself. "And now I 'ave to be married in this old dress."

He tipped her chin up. Looked into her embarrassed brown eyes.

"You are still the prettiest bride I've ever seen," he said.

Her cheeks turned rosy. "You're just being nice."

"Not nice—truthful." He managed to coax a smile from her. "I'm sorry we didn't have time to get you a proper wedding dress. We'll shop for your trousseau when we get to London."

"I'll never be as grand as you," she said wistfully. "You make a fine bridegroom, Knight."

Her unabashed feminine approval brought a rush of heat to his groin, threatening to ruin the crisp lines of his tailoring. At the same time, he noticed that her father and brothers had entered. The lads waved at him, grinning, and Severin nodded back. Seeing Milton Sheridan's troubled look, however, Severin decided not to dally.

"I wouldn't be a bridegroom without you." He offered Fancy his arm. "Ready, sweeting?"

She placed her small, ungloved hand on his sleeve, and her trusting smile caused a sweet pang in his chest.

"I'm ready," she said.

14

I'm married to Knight.

Fancy wanted to pinch herself to make sure she wasn't dreaming.

After the disaster of her wedding dress, the rest of the day had thankfully gone without a hitch. Truth be told, she'd been surprised at the swiftness of the ceremony that had bound her and Knight for life. Mr. Clewis, the blacksmith who'd officiated the ceremony, had instructed them to stand by the large anvil at the center of the room and join hands.

"Are ye o' age to marry?" he'd asked in a thick Scottish brogue.

She and Knight had both answered *yes.*

"Are ye free to marry?" Clewis went on.

The affirmatives had barely left her and Knight's lips before the blacksmith picked up a large black hammer and struck the anvil with a resounding swing that made her teeth chatter.

"You're married," he'd declared. "Best o' luck to ye. Now exit to the room on your right, if ye please, to complete the paperwork. Go on, now, the next couple's coming in."

That had been that.

Afterward, Knight had hosted a luncheon at a nearby inn for

her family. Much to the delight of her brothers, the meal had been a feast, including haddock and potato soup, roast beef and lamb, and savory game pies and puddings. For dessert, the innkeeper's wife had laid out an assortment of shortbreads, fruitcake studded with nuts, and a parfait made of raspberries, whipped cream, oats, and heather honey. The guests had washed down the delicious food with copious amounts of elderberry wine and whisky.

Knight had proved a cordial host. He'd borne her brothers' antics and ribald toasts with good grace, a smile reaching his eyes when he caught her blushing. Da had thawed toward Knight somewhat, his felicitations resigned rather than genuinely joyful. Fancy had spent the last two days reassuring her father that Knight was the man she wanted to marry.

After the feast ended, she'd gone up to the bridal suite Knight had reserved for her. A maid had been waiting to help her with her bath. After a luxurious rose-scented soak in a large copper tub, the maid had dressed her in her best nightgown. The night before, Fancy had used scraps of blue ribbon and lace to trim the neckline of the plain linen shift. She hoped Knight wouldn't notice the garment's worn state. At least her hair looked nice, the maid brushing it until it fell in a shining curtain to her waist.

Now Fancy sat in one of the overstuffed armchairs by the fire, waiting for Knight. Her husband. She supposed she ought to be nervous, but the truth was she was eager. She couldn't wait for her wedding night, to discover more of the passion he had begun to show her. She felt giddy as she glanced at the large bed.

She looked down at her left hand, where her wedding band gleamed. The plain circle of gold shone with possibility. Knight had given it to her before they'd left the blacksmith's shop. When he'd slid the ring onto her finger, her throat had clogged with wonder, and she'd struggled to get out her thanks.

"This was the best I could do on short notice," he'd said in a brusque manner. "I'll get you something better when we return to London."

Realizing that he had misinterpreted her silence for dislike, she blurted, "No, I *love* the ring. Thank you for thinking of it."

The door to the adjoining chamber opened, and her chest swelled as her new husband entered. Sweet Jaysus, he was handsome. Attired in a black silk dressing gown, he prowled toward her with virile grace. His thick hair was damp from his bath, the curling at his nape suggesting that his hair might have an appealing wave to it if he were to wear it longer.

When she rose to greet him, he reached for her hand. His fingers engulfed hers. The warm brush of his lips over her knuckles unleashed a shiver of anticipation.

"I like your hair this way, *chérie*," he murmured. "Did I give you sufficient time to recover from the day's festivities?"

His elegant endearment gave her a little thrill. Having done piecework for a French dressmaker, she knew *chérie* was French for "dear."

"I'm not tired," she said candidly. "I was waiting for you."

"Were you?" His slow smile caused her heart to flip-flop. "What a good little wife you are."

Blushing, she said, "It's still strange thinking o' myself as a wife."

"What about as the Duchess of Knighton?"

"That is even stranger," she admitted. "I can't believe we're married."

"Believe it because we are. There is no going back."

The firmness of his tone took her aback. As did the possessive flare of his pupils.

"I don't want to go back," she said.

"Good." He took her chin between finger and thumb, rubbing the latter gently over her bottom lip. "Because I would like nothing more than to move forward with our marriage."

"I want that too. Since our night in the forest, I've been thinking o' little else."

At her confession, he let out a warm, husky laugh. "Married a lusty wench, did I? Lucky me."

In the next instant, he swept her into his arms and carried her to the bed. He set her on her feet next to the mattress; as he perused the length of her, she felt a nervous flutter.

I 'ope 'e doesn't notice the patches, she fretted.

"Lift your arms up, sweetheart," he said.

When she obeyed, he pulled her shift over her head, tossing it aside without a glance.

So much for caring about my nightgown.

Her relief was short-lived as she was now standing fully naked before a man for the first time. Knight's proprietary gaze felt like a touch, awareness prickling over her skin. Her breasts rose and fell with her rapid breaths, the tips taut and straining toward him. When she instinctively squeezed her thighs together, she felt the slickness of her dew.

"By Jove, you're pretty," he said thickly. "I didn't get a good look the last time."

The molten silver in his eyes made her *feel* pretty, albeit a little embarrassed. While she found no shame in physical desire, especially between husband and wife, the intensity of what she felt was still new to her. A bit overwhelming.

Her gaze slipped from his as she mumbled, "You're getting an eyeful now."

He curled a finger under her chin, making her meet his eyes.

"I am your husband, and I like looking at you," he said simply. "There's nothing to be embarrassed about."

"Easy for you to say. You ain't standing 'ere naked," she pointed out.

He quirked a brow. "Would you like me to be?"

At her fervent nod, his lips tipped up at the corners. He untied the belt of his robe, shrugging off the fine black silk. He had a sleep shirt on beneath, and as his long fingers worked on the buttons, the vee of parting fabric revealed the hair-dusted planes of his chest. Then he tugged the shirt over his head, and the rippling display of maleness made her mouth go dry.

She blinked in awe. "You're...magnificent."

Knight was built in virile proportions. His wide shoulders and bulging arms were sculpted sinew. His chest was made up of taut blocks of the same, with a light covering of dark hair that narrowed into a trail over his lean, ridged belly, gathering in a dense nest around his...

Sweet Jaysus. She couldn't help but stare at his manhood—couldn't believe that something that huge had fit inside her. No sheltered miss, she'd had basic knowledge of what went on between a man and woman even before her first time with Knight. She'd known what part fit into where, how babes were made, and even how to prevent making them (whenever her brother Oliver had contraceptive sheaths on hand, they sold like hotcakes). Yet she'd never seen an aroused male before, and the sight was astonishing.

Hanging heavily between his muscled thighs, his male member had to be ten inches long and nearly as thick as her wrist. The fleshy shaft was ridged with veins, the thick burgundy tip dripping with his male essence. Feverish heat spread over her, and her body moistened in response to his manly display.

When he placed his hands on her shoulders, she gave a start.

"Nervous?" he asked quietly.

"More like admiring. Although, if I 'ad seen you last time," she said ruefully, "I might 'ave gone running for the 'ills. I don't understand 'ow you managed to fit."

"We fit perfectly." He slid a hand up, cupping the back of her neck, holding her to his intense gaze lit with shards of silver. "I will be gentle with you, Fancy. Always. I won't ever hurt you."

Then he lowered his head, and her neck arched into his hold as his lips skimmed over her cheek. He nuzzled her ear, the hot licks that followed dissolving the starch from her knees. He caught her and lay her upon the bed. Stretching on his side next to her, he caressed her flank with frank possession. His touch moved to her breasts, and she couldn't quell a whimper when he molded her flesh in his palms, his fingers playing with the sensitive tips.

"I was right about your nipples." He sounded quite satisfied with himself. "They are as red and plump as your lips."

"You thought about my...um, nipples?" She didn't know whether to be flattered or mortified.

"From the moment I met you." He caught one rosy bud between finger and thumb, and the gentle pinch seemed to connect to her sex, her intimate muscles fluttering.

"That can't be true." Her tones were breathy as he repeated the caress on her other breast. "You didn't even notice me at first."

"I noticed you from the start. Couldn't stop thinking about you, as a matter of fact."

She drew her brows together. "What were you thinking, exactly?"

A wolfish glint appeared in his eyes.

"Why don't I show you," he murmured.

∽

"Oh, Knight, oh you can't...oh, that's...that's...*don't stop*..."

With his bride's sweet litany in his ears and the taste of her even sweeter cunny on his tongue, Severin knew he was one lucky bastard. Fancy's reaction as he ate her pussy was one of the most erotic sights he'd ever beheld. Her initial shock when he'd put his mouth on her had turned into pure feminine surrender. Framed by her surging tits, her face glowed with sensual heat, her lush red lips parting on a moan.

God, she was beautiful. More wanton than his darkest fantasies.

And she's mine now.

His heart and cock pounded with that knowledge. With the rightness of the choice he'd made. For better or worse, Fancy belonged to him—and only him. Until now, he'd never placed particular value on marrying a virgin. Yet knowing that he would be Fancy's only lover, that she would belong to him that utterly, filled him with undeniable pride.

And hunger.

On either side of his head, her thighs trembled, a sign that her release was near. He wanted to see her go over. Parting her slick pink folds, he delved deeper, licking into her tightness. He sought out her pearl with his thumb, diddling her while he fucked her with his tongue. Her taste and scent made him ravenous, her abandon even more so.

His cockhead seeped pre-seed as she arched against his mouth.

"*Knight,*" she gasped as she came.

With her honey dripping from his lips, Severin rose over her. Over *his wife*, her hair a glossy fan on the bed, her face flushed with passion. His chest heaved, lust and possessiveness combining in a potent mix that darkened his vision. He had to have her *now*. Leaning over her, he kept his weight on one arm. With his other, he gripped his cock and notched it to her soft, ready entrance. He thrust into her slowly, panting at the lush constriction.

"All right, sweeting?" he said hoarsely. "Are you sore from the last time?"

"No." She gazed at him with languid eyes. "It feels good. Keep going."

Thank Christ.

Still, he took his time, not wanting to cause her any discomfort. He worked himself in to the balls, the silky, snug clasp of her passage an agonizing delight. Pleasure radiated from his cock to his limbs, tingling all the way to his scalp. Clenching his jaw, he resisted the urge to pick up the pace.

"How is this, *chérie*?" He rocked his hips gently. "Does it still feel good?"

"Yes, but..." She bit her lip and squirmed beneath him.

"But what, sweeting?" he asked with tender concern. "You can tell me anything."

"Do you think you could move, um, faster?"

At her unexpected request, he felt laughter rise. Amusement and lust was a novel yet potent blend for him. His cock jerked like a stallion at the starting gate.

"I think I can manage," he said huskily.

He gave into the demands of his body and of his adorable bride. As he took her harder, deeper, she moved with him, with a natural grace that stripped away his civilized intentions. Skewered by his prick, she moaned and wrapped her legs around his hips, letting him in even deeper. Savage need swept over him, and he answered her with vigorous thrusts.

His senses became absorbed by the intensity of their mating. By the slap of his hips against her thighs, the sensual bounce of his stones against her drenched slit. By the prick of her fingernails against his flexing biceps. By the deliciously wanton noises that left her, her berry-ripe lips tempting him to take a taste...

Feeling the warning sizzle at the base of his spine, he didn't want to go over alone. Reaching between them, he sought her love-knot, rubbing it against his pistoning shaft. The effect was instantaneous: her pussy clamped on his hardness, a demanding grip that made him growl with bliss.

"Come again, sweet," he demanded. "Milk me with your pussy, and I'll come with you."

Probably not words a gentleman should use with his wife, but Severin was too far gone to care. The voluptuous rippling of Fancy's cunny told him that she didn't mind his wicked vocabulary, and her climax summoned his own. Heat erupted from his balls, shooting up his shaft, exploding with a power that forced a shout from his throat. Shuddering, he spent and spent inside his bride.

When he was blissfully empty, he lay beside her and drew her against him. She tucked her head into his shoulder, sliding an arm over his torso and a leg over his own as if they were lovers who'd been doing this for years. Silence settled over them like a cozy blanket. He should probably say something—a lady had every right to expect a compliment from a husband after their wedding night. Yet he couldn't get his sated brain to come up with the appropriate words.

Just then, a wisp of a snore escaped her. Amused, he saw that she'd fallen asleep. He spent a few moments admiring his wife's pretty, relaxed features, his gaze lingering on her mouth.

Frowning at himself, he looked away. What he had begun to build with Fancy was solid and reliable, and he wouldn't ruin it. Holding her close, breathing in the sweet scent of her hair, he followed her into sleep.

15

Fancy opened her eyes to an unfamiliar view: a naked male torso.

Smiling dreamily, she rubbed her cheek against Knight's hair-covered chest, enjoying her first time waking up with her husband. The easy surges of his breathing told her he was still asleep. Even so, his arm kept her trapped against his side, and she snuggled in closer, taking the opportunity to admire him.

As her gaze roved over his powerful form, she recalled his tender concern for her last night, and her heart gave a silly hiccup. She ran her fingertips gently over the bulging planes of his chest...and frowned when she discovered a scar close to his heart. The dull red line was hidden beneath his hair, the bumpy ridge several inches long.

Without thinking, she pressed her lips against it.

He flinched, his eyes snapping open.

"I'm sorry," she said in surprise. "Does it 'urt?"

It took a moment for his gaze to clear, and he shook his head against the pillow. "It's old."

"'Ow did you get it?"

"It was an accident," he said shortly. "If you're interested in my scars, I have plenty more of them. The consequence of being a guard-for-hire, I'm afraid."

Seeing the lines slashing around his mouth, she wondered if he thought she would find the wounds of his past unattractive. Which couldn't be further from the truth. She touched his jaw, the muscle quivering beneath her fingertips.

"They're badges o' honor," she said softly. "Reminders of how you fought for your success."

The tension in his jaw eased.

"Do you always see the best in everything?" he asked wryly.

"I see the man that you are. A man I'm proud to call my 'usband."

His gaze warmed. "You're proud?"

She nodded. "You told me the things you like about me. Well, I like things about you too."

"I'm all ears." He arranged them so that they faced each other lying on their sides. Then in a pompous tone, he said, "Do expound upon my fine qualities, dear wife."

His teasing didn't quite hide his eagerness to hear her praise. The glimpse of his boyish side reminded her of their first meeting, the delight he'd taken in playing his small trick. Knowing what she now did about his past, she imagined he'd had to grow up quickly, and her chest softened.

"You're noble, of course," she began.

"Well, that's not enlightening. I already know I'm a duke."

"I don't mean noble in the sense o' your title." Rolling her eyes, she said, "I meant you're noble at 'eart. You look after the welfare o' others like your siblings. And like me. Even when it's not in your own interest. You rescued me time and again and married me to save my reputation."

"Marrying you wasn't entirely selfless, you know."

She blushed beneath his smoldering glance. "Nevertheless, I wasn't what you were looking for in a duchess. But, being a man o' honor, you gave me your name anyway. And you don't look down upon me or my family. You're kind to my brothers, who I know are a 'andful, and you've put up with Da's disapproval o' our marriage."

"I like your family." He sounded like he meant it.

"I'm glad. And I look forward to meeting yours."

"I shall consider it a triumph if you don't require smelling salts."

Unfortunately, he sounded like he meant this as well.

She snorted. "I've never succumbed to 'ysterics in my life."

"A tough little thing, aren't you?" He ran a finger along her nose, his touch playful, his gaze soft as smoke. "Thank you, Fancy. For taking me and my family on."

"Likewise," she said.

She smiled, enormously pleased with their progress. She and Knight had only been married a day, and already she felt closer to him. She wanted to learn more, to understand all the different parts that made up this complex man.

"A few days ago, when you told me about your parents," she said, "you didn't 'ave time to explain why your father left you and your mama. We 'ave time now."

His eyes grew guarded. "Why does it matter?"

"Because I want to know you better." She furrowed her brow. "You said we would be 'onest with one another, to communicate and work as a team."

"Hoisted by my own petard," he muttered.

"You mentioned meeting with your father," she prompted.

"Right." Heaving a sigh, he sat up against the headboard, the sheets bunching at his waist.

She did the same, pulling a sheet up modestly over her breasts...blinking when he prevented her from doing so.

"Since you are asking me to discuss an unpleasant topic, you owe me a distracting view." He looked at her breasts, the tips stiffening beneath his gleaming gaze. "This will do nicely."

Her cheeks burned, her pussy fluttered, but she would not be deterred.

"Go on, then," she said.

"My sire summoned me to his deathbed around a year ago. He told me that I was his legitimate son, that he'd met my mama in London when she was working as a seamstress in a shop. They fell in love, and he married her in secret. He was the youngest of the duke's three sons, not even the spare to the heir, and he thought he could convince his parents to accept his marriage. He was wrong. His parents threatened to disown him if he didn't seek an annulment. To make their point, they cut off his allowance, his only source of income."

"'Ow did 'e and your mama survive?" Fancy asked softly.

"Barely. He'd never worked a day in his life and was used to a life of luxury. After a few months, he'd had enough of poverty. My mama's pleading did no good, and he left her to go back to his old life in Mayfair. After he abandoned her, she must have discovered that she was with child."

Fancy's throat tightened. "Why didn't she go to him then?"

"Since my *maman* died when I was twenty and never spoke a word of this, I can only make a conjecture. Being a woman of great pride, she must have been furious at my sire for his desertion. She most likely thought he did not deserve to know he had a son; I think her taking "Knight" as our surname was her way of thumbing her nose at the Knightons." Knight's mouth formed a tight line. "My father had an additional theory. His parents were not kind to my mother. They accused her of tainting the family line and issued threats, trying to scare her into leaving my father. It's possible she thought they might force her to end the pregnancy if they found out about it."

"What sort o' people would do such a 'orrible thing?" Fancy burst out.

"According to my sire, there was no love lost between him and his parents," Knight said grimly. "But he was too cowardly to cut the ties of their purse strings. After his parents secured the annulment, my father rebelled by living the life of a libertine. He left England and dwelled in France, fathering my four half-siblings with two different mistresses. His parents didn't care as long as he didn't marry his lightskirts; by this point, they'd already secured their legacy via their older sons, both of whom had married and produced offspring.

"Two years ago, however, my sire's parents were aboard a ship that capsized. They died, along with their two older sons and grandchildren who were also on board."

Horrified at such a tragedy, she whispered, "Sweet Jaysus."

"That left my father as the sole remaining heir of the Knighton duchy. Since he had not remarried, he now had to go about finding himself a wife and producing a legitimate heir. Aging and in failing health due to decades of dissolute living, he didn't want the trouble of doing either. And then providence struck.

"My sire discovered correspondence between his father and a solicitor dated several years earlier. Apparently, there had been a mistake, and the annulment of my parents' marriage had never been fully codified. The solicitor had only discovered the oversight and wanted to know how to proceed. My grandfather had hired an investigator to discover what had become of my mama, which is how he found out about me. And reading those letters was how my sire discovered that he had a son."

"Your grandfather didn't tell your father about you?" she said incredulously.

"My grandfather wanted me kept a secret." Lines bracketed Knight's mouth. "Since my mama was already dead, there was no point in risking scandal in order to complete the annulment. My grandfather probably decided that the best thing to do was to hide any connection between me and the family. Even though I was legitimate, he wouldn't have been worried about my claim to the title: after all, he had two older sons and two grandsons who had precedence over my father and me. How was he to know that a single shipwreck would change everything?"

"But it did," she said quietly. "In the end, Fate worked everything out."

"Yes."

"What…what was it like seeing your father?"

"It was like meeting a stranger," Knight said emotionlessly. "After he died, my inheritance was held up in the courts when a distant cousin tried to contest it. The case took almost a year to resolve. The best part of that was when my relationship to my sire was finally recognized, the mourning period was over. I didn't have to pretend I cared about the death of the man who'd abandoned my mother."

"I'm sorry you went through all of that," she said tremulously. "And even prouder that you had the decency to take on your sire's legacy, including your half-siblings."

"I do believe I married a hopeless optimist." Crinkles fanned around his eyes. "Most people would assume that I wanted the title for its privileges, not because of some innate sense of honor."

"Those people don't know you like I do," she said firmly.

Emotion flashed like a falling star through his gaze. Just as quickly, it was gone.

"I cannot argue with that," he drawled. "Especially after the night we shared."

"I didn't mean it that way," she said, her cheeks warming.

He traced a circle over her bare shoulder. "Are you sore this morning?"

Feeling a twinge between her legs, she admitted, "Maybe a little."

"Poor wife." He trailed his fingers downward over the slope of her breast, circling the budded tip. "I suppose I can delay my husbandly plans and let you rest."

Trembling at his touch, she said, "Your husbandly plans? But it's morning…"

She dropped her gaze to his lap. Sweet Jaysus, he *was* raring to go. It looked like he had an iron bar hidden beneath the sheet.

"Did you think lovemaking was exclusively a nighttime activity?" He looked amused.

Embarrassed at her naïveté, she gave a small nod.

"That won't be the case for us." His smile was lazy and self-assuredly male. "In point of fact, there are variations on the theme that won't exacerbate your tender state, and I've a mind to introduce you to a few."

16

Later that morning, Severin descended to the inn's lobby. Since the establishment catered to eloping couples, the space was done up with romance in mind. Striped pink and cream paper covered the walls, the furnishings done up in maroon velvet. Vases of roses and heather bloomed on the front counter and in the cozy seating area by the hearth.

The innkeeper, a portly whiskered fellow, was puttering behind the counter.

Catching sight of Severin, he asked cheerfully, "Enjoying your stay, Your Grace?"

Severin thought of Fancy, whom he had left dozing upstairs. He had worn her out. To be fair, she'd done the same to him.

He had taught her how to frig him, and she'd proved an apt pupil. The image of her delicate, competent fingers pumping his cock brought a sizzle to his blood even now. Truth be told, he ought to be sated, considering how copiously he'd spent in his wife's pretty hands. He'd returned the favor, fingering her bold little pearl until she came, then licking her pleasure from her a second time.

With those memories fogging up his brain, he murmured, "Quite."

The innkeep winked. "Always said a bridegroom is the luckiest fellow on earth."

Severin knew he was a lucky fellow. Damned lucky. Not only because he and his wife set the bedsheets on fire. Waking up with Fancy this morning, he had felt...not alone. He'd enjoyed cuddling and talking with her. He was a bit discomfited by how good her words of praise had felt. And even though she *was* nosy, her intentions were good. He owed her the essential facts so that she understood the family she'd entered into.

Then he remembered the way she'd kissed his scar, and his gut seized. He told himself that he could let her in, but only so far. Some things were too ugly to share with a wife. Too ugly to share with anyone.

He expelled a breath, not wanting to think of such things now. He wanted to enjoy the delights of being a new groom. He thought he might begin by taking Fancy on a brief tour of Scotland, a wedding trip to mark the beginning of their married life. He wanted to show her the sights, take her shopping and buy her anything her heart desired, spend hours making love to her...

He decided to write follow-up letters to his man-of-business and Aunt Esther forthwith. He would inform them of his marriage and of another week's delay before he returned to London. It struck him that Fancy had a way of coming before his duties. That she made his existence less dreary and gave him something to look forward to. The fact that he now had a domestic life was strangely...satisfying.

Then he thought of Imogen. He would write her too, to break the news of his marriage before she heard it elsewhere. It seemed the right thing to do.

"Is there anything I can help you with, Your Grace?" the innkeeper was asking.

Severin recalled why he'd come down. "Do you have any newspapers from London?"

"As a matter of fact, we received a delivery this morning." The innkeep went to the table that served as his desk, returning with a stack. "Peruse at your pleasure, Your Grace."

Severin took the papers to the sitting area. Settling in a wingchair, he sifted through the pile—and froze as a headline jumped out at him:

ANGRY MOB DEMANDS JUSTICE FROM RAILWAY COMPANY.

He scanned the article, dated a few days ago, and his chest tightened.

Bloody hell, will the mayhem never cease?

Rising, he strode up the stairs to share the unwelcome news with his wife.

~

"I don't see why you 'ave to go to London." Crossing his arms, Da took a drag of his pipe.

Fancy stared at her father in disbelief. She and Knight had arrived at her family's camping ground a quarter hour ago. Standing outside the caravan, she'd shared in detail what Knight had read to her from the newspaper.

"But I explained, Da," she said urgently. "The price o' shares in Mr. Murray's railway company are plunging, the papers blaming Bea for it. They're calling 'er vile names, saying she's refusing to let Mr. Murray's company lay track through 'er land because she wants more money. Seems like everyone in London invested in 'is company, and now there are *mobs* after Bea and Mr. Murray's blood. I 'ave to go to London—to be by Bea's side."

Worry flashed in her father's bespectacled gaze, but he shook his head stubbornly. "Ain't nothing you can do to 'elp 'er, petal. Murray's a wealthy toff with connections, I'm sure 'e'll sort it all out—"

"This may be beyond Murray." Knight spoke up, his expression grave. "To ease Fancy's worry, I will offer him my resources and help him however I can."

She sent him a grateful look. He was such a noble man, the very best of husbands. Although no words passed between them, he seemed to read her thoughts, slight crinkles fanning from his eyes.

"But you be recently married to me girl." Da's voice vibrated with a tension that she didn't understand. "You ought to be taking 'er on a wedding trip—"

"Da, what is the matter with you?" Fancy exclaimed. "Bea is my bosom chum and a friend to all us Sheridans. You taught me to never let down a friend."

She couldn't hold her frustration in any longer. Her father was acting strange—had been since Knight had proposed to her. Something was going on with him. He brought his pipe to his mouth again, his hand a bit unsteady, as if he was...afraid?

"Whatever it is, Da," she said, gentling her tone, "you can tell me."

"Ah, Fancy. The truth is..."—his eyes glimmered, his beard trembling—"I be afeared for you."

"There's no need to be afraid," she said patiently. "I'll just be keeping Bea company."

"I ain't afeared on account o' Miss Bea." Da took a shaky breath. "It's on account o' you, Fancy, going to London. There be a reason why I've ne'er taken you there."

"I know you think the city isn't safe but—"

"It ain't because o' that. It's because o' *you*, me girl. Your past."

A tingle raced up her spine. "What do you mean?"

"Me and your ma, we didn't tell you everything about the day we found you in the fields." Da drew on his pipe as if to fortify himself. "We kept it a secret from you, me Fancy, because we wanted to protect you."

Premonition shivered through her. "Protect me? From what?"

"I don't know," Da said heavily. "But whoe'er left you in the fields that day...they did it because they thought you be in danger."

The tingle became a chill that spread over her insides. At the same time, a wall of reassuring warmth came up behind her: Knight. Although he was not touching her, she could feel his protective strength, and it anchored her.

"You will explain that statement, Sheridan," Knight said.

Da exhaled. "Wait 'ere. I 'ave something to show you."

He went into the caravan. The sounds of rummaging came from within, and he returned scant moments later. He held out a piece of folded fabric to her.

With brimming curiosity, she unfolded it, holding it up.

"It's a babe's christening gown...mine?" she asked, astonished.

The garment was of immaculate quality and showed no signs of aging. The thick ivory silk slid smoothly beneath her fingertips, and lace as delicate as a spider's web trimmed the neckline and wrists, a wide panel extending down the front.

"When I found you, petal, you be wearing this, wrapped in a velvet blanket as fine as any I'd seen. That is why I named you Fancy," Da said in a gruff voice. "You looked like a wee faerie creature, and when you saw me, you stopped crying. You looked at me with big, wondering eyes and cooed. I knew then I couldn't leave you there."

Shock percolated through her. "But who would abandon a babe in such finery...and why?"

"May I?" Knight took the garment from her, examining it with an expert eye. "French silk, first-rate. The lace looks equally expensive, Belgian most likely." He'd turned the gown around, pointing to a bit of embroidery on the left shoulder. "Did you see this?"

Fancy leaned in to take a closer look. The tiny, bell-shaped bloom was exquisitely rendered in shades of red and pink, flecks of yellow at its center.

She squinted at it. "Is it a rose?"

"Hard to say," Knight replied. "Pretty though."

Fancy's mind was whirling. The christening gown was undoubtedly costly. Did that mean she'd come from a background of wealth, perhaps even...nobility?

She turned to her father. "Why didn't you tell me any of this before now?"

"Because I was trying to protect you." His expression bleak, Da took a piece of paper from his pocket and gave it to her. "This be tucked in the basket next to you. Me and your ma 'ad a shop-keeper read it to us."

Fancy took the note with trembling hands. It was yellowing at the edges, the spidery handwriting difficult to read. Beneath Knight's gaze, she felt her cheeks warm. Her reading was improving, thanks to Bea's lessons, but under pressure she still had to sound out the words.

"May God...watch over...this babe," she managed to read aloud. *"For 'er own safety, she must never re...return to Lon...London."*

The words sunk in.

"Why must I be kept from London?" she asked, bewildered. "Who am I?"

"I don't know, petal," Da said heavily. "But me and your ma, we weren't going to risk you coming to 'arm. That's why we stayed away from London all these years. And that's why I didn't want you marrying Knighton: I knew 'e would take you there and deliver you into the arms o' danger."

"Fancy will come to no harm," Knight said. "You have my word."

Although his statement was calm, it had the lethality of a honed blade.

"I can't stop you from going to London. But now that you be

knowing the truth," Da said heavily, "you'll be taking extra caution with me girl, you 'ear?"

"I would take care of my wife regardless," Knight said evenly.

My wife. Fancy didn't miss his emphasis on the words, and his possessiveness thrilled her. Seeing the worry carved on her father's brow, however, she reached out and took Da's hand. She felt his calluses, the working man's strength that had taken care of her all her life, and love for him welled.

"Don't worry, Da." She gave him a smile and a reassuring squeeze. "All will be fine."

He returned her squeeze. "I 'ope you're right, petal. By the grace o' God, I 'ope you are."

17

THE JOURNEY TO LONDON TOOK FIVE DAYS. KNOWING HOW badly Fancy wanted to see her friend, Severin instructed his groom to make the trip as quickly as possible without compromising comfort. They drove most of the day, stopping only to refresh the horses and to stay the night at coaching inns along the way. While it wasn't the wedding trip Severin had wanted to give his new bride, the time nonetheless seemed to fly by.

He realized that it was the first time he'd spent this much time with a female before. With Imogen, his visits had always been limited and furtive. With his mistresses, he hadn't seen the point in lingering after the tupping.

Fancy was different.

Bedding her was sublime. Her blend of innocence and eagerness kept him in a perpetual state of arousal. Although she was inexperienced, she showed no shame about the pleasure she found at her husband's touch. She wasn't coy, didn't play games, and it made Severin want to fuck her constantly. It was a good thing she had no trouble napping in the carriage for he kept her up at night, plowing her until she cried out her pleasure, her snug sheath milking him of his own.

But his attraction to her was about more than just coupling.

She was a good companion, for starters. She didn't complain, need to make constant stops, or ask how much farther until the destination. Instead, she made the time pass quickly with her entertaining anecdotes about the travelling life. Her stories about Bertrand alone could fill a book.

She was also full of curiosity about Severin's everyday life. Luckily, his replies did not seem to bore her. Unlike others whose eyelids would begin to droop when he expounded upon the latest version of the Jacquard mechanism and other innovations of his trade, Fancy was inquisitive, asking thoughtful questions.

While he'd always admired her character, he was ashamed to admit that he hadn't fully appreciated her intellect. Her sweetness and honesty were accompanied by a clever and resourceful mind. Day by day, he was discovering that his wife was possessed of an astounding repertoire of skills.

Before they left Scotland, Milton Sheridan had taken Severin aside. Surprisingly, the tinker had decided not to accompany them to London.

"Fancy made 'er choice, and she be in your 'ands now," Sheridan had said gruffly. "But while she ain't mine to look after anymore, I'll be wanting your word you'll take good care o' me girl."

Having given his word, Severin did not like to repeat himself. But he'd made an exception for his wife's father. Now that he understood that Sheridan's reservations about their marriage stemmed from the mystery of Fancy's past, he could afford to be generous.

Moreover, he thought the tinker's decision not to go to London was for the best. Upon their arrival in Town, Fancy would face the daunting prospect of gaining the *ton*'s acceptance, for herself and his siblings. The presence of her tinkering family would exponentially increase the difficulty of that task.

"I'll look after her," Severin had said.

"Good." Sheridan had extended his hand.

Severin had taken it, surprised by the strength of the tinker's grip and his next words.

"As you know, me Fancy don't come with a dowry." Before Severin could aver that he had no need of one, Sheridan went on, "But what she brings be more valuable than money. She's learned the art o' tinkering from me, ain't nothing me girl can't fix."

Severin hadn't wanted to damage his father-in-law's pride or the present truce by stating the obvious: as a duke, he retained an army of people to fix things for him.

"Thank you, sir," he said with solemn gravity. "I am certain that will prove useful."

"I've a feeling it will," the tinker replied with a sage nod. "Fancy won't come to you entirely empty-'anded, 'owever. I've given 'er my best tinkering invention, and I also 'ave a special wedding gift for the both o' you."

Which was how Bertrand the donkey ended up leading Severin's team of horses. According to Sheridan, the damned donkey liked to be in the lead, and for some reason the thoroughbreds deferred to the mangy grey creature. Bertrand set a brisk pace for the team and kept it going.

Near the halfway point of their journey, a rainstorm descended out of nowhere. As drops pelted the carriage, Severin and Fancy sat side by side, discussing her father's revelations about her past.

"Growing up, did you wonder who your real parents were?" he asked.

"As strange as it sounds, not really," she admitted. "Even though I knew I was a foundling, I never felt like one. My parents didn't treat me any differently than my brothers and loved us all the same."

"You were lucky."

"Very." Her smile was wistful. "I wish you could've met my ma."

"What was she like?"

"Loving and kind. She told the best stories, faerie tales about princesses and 'appily ever afters."

That explained his wife's romantic streak.

"She was also practical and could tinker as well as Da," Fancy went on. "We 'ad these ironstone dishes that my brothers kept dropping. She mended those plates countless times, but you couldn't see the cracks—that's 'ow good she was at it."

"She sounds like a woman of many talents."

Nodding, she said, "Ma would've been shy around you...at first. She was like that with strangers. But once she got to know you, she would 'ave made you feel like part o' the family."

"You take after her," he murmured.

"I consider that the greatest compliment." Fancy paused, canting her head. "What was your mama like?"

She was beautiful, proud, and whored for us to survive. In the end, the poverty and desperation broke her. I failed to save her, and her ending was brutal.

"She was a good woman and did her best by me," he said. "Back to your parents. Do you have any curiosity now about who your true kin might be?"

Fancy's brow pleated, no doubt at his abrupt change of topic. But he had divulged as much as he meant to about that part of his past. That dark time before he became a gentleman.

"Yes and no," Fancy said slowly. "A part o' me *is* curious, but another part thinks it's best to let sleeping dogs lie. Why would a person abandon a 'elpless babe in a field? The only reason I can think o' is the obvious."

"The child was born out of wedlock," he stated.

She nodded, biting her lip.

"Are you worried about the note your father found?"

"It was written o'er two decades ago." She knit her brows. "Whatever the trouble was, I don't see 'ow it could find me now."

"It seems unlikely," he agreed. "But if you wish, I could hire an investigator—"

"What would be the point?" she asked with quiet dignity. "I'm 'appy knowing that I'm the daughter o' Milton and Annie Sheridan. They're my real parents. I don't need to know the identity o' whoe'er threw me away."

Severin couldn't argue with her logic. And, practically speaking, an investigator was unlikely to turn up much based on a christening gown and an old note.

The carriage suddenly went over a bump, careening with such force that Fancy soared off the seat. He caught her and held her securely, his other hand gripping the carriage strap while the conveyance came to an unpromising halt.

"Stay here, sweeting." He opened the door. "I'll see what's going on."

Outside, the rain had slowed to a drizzle, and he trudged through the slick mud to stand next to his driver, Rogers, and valet, Verney, both of whom had descended from the covered driver's perch to survey the damage.

"Apologies, Your Grace," Rogers muttered, droplets dripping off the brim of his hat and clinging to his dark whiskers. "I ran into a rock on account o' the rain. Now one o' the front wheels is broken."

Severin examined the wheel. Two of the spokes bore large cracks.

"Can you repair it?" he asked.

"Aye, with the proper tools. And I would need to prop up the cabin." Rogers looked resigned. "I'd best ride ahead to the next village and bring back 'elp."

"What 'appened?" Fancy called breathlessly.

Severin turned to see his wife coming up behind them, her braids bouncing against her shoulders as she navigated puddles. She hadn't even donned a cloak.

Removing his coat, he bundled her in it. "You shouldn't be out here, *chérie*. You'll get soaked."

Her gaze strayed to the wheel. "I wanted to see if I could 'elp."

"Rogers will ride ahead to the next village to obtain assistance. Let's get you back inside—"

Fancy had already gone to examine the wheel. "Mind if I 'ave a look?"

Rogers and the valet exchanged a glance that was just short of eye-rolling, but they stepped aside for their new mistress. Lucky for them because Severin wouldn't tolerate any disrespect toward his duchess.

"I see cracks in these two spokes." She ran her fingers over the fissures, heedless of the mud. "Any other damage, Rogers?"

"No, Your Grace," the driver said.

"Well, there's no point in you riding to the village and back in this weather. I 'ave something that ought to 'old the wheel together until we get to the village. Verney, would you mind fetching my travelling case? I need my tools."

The valet slid a questioning look at Severin, who inclined his head. "Do as Her Grace bids."

Fancy and Verney went to the luggage compartment, and she soon returned with a worn leather bag slung over her shoulder. Verney followed, holding an umbrella over her and a stack of toweling.

Crouching by the wheel, she instructed, "Be sure to keep the umbrella o'er the wheel. It needs to stay dry while I mend it."

"Yes, Your Grace." Verney dutifully positioned the umbrella.

Severin watched in fascination as Fancy spread a towel on the ground and took out a large jar from her bag. Using more of the toweling, she proceeded to dry off the wheel in brisk, meticulous motions. When she was done, she reached into her skirts, pulling out a...pocketknife? It was compact, about the length of her hand and half as wide.

"Da gave this to me as a wedding present. It's one o' 'is best inventions," she said proudly. "'E calls it *a tinker's friend* because no tinker should be without it. It 'as all the basic tools, and it folds up to save room. 'Ave a look."

Amused and intrigued, Severin looked on as she pulled out various tools that had been tucked inside the metal casing, attached to the contraption by a rotating bolt. The tools were scaled-down versions of the originals and included a screwdriver, blade, and spatula amongst others. Fancy reached for the jar, opening it to reveal a thick, dark substance. Scooping up the treacly stuff with the metal spatula, she began patching the wheel with it.

"What is in the jar?" Severin asked.

"Da's proprietary concoction." Her brow furrowed in concentration, she didn't take her eyes from the task. "It's a mixture o' tree sap, coal tar, and linseed oil, plus a few other ingredients. It dries in a blink and will 'old anything together."

"Amazing," he murmured.

"No one tinkers better than Milton Sheridan," she said proudly.

He wasn't referring to her father's inventions, handy as they were. His duchess finished filling the cracks in the wood, seeming oblivious to the astonished and admiring looks from the other men.

"There, that should do it." She stood, wiping her tinker's friend clean before folding it up and returning it to her skirts.

Rogers examined the wheel. "Blimey, you fixed the bleedin' thing," he said in awe. "And saved me a ride in the rain."

"It wasn't me but my da's concoction."

At Fancy's friendly smile, the driver looked spellbound.

Severin couldn't blame the man. Tendrils had escaped from her braids, curling delicately upon her pink cheeks. Her rain-spiked eyelashes made her brown eyes appear even bigger. She looked like a friendly faerie, one disarmingly unaware of her charms.

"I think Rogers can take it from here," he said.

He steered her back into the carriage, closing the door behind them. She shed his wet jacket and perched on the squabs, toweling off her braids. As the carriage began to move, Severin drew the curtains together.

She tilted her head. "Why are you closing the curtains?"

"We need to get you out of your wet things," he said.

"I'm not that wet—"

Her sentence was lost in a squeak as he tugged her onto his lap so that she straddled him. Flipping up her damp skirts, he found the slit in her drawers and ran a finger along her feminine cleft. The contrast between her silky thatch and slick flesh made him instantly hard.

"You're getting there," he said in satisfaction.

Her eyes widened, her hands clutching his shoulders. "But, Knight, we're in a carriage—"

She gasped. Probably because he'd released his erection and was running the burgeoned head along her dewy folds. As he breached her hole, warm honey bathed his cockhead.

Bloody heaven.

"What are you... It can be done *this* way?" she breathed.

He impaled her deeper onto his shaft, biting back a groan at the deliciously snug fit.

"Yes, sweet," he said. "I think you'll like it."

Her blissful moan told him that he was right.

18

THEY ARRIVED IN LONDON AT NIGHTFALL. DESCENDING THE carriage, Fancy stared up at the house—no, it was more than that. It was a blooming mansion, the size of which even the dimness could not obscure. Built of light-colored stone, the edifice stood four stories tall, complete with columns, pediments, and rows of arched windows from which light blazed.

"This is where you live?" she asked in a small voice.

"This is where we both live now, sweeting." Knight led her up the front steps, his hand at her waist. "I took residence here not long ago myself. We'll get used to this pile of stones together."

His comment was no doubt meant to be reassuring, but it didn't quell the fluttering of her nerves. Unlike her, *he* hadn't been living in a travelling wagon before this.

Until this moment, her confidence in their compatibility had been growing by leaps and bounds. The intimate sharing of their bodies and minds had made her feel like his equal. Moreover, Knight had a way of making her feel...special.

After making love to her in the carriage, for instance, he had cuddled her in his lap, murmuring in her ear, "Do you have any idea how adorable you are when you tinker, *chérie?*"

No one had called her adorable before. The fact that he found her so had rendered her speechless. She wanted so badly to be a good wife to him; unfortunately, the role included being a duchess.

'Old your 'ead up, then, she told herself. *Act as if you belong 'ere.*

Her resolve wavered as they entered the grand abode. Awaiting them in the stunning marble antechamber was a veritable army of servants. She gulped as she took in their formal livery, polished brass buttons winking beneath the chandelier. Although she'd donned her best pink dress for the occasion, the garment showed the signs of travel and needed a good sponging. She also regretted not taking more trouble with her hair; in her hurry to get on the road this morning, she'd wound her thick locks into their usual braids.

Knight introduced the staff to her one by one, and Fancy tried to remember everyone's names. It was difficult since there were so *many* of them. After going down the line, Knight dismissed all of the servants except the butler and housekeeper.

"Her Grace will need a lady's maid, Mrs. Treadwell," Knight said to the latter.

"I shall gather a list of candidates." Mrs. Treadwell had salt and pepper hair and a brisk yet friendly manner. "Does Her Grace have any specifications in mind?"

Hesitating, Fancy asked shyly, "Could you find someone who's good with 'air?"

"Of course, Your Grace." Mrs. Treadwell inclined her head.

Severin turned to address the butler, a man with an intimidatingly formal manner.

"Harvey, where is Lady Brambley?" he asked.

"She is in the drawing room with the rest of the family, Your Grace," Harvey said, his voice as sonorous as a church bell.

Knight took Fancy's hand, placing it on his sleeve.

"Come, sweet," he said. "Time to meet the family."

Family...or firing squad? she thought, swallowing.

Although Knight's face was impassive, the bunched muscles of his forearm quivered beneath her fingertips. He was as apprehensive about the meeting as she was. On the journey over, he'd revealed more details about his family situation. He'd told her that his Aunt Esther, Lady Brambley, had supported his claim to the title but was rather aloof and disapproving. He'd described his ambivalent relationships with his siblings, especially the older ones who resented a stranger appearing in their lives and taking charge.

And now Fancy had to somehow gain his family's approval. Knight hadn't put it as such, but she understood how important it was for him to have a helpmate, someone who could bring his family together and guide his siblings toward respectability. It was a daunting endeavor, even for a well-bred lady. For a tinker's daughter, the task would be Herculean.

Will I be worthy o' the task? Fancy fretted.

They entered the drawing room, and she found herself the focus of five pairs of eyes. On her best day, she wasn't comfortable with strangers, and she had to force herself to breathe in and out as Knight made the introductions. Even before he did so, she could guess who was who from his descriptions of them.

His Aunt Esther, Lady Brambley, sat stiffly upon a burgundy settee, her thin figure draped in a gown of black Parramatta silk. According to Knight, Esther had been in mourning since the death of her husband, Earl Brambley, over a decade ago. A sharp-featured woman in her sixties, Lady Esther had silver hair and narrow blue-grey eyes that tilted upward, giving her a feline appearance.

Beside her sat sixteen-year-old Cecily, a tawny-haired, green-eyed beauty. Her slender figure was draped in a muslin gown with a low neckline that straddled the line of respectability. Cecily had the kind of face that would stop a man in his tracks; unfortunately, her natural gifts were dimmed by her ill-tempered pout and excessive face paint.

It had to be Jonas, the eldest, who stood posed by the hearth, his arm propped on the mantel. He bore some similarity to Knight in his height and coloring. Yet there was nothing of Knight in the boy's air of superiority and contrivances. He carried himself like some brooding poet; his longish hair, arranged in a windswept style, kept falling into his eyes.

The thirteen-year-old twins, Eleanor and Toby, shared a divan. Both were brown-haired and freckled. Eleanor had an open book in her lap, her intelligent brandy-colored eyes owlishly scrutinizing Fancy from behind a pair of spectacles. She had a solemn little face, her hair in plaits not unlike Fancy's own. Beside her, Toby was eating a piece of cake, pausing to give Fancy an awkward wave that she nervously returned.

Knight led her to a pair of chairs across the coffee table from his aunt and Cecily and adjacent to the twins. Fancy perched on the edge of her seat, while Knight sat back, his expression stony.

"Welcome to the family, my dear," Esther, Lady Brambley, said in cool tones. "It was *such* a surprise to hear from my nephew that he'd married."

"It is a pleasure to make your acquaintance, ma'am," Fancy said timidly.

Esther's thin black brows inched toward her silver widow's peak. "You may address me as Aunt Esther, my dear. I shall call you Francesca for I detest pet names."

"Oh, Fancy ain't a pet name. It's my full name."

Aunt Esther's gaze narrowed. "How unfortunate. Nonetheless, it is considered ill-mannered to correct your elders. Mind you remember that."

"Yes, ma'am...I mean, Aunt Esther." Cheeks aflame, Fancy darted a glance at Knight.

He had a slight crease between his brows but said nothing.

"Now Knighton informs me that I am to guide you in the ways of Society," the lady went on. "You, in turn, will be responsible for the management of my brother's younger children."

"Yes, Aunt Esther. I would be e'er so grateful for your 'elp." Gathering up her courage, Fancy said earnestly, "I know I ain't polished yet, but I'll work 'ard, and I'm a quick learner."

"A *quick learner?*" Cecily gave a trilling laugh. "My dear sister-in-law, do you come with references?"

Jonas snickered, and Fancy's face heated even more.

"That is enough, Cecily." Knight gave both his siblings a quelling look. "You'll show Fancy the respect that is due to her."

"I didn't say anything wrong," Cecily said petulantly.

"Hell, I didn't even say anything," Jonas drawled.

"Language, Jonas," Aunt Esther chided. She turned to the niece beside her. "And you, Cecily, will mind your manners."

"Why am I the one who must be reminded of my manners?" Cecily's face reddened with remarkable speed. She waved a hand at Fancy. "She cannot even speak properly and dresses like a country bumpkin. If I have to wait for her to become fashionable so that she can bring me out into Society, then I shall be waiting forever!"

Mortification and shock at the girl's rudeness robbed Fancy of speech.

"Cecily, I believe I told you to desist," Knight said sharply.

"That is all you ever do, *brother.*" Cecily shot to her feet, her slender form vibrating with rage. "Papa never told me what to do; he wanted me to be happy. But because of you, I have been separated from my dearest Jacques and all my friends in France. My heart is broken, and it is all your fault. I hate London, and I hate you!"

She gave a sob and ran out of the drawing room.

A clock counted out the silence.

Stunned, Fancy turned to her taut-jawed husband, whispering, "Should you go after—"

"I wouldn't bother." The matter-of-fact statement came from Eleanor, who looked up from the book she'd been reading. "Cecily is prone to dramatics," she said calmly. "Her mama was an actress."

"Her mama was *my* mama." Jonas tossed a fussy wave of hair out of his eyes in order to glare at his younger sister.

Eleanor's brows rose above her spectacles. "Precisely."

Jonas' hands curled at his sides. "Why you uppity little bluestocking—"

"I would rather be a bluestocking than a rake."

"No one even knows you exist, you little twerp," Jonas retorted.

Eleanor directed a hard stare at him. "*Cogito, ergo sum.*"

"What in blazes does that mean?" Jonas snapped.

"I think, therefore I am." The girl's smile was smug. "According to Descartes' principle, you're the one who doesn't exist."

"Why you bloody *know-it-all*—"

"Jonas, do not attack your sister," Aunt Esther cut in. "Eleanor, stop provoking your brother."

"I've better things to do than put up with this nonsense," Jonas declared.

He, too, exited the room.

"He doesn't," Eleanor said. "Have anything better to do, that is."

Before Fancy could think of a reply, the girl buried her nose in her book again, seemingly shutting out the rest of the world.

Silence once again descended, the clock's ticking becoming deafening. Fancy looked at Knight, who sat with stiff shoulders and a stark expression.

"Well, Knighton, didn't I tell you this was a Sisyphean task?" Aunt Esther said coldly. "All my efforts trying to civilize these beastly children have come to naught. It is like trying to spin gold out of straw. One cannot alter the base material."

Knight's mouth tightened.

"Please don't be angry, Aunt Esther." Toby spoke for the first time, his voice high and timorous. "Would you like some cake? The cream slice is very good."

For some reason, Aunt Esther's features turned wary. "No, Toby. No cake for me."

"What about for you, Your Grace?" Toby turned shyly to Fancy. "Could I get you some?"

At the boy's eager-to-please expression, Fancy's heart melted. "Yes, please."

"I don't think that's a good—" Knight began.

Fancy hushed him, not wanting to hurt Toby's feelings or discourage the first sign of goodwill she'd had from his family. Toby put a slice of cake on a plate and headed over to her, but his foot somehow got caught on the leg of the coffee table. He tripped, the cake flying from the plate, and the rest seemed to happen in slowed time. Fancy's eyes widened as the slice arced through the air toward her; an instant later, cool cream and spongy cake pelted her in the face.

She sputtered and gasped.

His handkerchief already out, Knight went to her and began wiping at her cheeks.

"I'm s-so sorry," Toby whimpered.

Through the creamy crumbs, Fancy managed to smile at the distraught boy. "Ne'er mind, dear. Accidents 'appen."

"But do they have to happen every hour?" Aunt Esther said with an aggrieved sigh.

His eyes shimmering, Toby hung his head. He scurried to sit back down next to Eleanor, who'd remained lost in her book through all of this.

"Knighton, you are only spreading the cake about. I'll take Francesca to her suite to tidy up," Aunt Esther said imperiously.

Knight narrowed his eyes at his aunt. "For Christ's sake, her name isn't Francesca. It's—"

"Been lovely to meet you all," Fancy blurted, bouncing up.

"And I would appreciate your 'elp, Aunt Esther. Thank you for offering."

Knight gripped the cakey handkerchief. "You do not have to go with her."

"I want to." Seeing his grim expression, she managed a smile. "I'll be fine."

"Come along, Francesca." Aunt Esther rose in a sweep of black silk. "Before we are treated to any further surprises."

19

Later that evening, Severin paused at the door that separated his and Fancy's bedchambers. He felt like an idiot standing there, paralyzed by indecision. On the one hand, he wanted to spend the night with Fancy. On the other, his aunt had cornered him in his study after the family supper, which had been tense even though Cecily had taken a tray in her room and Jonas had gone God knows where. As was her wont, Esther hadn't minced words.

"You do not like things easy, do you, Knighton?" his aunt had said dryly. "Now not only do I have to contend with your wild siblings, I have your duchess to take in hand as well. She was supposed to help save the family name, not make doing so *more* difficult."

He'd reminded his aunt that Fancy had been grateful and willing to take her advice.

"I suppose that is something." Esther had given him a severe look. "Training her to be a duchess will be a monumental task, you understand. We will need the best of everything: a modiste, lady's maid, elocution expert, dancing master, and so forth."

"Whatever you need will be at your disposal."

"What I need is a miracle," Esther had harrumphed. "Short of that, I must needs rely on my good taste. Speaking of which, I want to speak with you about your manner with Francesca."

"Her name is Fancy," he had said through gritted teeth.

"A problem I am trying to rectify." Sniffing, Esther went on, "Couples of good breeding do not live in each other's pockets. People will make allowances for newlyweds but, in my opinion, it is best to begin as one means to go on. Francesca looks at you with stars in her eyes; while you might find that charming, you do her no favors by encouraging such a blatant show of emotion. She lacks sophistication and polish as it is. Do you want the Duchess of Knighton to be seen by the *ton* as a moonstruck ninny?"

Severin's face had heated like that of an errant schoolboy being scolded by a governess. Yet he hadn't been able to stem the reflexive warmth that flooded his chest. Did Fancy really look at him that way? With stars in her eyes?

A tide of guilt had swiftly followed. It was not fair of him to take advantage of his wife's sweetness when his own damaged heart could not offer anything in return.

He had cleared his throat. "Of course not."

Which led to his present predicament.

Esther was right. In good society, strong displays of emotion were discouraged, and excessive sentimentality was seen as common. The Hammonds, for instance, had always been self-possessed; their reactions to everything and each other had been pleasant and modulated. Imogen's motto had been, *If you do not have anything nice to say, then do not say anything at all.*

Severin pushed aside the thought. He didn't want to think of the past when he had his marriage to figure out. Things had seemed so much simpler when he and Fancy were on the road. Free from responsibilities, he had just been a newlywed groom with an itch for his pretty bride.

But they were back in London now, and he wasn't just a randy newlywed. He was a duke who needed a duchess, which meant he ought to treat his wife like one. He stared at the thick paneled door between them, the gleaming polished knob, and his fingers twitched to reach out and open the door. To not think about his deuced duties and family—to just lose himself in Fancy's passionate warmth.

You are only thinking of your own needs, you selfish bastard, he told himself starkly. *If you had married a well-bred lady, you wouldn't be tupping her every day...and some days more than once. Fancy deserves the same respect, doesn't she?*

He exhaled, turning to go.

Then the door opened, and he jerked around.

"Knight?" Fancy peered at him through the half-open door.

"Yes, sweeting?" He tried not to notice the fact that she was dressed for bed, her chestnut hair loose and shining. "Do you need something?"

"No...not, um, really." She bit her lip, her cheeks flushing. "I was just wondering if you might want, um, company?"

Her vulnerability loosened the knot in his chest.

"I was about to knock and ask you the same thing," he said ruefully.

"Were you?" Relief filled her brown eyes. "Aunt Esther said separate bedchambers are the appropriate arrangement between a lady and 'er 'usband. And she said it's always the 'usband's prerogative to open the door."

Hearing Fancy convey Esther's advice made him realize how stupid that advice was. It was *his* marriage—his and Fancy's. What went on in their private lives was nobody's business.

"Aunt Esther may be an expert on many things but not marital matters." He took his wife's hand, tugging her into his room and closing the door behind her. "Open the door whenever you like; I cannot think of a single occasion when I would not welcome your company."

Her eyes were like melted chocolate in the candlelight. "Truly?"

"Truly," he said.

She smiled, so beautifully that his heart gave a stutter. Reaching up, she fiddled with the lapel of his robe. "After the last week, it felt strange sleeping alone. And the bed in my chamber is as big as my family's entire caravan."

"You do not have to sleep alone."

And neither do I.

The realization came with a feeling of wonder. Before Fancy, he had rarely stayed the night with a woman. On occasion, he'd fallen asleep with his mistresses, but no cuddling had been involved. Yet since their very first night together, Fancy had fit perfectly in his arms. He had gotten accustomed to falling asleep to the scent of her hair and awakening tangled up with her.

He led her over to his bed, a giant mahogany tester draped with navy silk hangings.

"Climb in, *chérie*."

She did, and he followed suit. Tucking her against his side, with her head against his heart, felt like the most natural thing to do. They lay in companionable silence, which was another fine quality his wife possessed. Unlike other women he'd known, she didn't feel the need to fill the space with nonsensical chatter. She just curled against him as he traced a lazy circle on her shoulder.

"Your family doesn't like me," Fancy announced.

He stopped his doodling. "That is not true."

"Cecily thinks I'm rude and unfashionable. She didn't even come to supper on account o' me."

"She didn't come to supper on account of her being a spoiled brat," he countered. "Besides, if she despises anyone, it is me."

Fancy lifted her head to look at him. "Why? She ought to be grateful you are looking after 'er."

"As I've mentioned, my father did not spend time with his offspring. The rare instances when he bothered to notice them, he indulged them. He did not set rules or guide their behavior."

"But you do set rules," Fancy said slowly.

"As their guardian, it is my duty," Severin stated. "They must learn to conduct themselves properly and gain self-discipline. How else will they survive the world?"

"You're a good brother," she said softly.

He shifted uncomfortably. "I am merely managing the responsibility that was given to me. My family is not like yours. There's no feeling of kinship binding us."

"I disagree. Whether or not they show it, your siblings look up to you, and you care for them in return." Before he could dispute her, Fancy said, "Who is Jacques? The fellow Cecily mentioned."

"Just one of the many ne'er-do-wells that Cecily had sniffing after her back in France," Severin said in disgust. "She has a penchant for picking up fortune hunters and scoundrels."

"Luckily, she 'as you to protect her now. And me as well."

He looked at her. "*You* are going to protect Cecily? After the way she acted?"

"That is why you needed a duchess, isn't it?" she returned. "It will be up to me to get your siblings into shipshape. Now I know I ain't precisely ready myself, but Aunt Esther 'as a plan for me."

Amused at her determined expression, he asked, "What plan is that, sweeting?"

"In a nutshell? She's going to change everything about me and turn me into a lady."

"You don't need to change. All you need is superficial polish. A few lessons and trips to the modiste."

"I'm going to make you proud o' me," she vowed.

"I am proud of you." He rolled so that he lay atop her, balancing his weight on his arms. Looking into Fancy's solemn brown eyes, he felt a tug in his chest. "I know what you're taking on for me, and I...I appreciate it. Appreciate having you by my side."

He was mesmerized by the sweetness of her smile. By the feeling that he wasn't...alone.

"I appreciate you too," she whispered.

Emotion surged over him. He had to tear his gaze away from the temptation of her mouth, instead burying his lips at her throat. She sighed as he kissed her there, his tongue finding the flutter of her pulse. He was already hard, already hungry for her. With an impatient hand, he undid the buttons of her nightgown, and she helped him get the bloody thing off her.

He paused. By God, he would never tire of seeing his wife naked. He ran a possessive hand over her: her throat, her rounded tits, the dip of her waist and belly. She arched into his touch like a kitten. He cupped her dark silky pussy, massaging the peak of her mound with the heel of his hand. Lust sizzled in his veins when dew coated his palm.

"You're ready for me, aren't you, sweet?" he said thickly. "Nice and wet for my cock."

She looked at him with dazed, dark eyes. "Oh, please..."

"Please what? Rub your little pearl harder like this?"

When he ground his palm, she whimpered, inciting the beast in him.

"Maybe you want more," he said. "Do you, Fancy?"

"I need you," she panted. "Whate'er you'll give me."

The same thing she'd said to him that night in the tree. And her surrender had the same effect now as it had then: he felt the gentlemanly shell slipping away from him, giving way to his animal need, his darkest desires.

He penetrated her with a finger, the hungry clutch of her cunny unleashing a growl from his throat. "You have one finger, sweet. Want another?"

Her moan was sufficient answer. She gasped, her hips bucking as he stirred two digits inside her. He pumped them and grunted his approval at her squeezing response. His erection butted the front of his robe as he finger-fucked her harder, faster, his palm slapping her pussy the way his balls would soon be doing.

"Work yourself on my fingers," he rasped. "Come for me, Fancy."

With her plump bottom lip caught beneath her teeth, she obeyed, impaling herself on his driving touch. Her passage began to convulse, a tight, hot rippling that made his cock weep in eagerness. She cried his name as she found her completion.

He yanked off his robe, notching his burgeoned dome to her entrance. He pushed inside her, and a line of fire shot up his spine as he buried himself fully in his wife's snug pussy. Driven by pure craving, he plowed her furrow with vigorous thrusts. Her spasms continued, and he didn't know if she was still coming or coming again. The sound of their colliding flesh was a visceral, maddening pleasure.

When her convulsions stopped, he withdrew and flipped his startled wife onto her hands and knees. Grasping her by her hips, he entered her from behind. He felt her jolt of surprise, followed by the hot, sucking acceptance of her body. The lewd delight of watching his shaft sink into her pink slit almost finished him off. Shuddering, he dug his fingers into her hips and hilted himself to the root. He did it again and again, egged on by her mewling sounds, by his own need to be as deeply inside her as possible.

He felt his bollocks tighten, his seed rising. He reached under, finding her pearl, working it as he slammed his cock inside her. She gasped, her fingers bunching the sheets.

"Spend with me," he bit out.

His command came out strangled, but she did it anyway. The squeeze of her pussy demolished the rest of his control. Heat shot from his stones with mind-melting intensity. He drove in, then held, shuddering, filling her with his pleasure.

Panting, he placed a soft kiss on her nape before pulling her down to lay with him. He had sufficient energy left to tuck the coverlet over them. She snuggled against him, her contented sigh an echo of his own sentiments. Stroking her hair, his legs tangled with hers, he fell into a deep sleep.

When Fancy awoke the next morning, it took a moment for her to recognize her surroundings. She was in Knight's bed. He was gone, but his scent still lingered. Smiling dreamily, she rubbed her cheek against his pillow, reliving last night. The steamy passion they'd shared...and more.

I appreciate you. Having you by my side.

Happiness trembled through her. Along with trepidation.

Was she falling in love with Knight?

She admired him so. For the way he had survived a dark past and yet took care of others without expecting anything return. For the way he made her feel special and wanted. For the way he was a fighter and protector and yet had vulnerabilities of his own.

Vulnerabilities that she wanted to help him with, the way he was giving her pieces of her dream. But was she setting herself up for pain? The devastation of a broken heart?

From the start, Knight had told her that he would not love her. He was nothing if not honest. Even though they'd grown closer since that time, she had no right to expect that his view on love would change. Knowing that, she ought to be wise and guard her heart.

Alas, when am I wise? she thought with a sigh.

She had never been one to give up on her dreams. But maybe she didn't have to. Maybe if she succeeded in fixing herself up into a perfect duchess, then he might fall in love with her.

He liked her already, she thought with burgeoning hope. And he *definitely* desired her. Each time they made love, she felt closer to him, felt him letting down his guard more and more. Last night, he'd shown a raw side of him she'd never seen before; just thinking of the way he'd rutted her, like a barnyard animal, made her cheeks—and other parts—warm.

With friendship and passion checked off the list, all she needed was to win Knight's admiration, the sort he obviously had for Imogen. If Fancy dazzled the *ton* as the Duchess of Knighton, hostess and sister-in-law extraordinaire, then he would see her in the same way, wouldn't he? She *could* win his love after all.

Brimming with optimism over her new plan, Fancy returned to her room. Winning Knight's love wasn't the only important item on her agenda: she was going to see Bea. Because they'd arrived too late last night, Knight had promised to take her first thing.

Returning to her own chamber, she rang for help, and the maid Mrs. Treadwell had assigned her arrived with a cheery smile and a breakfast tray. After Fancy ate every bite of the coddled eggs and crisp buttered toast (last night had worked up her appetite), she dressed, completed her morning ablutions, and hurried downstairs to find her husband.

He wasn't in the breakfast parlor, and one of the footmen said His Grace was with a visitor in the drawing room. Fancy ventured over and heard voices coming from within. Putting on a bright smile—she wanted to make a good first impression on Knight's guests—she walked through the door and froze.

Knight was standing by the fire with the most beautiful creature Fancy had ever seen.

The woman had hair of reddish gold, bound up in swirls and curls that showed off the swan-like perfection of her neck. She was tall, just a few inches shorter than Knight. Her slender, willowy build was draped in an elegant carriage dress of cerulean blue. Her matching pelisse was cinched at her waist with a gold belt, and her slim fingers were encased in pristine white gloves. She was standing close to Knight, clutching a handkerchief, looking up at him with a longing expression that twisted Fancy's heart.

When Knight's gaze jerked to Fancy, the woman also turned, and her azure eyes widened in her sculpted face. The single tear rolling down her cheek enhanced her angelic beauty.

In a sickening, heart-crushing flash, Fancy knew who the woman was.

"Fancy, you're up early." Knight took a hasty step back from the woman. "This is an old friend, Lady Imogen Cardiff. She, er, had something caught in her eye, and I was just lending her my handkerchief."

Fancy's heart pounded at his gruff explanation, which rang false to her ears.

"I am so pleased to make your acquaintance, Your Grace, and wish to offer my sincere felicitations on your marriage." Imogen's voice was as musical as bells, her curtsy a masterpiece of grace. "And I must apologize for calling at this unfashionable hour. I was running an errand in the neighborhood and thought I would stop by for a quick visit. Knighton being an old family friend, he and I do not usually stand on formality."

"You are welcome to visit whene'er you wish, my lady." Fancy forced the words out. "And it's a pleasure to meet any friend o' my 'usband."

"You are too kind." Imogen smiled as if Fancy had done her the greatest favor. "I understand that this is your first trip to London?"

Fancy looked at Knight, wondering how much information he'd shared about their marriage with his former love. His expression was impassive, but the tense line of his shoulders betrayed his discomfort. In her heart, she trusted him not to betray her: he'd promised to be true, and he was a man of his word. Yet now that he was seeing her and Imogen together, was he comparing them...and finding Fancy lacking? Despair and hot humiliation welled in Fancy's breast. Why couldn't she have had some warning, maybe a week or two to prepare?

What difference would it make? You'll ne'er match the perfection o' Lady Imogen Cardiff.

"Yes, it's my first time 'ere," she said dully.

"Please, call me Imogen. It would be so lovely for us to be friends."

For some reason, which could very well be her own jealous heart, Fancy didn't find the other's smile convincing. "Then...I'm Fancy."

She sounded awkward and ungracious, but Imogen seemed to take no notice.

"If you need my help with anything at all, Fancy, do not hesitate to ask. I can recommend the most fashionable establishments for ladies of quality," Imogen said. "Some of these places do have a waiting list, but I would be happy to speak on your behalf. In light of your, ahem, circumstances."

Fancy found herself gritting her teeth. Although she wasn't cultured, she was plenty experienced when it came to being patronized. She would rather wear her pink dress *forever* than accept the lady's help.

"Aunt Esther 'as a plan," she said curtly. "I'm sure she'll take care o' me."

"How delightful. Well, I mustn't take up more of your time," Imogen said smoothly. "I hope to see you soon?"

The last was clearly directed at Knight, who gave a short bow. "Thank you for stopping by, my lady."

After Imogen departed, leaving a trail of Attar of Roses in her wake, silence blanketed the room. Emotions roiled in Fancy's breast. They were too confusing and too terrifying to share when her husband had that distant look in his eyes, his jaw taut and body braced. Her passionate, tender lover of the night before had vanished, and she wasn't sure who the stranger was before her.

No, she *had* seen him this way before. That night at the pond. Had he been brooding over Imogen then?

Unable to bear the silent agony, she said, "I wanted to ask you something."

His eyes were wary. "Yes?"

"You said you would take me to see Bea today. Could we go now?"

"Of course." Relief spread over his rugged features. "Will leaving in ten minutes suit you?"

She nodded.

"I'll see you then." He left the room as if the hounds of hell were at his heels.

Alone, she stared after him, torn between her deepest yearning and the realization of what she was up against if she wanted to win her husband's heart.

20

"I WANT *ALL* THE DETAILS, MY DEAR," BEA SAID THE INSTANT Knight and Mr. Murray left the room. "I leave you alone for less than a month, and you become a duchess!"

Fancy was seated with her bosom chum in the drawing room of Mr. Murray's townhouse. The carriage ride over had been strained, with Knight continuing to be remote and lost in thought. Upon their arrival, they'd received a surprised but delighted welcome from Bea and Mr. Murray. The pair had wonderful news to share: the villain who'd masterminded the attacks on Bea—and Fancy's kidnapping—had been defeated and could cause no further trouble.

The problem with the mobs blaming Bea for the crashing railways stocks was also over. After her harrowing adventures, Bea had discovered that true security lay in the love between her and Mr. Murray and not in a piece of land. She'd decided to sell her property to Great London National Railway; using the proceeds, she would purchase another estate nearby so that her tenants could continue to sustain their livelihoods. Bea and Mr. Murray had also shared the best news of all: in a little over a week, they would be getting married by special license.

"You'll be my maid of honor, won't you, Fancy?" Bea had said.

In the excitement of catching up on Bea and Mr. Murray's news, Fancy and Knight hadn't yet shared their own. She'd glanced over at her husband, who'd maintained his usual stoicism. He'd lifted his eyebrows as if to say, *You might as well tell them*.

Drawing a breath, she'd said to her bosom chum, "I can't be your maid o' honor."

Bea had furrowed her brow. "Why not?"

"Because I'd be...your matron o' honor."

"Matron? But you're not—oh my goodness!" In a heartbeat, Bea had put two and two together. "You and *Knighton*?"

"Fancy did me the honor of becoming my wife," Knight said. "We were married a week ago in Gretna Green."

"You sly devil." Grinning, Mr. Murray had gone over to shake Knight's hand. "Always the competitive fellow, eh? You had to get to the altar first."

"I was not aware that matrimony was a race." Knight's tone had been wry, his eyes amused. "In either case, I believe we are both winners."

"Very gallant, Your Grace," Bea said approvingly.

"He's just showing off," Mr. Murray muttered, but there was a good-natured twinkle in his hazel eyes. "This calls for champagne."

The celebratory beverage had been brought in, and the four had toasted to the happiness of both couples. Then Bea had suggested rather pointedly that Mr. Murray should offer Knight a cigar in his study.

"We're being dismissed, Knighton." Mr. Murray's teasing tones had carried as he led his guest out. "Is this what married life will be like, I wonder? We useless husbands being ordered about by our wives?"

"Speak for yourself." Knight had cast a look back at Fancy. "I intend to have my uses. I would not give my wife any cause to wonder why she married me."

Surprised by the warmth in his eyes, Fancy had blushed.

Now Knight was gone, and she was facing an inquisitive Bea.

"It's a long story," Fancy began.

"How long could it possibly be?" Bea arched her fair brows. "You met Knighton less than a month ago. Now you're married to him. Stop prevaricating, dearest, and tell me all."

So Fancy did. Starting from her encounter with Knighton at the stream to the camping at the farmhouse to her sleepwalking in the storm. She told her best friend about how good, kind, and noble Knight had been toward her. And she revealed the terms of their marriage: that the one thing Knight wasn't offering was love.

"Hold up," Bea said with a frown. "*You,* Fancy Sheridan, lifelong believer in faerie tales, married a man who wants nothing to do with love?"

"It's not as bad as it sounds." Seeing her friend's skepticism, Fancy added quickly, "Knight is a kind and generous 'usband. Why, this afternoon I'm to go shopping with 'is Aunt Esther, and 'e's given me,"—she tried to recall the phrase—"*carte blanche.* It means I can buy whate'er I want."

"I know what it means." A line formed between Bea brows. "And I also know that you don't give a whit about gowns and gewgaws. Haven't you always told me that nothing is more important than love? What you want—what you've *always* wanted—is a husband you love and who loves you in return."

It was true. That had been her dream, always.

It still is, her heart whispered.

"I 'aven't given up on my dream. I think...I think I'm falling in love with 'im, Bea." She swallowed against rising despair. "But 'is 'eart belongs to another, and I met 'er this morning. She looks like an *angel.*"

To her horror, her voice broke, heat pushing behind her eyes. The tears fell before she could stop them, and once they started, they wouldn't stop.

Bea put an arm around her shoulders, murmuring, "There, there, dear. Let it all out."

Fancy did, and when she was done, Bea handed her a handkerchief. "Feel better?"

"Yes." Sniffling, she wiped her eyes. "I 'aven't 'ad anyone to talk to about this."

"That's what bosom chums are for," Bea said. "Now tell me about this 'angel' you met."

Not wanting to betray Knight's confidence, Fancy kept the details to a minimum, enough so that her friend could understand the situation.

"'Er name is Imogen, and 'e's loved 'er since 'e saved 'er from a runaway carriage when 'e was fifteen. But she's a lady, and 'e wasn't grand enough back then to win 'er family's approval. She married an earl five years ago and,"—Fancy's breath hitched—"Knight still loves 'er."

"He told you this?" Bea asked.

Fancy blew her nose and nodded. "'E said loving 'er was a 'abit 'e couldn't break. 'E was being 'onest with me, see, because 'e wanted me to understand the kind o' marriage 'e was offering."

"A marriage of convenience?" Bea murmured.

"'E didn't call it that, exactly. 'E said that while 'e couldn't give me love, 'e would be true and take care o' me. That we would 'elp each other and be a team."

"How are things in the marital bower?"

Heat flooded Fancy's cheeks.

Bea laughed. "You don't need to answer me, dearest: your blush says it all. I'm not surprised, really, given the way Knighton looks at you."

"'Ow does he look at me?"

"How do I describe it?" Bea tilted her head. "Like you're a deer and he's a starved wolf?"

"Oh." She widened her eyes. "You think so?"

"I noticed it even before I left for London. While Knighton

was busy convincing himself that he had a duty to propose to me, he couldn't keep his eyes off *you*. That was why I warned you before I left. I was worried that he might propose something untoward, but instead..." A smile slowly spread across Bea's face. "Instead he's done the right thing and made you a duchess."

"I want to be the lady Knight needs me to be," she said earnestly, "one 'e'll be proud to 'ave on 'is arm. I want to 'elp 'im with 'is siblings too—who, by the by, make my brothers look like perfect princes. I didn't tell you all o' it, but Knight's road 'asn't been an easy one. 'E's ne'er 'ad anybody to lean on, not really, and I want 'im to know 'e ain't alone now."

As she spoke her thoughts aloud, her resolve grew. She could never be the angelic Imogen, but Knight wasn't married to Imogen, was he? He was married to her, Fancy, and she didn't come to this marriage empty-handed. She was her father's daughter: what tinkers lacked in wealth and prestige, they made up for in grit, determination, and adaptability.

Why, how many times had she mended a broken pot or piece of clothing? Or taken things she'd found in a rubbish pile and turned them into objects others would pay good money for? She would use all the skills at her disposal to become what Knight needed.

She would simply fix...*herself*.

I'll be what 'e needs, she thought fiercely. *I'll make myself o'er into a lady. I'll work to win my prince's 'eart.*

"You *are* what your husband needs." Bea reached over and squeezed her hand. "You are beautiful, loving, and sweet, which is probably what drew Knighton to you in the first place."

Fancy was too busy planning to pay full attention to her friend's words.

"Aunt Esther will 'elp me with my clothes and 'air," she said eagerly. "She says I must 'ave lessons as well."

Bea pursed her lips. "Lessons in what?"

"In *everything*. She says I must learn to speak, dress, and act like a lady." Fancy looked hopefully at her friend. "Would you mind 'elping me with..." She tried to recall Aunt Esther's term. "Proper comportment?"

"I'm hardly a shining example of propriety," Bea said dryly. "But I would be glad to point you in the general direction."

"Thank you." Bubbling with enthusiasm, Fancy suddenly realized there was something she had not yet mentioned. "And there's something else. A secret about my past."

She shared what Da had revealed about her origins.

"Goodness." Bea's lavender gaze rounded. "And there were no other clues about who your parents might be, other than the clothing you were wearing and the note?"

"None whatsoe'er. Da thinks—and Knight and I agree—that at least one o' my parents must 'ave been rich." She bit her lip. "Maybe a lady gave birth to me out o' wedlock, or I'm some toff's by-blow. Whate'er the case, they needed to be rid o' me."

Concern lined Bea's brow. "Is it safe for you to be in London?"

"It's been o'er two decades since that note was written. 'Ow could I be in danger now?" She shrugged. "But Knight says I'm not to take risks, and 'e won't let me go anywhere without an escort."

"I like your duke better already," Bea murmured.

"'E's a good man," she said staunchly. "And I'm going to make myself into a lady worthy o' 'im."

"That is utter claptrap."

At her chum's sharp tone, Fancy blinked.

"I've been around so-called ladies all my life, Fancy," Bea went on. "After I was scarred, they turned their backs on me, even those who professed to be my closest friends. None of them showed your goodness, loyalty, or heart. Any man who deserves you will see that: will see *you* for the jewel that you are."

Fancy was touched by her friend's words. Yet if she were a jewel, she would be a diamond in the rough compared to the sparkling perfection of Imogen, Countess of Cardiff. Being born a duke's daughter, Bea didn't understand certain things...and perhaps couldn't. Even when the winds of Fate had been cruel, she'd had wealth and privilege to buffer her.

Not having those things, Fancy would have to rely on her skills to win her husband's heart.

"Even a jewel needs the right setting and polishing up," she said lightly. "Speaking o' which, Aunt Esther is taking me shopping this afternoon."

"I wish I could come with you," Bea said, "but Wick is taking me to look at rings."

The glow of happiness on Bea's face warmed Fancy inside and out. They moved on to discuss the plans for Bea's wedding ceremony, and Fancy offered to help however she could. Listening to her once-jaded chum wax on about flowers and decorations, she felt her resolve and courage strengthen.

Love was everything, and she would fight for it in her own marriage.

21

That afternoon, Fancy followed Aunt Esther into a shop on Bond Street. The establishment's exclusivity was such that its name was not advertised. There was only a discreet sign in the window that read, "By Appointment Only."

The sparkling plate glass windows and royal blue awning piped with gold set the tone for the elegantly spartan interior. Gleaming rosewood counters and cabinets lined the shop's perimeter. Chairs upholstered in dark blue velvet were clustered next to small tables laid with gilt-rimmed teacups.

"*Bienvenue,* ladies." A dressmaker's assistant came to greet them with a diffident curtsy. "Madame Rousseau is finishing up with a client and will be with you shortly. Please have a seat."

Following Aunt Esther's lead, Fancy settled into one of the chairs, and before long they had tea and a plate of bite-sized pastries to enjoy as they waited.

Fancy peered at her surroundings with awe. "This is a grand shop, ain't it?"

"It *is* an exclusive establishment." Aunt Esther's blue-grey eyes were stern over the rim of teacup. "Elocution and grammar lessons begin tomorrow morning, but you might as well start reforming your speech now, Francesca."

"Yes, ma'am." Fancy didn't mind being corrected; as far as she was concerned, she needed all the help she could get to become a lady. "I'll try my best to speak proper-like."

"Proper*ly*. And don't try, gel." Aunt Esther sipped her tea. "Simply do it."

"Yes, aunt." Lowering her voice, Fancy said, "Do you think Madame Rousseau will be able to 'elp me look like a duchess?"

"Madame Rousseau is the most sought after modiste in London. Her patrons represent the *crème de la crème* of Society and include royalty." Aunt Esther did not whisper. "If she cannot help you, no one can. She only accepts clients by referral, and it takes months to get a booking with her. You are only getting in because I am giving you my appointment."

"That is kind o' you," Fancy said earnestly. "I appreciate everything you're doing for me."

Aunt Esther set down her cup. "I am not doing it for you, gel. I am doing it for the family."

"I know. But I'm still grateful for your 'elp. And for all you've done for Knight."

"What do you know about that?" the lady asked, her thin black brows arching.

"I know that you championed 'im when a cousin contested 'is legitimacy and right to the title. I know you supported 'im when you could 'ave looked the other way. And I know that you're one o' the few people in Knight's life who 'as stood up for 'im," Fancy said with trembling sincerity. "For that, you'll 'ave my gratitude always."

"Knighton told you this?" Aunt Esther looked astonished. "He said that I championed him?"

He had not said that in so many words. But Fancy knew that he *felt* it.

She recalled how solitary Knight had seemed when they first

met. And the way he had kept himself apart from her family and the Taylors, not because he was a snob but because, she suspected, he simply did not know *how* to be part of a family. She thought of his wry comments about his siblings' dislike of him and his stark resignation when that introductory meeting had gone awry. Her heart squeezing, she resolved to help him patch things up with his family...starting now.

"'E might not express 'is appreciation aloud," she said. "Knight ain't a gentleman who discusses 'is feelings—"

"As is proper for a gentleman," Aunt Esther said with an approving nod.

"But I know 'e appreciates all you've done for 'im, 'is siblings, and me. Since 'e grew up with only 'is mama, I think 'e never 'ad much o' a family, which makes 'im value 'aving one now all the more," Fancy mused.

"Well." Aunt Esther cleared her throat. "I would not have guessed it. But, as you say, Knighton is not a man to air his laundry, which is a sign of good breeding. You can tell me these things, Francesca, but mind you don't wag your tongue like an untrained puppy when we're out in Society. Best to keep matters in the family, do you understand? The Knighton name is never to be tarnished."

"Yes, Aunt Esther," she said.

She could see that reticence ran in the Knighton blood. Yet as Aunt Esther took a sip of tea, indicating the conversation was over, Fancy saw a glimmer of longing in the other's eyes. Her intuition told her the lady's blade-sharp tongue shielded a softer core. After all, Lady Brambley had outlived her husband, parents, and her siblings, and she had no children of her own. Such an existence must be lonely. Maybe she needed a family as much as Knight did.

A door opened at the back of the shop, and Fancy saw a woman emerging. While short of stature, the lady possessed a regal bearing and wore a bonnet with pink ostrich feathers that increased her vertical presence considerably. Her face was angular, with a hawkishness to her nose and dark eyes. Her steel-colored curls placed her in her fifties or sixties. The woman who held the door for her was thin, with dark silver-threaded hair, her immaculate black gown identifying her as the dressmaker. A maid followed diffidently in the stately lady's footsteps.

To Fancy's surprise, Aunt Esther surged to her feet, gesturing to Fancy to follow suit.

"Your Royal Highness," Aunt Esther said with a deep curtsy. "What an honor to see you."

Fancy hastily dipped her knees and bowed her head as well.

"Lady Brambley." The woman had an aristocratic accent that sounded...German? The imperiousness of her voice made Fancy keep her head ducked. "And who do you have with you there?"

"May I present to you my nephew's wife Francesca, the Duchess of Knighton? Francesca, you have the honor of being introduced to Her Royal Highness, Princess Adelaide of Hessenstein."

"I am pleased to make your acquaintance, Your Royal 'Ighness," Fancy blurted to the lady's embroidered shoes.

"A duchess, eh? Well, let's have a look at you."

At the command, Fancy slowly raised her head. She saw something flash through the princess's hooded gaze, and her heartbeat stuttered. Blooming hell, she didn't look *that* terrible, did she? She knew her gown wasn't the nicest, but the maid had managed to tame her hair into a creditable topknot. As Princess Adelaide continued to peruse her, looking at her as if she were some vile thing the cat dragged in, Fancy's stomach churned, her mortification growing.

Why couldn't I 'ave met 'er after I got new dresses and a few lessons under my belt? she thought miserably.

Fancy wanted so badly to be a duchess who would make Knight proud, the sort who could glide into any room with poise and grace. Instead, she'd fallen flat on her face on her very first outing. And she'd done so in front of *royalty*, no less. It was a nightmare coming true.

"Her Grace is newly arrived in London, Your Royal Highness." Aunt Esther's apologetic tones cut through Fancy's spiraling thoughts. "She is not yet accustomed to Town ways, but rest assured, I shall be offering my guidance."

"How fortunate for her." Princess Adelaide pinned Fancy with piercing eyes. "Where are you from, Your Grace?"

"Um, 'ere and there," Fancy said weakly.

"Here and there?" The princess's gaze narrowed. "What sort of an answer is that?"

"My family travels, Your 'Ighness." She swallowed. "My da is a tinker."

"A tinker, you say?" Princess Adelaide's brows shot ceilingward. "How extraordinary of Knighton to marry into a family of travelling peddlers."

As mortified as Fancy was, she did not like the woman's scornful tone. It was one thing to insult her and another to insult her family who'd done nothing to deserve it.

She pulled her shoulders back. "My da isn't a peddler. 'E's a tinker and gifted at 'is trade, Your 'Ighness."

"Well, that is not saying much, is it?"

"The name Milton Sheridan is famous in some parts for if 'e can't mend it, nobody can," she said through gritted teeth.

"I have never heard of him."

The princess's haughty dismissal of Da provoked Fancy into replying, "If you 'ad, you would know that 'e's known equally for 'is tinkering and for 'is good 'eart, and that I can speak to personally. If 'e and my ma 'adn't taken me in when I was a babe, I wouldn't be standing in front o' you today, and that's a fact."

Aunt Esther gasped, quickly covering the sound with a cough. Fancy's heart thumped with anger and fear as the princess regarded her for several long moments.

"You have pride," Princess Adelaide declared.

Fancy blinked.

"That will serve you well in your new life, Your Grace." She raked Fancy over with another assessing glance before turning to Aunt Esther. "Lady Brambley, you may bring her to my next monthly salon."

"How very kind of you, Your Royal Highness."

Aunt Esther sounded as shocked as Fancy felt. She curtsied, and at her sharp nudge, Fancy followed suit. Princess Adelaide inclined her head and walked out, her maid scampering behind her.

Once the door was closed, Aunt Esther expelled a breath. "That was a near disaster."

Shame clogging her throat, Fancy clasped her hands. "I'm sorry, Aunt Esther. I know I shouldn't 'ave—"

"You have no cause to be sorry, gel," Aunt Esther interrupted. "You just snatched victory from the jaws of defeat...in a manner worthy of Wellington himself! Princess Adelaide is one of the most fashionable hostesses in Society; a word from her can make or break a reputation. Do you know how difficult it is to secure an invitation to Her Royal Highness's monthly salons?"

"No," Fancy said truthfully. "Is it difficult?"

"More difficult than getting an appointment with Madame Rousseau. Is that not so, Madame?"

Aunt Esther turned to the dressmaker, who'd been standing there, Fancy realized, discreetly observing all the while. Madame Rousseau had a handsome face and intelligent eyes that gave the impression of missing little.

"Lady Brambley speaks the truth," Madame Rousseau said. "My establishment, it is exclusive. But only a select few of *my* clients can secure vouchers to Princess Adelaide's salon. It is open only to the *crème* of the *crème de la crème*."

"And *you* will be amongst them, Francesca." Aunt Esther's look of awe turned into one of determination. "The princess's salons fall on the last Friday of the month...which means we have just over a fortnight to get you ready. We do not have time for shilly-shallying!" The lady turned to the dressmaker. "Madame Rousseau, Francesca needs a new wardrobe, top to bottom, immediately. You will have *carte blanche*, of course."

"Would you please 'elp me, Madame Rousseau?" Fancy asked anxiously. "I 'ave to make myself o'er into a proper lady."

"In terms of the outer trappings, *oui*, this is true. The rest, I think, requires no transformation." Madame Rousseau smiled, then said crisply, "Follow me, ladies. Let us begin the preparations."

22

Although Severin owned multiple manufactories, he spent the bulk of his time at his main office. His mentor and former business partner, James Hessard, had converted this block of terraced houses close to Petticoat Lane Market into weaving ateliers. The buildings had been built for the craft, the floor to ceiling windows letting in ample natural light. Having lived in dingy, windowless dens for the first half of his life, Severin liked having a view of the sky.

In accordance to the customs of weavers, the lower floors of the buildings were used as residences for the workers. He kept the rents low to make his weavers happy. Happy employees, to his mind, made for enhanced productivity. On the upper floors were the weaving rooms, vast spaces occupied by the looms.

Severin's office was on the top floor. Antique tapestries hung on the walls, muffling the clacking of the looms outside. The mahogany furnishings that graced his sanctum were of the highest quality. To the left of his large desk was a wall of windows that gave him a bird's eye view of the bustling Spitalfields markets.

At present, he was sitting in his chair, looking out the window as Dutton, his man-of-business, delivered the monthly report in a droning voice. Typically, he didn't have difficulty concentrating, but this afternoon his mind was elsewhere. Thoughts of Fancy kept distracting him, along with feelings of guilt.

Since Imogen's unplanned visit two days ago, he'd been working late every night. It wasn't just because he had much to catch up on after his hiatus. The truth was he was avoiding his wife.

Fancy deserved better than to be around him when he was in a brooding mood. The state that seeing Imogen often put him in. This time, it had been worse because Imogen had arrived unannounced, taking him off guard with her rare agitation.

I am s-sorry, Knight. She had dabbed her eyes with the handkerchief he'd given her. *It is just that your letter...it came as a shock. Are you happy, my dear?*

My wife is a fine woman, he'd said gruffly.

I am certain that she is. Imogen had bit her lip, the glimmer in her cornflower blue eyes causing a reflexive tightening in his chest. *If only things had been different, then* I *could have been your duchess...*

Then Fancy had come in, and Severin had jerked away from Imogen like a criminal caught red-handed. His excuse had been asinine. He didn't know why he'd made it; he had not done anything wrong. Yet the look on Fancy's face when she realized who their visitor was had twisted his gut, filled him with a strange panic. For an instant, he'd regretted telling Fancy as much as he had about Imogen...but that was one of the things he valued most about his new wife: her candor and frankness, her acceptance of him and his shortcomings.

Since then, she hadn't asked him about Imogen's visit, and for that he was profoundly grateful. Because he, himself, was confused. When Imogen had asked him if he was happy, he hadn't known how to answer.

What he felt for Fancy wasn't the adoration he felt for Imogen; he acknowledged that. In his mind, Imogen rested upon a pedestal of perfection whereas Fancy was, well, *Fancy*. A cheery, tender, and down-to-earth tinker's daughter with a whimsical streak. Comparing the two women was like comparing apples and oranges and did neither of them justice. Moreover, his reaction to them was different. Imogen elevated his thoughts, made them pure and gallant. She inspired him to be a gentleman.

His thoughts about Fancy, on the other hand, were far from civilized. His desire for his wife was proving insatiable; he hadn't been this lusty, this needful with any of his former bedpartners. Luckily for him, Fancy seemed to welcome his attentions, and not only was she sweet in bed—God, the *taste* of her honey—she was just as sweet out of it.

He could talk to her, share his problems, laugh with her. He'd never had anyone like her in his life before. Given the less than auspicious beginnings of their marriage, they were off to as good a start as any he could imagine.

Then why did Imogen's visit unsettle me?

"Shall I proceed, Your Grace?"

He snapped his attention back to his man of business. Annoyed at himself for losing track of what the other was saying, he asked, "What are you referring to, Dutton?"

"The order for the Jacquard mechanism, Your Grace."

Right. An innovation in weaving, the Jacquard mechanism automated operations that previously required skilled weavers to carry out. Attached to a loom, the device consisted of a chain of punched cards that controlled the raising of the warp threads and, thus, the pattern of the fabric. As a result, complex designs including damasks, brocades, and matelassé could be achieved in a fraction of the time and at a lower cost.

Severin's mentor, Hessard, had resisted the technology, stating that no machine could produce fabrics as exquisite as those created by his skilled weavers. At first, Severin had been willing to follow in his predecessor's footsteps since their handcrafted silks commanded a hefty sum from a select group of clientele. The latest version of the Jacquard mechanism, however, had changed Severin's way of thinking. The intricacy and beauty of the fabrics produced by this new generation of technology surpassed anything made by even his most experienced weavers.

Severin had to face facts: he could not compete with other companies using this mechanism. He would have to adapt to the times...and his weavers were not going to like it. In truth, they weren't wrong to fear that their specialized skills could soon be replaced by a machine. He had to convince them that the wisest course of action was not to resist inevitable change but to find a way to profit from it. He would train his workers in new skills—how to design the patterns and create the Jacquard cards, for instance—but they had to work with him.

And therein lay the crux of the problem. He hadn't lied when he told Fancy that weavers were a contentious lot, and the most contentious amongst them was a head weaver named William Bodin. Fiery and defiant, Bodin was a natural leader who had the ear of the other workers. He'd made trouble for Severin before, yet he had the backing of his peers, which made it difficult to oust him without causing a work stoppage or, worse, riot. Bodin would no doubt oppose the use of the new Jacquard looms.

Severin's temples tightened as he contemplated the pitfalls ahead. Then again, when had anything in his life been easy? Nothing had been given to him without a fight.

"Order the device," he said brusquely. "Have it set up in one of the empty warehouses and use discretion. I do not wish for word of the machine to leak until I have done a trial run."

"Very good, Your Grace," Dutton said. "If there is nothing else..."

Dismissing the man of business, Severin went to stare broodingly out the window. He was literally standing at the height of success, and he ought to be content. But he wasn't. He felt isolated...alone. In and of itself, this was not unusual. What was unusual was that it bothered him.

Severin became aware of the craving he had been keeping at bay for the past two days. He hadn't felt right going to his wife's bed when he was brooding over another woman. Yet now as his rumination over Imogen subsided, he realized how much he'd missed Fancy, spending time with her even if they were just talking.

While he hadn't knocked on her bedchamber door, she hadn't knocked on his either. He thought that she was probably tired. Aunt Esther had been keeping her busy with shopping expeditions, elocution lessons, and the like. The old dragon had even cornered him on his way out this morning to pay Fancy a compliment.

Francesca has a long way to go, Knighton, no doubt about that, Aunt Esther had said. *Nonetheless, there is no lack of effort on the gel's part. She is determined to become a proper duchess and to do you and the family name proud.*

It might not sound like a glowing compliment. From Aunt Esther, however, this was nothing short of an accolade. Somehow it didn't surprise him that Fancy was managing to win over his prickly aunt: his wife's warm and cheerful manner would please anyone but the most dyed-in-the-wool ogre.

Severin hungered for a taste of Fancy's sweetness and that feeling of closeness that had begun to grow between them. Now that his head was clear and his mood had passed, he could go to her without feeling like a bastard. A sudden inspiration struck him. He decided to make a stop on the way home to pick up a gift for his wife. Such a tribute was long overdue, and he couldn't wait to see Fancy's reaction when he gave her his surprise.

∼

After her bath that evening, Fancy sat at her dressing table while her new lady's maid Gemma combed out her hair. Mrs. Treadwell had lined up three applicants for Fancy to interview today; Fancy had hired Gemma on the spot when the other expertly styled her hair into a coiffure that even Aunt Esther deemed acceptable. Resourceful and discreet, the little blonde maid was a fount of information about the latest fashions, having worked with many ladies of quality in the past.

When the knock sounded on the door between her and Knight's bedchamber, Fancy gave a start of surprise. Given Knight's absence the past two nights, she hadn't expected him to pay her a visit.

Gemma gave her a conspiratorial smile. "Shall I get the door, Your Grace?"

"Yes. No. Wait." Fancy hurriedly inspected herself in the mirror. "'Ow do I look?"

"Beautiful, Your Grace." There was a twinkle in Gemma's eyes. "The new nightgown suits you ever so well."

The matching negligee and peignoir had been amongst the first of the items to arrive from the modiste and were unlike anything Fancy had owned or worn before. At the fitting, Madame Rousseau had assured her that this design was all the rage in Paris and a favorite of aristocratic clients and *especially* their husbands. Indeed, the dressmaker had said with a secret smile, she always encouraged clients to order duplicates. Although Fancy didn't see why she would need two of the expensive negligees—she made it a habit to take good care of her clothing— she'd nonetheless put herself completely in the modiste's hands.

Madame had constructed the negligee and peignoir out of fine ivory silk, the clever cut designed to show off Fancy's curves. Both garments were trimmed with bronze ribbon, and the back of the peignoir was embroidered with a Chinoiserie scene in matching bronze thread. The workmanship was flawless. In Fancy's estimation, Madame's genius lay in her ability to create garments that were simple yet extraordinarily flattering.

As Fancy looked into the mirror now, her confidence grew. There was a reason she was wearing her new garments tonight:

she had decided that if Knight wasn't going to come to her, *she* would go to him, even though Aunt Esther would likely disapprove of her plan.

You mustn't be so eager to please, Francesca, Esther had lectured during today's lesson in etiquette. *In our world, being too accommodating is considered bourgeois. You are not a puppy to do as its master commands. A true lady knows her worth—and knows she is worth the trouble. Do you understand?*

Fancy did, yet spending two nights apart from Knight was enough in her opinion. He'd given her permission to open the door whenever she wanted, hadn't he? At supper tonight, he'd seemed less remote and more like his old self before that scene with Imogen. Fancy had resolved to take the bull by the horns and go to him that evening and thus the pains she'd taken with her toilette.

When Knight's imperious knock sounded again, happiness and relief swirled through Fancy. If he was taking the initiative, then maybe he'd missed her too.

"Please let 'Is Grace in," she told her waiting maid. "Then you may go."

As Gemma did as she bade, Fancy rose and nervously adjusted the belt of her robe. The slide of silk against her skin felt different from her old flannel. It made her feel more sensual... more daring. She wondered what her husband would think of her new attire.

She didn't have long to wait. Dressed in his black dressing gown, Knight prowled toward her, the glint in his eyes turning predatory as he took her in. His male hunger was unmistakable, filling the room, making her heart knock against her ribs. Some age-old instinct made her retreat a step, the back of her legs hitting the dressing table, rattling the contents on its surface.

He stopped a hairsbreadth away.

Staring down at her, he murmured, "What are you wearing, *chérie?*"

"It's part o' my new wardrobe," she said. "Do you, um, like it?"

"I cannot say for certain." As her heart plummeted, he lifted a hand, running a finger down the slope of her shoulder. "Not until you show me the rest, hmm?"

Emboldened by his sensual demand, she undid the belt of the peignoir and shrugged it off. It cascaded down her body, pooling at her feet. The negligee was held up by thin straps, an elegant column that bared her shoulders and dipped in the front to show the shadowed crevice between her breasts. The silk flowed downward, loose but not billowing, skimming over her curves. She felt her husband's smoldering gaze rake over her. Her nipples stiffened to hard points visible against the silk.

"What do you think now?" she dared to ask.

"I think," he said, a growly edge to his voice, "that you look good enough to eat. As it happens, I have not yet had my dessert."

He swept his arm over her dressing table. Shocked, she watched as toiletries went flying left and right, thumping onto the carpet.

"Knight, those were expensive—"

"I'll buy you more." He hauled her onto the dressing table, her spine pressing against the mirror and legs dangling off the edge. He yanked on her neckline.

Hearing seams tearing, she gasped, "This is *new*. You're ruining—"

"I'll buy you another."

So that's why Madame said I needed a duplicate. The realization dispersed like a dandelion puff at the force of Knight's ravening gaze upon her bared breasts.

"By Jove," he rasped, "you have the most delectable tits."

Her reply became a moan for he'd fastened his lips over a straining nipple. He suckled her, the feeling shooting straight between her thighs. Her pussy clenched helplessly as he tongued her taut buds, going back and forth until her breasts glistened from his kisses. When he grazed her with his teeth, her hips bucked, a gasp leaving her.

"Too much?" His gaze searched her face, and whatever he saw made his lips curve into a wicked smile. "I didn't think so."

Before she could reply, he crowded in closer, making room for himself between her splayed legs. He lowered his head again, giving her a nip. At the bite of pleasure-pain, she arched into him, whimpering when the motion brought her pussy up against his muscled thigh, giving her friction where she needed it. She felt herself dampening the silk of her negligee.

"Ride my leg, sweetheart," he said huskily. "Come for me while I kiss your tits."

Panting, she gave into his naughty order. She clutched onto his hard shoulders and squirmed wantonly against him. He redoubled his attentions on her breasts, cupping and kneading them, his fierce sucking pulling at her core. Her pussy contracted as he drew hard on her nipples. Desperate for relief, for *him*, she rubbed herself against the firm ridge of his leg, moaning his name as she soared on a crest of pleasure.

~

His wife was always pretty, but at the height of rapture, she was incomparable. Severin took an instant to drink in her beauty: her passion-flushed cheeks, her big brown eyes dazed with bliss. Her beauty mark quivered as she panted, her lush, rosy lips parted like the gate to temptation. For a wild instant, he saw himself taking her mouth, kissing her with all the need burning inside him.

He had just enough willpower to resist the urge. It wasn't fair to her; she deserved more than an imitation of the real thing. The one request she'd made of him was not to kiss her unless he meant it. Thus, he couldn't do it. But he could do other things to her.

Christ, he *needed* to.

Although he'd planned to have a talk with her this eve, lust got the better of him. Conversation could wait; his desire for his wife could not. He stripped off his robe and threw it aside. Fancy's eyes followed his movements. He dragged his nightshirt over his head, and she ran her gaze over his bulging chest muscles, the flexing ridges of his belly, all the way to his erect cock.

When she wetted her lips, he nearly groaned. He fisted his rod, running his hand up and down the heavy shaft.

"Like what you see, *chérie?*" he asked silkily.

"Yes." The unabashed approval in her eyes lured a drop of seed from his tip. "I take it this means you approve o' the nightclothes Madame Rousseau made for me?"

Her satisfied little smile made him grow even harder.

"I like them," he said. "But I like what's underneath even more. Raise that skirt for me, sweeting, so that I can see what's mine."

Her bared breasts rose and fell at his command, the tips taut and cherry red. Slowly, she reached for the hem of her negligee and pulled it up her shapely legs.

"All the way, sweet," he coaxed. "Let me see your pussy."

Blushing, she did as he asked, squirming to get the silk past her hips. His nostrils flared as he drank in the sight of his duchess on her dressing table, her nightgown now bunched at her waist, her beautiful breasts, legs, and cunny exposed. Feral instincts tore through his gentlemanly restraint.

"Are you wet for me?" he asked.

She gave a shy nod.

"Show me."

She blinked at him.

"Touch your cunny, sweet," he said thickly. "Show me how ready you are for my cock."

Her lips parted on a shocked breath, and he wondered if he'd pushed her too far. If he'd revealed too much of his bestial nature. Then her hand crept bashfully downward, and his heart drummed as her fingertips brushed her dark nest. She touched herself furtively, dipping a fingertip into the top of her slit, her bottom lip catching beneath her teeth.

"I'm ready," she whispered.

Lust seared him at the sight of her finger glistening with her dew. His erection swelled, testing the limits of his grip. He brought his weeping cockhead to her tender opening, and when she would have moved her hand, he stopped her.

"Keep petting yourself," he grated out.

He pushed inside, watching with animal greed as his thick shaft spread his wife's pretty pink folds. She was watching too—and feeling his penetration not just with her pussy but with her fingers. Obeying his instruction, she was petting herself, rubbing her pearl, her fingertips brushing over his invading rod.

Feeling her delicate touch as he debauched her was too much. With a growl, he slammed his hips, burying himself fully. Pleasure blazed up his spine at the exquisite constriction. His wife's hot, wet hole was bloody *made* for his cock. Gripping her hips, he plowed her with bestial urgency, with desperate need he couldn't contain. Her sweet moans accompanied the hard slaps of his thighs as he pounded into her, her back thumping against the mirror.

Feeling the pressure in his stones, he gritted out, "Rub your pearl harder, Fancy. Spend on my cock like a good little wife."

His words seemed to electrify her. Her beautiful eyes widened, her legs tightening around him, her fingers swirling in a frantic rhythm. Moments later, she cried out, her rippling climax drawing forth his own. With a shout, he surged into her, his neck arching as he spent in lavish bursts.

Thrusting languidly, he gazed into Fancy's flushed face. Bliss thrummed in his veins along with a feeling he couldn't quite put a finger on. Contentment, maybe. Not a man to linger over sentiment, especially when he was still inside his wife, he leaned in to kiss her forehead. As he moved, his cock burrowed deeper inside her snug sheath, and her responding clench had an instant stiffening effect on him.

He raised his eyebrows. "Again?"

A shy yet sultry smile tucked into her cheeks. "Yes, please."

He was amazed by his renewed hunger. By all rights, he ought to have been sated. But the sweetness of her expression and the lush hold of her pussy were too much to resist.

"You're going to kill me," he murmured.

Then he set about finding *le petit mort* with his wife once more.

23

Fancy awoke with a dreamy feeling. That feeling grew when she realized that her cheek was tucked against her husband's chest. Memories of their passion enveloped her, and her lips curved.

Knight had liked her nightgown. Her efforts at becoming a lady were succeeding. Her marriage was once again on track, and last night had been a heady reminder of what a passionate, tender, and virile lover her husband could be.

A happy sigh in her heart, she was content to enjoy the view. She loved her husband's body, the taut bulges of muscle, the virile covering of hair. She even liked that scar near his heart because it showed that he was a warrior who could survive the toughest of battles. Her gaze veered downward past his ridged belly. The blanket was draped over his hips, cutting off her view of his superb form...but not entirely.

Her eyes widened. Over her husband's groin, the blanket was unmistakably tented.

"Keep looking, and it is liable to get bigger," Knight's amused voice rumbled.

She tilted her head back to meet his alert grey eyes. "You're awake?"

"I have been for a while. I was watching you sleep."

"Oh." She wasn't certain how she felt about that. "Was I, um, drooling?"

"No. Although you were snoring a little... I'm only teasing," he said, correctly interpreting her look of horror. "You were adorable as always."

"That's, um, nice o' you to say."

She sat up, keeping the sheet up over her breasts. She ran her fingers through her hair, relieved that she didn't encounter any bird's nests.

"I'm saying it because it's true. You are adorable." A line deepened between his brows, and his voice had a stark quality as he sat up next to her. "If I've given you cause to doubt that, then the fault is mine."

"You 'aven't done anything," she said quickly.

"Haven't I?" A pause. Then, "I owe you an apology, Fancy."

Seeing the brooding intensity enter his eyes, she had a sinking feeling. "What for?"

"I haven't been myself since seeing Imogen."

Her throat cinched at his blunt statement, which confirmed her suspicions.

He dragged a hand through his hair, his biceps bunching. "I know I've been...distant. Although you haven't asked, I want to explain what happened. Not that anything happened," he said hastily. "You do know that, don't you?"

"I know you wouldn't betray your vows," she said quietly.

"Thank you, sweeting."

"But Imogen..." She hesitated.

"Ask whatever you want, Fancy. You are my wife and have a right to know."

"She didn't 'ave something in 'er eye, did she?"

"She did not." Grooves lined his brow as he said, "It was

stupid of me to make that excuse; I don't know why I did. It just...came out."

"Maybe you were flustered over 'er tears?" she ventured.

"I don't get flustered." He looked disgruntled. "I was, however, taken aback by her unexpected arrival. I had written her, just a brief note informing her that you and I had wed." He gave her a direct look. "Given our history, it seemed the right thing to do."

She nodded, although her heart lurched at the knowledge that her husband had written to his former sweetheart. "Why was she crying?"

"She was surprised by my marriage," he said. "Truthfully, she has no cause to be. After I inherited the title, there was no question that I would need a wife to produce heirs and introduce my siblings into society."

Pain lanced through Fancy, and she lowered her gaze to her hands, which were twisting the coverlet. She didn't know what to say. How to respond to the fact that the woman her husband loved was hurt by his marriage. Hearing him state so plainly that he married her, Fancy, not out of desire but necessity felt like a blow.

"Not that those were the only reasons I married you." Frustration threaded Knight's voice. "Bloody hell, I'm making a hash of this. Fancy, look at me, please."

She raised her eyes.

"Imogen is in my past, and I am damned lucky that you are my wife and here with me now," he said with quiet intensity. "I know that you and I didn't marry under the best of circumstances, but we're making a go of things, aren't we?"

A go of things. If he'd married Imogen, would he have described their marriage in those terms? Fancy wondered morosely.

"Are we?" Her voice cracked a little.

"I think so." He cupped her cheek, his grey eyes as warm as the sky during a summer rain. "I have never wanted a woman the way I want you, Fancy."

That was something, at least. A balm to soothe the soreness of her heart. Even if he didn't love her, he desired her physically, and according to him, more than any woman he'd known.

More than Imogen? The question popped into her head; she wasn't ready to know the answer.

"I'm sorry I have not been attentive these past few days," he went on. "Will you forgive me?"

It was not in her nature to hold onto hurt. Knight had apologized and explained things, and he'd been honest about Imogen from the start. Fancy couldn't expect his feelings to change overnight; she had to give their marriage time to grow and blossom.

She nodded, ready to move on.

The tension eased from his features, a smile reaching his eyes. "Tell me what you have been up to, sweeting. I know you've been busy. Aunt Esther has been singing your praises to me."

"Really?" she said in surprise.

His lips quirked. "She said, and I quote, *there's no lack of effort on the gel's part. She is determined to become a proper duchess and to do you and the family name proud.* Trust me, coming from Esther that is the highest of accolades. And she is tickled that you managed to wrangle an invitation to Princess Adelaide of Hessenstein's salon."

"Aunt Esther 'as been a good mentor to me. 'Er bark is worse than 'er bite, and I think she's 'appy to 'ave something to do," Fancy mused. "It must 'ave been lonely for 'er until you and your siblings came along and gave 'er a family."

"We hardly qualify as a family," Knight said dryly. "We are more like strangers stuck at an interminable house party with no hope of escape."

Fancy had to grin at the description, which wasn't far from the truth. Yet hearing his unspoken longing, she wanted to encourage him.

"I thought everyone was on better behavior at supper last night," she said diplomatically.

"Because you, *chérie*, think the best of everyone." He brushed his finger along her nose. "In reality, Cecily was sulking, Jonas drinking excessively, and Eleanor reading the book she had hidden beneath her napkin."

"Toby was sociable," she pointed out.

"And nearly hit you in the face with an oyster," Knight muttered.

"Not on purpose," she countered. "'E apologized for it."

"The boy is a walking disaster."

"Don't lose 'eart in your family," Fancy said earnestly. "They'll come around. Why, if I can change into a duchess, then surely your siblings can learn to behave better."

And I'll 'elp them, she thought determinedly. *They're my family now, too.*

For better or worse, family stuck together.

"Don't change too much, my dear," Knight said softly. "I like you the way you are."

His tender words caused her heart to constrict with hope. "I like you too."

"I don't know what I did to get myself such a good little wife," he said huskily. "Which reminds me...I have something for you."

He left the bed, striding over to pick up his dressing gown. She couldn't help but stare at his backside, the taut curves and hollowed grooves of his arse, the flexing muscles of his back. When he headed back toward her, his virility arrested her breath. Even at rest, his male equipment was weighty, swaying heavily between his corded thighs.

"This is for you," he said. "Unless there is something else you would like, my sweet?"

She'd been so busy ogling him that she hadn't noticed that he was holding out a black velvet box tied with a silver ribbon. His knowing expression told her that he'd caught her staring at him, and he didn't mind one bit.

Blushing, she took the box. "Thank you."

He looked amused as he settled on the mattress beside her. "You haven't opened it yet."

"I don't 'ave to open it to know that it was thoughtful o' you to get me a gift."

"Will you stop being sweet long enough to open the damned thing?"

The warmth in his eyes told her he was teasing. Dutifully, she untied the ribbon and lifted the lid. There was another box inside, this one made of silver. Taking it out, she opened it, and her breath lodged.

"Do you like it?" he asked.

She couldn't reply. Couldn't get the words out as she stared at the ring nestled in white satin.

The center stone was a flawless ruby the size of her thumbnail. A halo of diamonds surrounded the blood-red gem. The combination of fire and ice was utterly breathtaking.

"Here, try it on." Taking the ring, Knight lifted her hand and slipped it onto her finger: it fit perfectly above her wedding band. "That looks nice, don't you think?"

"It's more than nice." Her voice wasn't quite steady. "Knight... it's the most splendid thing anyone has given me."

"Well, it is no tinker's friend, but I am glad you like it." Smiling, he stroked his thumb over the stacked rings. "When I saw the ruby, I was reminded of you."

"You were?" She couldn't see what she had in common with this precious jewel. "Why?"

"For starters, your price is beyond rubies."

"Oh, Knight." Her heart hiccupped at his gallantry.

"Then there's the color of the ruby. At first, I was looking for something to match your eyes but they are peerless, I'm afraid. No jewel can capture their velvety warmth."

If she were the swooning type, she would have swooned then and there.

"So I decided to match the gem to something else instead," he went on.

Tilting her head, she gave him a dreamy look. "What did you match it to?"

"Your pretty mouth." He rubbed his thumb along her bottom lip. "And your lovely nipples."

She blinked. "You bought me a ring to match my *nipples*?"

"The most beautiful nipples I've seen."

He tugged down her sheet. Lifting her left hand, he positioned it on her left breast so that her nipple rose proudly between her ring and middle fingers. The stiff bud and the gem were indeed of a similar hue.

His gaze molten, he said, "See? A perfect match."

"That's wicked," she sputtered.

"It is rather."

He tumbled her backward onto the mattress. She gasped at the filling thrust of his manhood, the long, proud heat of him drilling into her core. Of their own accord, her hips arched for more.

A devilish smile lit his eyes.

"Lucky for me," he murmured, "I have a sweet, accommodating wife who doesn't mind a bit of wicked."

24

After Fancy accommodated her husband not once but twice, Knight left for his office. He'd promised to be back for supper and, with that irresistibly wicked glint in his eyes, told her to expect him afterward. Then he went on with his day and Fancy went on with hers.

After Fancy ate her breakfast on a tray, Gemma helped her don one of the latest items Madame Rousseau had sent. The visiting dress of peach silk had a long bodice, narrow sleeves, and skirts that flared in an elegant dome. The crisscrossed bodice was ornamented with ruched ribbon of paler peach, the ruching repeated on the double tiers of the skirts.

Fancy adored her new dress. Not only was it the most stylish frock she'd ever owned, but the modiste had granted her request as well: there were hidden pockets in the skirts. Stashing her tinker's friend and Knight's old button, which she carried around as a secret good luck token, Fancy put on her new ruby ring, squared her shoulders, and descended to her lessons.

Her mornings were split between classes with her dancing master, Maestro Agostino and her elocution master, Mr. Stanton. Her hour with the former passed quickly for she enjoyed dancing and, to her instructor's delight, had no trouble learning the steps to the more formal dances that had not been in her repertoire.

Her time with Mr. Stanton, however, required more concentration and effort.

"Today we are focusing on the letter *H*." The teacher, who had a ring of hair around his gleaming pate, stood before a chalkboard with a pointer in hand. "I'll read first, Your Grace."

He read the lines he'd written, his pointer following the words:

Does Harry Hunt hunt heavy hares? If Harry Hunt hunts heavy hares, then where are the heavy hares Harry Hunt hunts?

"Your Grace?" Mr. Stanton asked.

"In 'Arry 'Unt's belly?" Fancy guessed.

Mr. Stanton frowned. "I meant it is your turn, Your Grace. To repeat the phrase."

"Oh, I see." Clearing her throat, Fancy followed the crisp movement of Mr. Stanton's pointer as it went from word to word. "Does 'Arry 'Unt...hunt 'eavy...*h*eavy 'ares? If 'Arry 'Unt 'unts...*h*unts...*h*eavy 'ares, then where are the *h*eavy 'ares 'Arry 'Unt *h*unts?"

She peered hopefully at her teacher.

He sighed. "Again, if you please."

By the time the lesson was over, poor Mr. Stanton looked ready to tear out what little hair he had left, and Fancy wished she'd never heard of Harry Hunt and his fat rabbits. Luckily, it was time for luncheon; she was starved and ready for a break.

She arrived at the cavernous dining room to see Aunt Esther already seated at one end of the long table. The lady wore her customary black and an impatient expression. The only other setting on the table was to the right of her.

"You and I will be taking lunch without the others in order to minimize distractions," Aunt Esther said crisply. "Today I will be covering the fundamentals of proper dining. I have asked Harvey to set our places for a formal supper. Don't dawdle, Francesca. Come have a seat next to me."

Fancy obediently headed to the chair, halting halfway at Aunt Esther's command.

"No, gel, don't rush about like a milk maid. You are a duchess; walk like one."

"'Ow...*h*ow does a duchess walk?" Fancy asked.

"At her own pace, to begin with. As you are not a puppy, you do not need to scamper at anyone's command. Do you understand?"

"Yes, Aunt Esther."

Fancy took a cautious step forward on the parqueted floor, freezing when Aunt Esther snapped out another order.

"No, *no*. Are you carrying something heavy, gel?"

Fancy gave the other a puzzled look. "I don't think so."

"Then why are your shoulders slumped forward? After lunch, you shall practice proper posture by walking with a book balanced upon your head," Aunt Esther said decisively. "When I was your age, I could walk up and down stairs balancing all of Shakespeare's tragedies."

The image floated through Fancy's mind.

"That's amazing," she said wonderingly. "My brothers learned similar tricks to earn money at the fairs. Godfrey can walk with a dozen plates on 'is 'ead while juggling apples—"

"I am not a circus performer," Aunt Esther said coldly. "Neither do I wish for your debut at Princess Adelaide's salon to be a vulgar exhibition. Now, come here, gel, with your shoulders back, your back straight but not too stiff, and your head balanced on your neck, not to the right, not to the left, but aligned with your spine."

Fancy managed to make it to the chair. "'Ow...*h*ow was that?"

"Like a performance given by a foxed puppeteer." Aunt Esther sighed. "Never mind. Sit so that we may review the use of utensils."

Fancy looked down at the battalion of gleaming silverware... and gulped.

∽

It was nearing three o'clock by the time Aunt Esther declared that she had had enough for the day. While the lady went up for a nap, Fancy decided to get a breath of fresh air. Guilt prickled her when she remembered that she hadn't visited Bertrand for two days, and she decided to kill two birds with one stone and head to the stables behind the house.

On her way out, a sound caught her attention. It came from the half-open door of the library. She hesitated, and when she heard the noise again, she went in.

The library was a high-ceilinged room that smelled pleasantly of parchment, wood polish, and leather. Tufted seating occupied the area in front of the hearth, and shelves of books lined the walls. Fancy followed the sound, like that made by an injured puppy, to the leather divan. Toby was sitting on the floor behind it, hugging his knees to his chest, his dark head buried in his arms.

His head jerked up at Fancy's approach, and her heart ached at his reddened eyes, the wet tracks running down his cheeks.

"What's the matter, dear?" she asked.

"Nothing." He wiped his sleeve over his face and only succeeded in smearing snot over the fabric. "I'm fine."

"You don't look fine." Easing herself to the ground—which wasn't the easiest thing with her voluminous skirts and tight lacing—she sat beside him. "You look like someone who's 'aving...*h*aving a rough go o' it."

Tears welled in his brown eyes.

"Everyone hates me," he said between hitched breaths. "I can't do anything right."

He buried his head in his arms again.

Fancy placed a light hand on his shoulder, which shook with his sobs. When he didn't pull away, she put her arm around him and sat with him while he got it out, the way her ma had done for her and her siblings whenever they had a low moment.

Eventually, Toby quieted, and she said, "Feeling better?"

"Yes, Your Grace." His cheeks stained red, he averted his gaze.

When he pulled away, Fancy didn't stop him. Growing up with her brothers, she knew how embarrassed males could get when it came to tears or any sign of perceived weakness. Her brothers would rather get a bloody nose than be caught crying.

"You needn't stand on formality with me, dear," she said gently. "Call me Fancy."

Nodding, Toby wiped his sleeve over his eyes. "Will you promise not to tell anybody that you saw me crying?"

Fancy made a quick decision. "I will on one condition."

"What is it?" he sniffled.

"I want to know why you were crying."

He looked at her, his bottom lip quivering. "You wouldn't understand."

"Try me," she suggested.

"It's just that I try to get things right, but I always get everything wrong," he blurted. "Last night, I nearly pelted you with an oyster. This morning I wanted to see if Jonas would take me riding, but when I went to ask him, I accidentally ran into him and made him spill the whisky he was holding all over his waistcoat. He called me a cl-clumsy oaf and told me to stay clear of him in the f-future."

Toby looked away, clearly trying to stop himself from crying again.

Fancy briefly wondered why Jonas was drinking whisky in the morning.

Aloud, she said, "Accidents do 'appen...*h*appen, I mean. To everyone."

"Does everyone have multiple accidents *every single day?*" Toby asked morosely.

Oh dear. The boy had a point.

"Have you always been, um, prone to accidents?" Fancy asked.

Toby gave a forlorn nod. "When Papa visited Mama when they were both alive, Mama only let me see Papa for a few minutes. She didn't want me to embarrass her. Eleanor got to visit as long as she wanted because she's perfect."

Fancy's heart hurt for the boy. "No one's perfect, Toby."

"You wouldn't understand," he said with a quivery sigh. "You don't know what it's like when everything you do is wrong."

"I understand that more than you know," Fancy said with feeling.

"How could you? You're so pretty, grown-up, and nice. Everyone likes you."

Touched, and a bit astonished by the boy's perceptions, Fancy felt that she had to be honest.

"That's flattering, Toby, but it isn't true," she said earnestly. "I spent the entire morning trying to improve my manner o' speaking so that I won't embarrass the family name. And my lessons didn't go well."

Toby blinked. "Why not?"

"I keep dropping my *h*'s no matter 'ow...*h*ow *h*ard I try not to," she said ruefully. "I almost gave poor Mr. Stanton a fit of apoplexy. And when Aunt Esther tried to teach me table manners, I kept confusing the salad fork and the fish fork. And I spoon my soup the wrong way."

"There is a wrong way?" Toby's freckled brow wrinkled.

"Not in my family," Fancy admitted. "But according to Aunt Esther, you're supposed to spoon *away* from you."

Toby pursed his lips. "I never thought about it before."

"That's probably because you are doing it right." Fancy smiled at him. "See? You do plenty of things well. But I suppose it's 'uman...*h*uman nature to remember the things we do wrong."

"I guess," Toby said doubtfully. "But I'm not good at anything important."

Fancy was beginning to wonder if Toby's lack of self-confidence had something to do with his accidents. Maybe if he doubted himself less, he might be more surefooted in the things that he did.

On impulse, she said, "I don't believe you, Toby. Everyone is good at something."

"Not me."

"Yes, you are," she insisted. "It's like the soup…you might not even realize you're good at something because it comes to you so naturally that you take it for granted."

Toby chewed on his lip. Then hesitantly, he said, "It is not a real skill. Or an important one."

"Tell me," she urged.

"I like animals." He hitched his shoulders, looking embarrassed. "And they seem to like me. Or, at least, they like me more than people do."

"Why, Toby, that is a marvelous talent to have," Fancy said excitedly.

Doubt warred with flickering hope in his eyes. "You think so?"

"I *know* it. My da is famous for 'is…*h*is ability to handle horses and beasts of burden. Everyone wants a horse trained by him," Fancy said proudly. "He's a successful tinker, you know."

"I wish my father had been like yours," Toby said wistfully. "Papa didn't care for animals."

"My da always said there's no truer friend than an animal. In fact, as part of my wedding present, he gave me a donkey—"

"A *donkey?*" Toby bolted upright. "Donkeys are tip-top! You are so *lucky*, Fancy."

"Well, Bertrand can be a bit grumpy, and he doesn't listen to me the way he does to Da. Actually," Fancy said, on a stroke of inspiration, "I was on my way to the stables. Would you like to come with me and meet him?"

"I would like that more than anything!" Toby cried, bounding to his feet. "May I bring Bertrand some carrots?"

Smiling, Fancy took the small hand he gallantly offered her and rose in a swish of silk.

"That is an excellent idea," she said. "Since I neglected to visit Bertrand for two days, we may need a bribe to win him over."

25

Two nights later, Severin found himself in his wife's bed, and for the second night, he did not make love to her. Not because he didn't want to. Last night, she had told him with rosy cheeks that her monthly visitor had arrived, and she couldn't engage in their usual bedtime activities. He'd surprised them both by saying that he would like to stay anyway, if she didn't mind the company, and her smile, as well as her words, had told him that she didn't mind at all.

Cuddling Fancy close, Severin savored the tranquil moment. The fire crackling in the hearth, the scent of his wife's hair. Was this what men referred to as domestic bliss?

"'Ow was your day?" Fancy asked in her charming way.

Severin found himself telling her about his troubles at work.

"'Ave...*h*ave you met with Mr. Bodin to discuss the new loom?" she asked.

"No, *chérie*. There's no point in talking with men like Bodin."

She furrowed her brow. "Why not?"

"He is distrustful of anything I have to say. He'll twist our conversation, use it to rile up the other workers like he's done in the past. He's a rabble-rouser," Severin said dismissively. "I'm not giving him a voice. If he objects, then I'll toss him out on his arse."

"But you said Mr. Bodin has made trouble in the past," she pointed out. "If it were so easy to be rid of 'im...*h*im, why didn't you just fire him before?"

Behind his wife's innocent face lay an astute mind.

"Because Bodin has too much sway with other workers," he admitted. "He could convince them to riot or walk off the job. Either way, it would be a mess of a situation. I don't want to fire him unless it's a last resort."

"Is there a way you could appeal to him? Convince him that you are only doing what's best for the workers? That, without the new technology, the weavers might be out of jobs altogether?"

"He works for me," Severin said with a scowl. "I don't have to convince him of anything. Besides, he's a hard-headed bugger, incapable of listening to reason."

"Hmm."

He raised his brows. "What does *hmm* mean?"

"Da always said that it takes two to negotiate. Maybe Mr. Bodin doesn't listen because he thinks you're not willing to do the same."

Disgruntled, Severin said, "It is not my job to listen to him. He is my employee, not vice versa. Trust me, when I fought my way up through the ranks, none of my employers asked my opinion. And I didn't go around offering it either. I just did my bloody job and was grateful to have one."

"You would know best." She smiled at him. "I'd like to see your office someday."

"I'll give you a tour." Ready to change the topic, he asked, "How was your day?"

This led to Fancy giving him an account of her activities. He found it oddly soothing to hear her domestic anecdotes. Perhaps it was the way she told her stories: she seemed to see the world through a lens that, while not precisely rose-colored, let in mostly the good. She saw the best in everything, even his siblings.

"You wouldn't believe how well Toby is doing with Bertrand," she said. "'E...he has the donkey literally eating out of his hand. Bertrand ate so many carrots that Cook ran out and had to send for more."

Severin felt his lips quirk at her enthusiasm. Leave it to Fancy to find something Toby could do without hurting himself or others.

"The boy could talk of nothing else at supper," he commented.

"He seems more confident, don't you think?" she asked. "I think that's the root of 'is...his problem. If he becomes surer of himself, then maybe he'll have less accidents."

As he looked at his wife's eager expression, warmth spread through his chest. How could he have doubted Fancy's ability to manage his siblings? With her kind and loving nature, she could win anyone over.

"Maybe Toby just likes having your attention," he said softly.

And I don't blame the lad.

"That's true too." She rolled so that she lay partly atop him, her chin propped on her folded arms. "But I think he would like your attention even more."

He threaded his fingers through her hair, enjoying the satiny texture and the privilege of touching her.

"Toby doesn't want my attention. He's a bundle of nerves when I'm around," Severin said. "I'm not a soft touch like you."

"He's only nervous because he wants you to like him. During the visits with Bertrand, he's told me some things about his life in France. It sounded lonely," Fancy said, her expression troubled. "He wanted your father's approval, I think, but the duke was never around to give it."

"My sire was hardly a shining example of fatherhood," he said dryly.

"Exactly. Which is why it would be nice for you to spend more time with Toby and your other siblings."

"Me?" He stared at her.

"Yes, you."

"I am not their father. I'm not even their full-blooded kin."

"But you are their guardian. The only one who's cared enough to take an interest in them."

"It was out of necessity, not caring," he said bluntly.

"Why didn't you just leave them in that drafty old chateau?"

"I beg your pardon?"

"You could've left Toby and Eleanor there with their governess, and Cecily and Jonas to their own devices. But you brought them all to London. Why?"

"Because our father made me their guardian. I was only doing my duty."

"You could have done it from London and left them in France," she insisted.

"I could not. They weren't living respectably—"

"Why do you care?"

"I didn't want them to live the way I did," he bit out. "I didn't want them fending for themselves and acting like damned heathens."

He realized that his chest was heaving beneath her palms. The gentle, understanding look in her eyes made his lungs work even harder, everything in him tautening...waiting.

"Because you are a good man," she said. "You care about them, virtual strangers, more than your father ever did about any of his children."

He didn't know what to say so he kept his mouth shut.

"Toby looks up to you, and a little encouragement would go a long way," she went on. "He's a charming fellow, much cleverer than he lets on. He volunteered to escort me to Madame Rousseau's tomorrow for the final fitting of my dress for Bea's wedding, and afterward we're going to Gunter's. Gemma said children adore the ices served there. I invited Eleanor along as well."

"Eleanor at a dress shop?" He smiled humorlessly. "I would have a care, if I were you. She might read a treatise on the rights of workers and encourage the seamstresses to riot."

"I doubt that since Madame Rousseau pays her seamstresses twice the going wage."

He canted his head at her. "How would you know that?"

"Fittings take a long time; you have to chat about something," his duchess said blithely. "I was wearing one of my old gowns, and Madame—her name is Amelie, by the way—commented on the fine workmanship. I told her I made it myself and that I'd done piecework from time to time. That led to a conversation about the trade in London, and Amelie told me that since she'd worked her way up as a seamstress, she knew 'ow...*h*ow hard the work was and how little it paid. So she pays her own apprentices better and... Why are you staring at me like that?"

"Because I'm sure that while Madame is privy to plenty of gossip, this was undoubtedly the first time a duchess confessed to working as a seamstress," he said.

"Oh." Fancy bit her lip. "Was it wrong of me to tell her? She seemed so nice...and Aunt Esther says Amelie's discretion is even more famous than her dressmaking."

"Tell her whatever you want, sweeting." He brushed his knuckles against the curve of her cheek. "I find your candor charming."

A notch formed between her brows. "I wasn't trying to be charming."

"I know. You are naturally that way."

Her gaze shimmered with emotion, and her gaze darted to his mouth before she tucked her head against his shoulder. She let out a quivery sigh that he felt in his balls. Even though it had only been two days since their last bedding, he was already hungry for her. He didn't know why talking with her about everyday matters should make him feel randy, but it did.

"I'm so lucky you're my 'usb...*h*usband," she whispered.

"I am the lucky one, Fancy." He meant it; he couldn't think of another woman who could bring out the best in Toby and try to lure Eleanor from her shell. Who would care enough to do so.

While Imogen had given him the names of dressmakers, tutors, and the like who she'd claimed could make his siblings respectable, she had not offered to provide them guidance herself. Not that he had any right to expect that from her, especially not after the one disastrous meeting she'd had with them. Imogen had been subjected to Cecily's vulgar fawning over her jewels, Jonas's inexpert flirtation, and Eleanor's utter indifference. Toby had capped things off by upending a cup of tea on her lap.

Imogen had not come for a return visit.

Yet Fancy was somehow making inroads with his siblings, a feat he had frankly begun to think was impossible. She shouldn't have to go at it alone. They were his kin, after all, and his responsibility.

Clearing his throat, he said, "I have some time tomorrow. I shall escort you on your outing."

Her lips curved against his chest. "That would be lovely."

∽

The following afternoon, Severin accompanied Fancy, Toby, and Eleanor to the modiste. He was relieved that Amelie Rousseau was as discreet as his wife had said. The modiste seemed to have taken a genuine liking to her new patron.

While Fancy was changing, the dressmaker murmured to him, "In designing Her Grace's new wardrobe, I chose simplicity over ornamentation. True beauty, the kind that glows from within, has no need of excessive polish, yes? No need to gild the lily."

Severin could not agree more.

Afterward, he took his wife and the children to Gunter's Tea Shoppe on Berkeley Square. Amongst the fashionable set, it was the place to see and be seen, and waiters brought ices out to the lords and ladies, who enjoyed the treats in their carriages parked along the square. Since it was Fancy and the children's first visit, all three wanted to eat inside the shop.

Severin secured them a table, and after deliberations worthy of Parliament over the ice menu, Fancy chose chocolate, Toby praline, and Eleanor pineapple. Severin opted for a plate of teacakes. When the sweets arrived, he enjoyed the delight on his wife and siblings' faces even more than the delicious confections. Eleanor, who'd had her nose buried in a book during the fitting, laid the volume aside as she, Fancy, and Toby sampled one another's flavors and debated which was the best.

Watching Fancy interact with the children, Severin had a sudden thought that one day she would be doing this with their own children. Given the frequency of their beddings, chances were good that she would be increasing soon. Part of his motivation to wed had been to secure an heir, but seeing Fancy wipe a smudge of cream from Toby's nose—shockingly, the only mess he'd made thus far—turned the hypothetical into something...visceral.

Severin pictured her belly swollen with his child, her eyes in the face of their son, her sweetness in the smile of their daughter, and his chest constricted with a feeling he couldn't quite name.

Possessiveness, maybe.

Fancy smiled at him over the empty dishes. "May we go for a stroll around the square, Knight?"

Although he had planned to return to work, he didn't have the heart to deny her.

Thus, they ambled along the tree-lined street gilded by the autumn sunshine. Fancy and Eleanor walked ahead, Severin and Toby following behind. To keep Eleanor out of her book, Fancy had taken the girl by the hand, pointing out things in shop windows, their bonneted heads leaning together like blooms.

"Thank you for taking Eleanor and me out today, Your Grace," Toby said.

Severin returned his gaze to his half-brother's freckled face. "It is my pleasure, Toby. You needn't stand on formality: Knighton will do." During the awkward pause that followed, he heard Fancy's voice in his head: *A little encouragement would go a long way.* He cleared his throat. "Fancy tells me that you have, er, an interest in animals."

"Yes, and especially Bertrand," Toby said enthusiastically. "Donkeys are clever, but Bertrand is the cleverest of donkeys—"

"Right." To spare himself further adulation of the mangy beast, Severin asked, "What about other animals? Have you had a pet?"

Toby shook his head. "My papa—our papa, I mean—didn't like animals. He had hounds, but they were kept in the kennel and not allowed in the house. I did secretly go to pet them sometimes."

"Would you like a pet?"

Toby halted, his eyes widening. "You mean...one of my own?"

"Well, yes. A dog or cat, whatever you like. Although perhaps not a donkey," Severin added hastily. "One is quite enough for the stables."

Toby stared at him, and Severin felt a jolt of alarm at the shimmer in the boy's eyes.

"Oh, Your Grace...I mean, Knighton," he said in a quivering voice. "Thank you. That would be the nicest present anyone ever gave me."

"It's nothing," Severin said brusquely. "We'll go to the pet shop this week."

"Wait until I tell Eleanor and Fancy!" Toby cried.

Wild joy shone in his eyes, and he craned his neck, looking for their female companions. His brow furrowed. "Knighton, what is that...?"

Severin swung his gaze alertly to Fancy and Eleanor. The pair had almost reached a building that looked to be in the midst of renovation, scaffolding obscuring the façade. He stared at the roof, seeing something on its edge—a large sack, teetering, about to fall.

Straight into Fancy's path.

An icy blade knifed his heart. He sprinted toward her, shouting, "Fancy, watch out!"

He reached her and Eleanor, glimpsed their surprised faces as he shoved them out of harm's way. Seconds later, a sound exploded behind them, the ground vibrating beneath his feet. Whirling, he saw plumes of dust rising from the toppled bag, its innards of smashed bricks spilling out where Fancy and Eleanor had been standing moments ago.

Breathing harshly, he saw his wife's stricken expression.

She could have been taken from me. Cold sweat prickled over his skin, the scar by his heart burning.

"Good 'eavens," Fancy said shakily, her arm around Eleanor. "What 'appened?"

Her voice jerked Severin out of his momentary daze. Locking his demons back in the cage where they belonged, he directed his gaze to the roof. No movement, no one up there that he could see. How had a bag of bricks plummeted from there?

Had this been an accident...or something more sinister?

"I don't know," he said tersely. "But I am going to find out."

26

THE MORNING AFTER NEXT, FANCY STOOD BY BEA'S SIDE AS SHE exchanged marriage vows with Mr. Murray. Flowers festooned the drawing room of his townhouse, swaths of white gauze adding to the romantic ambience. Mr. Murray's groomsman was his older brother Viscount Carlisle, a rugged Scotsman who looked on with approval as the vicar conducted the special license ceremony. A solemn stillness fell as the lovers repeated the words that would bind them for life.

Fancy became a bit teary-eyed as Bea, resplendent in a pale blue wedding dress trimmed with seed pearls, promised to have and to hold Mr. Murray through all the travails and blessings of a lifetime. The way Mr. Murray gazed back at his bride, his hazel eyes lit with adoration, made Fancy's chest ache with joy and longing.

She sneaked a peek at her husband. Chairs had been set in rows to accommodate the couple's closest friends and family, and Knight sat near the back of the room. He looked handsome and distinguished in his charcoal cutaway coat, silver brocade waistcoat, and silver cravat. As usual, his expression was impassive, but when his eyes met hers, the smoldering intensity in those smoky depths made her heart thump with hope.

While her own marriage hadn't started as a love match, she felt in her bones that, day by day, things were changing. Knight was sharing more of himself with her and showing through his actions that he cared for her. Since the accident, he'd assigned a coterie of guards to accompany her wherever she went. Although she'd protested that the bag of bricks had probably fallen by accident, Knight had held firm.

"I'm not taking any chances with your safety," he'd stated. "You are too important."

All arguments had vanished from her brain, replaced by wild joy. Not only did he appreciate her, now she had become *important* to him. It was definitely a step in the right direction.

Yesterday, when she'd come to help Bea with the last-minute preparations for the ceremony, she'd giddily shared what Knight had said. Frowning, Bea had wanted to know more about the accident itself. Fancy hadn't wanted to worry Bea before her wedding day, but the other had insisted on knowing all the details.

"It was likely an accident," Fancy said reassuringly.

"I agree with Knighton." Concern creased Bea's forehead. "You mustn't take any chances, especially given that note your father found."

"That note was from twenty-two years ago," Fancy replied. "'Ow...*h*ow would anyone know that I was that babe? Or that the babe had survived? The bricks were just an unlucky mishap."

"I wish Wick and I didn't have to go back to Staffordshire straightaway," Bea fretted. "But now that I'm selling my estate to Wick and his partners, I have to find a new property for my tenants—"

"Of course you must attend to your tenants. I have Knight to look after me. Not that I need looking after," Fancy had added.

Luckily, she'd managed to convince Bea that there was no need to change her travel plans. Fancy would never forgive herself if Bea missed out on her wedding trip. Bea had waited so long to find her prince, and she deserved to enjoy every moment of her long-awaited happily ever after.

"With this ring, I thee wed." Mr. Murray's deep voice rang clearly through the room. "With my body, I thee worship, and with all my worldly goods, I thee endow. In the name of the Father, and of the Son, and of the Holy Ghost. Amen."

Fancy's heart sighed as he slid a gold band on Bea's finger, and then Bea repeated the vows, her lavender eyes glowing as she presented him with his matching ring. The vicar proclaimed the couple man and wife, declaring, "Those whom God has joined, let no one tear asunder. You may now kiss the bride."

Mr. Murray bent his head and kissed his new wife with enough gusto to elicit giggles from the ladies and clearing of throats from the gentlemen in the audience. Even as Fancy's lips twitched, longing pierced her heart.

Will Knight one day want to kiss me? she thought with painful yearning.

Given all the other intimacies they shared, it was strange that a simple kiss remained forbidden. More and more, she found herself tempted to kiss him, yet pride and fear stopped her. Knowing what a kiss meant to Knight, that it was a pledge of his love, she needed *him* to bestow it upon her. Only then would she know that Imogen's spell was broken. Only then would she have her faerie tale ending. For only then would she know that she truly had her husband's heart.

With the official part of the ceremony concluded, Fancy shelved her thoughts and was the first to congratulate her best friend. Giving Bea back her bouquet of roses and lilies, she whispered, "You're going to be so happy!"

"I know," Bea whispered back. "Now we both have our faerie tale endings."

After a bit of mingling, it was time for the wedding breakfast. To accommodate all the guests, doors had been folded back between the dining and drawing rooms, and tables had been set up throughout.

"I hope you don't mind being at a different table," Bea said.

"Not at all," Fancy assured her. "Your table is for family, after all."

"You *are* family to me, dear. But I had to find a way to accommodate Wick's kin,"—Bea lowered her voice—"and shield the rest of the guests from his mama. Complaining is the dowager's favorite hobby; Violet and I will have our hands full."

Fancy had met Violet, Viscount Carlisle's wife, earlier. The vivacious brunette had been friendly, a sparkle of mischief in her caramel-colored eyes, and Fancy was glad that Bea had an ally in dealing with her new mama-in-law.

"Anyway, I've put you with those friends I told you about, Wick's business partners and their wives," Bea went on. "You'll like them. And you can trust them with anything."

On that rather enigmatic note, Bea had to leave to lead the guests in. Fancy arrived at her assigned table with Knight and found Bea's friends waiting for her.

Introductions were made, and they all took their seats. Normally, Fancy would be intimidated by meeting so many strangers, especially women as stunning as petite, raven-haired Tessa Kent and voluptuous, redheaded Gabriella Garrity and their handsome husbands, who were Mr. Murray's partners at Great London National Railway. Bea had told Fancy that the Kents and Garritys had assisted her during her recent ordeals, and gratitude eased Fancy's nervousness.

As it turned out, Knight was acquainted with them.

"Well met, Knight," Harry Kent said. "Been some time, hasn't it?"

Mr. Kent had unruly dark hair and boyishly handsome features. Although he had the lean build of an athlete, his wire-rimmed spectacles gave him a scholarly air, which made sense since he was apparently a scientist and in charge of technological development at GLNR.

"It's Your Grace now," his wife reminded him.

According to Bea, Tessa Kent was a force to be reckoned with in the London underworld. Just as Knight was known as the Duke of Silk for the power he wielded in Spitalfields, Tessa was the Duchess of Covent Garden for the territory she oversaw. Although one wouldn't think it looking at the elfin lady with wide jade eyes, her waifish figure clad in a blush muslin dress trimmed with pink ribbon, she purportedly kept the peace with an iron fist. She had a special dislike of brutes who tried to abuse the prostitutes and children under her protection.

"Right, sprite. Almost forgot about the new title," her husband said good-naturedly. "Welcome, Your Graces."

"Knighton will suffice," Knight muttered.

"Bea has told us ever so much about you, Your Grace." Gabriella Garrity, who was sitting next to Mrs. Kent, addressed Fancy. Framed by fiery upswept curls, Mrs. Garrity's face was sweetly rounded, and her guileless eyes, which matched her sky-blue taffeta gown, emanated genuine niceness. "Your gown is ravishing. The color reminds me of sunshine."

Using silk of a pale golden color, Madame Rousseau had created a masterpiece with a corsage à la grecque, an elongated, nipped-in bodice, and full, flowy skirts. When Fancy had first tried it on, she'd felt like a princess.

"I like your gown as well," she said truthfully. "Please call me Fancy."

"And I'm Gabby," Mrs. Garrity said warmly. "Since our husbands are colleagues of a sort, I feel as if we know one another already."

Bea had mentioned that Adam Garrity was, like Knight, a powerful man with underclass roots. Mr. Garrity had made his fortune as a moneylender before taking the helm of GLNR. Sitting beside his wife, he was ice to Gabby's fire, a ruthless quality to his pale, sharp features, slicked-back inky hair, and pitch-black eyes. Bea had described him as a cold and cunning man, except when it came to his lady.

"Colleagues." He sent his wife an amused look before addressing Knight. "Is that how you would describe it, Knighton?"

"At a wedding breakfast and in polite company? Probably," Knight said.

"Anyway," Gabby said with cheerful aplomb, "I'm so glad you're sitting with us, Fancy. Bea mentioned that you were recently married in Gretna Green. That sounds ever so romantic, and I should love to hear about it!"

As the delicious meal was served, along with flutes of champagne, Fancy found herself chatting easily with the group. Bea's friends seemed interested in learning more about her life as the daughter of a travelling tinker. No one showed any sign of judgement—perhaps because they, too, came from unconventional backgrounds.

Tessa shared proudly that she was the granddaughter of London's most notorious cutthroat and described her toddler son as an even bigger terror. Mr. Kent pointed out that since she'd insisted on naming their boy Bartholomew after her grandfather, it should only be expected that the tot take after his namesake. Tessa had them all in stitches with her tales of how little Bart liked to ransack the pantry, waving his play sword with one hand and keeping up his listing nappy with the other.

What was striking to Fancy was not only the kindness of the people at the table, but the passionate devotion she saw between the husbands and their wives. Impish Tessa obviously enjoyed teasing her husband, who bantered good-naturedly with her. Gabby was sweetness and light, her flame glowing brighter against the dark foil of her husband. When Adam Garrity looked at his wife, his black eyes had a proprietary gleam that sent tingles over Fancy's skin.

She couldn't help but wonder how she and Knight appeared to the other couples. Her husband wasn't a demonstrative man, and she knew he didn't yet love her the way these men clearly loved their wives. At present, his emotions were masked by a neutral expression. Weddings, she realized, had a way of bringing love and relationships to the forefront of one's mind. As she was yearning for Knight...was he thinking of Imogen?

Her heart clenching, she finished her champagne, and a helpful footman refilled it.

"I hope I'm not being too forward, Fancy," Gabby was saying, "but Bea told us about your recent accident. Or rather, she said she was afraid that it was *not* an accident. She asked us to look out for you while she and Mr. Murray return to Staffordshire, and we would like to help in any way we can."

Gabby's husband uttered something under his breath that sounded like, "Here we go again."

"That's very kind o'...of you," Fancy said. "But unnecessary as it probably was a mishap."

"I wouldn't be so sure," Tessa said matter-of-factly. "In my experience, bags of bricks don't fall from rooftops and nearly smash people to smithereens without being nudged. What is your take on the situation, Knighton?"

"I don't like it," Knight said flatly. "My men located the builder working on the house where the bricks fell. While he confirmed that he was using those bricks on the façade, he said there was no reason for that bag to be up on the roof."

"You didn't tell me this," Fancy said in surprise.

"I only learned of it this morning." Knight's eyes softened as he looked at her. "I was going to tell you after the wedding, *chérie*; I didn't want to ruin the day for you."

She was touched by his thoughtfulness and a bit intrigued by his openness with this group. Then again, he was amongst people who had come up in the same world as he had and who'd likely dealt with their fair share of murder and mayhem.

Murder. She swallowed. *Is someone truly out to 'urt me? Why?*

"Do you have any enemies, Fancy?" Tessa asked as if reading her mind.

"Not that I, um, know of."

She cast an uncertain look at Knight, and he responded with a slight nod. Bea's words rang in her head. *You can trust them with anything.* If Bea had faith in the Kents and Garritys, then surely Fancy could as well.

Inhaling, she told her new friends about her father's revelations regarding her past.

"I 'ave…*h*ave no idea why anyone would want to 'urt…*h*urt me." It was difficult to remember proper enunciation when discussing such disquieting matters. "I'm not important. And I've harmed no one, at least not knowingly."

"If the note your father found is to be believed, then an attack would have nothing to do with your actions per se. The danger would have been put into play by your mere birth," Mr. Kent reasoned. "In other words, you did nothing to cause this, Your Grace."

"Excellent logic, darling," his wife said with clear admiration. "I always said that you were the brains of our operation."

Mr. Kent lifted his brows. "And you, I take it, are the brawn?"

"You have plenty of brawn when it counts," Tessa said in a flirtatious tone.

Grinning, her husband chucked her under the chin. "Nice try, sprite. We both know little Bart gets his bloodthirsty streak from his mama."

"Being bloodthirsty has its uses. Now, Knighton," Tessa said in an imperious tone, "ever since you participated in the rescue of my grandpapa, I've been in your debt. It's time to clean the slate. How may Harry and I assist in safeguarding your lady?"

"We want to help too," Gabby said in a soft rush. "We cannot just stand by while some villain threatens Fancy, can we, Mr. Garrity?"

"I suppose not, my love." There was a hint of irony in Mr. Garrity's voice. "Well, Knighton? What is your plan?"

"I've assigned guards to Fancy. She won't go anywhere unless she's accompanied by them or me," Knight said grimly. "I also need to look into her origins. To discover who she is and why someone might wish her harm."

Icicles prickled over Fancy's skin. The seriousness of the situation was sinking in. She reached for her champagne glass, once again overflowing with bubbles, and took a fortifying gulp.

"The note and christening gown Her Grace mentioned," Mr. Garrity said. "Do you have those items in your possession?"

Knight inclined his head. "They don't offer much in the way of clues, however. The note is written on plain parchment, in an indistinct hand...a woman's, if I had to guess. I can vouch for the quality of the gown—hand-woven silk of the highest grade—but there's nothing to signify where it was made. There is a bit of embroidery on the gown, a flower that might bear some significance, but that is the only thing to go on."

"I would like to have a look at the items," Tessa said.

"Me too," Gabby chimed in. "May we call upon you tomorrow, Fancy? Maybe our fresh eyes will yield something new?"

"That would be lovely," Fancy said tremulously. "Thank you."

The tapping of a glass signaled that the toasts were about to begin, and for the next little while at least, Fancy was distracted from thoughts of murder and mayhem, her mind on more pleasant things.

27

AFTER THE BREAKFAST ENDED AND THE WELL-WISHERS SAW THE bride and groom off on their wedding trip, a few guests lingered to chat, hosted by the groom's brother and sister-in-law. Severin took the opportunity to speak with Garrity and Kent whilst their ladies carried on in their own group.

Having known Garrity for years and fought side by side with both men during the rescue of Tessa Kent's grandfather, Severin respected and trusted their judgement. Kent and Garrity knew the darker side of life just as he did. The three of them might have had territorial disputes and other minor skirmishes, but as men of honor they shared a sacrosanct code: women and children were to be protected.

In the past, when the mates of these men were threatened, they had set aside their differences to help one another. Knight knew they would do the same for him. Especially since their wives had taken a liking to Fancy.

"Her Grace's origin is the key to all this," Kent said, his bespectacled gaze thoughtful. "Why would someone want to harm a babe?"

Severin shared his theory. "Perhaps the babe was born out of wedlock, and the parents needed to get rid of her for fear of scandal."

"True," Kent allowed, "but why dress the babe in such finery? Why leave the babe in a field and not some place like an orphanage or foundling hospital? And I hate to say this, but if someone wanted to be rid of a babe, they could have done so in a more...permanent fashion."

Severin nodded starkly. These were questions he'd also mulled over.

"Don't forget money and revenge as motives." Shadowy emotion flickered in Garrity's dark gaze. "In my experience, those are the most common roots of evil."

"You think someone might have taken the babe out of revenge?" Kent asked.

"Anything is possible," Garrity said coolly. "It could also be a kidnapping gone wrong. Someone might have taken the babe and perhaps they didn't receive the ransom they demanded. Or they did, but they didn't bother returning the babe."

"Why leave that note?" Kent pondered aloud. "If some bastard was heartless enough to steal an infant, then surely he wouldn't pen a missive trying to keep the babe safe."

"You are assuming that the point of the note was to protect the babe. But perhaps the real impetus behind the note was to keep the babe away from London so that she was never found. Which brings us back to revenge as a possible motive."

Kent stared at his business partner. "Devil and damn, that's a pessimistic take on the matter."

"I call it realistic. One of us has to leave off the rose-colored glasses," Garrity said wryly.

Garrity's hypothesis about kidnapping sparked a thought in Severin.

"How would one go about seeing if a babe, likely from a wealthy family, went missing in London twenty-two years ago?" Severin asked.

"Good question." Kent stroked his chin. "Back then, before the establishment of the police force, I suppose a family with means would hire Bow Street Runners or other investigators to look into the case."

"The Charleys might have sounded the alarm that a child had gone missing," Garrity added.

Charleys were the night watchmen who had patrolled the streets prior to the establishment of Sir Robert Peel's policing force. There were still a few around, mostly in wealthier enclaves where the householders could afford to pay the parish fee for additional security.

"I could have my men locate Charleys who were working at the time," Severin said. "It won't be easy, given that it was over two decades ago, but if Fancy was indeed taken from a wealthy family, that would narrow down the neighborhoods at least."

"You could concentrate on the Charleys of the most affluent parishes," Kent agreed. "St. James's, St. George Hanover Square, and Piccadilly."

"Even so, it will be no small task hunting down the old watchmen," Garrity remarked. "I'll lend you some of my men."

"My brother Ambrose runs an investigative agency," Kent said, "and he has old contacts who were Bow Street Runners. He could see if any of his cronies recall a case of a missing child fitting our time frame."

"I am in your debt, gentlemen," Severin said.

He wasn't someone who accepted help easily. Perhaps because help had been so rarely offered. He would, however, do whatever it took to ensure Fancy's safety.

"We shall call it even," Kent said. "After all, you helped Tessa and I in our time of need."

"As much as I would like to accept your marker," Garrity said, "my wife will not hear of it. Mrs. Garrity has taken a liking to Her Grace, and she has this strange notion that favors amongst friends should come for free."

Although Garrity had adopted the tone of a long-suffering husband, Severin didn't miss the pride in the man's eyes as he searched out his redheaded wife.

Across the drawing room, Mrs. Garrity, Fancy, Mrs. Kent, and Viscountess Carlisle occupied a cluster of curricle chairs. The four ladies looked like frolicking nymphs from an oil painting, their pretty heads bent together, their expressions merry. As Severin watched, Viscountess Carlisle said something, and all four burst into laughter.

"What do you think they are giggling about?" he mused.

"We don't want to know," Kent said ruefully. "My sister Violet may be a viscountess and mama of three, but that hasn't stopped her from being a hoyden. Carlisle indulges her quite shamelessly. That last comment she made was probably outrageous."

"You do realize that is not tea they've been drinking?" Garrity's gaze narrowed on his pink-cheeked and, indeed, rather tipsy-looking wife.

Severin studied his own bride. Fancy was also flushed, her eyes sparkling as she finished a glass of champagne. He thought back to the breakfast...how many glasses had she had? Before his bemused gaze, she whispered something to Mrs. Garrity, and the pair dissolved into a paroxysm of giggles.

"Gentlemen," Garrity said. "I do believe it is time for us to collect our wives."

"Probably a good idea," Severin muttered. "If Fancy doesn't stop now, she will have a megrim on the morrow."

"The trick, Your Grace, is to take good care of your lady this eve," Garrity said silkily. "Adieu."

He advanced toward his wife, his stride distinctly predatory.

A wolfish gleam entered Kent's gaze as well as he headed after his own lady, murmuring under his breath, "Devil and damn, I like weddings."

"You don't 'ave to carry me up the stairs, Knight," his wife said, giggling. "I can walk."

Glancing at his duchess's languid, rosy features, Severin hid a smile.

"Since you nearly toppled out of the carriage, I am not taking any chances," he told her.

"I tripped," she said blithely.

"Over your own feet."

"I'm not usually prone to accidents," she said.

Then a worried crease formed between her brows, and he knew she was thinking about the bricks and the invisible menace.

"Nothing is going to happen to you," he said firmly. "I will take care of you, Fancy. You know that, don't you?"

Her forehead smoothed, his declaration—and no doubt the champagne—easing her anxiety.

"I trust you," she said with a simplicity that made his chest expand with pride.

"Put it out of your mind, then," he said. "We'll deal with it in the morning."

Arriving at her bedchamber, he dismissed her waiting maid. He sat his wife on the edge of the bed. Planting her hands on the mattress behind her, Fancy leaned back, chuckling as he knelt to remove her shoes.

"Are you my lady's maid tonight?" she asked.

Fancy unsubtly batted her lashes at him. She was tipsy all right...but not so drunk that they couldn't have some fun. Tonight, he wanted to take her mind off the looming threat; he had a plan and would contend with the dark business in the morning. At present, he had his wife to himself, and she was endearingly playful. It had been days since he'd tupped her, his loins burgeoning with the need to claim her once more.

He slid his hands beneath her golden skirts, up the silk-covered curve of her calf. He felt a pulse of satisfaction at the way her breath hitched, her eyelids lowering as he hooked a finger under her garter, unfastening it. His cock stiffened when she spread her legs wider for him, an invitation to touch her higher up.

Two could play at flirtation. After days of going without, he wanted to savor his pretty bride.

He took his time untying her other garter and rolling down her stockings. Then he pulled her to her feet, turning her around so that he could work on the buttons of her gown. She swayed a little as he divested her of the garment. Taking her hands, he placed them on a poster of the bed.

"Hold on to the bedpost, *chérie*," he murmured against her ear. "We don't want you falling while I get the rest of these layers off, hmm?"

She shivered against him. "Whate'er you say, Knight."

"What an obedient little wife you are." He untied her petticoats, the layers pooling around her. "By the by, you looked beautiful tonight."

Her breath caught as he tugged at a knot in her corset lacing. Holding the strings that controlled her respiration fanned his arousal. She was so exquisitely trusting in his hands. He tugged, then released, her sensual sigh engorging his prick.

"I'm glad you think so." She looked over her shoulder at him with her big brown eyes. "I wanted to make you proud."

God, she made him hard.

He chucked the corset aside and cupped her curvy backside, now covered only by a thin linen chemise. She quivered as he squeezed her luscious arse.

"I am proud of you." He pushed her chemise up, his touch proprietary. His nostrils flared as he took stock of his lady: her lush hips, indented waist, the firm perfection of her breasts.

"Even if my speech isn't perfect?" she gasped out.

He stilled in the act of playing with her tits which were, indeed, perfect. He took her hands from the bed post and turned her to face him. With her hair still in its elegant coronet, she looked like a debauched princess in her transparent chemise that displayed her budded red nipples and alluring dark thatch. Lust pounded urgently in his veins, but even more pressing was the worry he heard in her voice.

"Your speech is fine," he said.

"I made mistakes," she said, her expression forlorn. "Even though I tried not to. I'm still 'aving...having trouble with my *h*'s."

Her vulnerability unleashed a wave of tenderness in him. Her cheerful disposition sometimes made him forget how much she was doing to become a proper duchess. All that she was undertaking...for him.

He cupped her cheek. "You're doing a smashing job, sweeting."

"Mr. Stanton doesn't think so." She wrinkled her nose, adding candidly, "He's tearing out what's left of 'is...*h*is hair trying to get me to say my *h*'s properly."

It struck Severin that Fancy didn't usually complain to him about...well, anything. It was probably the champagne loosening her inhibitions. He wanted her to know that, tipsy or not, she didn't have to hide how she felt from him.

"Tell me more," he encouraged. "Maybe I can help."

"I don't think you can," she mumbled.

"Try me." After a pause, he added, "I had to polish up my own speech, you know."

"You did?"

Her surprised look reminded him that he'd glossed over the details of his past.

"'Ad to, luv, didn't I?" he said in the Cockney accents of his youth. "Wanted to be a nob, so I 'ad to learn to walk and talk like one."

"'Ow...*h*ow did you learn?"

Gazing into her wide, curious eyes, he hesitated. He wasn't sure he wanted to tell his wife that it had been Imogen who'd coached him. Back then, he couldn't afford elocution lessons, so he'd learned by aping Imogen and her family. Day in and day out, he had listened to the Hammonds and privately rehearsed their accents and manner of speech. When he practiced with Imogen, she'd giggled, calling him her Knight-in-training and giving him pointers on how to further polish his accent.

But Imogen had no place in his marital bower, and he didn't want Fancy to be distracted by his past. In truth, he had no problem concentrating on the present, not when his nearly naked wife was gazing at him with her soft doe's eyes.

"I practiced." He stroked her downy cheek. "It takes time."

Fancy blew out a breath, her rosy lips rounding in a pout that made his cock strain with longing.

"That's the problem," she said. "I only 'ave...*h*ave a week until Princess Adelaide's soiree."

Ignoring his arousal, he said, "Tell me how I can help, *chérie*."

"I don't know that you can. I think...I think there's something wrong with my mouth."

"There is absolutely nothing wrong with your mouth," he said with conviction.

In fact, he was about to explode watching her tongue wet those perfect, plump lips.

"Well, *something* ain't working. Mr. Stanton keeps telling me to keep my jaw loose, to breathe the sound from the back o' my throat, and I 'ave...*h*ave no idea what he means," she said mournfully.

A proper gentleman would console his wife. Perhaps utter a few soft words of encouragement. He would definitely not have the depraved thoughts that Severin was having.

Truth be told, he had been entertaining the idea and waiting for the right time to introduce this particular variation on the theme to his wife. Now was probably not the right time but... He struggled briefly with his lust.

To hell with being a gentleman, he thought.

"I think I can help you with that, sweeting," he said.

She tilted her head. "How?"

Anticipation sizzled up his spine. He kept his expression bland.

"Take off your chemise, and I'll show you."

~

Fancy blinked at her husband. "I 'ave to be naked for this lesson?"

He arched his brows. "Do you want my help or not?"

She *did* want help, and the truth was she wouldn't mind something else either. Now that her flux was over, she was eager to resume her marital activities. She had enough liquid courage left in her to reach for her chemise and pull it over her head.

She looked up into her husband's eyes. What she saw in his smoldering gaze was more intoxicating than any beverage. Her heart thumped giddily.

"Nicely done," he said.

His calm, almost cool reply heightened her excitement. Grabbing a pillow from the bed, he tossed it onto the floor in front of him.

"Now kneel, sweetheart," he said.

Her pulse raced. Was he in *earnest*? His expression said that he was. They'd never done anything like this before, and the idea of being on her knees, naked at the feet of her fully clothed husband, stirred the darker shadows of her desire. There were faint crinkles around his eyes, a sensual slant to his mouth that suggested they were playing a game. A new, sophisticated sort of game that a duke could apparently play with his duchess.

With the danger lurking in her life, Fancy experienced a wild need to lose herself in the fantasy Knight was offering. To surrender her worries and fears for the night. To not think about anything but the pleasure she felt in his arms.

Her knees quivered as they bent, touching the feathery cushion. She gazed up at him, and the molten approval in those grey eyes made her feel faint with wanting. He unbuttoned his jacket, his manner leisurely while her heart pounded as if she'd run for miles. His waistcoat went the way of his jacket, and he began to work on his shirt. The parting panels of linen revealed the bulging, hairy planes of his chest, the taut stack of muscle below. And below that...she swallowed.

A thick, vertical bar strained the front of his trousers.

It was good that she was kneeling for her knees went utterly weak.

He reached for his waistband, began unbuttoning the fall, his unhurried pace ratcheting up the sensual tension. The wobbly feeling spread from her knees to her center when he took out his cock. By all rights, she ought to be used to his size by now, but she'd never seen his manhood from this angle. It loomed over her, jutting from his open placket like a weighty branch, bobbing under its own weight.

He fisted himself, pumping the veined rod while her palms itched with the memory of how it felt to stroke the velvety skin over the rigid core. She wanted to touch him now, but she had a feeling that he had something else in mind.

"We're going to work on an exercise to keep your jaw loose," he said in a conversational tone.

An image flashed, causing a hot quickening between her thighs.

"'Ow?" Her voice sounded throaty.

"You'll practice by taking my cock in your mouth." He kept pumping his huge erection, teasing her with it. "Only if you want to, of course. Do you want to, sweeting? Do you want to suck your husband's cock?"

"Yes," she breathed.

"What a good wife you are. Now open your mouth, and I'll give you a taste."

Shivering, she obeyed, and he brought his member to her parted lips. She saw a pearly drop leak from the slit in the tip, glossing the fat head. He laid his cock upon her tongue, and the taste of him, salt and clean male musk, spread through her like a drug. Pleasure and craving swirled in her blood.

"That feels nice," he said thickly. "Shall we practice having you take more?"

She made a sound, muffled by the heft of his cock, but he seemed to know her answer. Steadying her head with one hand, he guided his hardness deeper into her mouth.

"Keep your jaw as relaxed as you can. That way I can get deeper." His voice sounded hoarse as she followed his instruction. "God, yes. Just like that."

He began to thrust slowly, taking her mouth the way he did her pussy. She moaned around his plunging thickness, her hands latching onto his cloth-covered thighs. The reminder that he was still mostly clothed heightened the depravity of what they were doing. She clenched her thighs together, feeling their slickness and her own throbbing need.

"Let go, my sweet Fancy." His touch was gentle on her jaw, his eyes burning as he drove his prick in deeper and deeper. "I'll take care of you. You know that, don't you?"

"I know," she said, her reply garbled by the fleshy pole he fed her.

He seemed to understand, his thrusts becoming harder, heavier. She had the exhilarating feeling that he was as lost in their passion as she was. She managed to relax the hinge of her jaw even more, and he groaned as he went deeper than he ever had. On his next thrust, he nudged her throat, and her eyes watered, her muscles clenching in reflex.

He withdrew, gasping, "God, Fancy, sorry…"

"Don't stop," she panted. "I want more. All of you Knight… the way you've had all of me."

His eyes blazed with feral hunger. Then he was inside her mouth again, his big cock moving between her lips, stoking the need in her pussy. All she could taste, smell, feel was her mate.

"I'm going to spend," he gritted out. "Tell me to stop if you don't want to take my seed in your mouth."

She dug her fingers into his thighs, holding on. His muscles turned to rock beneath her fingertips, his hands clenching the back of her head, his hips bucking. She heard him roar her name, then a hot, salty burst drenched her senses. His fingers dug into her scalp as he ejaculated, and she swallowed the scalding shots, taking them as her due. Tremors wracked his strapping frame, and knowing that she had caused them filled her with a heady sense of power.

Chest heaving, he pulled out, and the world spun as he hoisted her off her knees and tossed her onto the bed. She giggled as he crawled over her, then moaned when he entered her with a commanding thrust.

He was hard, throbbing, huge inside her.

"Already?" she gasped.

"For you, wife, I'm always ready," he said in a guttural voice.

He spent the rest of the night proving his words.

28

The next morning, Fancy awoke alone. She was curled up on her side, facing the empty space that Knight had vacated, his pillow still bearing his musk. Memories of the night washed through her, accompanied by the faint ache of well-used muscles and the twinges of a megrim. Despite the reminders of her excesses, she couldn't help but smile.

Goodness, her husband was wicked...and insatiable.

Then again, so am I.

As she stretched like a contented kitten, a sweet fragrance wafted to her, and she turned her head toward the table by her bedside. Her heart fluttered when she saw the bouquet of red roses, each bloom large and perfect, arranged in a porcelain vase. Next to them was a small paper packet and a glass of water. Sitting up, she reached for the note propped against the vase and read Knight's bold scrawl:

My sweet Fancy,

Please accept the roses as a token of my esteem. The packet contains willow bark and will help with any megrim. I have placed extra guards on duty and informed the family that, for safety's sake, you must all stay home today.

See you at supper.
 -K

P.S. I am proud of you. Always. And if you need further help with your lessons, I shall be happy to assist.

Smiling dreamily, she plucked a flower from the bunch, the dethorned stem smooth between her fingertips. She brushed the silky petals against her nose, inhaling the delicate scent and reveling in her husband's gesture. The note and flowers were so *Knight*: thoughtful, sensually teasing, and gallantly protective.

Even if some mysterious villain wanted to harm her, she felt safe...because of Knight. Because, with him, she'd found her place of belonging. She had fallen in love with him, her prince who gave her a home and made her feel special. An image flashed of their future together: they would have darkly handsome boys who Knight could teach to be gentlemen and successful men of business, pretty girls to whom she could impart the skills of being a lady and a tinker.

Confidence and clarity bolstered her resolve. Her plan to make herself over into a duchess was working, but there was more to be done. Now that she had admitted the truth of her own heart, she could not settle for anything less than Knight's love. Princess Adelaide's soiree was in a few days. If Fancy could pull off a dazzling debut as the Duchess of Knighton, then maybe Knight would finally kiss her. In that magical moment, she would know she had his whole heart.

With all that in mind, Fancy did not want to waste a single moment of the day. After taking the willow bark powder, she breakfasted, dressed, and threw herself into her daily tasks.

She didn't know whether it was her positive attitude or

Knight's "lesson" that was the cause, but her session with Mr. Stanton went exceptionally well. When her tutor exclaimed over her progress with *h*'s, commenting that she must be doing the oral exercises he'd prescribed, her cheeks flamed. She was, nonetheless, thrilled with her success.

The improvements extended into her time with Aunt Esther, who was astounded when Fancy managed to recite by heart several distinguished family trees from Debrett's *and* walked the length of the library with three books balanced upon her head.

The triumphs continued into luncheon. Instead of strained silence, conversation reigned over the table. It was led by Toby, who was over the moon about Knight's promise to get him a puppy. He also chatted about the tricks he was teaching Bertrand. Eleanor, who'd been joining him and Fancy on their visits to the stables, agreed that Bertrand was a creature of singular intellect. She had decided that donkeys were vastly underrated due to commonly held prejudices against them.

To that end, Eleanor had started a club called The Society for the Equalization and Protection of the Rights of Asses, with Toby acting as Club Secretary and Fancy as Treasurer. The girl had even managed to rope Aunt Esther into being a member. Her aunt had agreed to join on one condition: Eleanor was not to bring books to the dining table.

A masterful stroke, Fancy thought admiringly.

Unfortunately, less progress was being made with Knight's older siblings. Jonas, Fancy noted, acted bored throughout the meal and drank too much wine. To draw him into the conversation, Fancy asked him about his interests and possible professions he might like to pursue.

"A gentleman doesn't work," he said, aghast. "Unless it is an absolute necessity."

"Knight does," she pointed out.

"Well, my dear brother isn't exactly a gentleman, is he?" Jonas said, sipping his wine.

"You will take that back." Fancy scowled at him. "Knight is the definition of a gentleman."

"No need to fly into the boughs." Jonas set down his glass, his expression turning wary. "I only meant that he's not a *conventional* sort of gent. Sons of dukes aren't usually raised in London's rookeries, nor do they own factories."

"You ought to be proud that your brother made his own fortune." Fancy wasn't going to allow him—or anyone—to disparage her husband. "And perhaps if you found something to occupy your time, you would be less inclined to waste it on frivolous pursuits. Idle hands are the devil's work, my da always says."

"What do you expect me to do?" Jonas muttered, pushing a drooping wave of hair out of his eyes. "Ain't much for a well-bred bastard to do *but* frivolous pursuits."

Despite the lad's defiant posturing, which all of her brothers had adopted at one time or another, Fancy heard his underlying insecurity. Like Knight, Jonas was the son of a duke, but he'd been born on the wrong side of the blanket. And that could not be easy.

Gentling her tone, she said, "It wouldn't hurt to try to find something useful to do." A kernel of an idea sprouted. "Why don't you ask Knight to show you one of his manufactories? Maybe he could teach you about his business."

"I've no interest in becoming a businessman." Jonas gripped his wine glass, saying with a slight sneer, "Besides, Knighton thinks he's better than the rest of us bastards. To him, I'm just a wastrel and an unwanted obligation. He ain't got time for the likes of me. For any of us."

"You have got the right of it, Jonas," Cecily cut in.

Fancy stifled a sigh. It figured that when Cecily joined in, it would be to support a rebellion.

"Knighton just wants to sweep us under the carpet," the girl claimed with a dramatic wave of her arm. "To him, we are less than dirt."

"You two would be wise to show more gratitude." Aunt Esther's gaze slitted. "A lesser man than Knighton would not have taken on the responsibilities your papa left behind."

"That's true," Toby piped up. "If not for Knighton, we would still be trapped in that musty old chateau with only that horrid governess for company."

"Mademoiselle Grigeaux." Eleanor shuddered. "I do not miss her canings, that's for certain."

The girl's revelation distracted Fancy from the war with the older siblings.

"Your governess beat you?" Fancy asked, horrified.

When Toby and Eleanor nodded their heads solemnly, Fancy's throat cinched. The poor dears. They needed Knight and her more than she had even known.

"No one is ever hurting you again," she said with fierce conviction. "If anyone dares to try, you come directly to me. Or to Knight. Do you understand?"

"Yes, Fancy," the children chorused.

Brow furrowed, Jonas said, "You never told me old Grigeaux caned you."

"You weren't there," Eleanor said in no-nonsense tones. "You had your own separate wing, and you were busy with your tarts."

"Young girls do not speak of tarts," Aunt Esther reprimanded.

Eleanor turned her bespectacled gaze to the dessert tray. "What about strawberry tarts? Or treacle tarts? Or lemon tarts—"

"The edible kind are allowed," Aunt Esther amended with a sigh.

She aimed a look at Fancy, as if to say, *See what I have been managing, gel?*

Fancy gave a reassuring nod back.

"I, for one, miss our lovely chateau in France," Cecily carried on. When it came to complaints, she was like a dog with a bone. "At least there I was allowed to have friends. Here, thanks to whatever trouble is following Fancy, I am a prisoner in my own house!"

"It is only temporary." Fancy clung to her patience. "Until Knight puts a stop to the threat."

"That could take forever." Bright spots stood out on Cecily's cheeks as she rose in a theatric swish. "I will be a spinster by the time I'm allowed to leave this gaol!"

She flounced off in a manner that Fancy was finding increasingly tiresome.

Thus, Fancy was more than ready to see Tessa and Gabby's friendly faces when they arrived later that afternoon for their promised visit. While Aunt Esther had been less than enthusiastic about meeting Fancy's new friends, who according to her were "not good *ton,*" her tune changed considerably when she saw the beautiful cinnamon-haired lady Tessa and Gabby brought with them.

"Your Grace," Aunt Esther said with a curtsy.

"How lovely to see you again, Lady Brambley," the Duchess of Ranelagh and Somerville said in pleasant tones. "I hope you do not mind my arriving uninvited. But Mrs. Kent and Mrs. Garrity spoke so glowingly of the Duchess of Knighton that I could not wait to meet her."

The duchess smiled warmly at Fancy, who smiled back. The other had a straightforward and unfussy manner that put her at ease.

"It is an honor to receive you, Your Grace." Aunt Esther gestured for everyone to sit, and Fancy poured out the tea. "And a welcome opportunity for Francesca to meet some of her peers. As she is new to London, we are giving her some polish before introducing her officially to Society."

"I know a thing or two about polish." The Duchess of Ranelagh and Somerville's tip-tilted emerald eyes shone with amusement. "Since my marriage, I have had quite a few layers lacquered on myself."

"Truly, Your Grace?" Fancy asked, fascinated.

She found it hard to believe that this poised, confident duchess had needed refinement. The lady was a vision of flawlessness in her flounced russet carriage dress with Bishop's sleeves.

"Do call me Maggie. And, yes, it was no small feat to transform the proprietress of a Dorset fossils shop into a duchess." The lady sipped her tea, her eyes rueful. "But I was determined, you see, to be the duchess my husband deserved."

Fancy understood that feeling wholeheartedly. The fact that Maggie had started off with less than noble origins and ended up a celebrated pillar of society buoyed Fancy's hopes.

"I don't know why you were worried, Maggie. Your husband adores you: he would have married you if you were wearing a flour sack and talking cant." Dressed in a maroon promenade gown styled *à la militaire*, Tessa polished off a biscuit and addressed the rest of the group. "You should have seen the way Ransom—the Duke of Ranelagh and Somerville, that is—proposed to her. I am not one for grand romantic gestures, but even my heart went pitter-patter."

Maggie blushed.

"We asked Maggie to come with us today, not only because we wanted the two of you to meet," Gabby said, her blue eyes earnest, "but because we thought she could help."

Fancy looked dubiously at the serene duchess. "That is very kind of you all, but I wouldn't want to involve Maggie, or any of you, in what could prove to be dangerous business."

"Danger *is* my business," Tessa said smartly. "But we'll get to that in a moment."

"When you told us that you wished to become a lady of fashion, we thought immediately of Maggie," Gabby explained. "She does not just know style, she *sets* it."

"I am more than a fashion plate, you know," Maggie said with a touch of wryness. "As you'll recall, I've had my share of perilous adventures. But, yes, I would like to assist in your venture, Fancy, in any way that I can. In fact, I'm holding a small *fête* in three days and would be honored if you and Knighton would be my guests of honor."

"Oh...thank you." Fancy glanced at Aunt Esther, who gave a fervent nod. "We would like that."

"Lovely," Maggie said, beaming. "Lady Brambley, I hope you will join us. And I understand Knighton has siblings who are, ahem, newly arrived from France. They are welcome as well."

Fancy admired Maggie's delicacy. The duchess was implying that she knew the illegitimate status of Knight's brothers and sisters and would still receive them. Having Maggie's stamp of approval would no doubt give the campaign to launch Jonas and Cecily into Society a much-needed boost.

Fancy knew she had interpreted the situation correctly when Aunt Esther said with gruff gratitude, "You are very kind, Your Grace."

After a bit more chitchat, Aunt Esther excused herself, leaving Fancy alone with her friends.

"Now that we are done with the fashionable talk," Tessa declared, "onto more pressing matters. Fancy, do you have the note and christening gown you mentioned?"

"Yes." Fancy retrieved the objects from a nearby table, where she'd set them earlier. "Here they are."

They all gathered around as Tessa started with the note.

"*May God watch over this babe. For her own safety, she must never return to London,*" she read aloud. "Sounds to me like someone was trying to protect you, Fancy. What do you think about the hand-writing?"

"The penmanship is rather unrefined," Maggie mused. "There are not the usual flourishes that I associate with an upper class lady's hand."

"Maybe it was written in a hurry?" Gabby suggested. "I leave out the curlicues when I have to scribble a quick note."

"Or it could have been written by a woman with less formal education," Maggie said. "A servant, perhaps."

Impressed with her friends' observations, Fancy said, "You all make excellent points."

"Now for the gown." Tessa held up the silk garment, tilting her head this way and that as she studied the embroidered flower. "Flora and fauna are not my strength. I cannot tell a cornflower from a cabbage. What do you think, Gabby and Maggie?"

"Is it a rose, perhaps?" Gabby squinted at the embroidery. "I wish it wasn't so small..."

"I have something that'll help." Reaching into the pocket of her skirts, Fancy took out her tinker's friend. She found the correct handle and swiveled out a small magnifying glass.

"How clever!" Gabby exclaimed.

"And handy," Tessa said. "Wherever did you come by such a contraption?"

"My da made it. He calls it *a tinker's friend*, and I never go anywhere without it." Fancy showed her friends the other tools and smiled at their *oohs* and *ahs* of delight. When they were done admiring, she held the magnifying glass over the embroidered flower.

"The bell-shaped petals resemble a rhododendron or azalea, I think," Maggie said. "What do you make of those yellow specks?"

She pointed at the tiny stitches at the center of the flower.

"Stamen?" Gabby guessed. "I count ten of them."

"Why don't I do a drawing?" Maggie suggested. "I'll show it to my gardener; he is quite knowledgeable about such things."

"That is a wonderful idea," Gabby said brightly. "We could also consult with the Ladies' Botanical Society, if needed. I am a member."

Looking at the ladies' determined faces, Fancy felt a welling of gratitude.

"Thank you," she said sincerely. "I don't know how I would manage without you."

"That is the point of having friends, isn't it?" Tessa's wink was roguish and heart-warming. "None of us have to manage alone."

29

THE NEXT DAY, AS THE CARRIAGE WOUND INTO THE HEART OF Spitalfields, Severin wasn't certain how Fancy had talked him into the current undertaking. Well, that was a lie: he did have *some* inkling. He suspected it had to do with the conversation he and his duchess had shared in bed the night before.

She had been telling him about her day and visits with her new friends whilst simultaneously wending a trail down his body with her lips. She'd apparently enjoyed his prior eve's lesson and wanted to try it again. He'd known, without a doubt, that he was a lucky bastard. Just as she had done something with her tongue that made his hips buck and his hands clench the sheets, she'd asked him for a favor.

"Anything," he'd said hoarsely.

Had she asked him to take down the moon and stars for her, he would have put in his best effort just to have more of her sweet kisses.

After he came down from the scalp-tingling bliss of spending in his wife's mouth (and returned the favor), he'd cuddled her close and asked her what she wanted. She'd requested that he give her and Jonas a tour of his offices. His first inclination had been to deny her, for the sake of her safety and his own sanity. The last thing he needed was Jonas running amok in his manufactory.

"You said I could have anything I wanted," she'd said reasonably. "I'll be safe with you and the half-dozen guards you've assigned to me. I think Jonas would benefit from seeing you at work. He might become less of a rabble-rouser if you gave him something productive to do."

Knight had sincerely doubted that Jonas was capable of producing anything but trouble. Yet seeing Fancy's determination —and the droplet glinting at the corner of her mouth—had softened his perspective. It had hardened another part of him, however. Not wanting to waste time arguing over his brother, he'd given in and gotten down to the important business of making love to his wife until dawn.

Which explained why he was now leading Fancy and Jonas into his offices. Not taking any chances with Fancy's safety, he had ten guards on watch; no one was getting within an inch of his wife. He gave a brief history of the company as they headed up the stairs to the top floors where the weaving took place. Fancy was full of questions and, surprisingly, so was Jonas.

"Why are the looms on the upper floors?" Jonas mopped his brow as they mounted the steps. "Wouldn't it be easier not to have to lug supplies up and down all these flights?"

"A good point," Severin acknowledged. "Weaving, however, depends on light, which is better the higher up one goes."

He led them to the uppermost floor, his lips quirking at Fancy's gasp of awe.

"It's beautiful up here," she exclaimed. "Look at that *view*... and all those looms."

His sense of pride grew as he introduced some of his senior weavers to her and watched her win them over one by one. Fancy looked every inch the duchess in a navy and white striped walking dress, matching feathers in her bonnet. A navy belt with a square gold buckle circled her narrow waist. Her hands were encased in white gloves, a striped reticule that matched her dress dangling from her wrist.

As beautiful as she was, he knew his men weren't just responding to her physical charms. Fancy exuded natural warmth as she asked questions about their craft. The weavers eagerly showed her the basic operations: the laying down of the warp threads, the task of the weaver's assistant who arranged those threads for a specific design, and the use of the shuttle to interlace the weft and warp threads. To the delight of the weavers, Fancy even tried her hand at passing the shuttle. The friendliness in her brown eyes was capable of disarming even the most hardened of men. This came into play in an unexpected way soon after Severin showed his wife and Jonas into his office.

He was pointing out buildings through his window when he heard his secretary's voice outside the door. "You cannot barge in there, Mr. Bodin. His Grace is in a meeting—"

"I don't give a rat's arse who Knighton's meeting with," came the surly reply. "Get out o' my way."

The door swung open with Potts, his secretary, clinging valiantly to it.

"I beg your pardon, Your Grace," Potts sputtered. "I tried to stop him but—"

"I'll handle this," Severin said. "You may go."

Bodin stormed in. He was a stocky, dark-haired fellow who reminded Severin of a bulldog. Bodin had his barrel-chest thrust out, his square-jawed face the essence of belligerence. His gaze veered to Fancy and Jonas, who stood frozen by the window. Severin immediately stepped in front of his wife and brother, his gaze narrowing on his erstwhile employee.

"State your business, Bodin," he said in glacial tones.

"I'm 'ere to discuss the machines you purchased to replace your workers," Bodin barked.

"You had better know your place," Severin said. "Or you will be seeking employ elsewhere."

"I ain't afraid o' you," the weaver taunted. "I've 'ad masters before you, and I'll 'ave masters after. What I won't 'ave is you destroying the livelihoods o' decent working men with damned machines."

"Christ," Severin heard Jonas mutter. "The cove sounds like Eleanor."

Severin clenched his jaw. "If you don't like how I run my business, then you are free to leave."

"Oh, I wouldn't make it that easy for you, Your Grace," Bodin vowed. "If I leave, I'm taking the rest o' the weavers with me. I'll shut you down; not even your bleeding machines can run without men, and after I'm done, I'll see to it that no one works for you."

Severin's nape chilled. Bodin was not the sort to make empty threats. He wouldn't claim he could bring about a walk-out unless he knew he could.

The bloody bastard's been campaigning behind my back. Severin curled his hands. *I ought to pound him to a fare-thee-well.*

"I am sure there is a better solution than that," Fancy's clear voice declared.

Before Severin could stop her, she wriggled around him to face the angry weaver.

"Who the devil are you?" Bodin demanded.

"I'm Fancy Sheridan Knight," she said. "Um, the Duchess of Knighton."

"Seeing as this is men's business, *Your Grace*," Bodin said with an insolence that made Severin tighten his fists, "you'd best leave the talking to me and your 'usband."

"I would, if you were *actually* talking to one another," Fancy said brightly. "But as my da always says, bargaining involves more than flapping your lips. You 'ave to listen as well."

Bodin narrowed his eyes. "'Ow does your sainted father know so much about bargaining, eh?"

"'E's a tinker," Fancy said promptly. "Bartering is 'is livelihood."

"Is this some sort o' jest?" Bodin swung an incredulous glance at Severin. "You expect me to believe that you married a tinker's daughter?"

"You'll show Her Grace the proper respect," Severin snapped.

"I'm sure Mr. Bodin meant no disrespect." Fancy smiled—actually *smiled*—at the bugger. "After all, 'e's just calling me what I am. I ain't ashamed o' my da's trade."

"Nor should you be," Bodin said sternly, crossing his arms over his burly chest. "Working men 'ave no cause to be ashamed o' their 'ard-earned living."

"I couldn't agree more," Fancy said earnestly. "I was brought up to value a good day's work. My da taught me the skills o' 'is trade."

"Good for you, missy—" Bodin frowned and caught himself. "I mean, Your Grace."

"It's all right. I'm still not used to being addressed by my title," Fancy admitted. "For most o' my life, people just called me by my first name."

"Fancy—" Severin said in a warning tone.

"See?" she said cheerfully to Bodin.

"Fancy's a fine name," the weaver said. "And it's a breath o' fresh air to meet a lady who doesn't put on airs."

"Putting on airs is 'arder than you think," Fancy confided. "I'm trying to learn 'ow to do it."

"I prefer 'onesty to uppity manners. My wife Meg is as blunt as a 'ammer, and I like it that way." After a pause, he added, "As it 'appens, Meg's pa is a tinker."

"No! Really?" Fancy exclaimed. "Does 'er pa travel in the countryside? Maybe 'e knows my da, Milton Sheridan?"

"My father-in-law is based in London. Couldn't say one way or another whether 'e's acquainted with your family, ma'am." Bodin cleared his throat. "Now as much as I've enjoyed talking to you, I've business to discuss with your 'usband—"

"Important business, I know," Fancy said, nodding. "Knight 'as told me all about it."

"'As 'e now?" Bodin raised his heavy brows. "What did 'is lordship 'ave to say on the matter?"

This had gone far enough. Too far already, by Severin's reckoning. When he looked at Fancy, however, he saw the imploring look in her eyes.

Trust me, she seemed to be saying. *You wanted to be a team, remember?*

He found he couldn't bring himself to put a stop to her stratagem. He wanted to see where she meant to take things and was prepared to jump in with both fists if Bodin showed her the slightest insult. For once, however, the weaver's belligerence seemed tempered by what Severin was beginning to recognize as...respect.

"Knight said you were a man o' principle," Fancy was saying.

Bodin snorted. "Pull my other leg, ma'am. It's shorter."

"It's true. My 'usband said you truly believe that you're doing the right thing by your fellow workers, and I believe 'e admires you for it. Because 'e wants the same thing."

"If that were true, 'e 'as a peculiar way o' showing it. 'E's building machines in secret at one o' 'is warehouses to replace us weavers," Bodin accused.

"I am *testing* the machines," Severin corrected. "Until I know for certain that they will improve productivity, I see no need to disclose my actions to the competition."

"You see? 'E's not keeping a secret, merely trying to gain a competitive edge." Fancy's tone was calming. "An edge that will 'elp preserve the jobs o' 'is workers."

"Workers 'e means to replace with machines," Bodin shot back.

"Machines can't run themselves, can they?" she asked in a sensible tone. "Men will still be needed. Now their work might be changing, but it'll be work just the same. As my da always says, the key to tinkering ain't about skills: it's about the ability to *adapt* those skills to any situation."

"'Ow are weavers supposed to adapt to these bloody modern contraptions?"

Although Bodin's expression remained suspicious, he sounded less hostile. Could it be that the weaver was actually *listening* for once? Then Severin was flummoxed to realize that he, himself, was picking up something new: worry threaded the other's tone. Perhaps it had always been there, hidden beneath that bellicosity.

Severin's own anger began to wane as he realized Bodin was awaiting an answer.

"I'll provide training," he said curtly. "Once I verify that the machines are, indeed, of use."

Bodin squared his shoulders. "You'll guarantee that no weaver will lose 'is livelihood?"

"I make no guarantees. But any man who is willing to learn the new technology will have a chance to continue working for me. Change is going to happen, whether or not you, or I, like it," Severin said. "Factories in other countries are modernizing, producing silk and other fabrics in greater quantities and cheaper prices. If we don't adapt and embrace the new technology, our entire industry will die, and there will be no jobs of any kind for weavers, *that* I can guarantee you."

Bodin's jaw worked, but he said nothing.

"So you see, sir, you and Knight are fighting on the same side." Fancy's tone was soft and persuasive, Severin noted with amusement, even as she went in for the kill. "The futures o' the weavers depend on making this new technology work. And that would go a lot easier if you and Knight could band together, convince the other men that this is the path to the future."

She gave Severin a meaningful look. Taking her cue, he extended his hand.

"What say you, Bodin? Shall we work together?" he asked.

Bodin stared at the hand offered to him and made no move to

take it. Severin told himself that he'd expected this. Nothing in life came easy, and if a bloodbath was what Bodin wanted, then that was what he would get.

Severin began to withdraw his hand, only to find it grasped in a beefy grip.

"All right, Your Grace," Bodin said. "We'll give the machine a shot."

Hiding his surprise, Severin returned the crushing handshake. "I am glad to hear it."

Fancy beamed at both of them. "So am I."

"It was a pleasure meeting you, Your Grace," Bodin said. "My Meg will be tickled when I tell 'er I met another tinker's daughter."

"I'd like to meet Mrs. Bodin," Fancy said warmly. "Would she come by for tea one afternoon?"

"I'm sure she'd enjoy that." With gruff admiration, the weaver added, "Ain't often she gets invited to tea by a true lady."

30

A COUPLE EVENINGS LATER, FANCY WAITED ANXIOUSLY TO BE announced at Maggie's ball. She and Knight were standing in the receiving line that led into the ballroom; Esther, Jonas, and Cecily were behind them. Peering into the glittering sea, Fancy felt her heart flip-flop like a fish out of water. She nervously ran her gloved hands over the skirts of her new wine-colored gown.

"Stop fidgeting," Knight said in an undertone. "You will do fine."

"I'm not fidgeting," Fancy whispered back. "I was straightening my dress."

"I can see you tapping your slipper from here," Cecily said from behind her.

There was no heat in Cecily's voice, however. When Fancy turned to look at Knight's sister, she saw that the girl wasn't sulking. In fact, Cecily's face glowed with excitement unobscured by any cosmetic. Learning from wily Aunt Esther, Fancy had made Cecily's invitation to Maggie's ball conditional upon two things: the girl had to forgo the face paint and allow Fancy to have the final say on her gown.

Although Cecily had pouted, she'd agreed to the terms. She was a natural beauty, with her tawny hair in dangling ringlets, her green eyes sparkling as she took in the gaiety of the ball. She wore a lilac satin ballgown that showed off her slender figure yet remained modest, thanks to the demure ruffle Fancy had sewn to the neckline. Cecily had been over the moon when she'd learned Fancy had secured her an appointment with Madame Rousseau to have new dresses made.

"You have no reason to be nervous, Fancy," Jonas drawled.

He had Cecily on one arm, Aunt Esther on the other, and looked quite dashing in his formal evening wear. Fancy had convinced him to trim his hair, and he'd blushed when she told him the ladies would find him even more handsome now that they could see his eyes.

"If you can defend Knighton against an angry weaver," he added, "then surely you can take on the *beau monde*."

Fancy darted a glance at Knight and was relieved to see amusement in his eyes. She'd been worried that she'd overstepped yesterday during the encounter with Mr. Bodin. When she'd fretted about it last night, Knight had reassured her that he valued her help. Then he'd expressed his appreciation in another way. A way that made her toes curl in her slippers just thinking about it now.

As if he had gleaned her thoughts, Knight's gaze heated.

"What a lucky fellow I am," he said softly. "To have a duchess who is not only beautiful but an invaluable helpmate as well. Now, relax, my sweet." He brought her gloved hand to his lips. "Tonight, we Knightons will take the *ton* by storm."

Smiling tremulously, she nodded.

"Not the kind that leaves a trail of destruction in its wake, one hopes," Aunt Esther said.

The lady's flawless delivery of the witticism dispelled Fancy's tension.

She was giggling, and Knight's eyes were gleaming with

laughter when the butler announced, "The Duke and Duchess of Knighton!"

∼

As Severin watched his wife whirl around the dance floor with their host, the Duke of Ranelagh and Somerville, pride inflated his chest.

Fancy's debut in Society was a success. He didn't know how he could have doubted her. Through her hard work and ingenuity, she had transformed herself from a tinker's daughter into the belle of the ball.

She looked breathtaking in a gown of claret velvet that matched her lips and the ruby ring he'd given her. The rich shade suited her coloring, and Madame Rousseau had earned every penny of her hefty bill with the design of the gown. The off-the-shoulder bodice showcased Fancy's smooth shoulders, accentuating the fullness of her bosom and slenderness of her waist. The sleeves and hem of the domed skirts had been artfully adorned with vibrant silk flowers.

With a touch of whimsy, Severin thought that his wife could be a storybook faerie queen cavorting with mortals for the eve. As she laughed at something her partner said, he felt a tug of jealousy. Not because he questioned Fancy's fidelity or that of the Duke of Ranelagh and Somerville, whose devotion to his own beautiful duchess was the stuff of legend. No, Severin was jealous simply because he wanted his wife—all of her, even her laughter—to himself.

The realization caused a rattling of a dark cage inside him. He flashed to the teetering bag of bricks, the smashed rubble, how fragile and stricken Fancy had looked. He saw his own mama, blade in hand, her eyes unrecognizable. And he felt the icy burn of the scar, a reminder that everything that mattered could be taken away in an instant.

"Knighton, I did not expect to see you here," came the familiar, bell-like tones.

Seeing Imogen gliding toward him, he exhaled, slamming the lid on chaos.

"Good evening, Lady Cardiff." He bowed politely over her hand.

Imogen carried herself with the confidence of a woman who knows that she will stand out in any room she enters. She was as perfect as an oil painting. Her rose-gold hair was artfully twisted upon her head, her lissome figure draped in ice-blue silk. The collar of sapphires circling her slender neck was no match for her eyes.

She smiled at him. "Your siblings are doing well this eve."

"They are, aren't they?" He looked out into the ballroom. "The credit goes to my wife."

Cecily, he saw, was taking a turn around the dance floor with a respectable lord, Aunt Esther watching the pair with eagle eyes. Jonas was fetching lemonade for a debutante. And Fancy...he frowned. She had been asked to dance again, this time by a handsome buck he did not know.

"Your duchess is making quite the splash. That is Lord Egerton dancing with her," Imogen said. "He is newly returned from Italy, where he is studying to be a sculptor, I believe."

Sculptor, is he? Severin narrowed his eyes as Egerton pulled Fancy closer than necessary during a spin. *If the bastard wants to keep his hands, then he had better keep them off my wife.*

"He has a reputation for being a rake, but I shouldn't worry. Lady Knighton strikes me as a lady who can take care of herself."

Hearing the light rebuff in Imogen's words, Severin felt his neck heat. Was his possessiveness obvious? Did he look like a fool?

"I am not worried," he said brusquely.

"Of course not. I apologize for misspeaking."

Hearing the quiver in Imogen's voice, he cursed himself

inwardly. He thought back to the hours she'd spent teaching him how to be a gentleman, what a good friend she had been to him when he had had no others. It wasn't her fault that he was distracted. That he was a jealous fool who wanted to punch any man who danced with his wife.

"You said nothing wrong." He softened his tone. "Did I mention how lovely you look tonight?"

"You think so?" Her eyes shone. "Cardiff didn't like my gown. He prefers darker colors, but you have always liked me in the lighter shades. Remember the gown I wore to my debut? You told me I looked like an angel."

Discomfort tread up Severin's spine. "That was a long time ago."

"Forever, it seems," she said wistfully. "And yet also like yesterday...at least for me."

Guilt constricted his chest. He felt suddenly as if a chasm had opened between the past and the present, and he had a foothold in each. He struggled to maintain his balance, to not fall into the dark abyss. All he knew was that standing here, talking with Imogen, he didn't feel...right.

He scanned the room for Fancy. She'd left the dance floor and was standing with a circle of ladies—the hostess and the wives of Kent and Garrity. His wife was laughing, bright as a flame in her red gown, and he had the urge to warm himself by her fire.

He turned to Imogen. "I must speak with some friends. Shall I return you to your husband?"

"Cardiff isn't here," she said. "That is for the better."

The look that flashed through Imogen's eyes made him frown. Before he could ask her what she meant, she drew her shoulders back.

"I shan't keep you from your friends, Knighton," she said stiffly. "Good evening."

She walked away.

Fancy laughed with her friends even though she had no idea what they were saying.

The evening had started with such triumph. She had managed to enter the ballroom with dignity and grace...at least, she hadn't fallen on her face as she'd feared. Jonas and Cecily were behaving. Knight had partnered Fancy in a waltz, the first time they'd danced together. He was a masterful leader, and she'd floated in his arms, cherishing every moment of it.

Although she would have been content to dance the night away in her husband's arms, she'd learned enough from Aunt Esther to know that a fashionable couple did not live in each other's pockets. Her dance card had filled with astonishing quickness, and she'd obligingly twirled around the floor with a number of partners.

After the last dance had ended, she'd been claimed by Tessa, Gabby, and Maggie. The ladies were delightful company as usual, and while chatting and sipping champagne with them, she'd looked around the room for Knight. It had taken her awhile to find him because he'd been standing half-hidden by some potted palms...with Imogen.

Fancy's pleasure in the evening had faded as she saw, between the fronds, her husband lean his head down to catch something Imogen was saying. With a sickening pang of jealousy, she'd had to confront what a perfect picture they made. Imogen was breathtaking in an icy blue gown that showcased her willowy figure. Knight, tall and darkly handsome in his elegant evening wear, was her natural foil.

Heart hammering, Fancy had made herself look away. She'd chided herself for being silly, a jealous fishwife. Knight had never lied about his past with Imogen; their history was complicated. And if the two were to meet up in public, of course they wouldn't ignore one another. It made sense that they would have a chat as old friends.

"Fancy, is something the matter?"

Her gaze flew to Maggie, who was regarding her with concerned green eyes.

"N-no," she stammered. "I was just, um, woolgathering."

"You are a bit flushed." Maggie's brow pleated. "Is it too stuffy in here? I could have the windows opened."

"No, I'm fine," Fancy said quickly.

"I don't think it's the room temperature that has her blood boiling," Tessa said.

Fancy's face heated at the shrewd observation. Tessa wasn't the Duchess of Covent Garden for nothing. The lady had a sharp mind and blunt tongue to go with her generous heart.

"What is it then?" Gabby asked, her blue eyes confused.

"Over by the potted palms," Tessa muttered. "Well, don't all look *at once*. He'll see you looking, and Fancy wouldn't want that."

Taking turns, Gabby and Maggie peered over at Knight and Imogen before quickly turning back to the group.

"Who is she?" Gabby asked in a hushed voice.

"Lady Imogen Cardiff," Maggie said. "I don't know her well. Her husband is an acquaintance of Ransom's."

"She and Knight knew each other as children." Fancy spoke up before her friends could speculate any further. "They're just old friends."

"Then why do you look like a puppy that just got kicked?" Tessa asked.

"Fancy doesn't look like a puppy." Gabby paused, her auburn brows knitting. "Well, except around the eyes, but I mean that as the greatest compliment. Your eyes are ever so soulful, Fancy."

"Um, thank you." Swallowing, Fancy confided, "I just wish I was as elegant as Lady Cardiff."

"She's not *that* elegant," Tessa said in the way of a loyal friend. "And you're prettier."

"Sometimes it is not just about *being* pretty though, is it?" Gabby's eyes rounded with sympathy. "It's about *feeling* like you are. It took me a long time to feel confident in my looks...and in myself."

Fancy stared at the redhead, who looked ravishing in a violet taffeta gown that showed off her ample curves. "But you're so lovely."

"So are you," Gabby returned. "But it doesn't mean anything unless you *feel* your own worth."

"If a lady doesn't feel beautiful," Tessa put in, "then I blame the husband."

"Knight is the most considerate of husbands," Fancy protested.

"Drawing room considerate?" Tessa raised her brows. "Or bedchamber considerate?"

"Tessa," Gabby said, giggling. "That's wicked. You'll shock poor Fancy."

"I'm not shocked," Fancy said, although her cheeks throbbed with heat. "He's considerate...um, everywhere."

"Then you have nothing to worry about," Tessa declared.

"I second that notion, and I can do that without inquiring about the, ahem, rooms of your marriage." Maggie leaned forward, her smile conspiratorial. "Knighton might be conversing with Lady Cardiff, but he has been secretly looking your way this entire time."

"Truly?" Fancy breathed.

"Not only is he *looking* your way, now he's headed here," Tessa said in an urgent rush. "We cannot let him know we were talking about him. Quick, ladies, *laugh*."

Thus, Fancy found herself joining in, with no idea what she was laughing at.

"Good evening, ladies." Knight's deep voice cut in. "May I join the loveliest and merriest group at the ball?"

"Of course you may, Your Grace," Maggie said with a smile.

Knight picked up Fancy's hand, casually kissing the gloved knuckles. "Care to share the source of your hilarity, sweeting?"

Fancy stammered, "W-we were, um, just laughing over...over..."

Her brain froze; she was a terrible liar.

"Puppies," Gabby blurted.

Knight tilted his head quizzically. "What is so amusing about puppies, Mrs. Garrity?"

"Oh, you know, they're round and, um, ever so soft...and have such big, soulful eyes. Some have the cutest spots, too," Gabby babbled, her face as red as her hair.

Clearly, she was no better at lying than Fancy was.

"I...see," Knight said, giving her a strange look.

Luckily, the other husbands materialized at their wives' sides, providing a welcome distraction. Ransom, a dashing fellow with a short beard and mustache, apologized to the group, saying that he had a dancing emergency...and whisked his duchess off to the dance floor.

"I saw you ladies laughing uproariously," Mr. Kent said to Tessa. "Care to share, sprite?"

"We were just gossiping, that's all," Tessa said blithely.

"I thought you were talking about puppies?" Knight lifted his brows.

"Amongst other topics, none of which were of consequence," Tessa evaded deftly. "Gentlemen, now that we have you here, how goes the investigation of Fancy's origins?"

Fancy had to hand it to Tessa: the lady knew how to take a situation in hand.

Mr. Garrity spoke first. "My men have located three Charleys who worked the streets of St. James's. One recalled that a child went missing from a well-to-do merchant around the time in question, but the child was a boy."

"We've had disappointing results in St. George Hanover Square," Mr. Kent said, his bespectacled gaze somber. "Finding those Charleys takes leg work. When we do find them, I cannot tell if their reporting is reliable or if they are making up a story to get some coin."

"That is because you're honest, darling," his wife said. "I can always tell when someone is lying."

"Takes one to know one?" Mr. Kent said dryly. "Should I be worried?"

She batted her eyelashes at him. "I would never lie to you, of course."

Fancy had to giggle at Mr. Kent's long-suffering look.

Lips twitching, Knight said, "The Charleys we located in Piccadilly didn't recall anything useful either. On the bright side, my guards have been keeping a close watch, and they've seen nothing suspicious and no signs of threat to Fancy."

"That is good news," Mr. Kent said. "And I also spoke with my brother Ambrose. He's consulting with his Bow Street Runner contacts, and I should hear back from him soon."

"Maggie told us her gardener identified the flower on Fancy's christening gown," Tessa said. "He thinks it is a species of rhododendron, due to the shape of the petals and number of stamen."

"Interesting, but not enough to lead us anywhere," Mr. Garrity said. "We'll keep interrogating the Charleys. At present, however, I believe I will claim my wife for this waltz."

He held his arm out to Gabby, who gazed dreamily at him as they headed to the dance floor.

"Chérie?" Knight's eyes smiled at Fancy, and he was so handsome that her heart hurt. "May I have the pleasure of a second waltz?"

She nodded mutely and took his arm.

Behind her, she heard Mr. Kent say, "Well, my dear, if you can't beat them..."

"Let's join them," his wife replied with a laugh.

31

Leaving Maggie and Ransom's ball that night, Fancy felt like she was floating on air. The waltz still played in her head, and she hummed along as they exited the gracious townhouse with Jonas, Cecily, and Aunt Esther.

"Did you enjoy the evening, sweeting?" Knight asked.

"I did," she said. "Especially dancing with you."

"The pleasure was mine." His eyes soft as smoke, he said, "Wait here. I'll see where our carriage is."

Leaving her and their family in the care of guards, he headed out into the foggy cobblestone street crammed with vehicles.

"That went passably well I thought," Aunt Esther remarked.

From Aunt Esther, that was praise indeed.

"Yes, it was—" Fancy began.

"Your Highness," an urgent voice said. "I must speak to you."

Confused, Fancy turned in the direction of the raspy female voice. A woman stood several yards away beneath a streetlamp. The yellow light limned her cloaked figure, her loose and scraggly hair, the deep fissures age had worn into her face. Her deep-set eyes had a wild glow.

Before Fancy could react, the guards closed ranks around her.

"Stay back, Your Grace. We'll 'andle this," one said.

Another addressed the woman. "Keep your distance, mort."

"You must listen to me, Your Highness..." The woman advanced.

"Stay back," one of the guards warned, drawing his pistol.

"I mean no harm—"

The woman never finished her sentence for a carriage stopped beside her, a group of men in dark coats alighting and descending upon her like a flock of vultures. They circled her, blocking her from Fancy's view. The woman screamed and then...nothing.

"Fancy!" Knight's voice, his pounding footsteps. He appeared at her side, his breaths harsh, his eyes blazing. "Are you all right?"

"I-I'm fine." Numbly, Fancy realized that her teeth were chattering. "A w-woman came out of nowhere. The g-guards protected me."

"Stay with Her Grace," Knight told the guards grimly. "I'll see what this is about."

She grabbed his arm. "Be careful—"

"I'll be right back, sweeting. Stay here."

He strode off toward the huddle of dark coats. Fancy watched, pulse racing, as he spoke with the group's leader, a short, thin man wearing a dark hat. After a few moments, the men stepped aside for Knight to have a look at the woman. Fancy's chest clenched when she glimpsed the piteous figure slumped like a ragdoll against the lamppost.

Her thoughts whirled. *Why would that woman want to hurt me? What is going on?*

A wagon stopped next to Knight and the gathered group. The cabin was enclosed, with bars over the windows, the kind of conveyance used to transport criminals and madmen. The back of the cabin opened, more men in black coats descending. They hefted the unconscious woman into the wagon as if she were a sack of coal and shut the door.

Knight exchanged a few words with the leader before the

latter joined the driver on the perch of the wagon, and the vehicle rattled off into the night.

"What was that about?" Fancy blurted the instant Knight returned.

"We'll talk in the carriage," he said.

They piled into their conveyance, ladies on one side, gentlemen on the other, and Knight shared what he learned. The man he'd been talking to was Dr. Karl Erlenmeyer, an Austrian physician specializing in mental disease. Dr. Erlenmeyer ran Brookfield Asylum, a private institute for the insane located in Highgate. The woman who'd accosted Fancy was one of his patients.

"Her name is Anna Smith," Knight said in a cold, detached voice. "According to Dr. Erlenmeyer, she was committed to the madhouse because of a long history of delusions. Evidently, she believes that she is a spy and has a history of attacking strangers whom she believes she's been sent on a mission to harm."

"Heavens," Aunt Esther said faintly.

With a shiver, Fancy remembered the woman's greeting. "She called me *Your Highness*."

"It is likely Miss Smith thinks you are royalty she's been sent to assassinate." Passing lights and shadows waved over Knight's stark features. "Dr. Erlenmeyer said that the last time that happened, Miss Smith assaulted a lady walking down the street... with an axe."

"Bloody hell," Jonas said, his eyes wide.

"Miss Smith escaped from the madhouse a week ago, and Dr. Erlenmeyer and his men have been searching for her. They glimpsed her near Berkeley Square five days ago, but she lost them."

"That was the day of the falling bricks." Fancy's throat cinched. "Miss Smith was in the area?"

Jaw taut, Knight nodded. "She's likely the one behind the 'accident'."

"But why would she target me?" Fancy asked.

"Dr. Erlenmeyer says there's no rhyme or reason to it. The last time Miss Smith escaped, she began stalking a lady she spotted at a milliner's. She probably saw you when you were out shopping—the doctor and his men said she migrates to Bond Street—and the voices in her head told her you were her next victim."

"To think, that wretched woman may have been spying on us when we were at Madame Rousseau's." Shuddering, Aunt Esther gave Fancy's hand a pat. "At least this dreadful business is over. It is, isn't it, Knighton?"

"I believe so," he said quietly.

The truth struck Fancy. "Then the danger…it had nothing to do with my past?"

"It would seem that the attacks were unrelated to your origins," Knight confirmed. "You were just a victim of bad luck, attracting the notice of a madwoman."

She expelled a breath. "I don't know whether or not to feel relieved."

"I, for one, am definitely relieved that the threat is over," Aunt Esther declared. "We will once again be able to circulate in Society without murder and mayhem hanging over our heads."

"Does that mean we can stop being hermits?" Cecily asked brightly.

"Not until I pay a visit to Dr. Erlenmeyer tomorrow," Knight said in flat tones. "I will not rest easy until I know that Anna Smith is securely confined and no longer poses a threat to my wife or my family."

∾

The next morning, Severin travelled to Brookfield Asylum. Fancy had wanted to come, but he had drawn the line at his wife visiting the woman who'd tried to kill her. He refused to expose Fancy to such darkness...and didn't want her there when he had to confront his demons.

For he was no stranger to madhouses. From the ages of fourteen to twenty, he'd visited his *maman* in Bedlam. He knew what to expect and braced himself.

In some ways, Brookfield was superior to Bedlam. Situated on the bucolic outskirts of Highgate, a village just north of London, the asylum was smaller, cleaner, the manicured grounds surrounded by a tall stone wall that managed to look decorative even though its function was to keep the residents in. The main building was flanked by two smaller wings, the elegant architecture marred by the barred windows and padlocked doors. As Severin passed through the front entrance, he heard a pitiful wail that knotted his stomach.

Dr. Erlenmeyer was waiting for him. The daylight revealed the milky translucence of the Austrian doctor's skin, the tracery of veins beneath. His sandy hair was combed in thin lines over his balding pate, and his pale blue eyes were bloodshot in his narrow face. The hand he extended to shake Severin's was hairless and smooth.

"Welcome to Brookfield, Your Grace," Erlenmeyer said. "It was unnecessary, however, for you to make the trip. I assure you that I have Miss Smith well in hand."

"Nonetheless, I would like to see for myself," Severin said.

"Follow me, then."

Erlenmeyer led the way through doors that he unlocked with a key. Inside the ward, rooms sprung from an arterial corridor, each containing two cots rather than the ten or more that had been crammed into the dungeon Severin's *maman* had occupied in Bedlam. Yet both madhouses shared a particular smell: boiled food mingled with caustic lye and urine. The odor of misery seeped from the brick and mortar, the very bones of a prison for the mad.

They arrived at a small, spartan cell. Severin looked at the woman lying on the single cot. The manacle on her ankle kept her chained to the bed. She was wearing a white jacket with ties that bound her arms to her chest; she looked like one of the mummies on display at the British Museum. Her eyes were lifeless, her tongue lolling and saliva trickling out of her mouth.

Severin couldn't stop the flood of memories: his own mother bound in similar restraints. Her glassy eyes, rambling words, and frothing obscenities. Even worse had been her flashes of lucidity, when suffering had bled over her worn features.

Severin, forgive me. I didn't mean to hurt you, she'd wept.

Pain raked his insides. He had told her time and again that he'd forgiven her—that he knew she hadn't meant to attack him. Bleeding in the street, he had begged the constables not to take her away. In the end, he was the one who had failed her. He hadn't been able to ease her anguish or get her out of Bedlam...until it was too late.

She had died in that hellhole, alone and afraid.

"As you can see, Miss Smith poses no risk," Erlenmeyer said brusquely.

Concentrate, Severin told himself.

Tamping down the swirling chaos, he asked, "How did she come into your care?"

"After her first attack on an unwitting victim, she was apprehended and found insane," Erlenmeyer said in precise accents. "As I have experience working with violent patients, it was deemed that she would benefit from my care. My hospital receives funding from generous benefactors to carry out its good works, even for destitute lunatics like Miss Smith."

"By good works, you mean you keep her chained and drugged," Severin said.

"We have to keep Miss Smith sedated." Erlenmeyer drew himself up, his tone defensive. "She is otherwise a danger to herself and others. There is no other way, Your Grace."

Severin couldn't stem his antipathy toward the mad-doctor

even though he knew it wasn't fair. The man was doing his job. Erlenmeyer had nothing to do with the way Severin's *maman* had been treated in Bedlam, the bruises and cigar burns Severin had found on her...the dried blood on her thighs.

Darkness welled. Years of self-discipline allowed him to shove back the rage of powerlessness before it swamped him. He faced the mad-doctor with the polished control of a gentleman—a duke. Although he knew that his past colored his perception of Erlenmeyer, his instincts told him that something wasn't right with this bloodless fellow.

"For my wife's safety, Miss Smith must be kept confined here at the asylum," Severin said. "I will not have it done in an inhumane fashion, however. See that she has regular meals and a chance to take air in the garden daily. She will have a female attendant with her at all times. If you do not have one, hire one, and send the bill to me."

"Very good, Your Grace," Erlenmeyer said. "Will there be anything else?"

The mad-doctor's apparent deference did not hide the resentful glint in his eyes. He didn't like having his authority questioned, which was too bloody bad. Severin couldn't shake his feeling of suspicion. Recalling that Harry Kent's older brother Ambrose was a renowned investigator, he decided to retain the services of the senior Kent forthwith to make enquiries into Erlenmeyer's past.

"I will expect weekly reports on Miss Smith's treatment," Severin said coldly. "If anything happens, I want to be the first to know. And if Miss Smith manages to escape again...you will have to answer to me."

32

ALTHOUGH THE THREAT TO HER LIFE HAD ENDED, FANCY FOUND herself more worried than ever. This time her concern was over the state of her marriage. Knight was behaving strangely, and she feared she knew the reason why. Since the attack by Anna Smith two nights ago, Knight had retreated into himself. He was polite, speaking when spoken to, his gaze cool and remote. To Fancy, he seemed to be going through the motions, and she had asked him if he was all right.

Predictably his answer had been, "I am fine."

Then why was he avoiding her?

The night of the attack, Knight had come to her bed, and they'd both fallen into an exhausted sleep. When she woke up, he was gone; there was no affectionate note to tell her where, although she knew he had gone to see Anna Smith at the asylum. Perhaps he hadn't wanted to rouse Fancy's anxieties by reminding her of the sad and terrifying affair. The next evening, he had stayed late at work. She had fallen asleep before he returned, and when she'd knocked on his door in the morning, he had already left.

The pattern was becoming undeniable.

Until two nights ago, their intimacy had been growing day by day. Fancy could only think of one thing that could have brought on Knight's brooding mood—the same thing that had brought it on the time before: Imogen.

Fancy tried to battle her insecurities, remembering what Maggie had said about Knight watching *her* whilst talking to the other woman, but her doubts proliferated like weeds. Could she ever replace the angelic Imogen in Knight's affections? Could she win her husband's heart? Would he ever want to kiss her and only her?

Fancy didn't know the answers. What she *did* know was that she loved her husband. She couldn't allow him to build a wall—or close the door—between them when they'd been making such good progress. Thus, that evening, she nursed a pot of tea and waited up for Knight.

At half-past midnight, she heard him enter his chamber. He had a murmured exchange with Verney, followed by the sounds of the valet readying him for bed. Hearing Verney leave, Fancy pounced on the opportunity and knocked on the door. Her pulse thrummed as footsteps sounded on the other side.

The barrier opened, revealing Knight. He was ready for bed. The vee of his dressing gown showed the hard, hair-dusted contours of his chest, his muscular calves bulging below the hem. The fact that he was obviously naked beneath his robe caused a flutter between her legs to accompany the one in her heart.

"Yes, sweeting?" He gave her an inquiring look. "Do you need something?"

You, she thought in frustration. *Why are you acting differently? Did one look from Imogen destroy all the progress we've made?*

His polite tone and veiled gaze made her afraid of the answers. She flashed back to the perfection of Knight and Imogen beneath the potted palm. Imogen, slender, beautiful, and breathtakingly fragile staring up at Knight with her heaven-blue eyes. And Knight, tall, dark, and handsome, bending to murmur a reply. It could be the perfect scene from a faerie tale—except the prince was with the wrong princess.

Knight's mine, Fancy thought with a surge of possessiveness. *He lives with me, sleeps with me, and he is blooming well going to love* me.

"Fancy? Are you all right?"

Seeing Knight's quizzical expression, she summoned her courage.

"I was wondering if you would like company tonight," she said.

Her breath held as his brows drew together. He'd told her once that he would always welcome her in his bedchamber; had he lied? Had his desire for her faded after seeing Imogen?

Clearing his throat, he stepped aside. "Yes, of course. Come in."

Exhaling, she entered his bedchamber. His gaze grew heavy-lidded as it roamed over her, building her confidence. She was wearing another of Madame Rousseau's creations, this bedtime set the most daring of them all. The cherry satin peignoir and negligee were cut to cling to her curves. The neckline plunged in a deep vee and was covered in scandalous black lace, which gave a peekaboo view of her breasts.

She might not possess Lady Cardiff's cool, fair beauty, but she had her own attractions. She knew Knight liked her breasts because he'd told her repeatedly as well as shown it. Determination unfurled in her to stake her claim on her husband…and she knew exactly how to do it.

Trying her best to be seductive and sophisticated, she walked over to his bed, giving her hips an extra wriggle. Her attempt to be a temptress was somewhat marred by the fact that she wasn't tall enough to slide sinuously onto the bed. She had to give an inelegant little hop to boost herself up, her bottom bouncing when it hit the mattress.

Recovering, she leaned back in what she hoped was a languid pose, giving Knight a come-hither look. She felt a charge of power when he prowled toward her. He towered over her like a stern yet sensual god, silver lightning in his eyes. His smoldering intensity fed the reckless beat in her blood, as did the prominent bulge at the front of his robe.

"What are you up to, sweeting?" he said.

"I wanted to show you my new negligee." She fluttered her lashes. "Do you like it?"

She let the peignoir slip off her shoulders, revealing the black straps of her negligee beneath.

His nostrils quivered like those of a stallion scenting its mate. "Take off the peignoir, and I'll decide."

She reached for the belt of her robe, his gaze tracking her movements. Deciding to give him a show, she untied the satin cord with slow teasing movements. She wiggled her shoulders to ease the satin down her arms, knowing that the action would also jiggle her breasts.

Her husband's gaze was trained on those mounds, straining against the net of black lace. His eyes moved upward, to her chemise's black satin straps, tied in a bow on each shoulder.

"What do you think?" she asked in the sultriest voice she could muster.

He fingered the bow on her left shoulder, the lazy caress scattering sparks over her skin.

"You look like a present waiting to be unwrapped," he murmured.

Feeling very daring, she said, "I'm *your* present."

And you're mine. You're my husband, my prince.

"Lucky me."

He tugged on the bow. It unraveled at his touch; that side of her bodice, no longer anchored, slipped downward, catching at her waist. His pupils darkened, and he repeated the action on the other side. It took all her courage to remain as she was, her palms planted on the mattress, letting him look his fill of her bare, heaving breasts. The stiff peaks strained beneath his hungry gaze.

Her heart pounded as he trailed a finger from her chin to her throat, downward to her collarbone, the surging slope of her right breast. He circled the red tip, catching it between finger and thumb. When he gave the ripe berry a light pinch, juice trickled from her pussy.

"Such pretty tits," he said in a casual tone that made her even wetter. "I'm going to enjoy licking them while you ride my cock."

Sweet Jaysus, yes.

Triumph filled her as she saw the need in him take over. His eyes were no longer cool or remote; ravening appetite spread like ink through those grey depths. He removed his dressing gown, and a breath puffed from her at the extent of his arousal.

She had roused the beast, all right.

His long, thick cock was primed for mating. The burgeoned tip pointed to her the way a hound points to its prey. Her body responded with a primal clench. Hot longing rushed beneath her skin.

He mounted the bed, sitting against the headboard. He had a king's arrogance with his knees cocked, one hand stroking his majestic shaft. He crooked his finger; with trembling anticipation, she crawled over the mattress toward him.

"Climb on, sweetheart," he said.

She did so with an eagerness that she couldn't quite contain. Her knees braced his thick thighs, and she placed her hands on his shoulders, the hard muscles bulging beneath her touch. When he rubbed his blunt dome against her slick petals, a needy whimper left her.

"You're nice and wet, ready for my cock," he purred. "This is what you wanted, isn't it?"

She bit her lip as his wide head breached her opening. She wanted it, yes, the wild pleasure. But she wanted more too. Fear held her back from saying what was in her heart. His brooding withdrawal had shaken her self-confidence, and she would have to work up to baring her soul.

She settled for, "I want you, Knight."

Savage satisfaction lit his eyes. "Then take me."

He gripped her satin-clad hips, pushing her onto his cock at the same time that he thrust upward. The hard penetration stole her breath, her senses, all her awareness focused on the thick pole drilling upward into her center. Her spine arched at the fullness, but he didn't give her time to adjust. Grunting, he wrenched her along his shaft, making her take him deeper and deeper, his virile presence setting off tremors deep in her womb.

"Ride me until you come," he rasped. "I want to feel your pussy milking my prick."

Primal need unspooled her inhibitions. She abandoned herself to the carnal heat, her bottom smacking against her mate's thighs as she rode his cock, chasing the wild finish. With a growl of approval, he cupped her breasts, teasing them with his lips and fingers. When he took a tip deep into his mouth, her intimate muscles clenched on his hardness. He sucked harder, and she moaned, grinding against him, impaling herself on his meaty shaft.

"Christ, yes," he gritted out. "You're almost there. Spend on my cock."

She looked into his face; in that moment of raw pleasure, he was open to her, his eyes burning with desire…and *love*. The power of their connection surged through her. Longing burst in her heart, breaking the dam of her control.

"I love you," she gasped and leaned in to kiss him.

The next instant, she was moving through the air. She found herself no longer on his lap, but on her hands and knees facing the other direction. Before she could make sense of what had happened, he thrust into her from behind, with a force that shoved a surprised cry from her throat.

She tried to look at him, but he planted his palm on the middle of her back, pressing her down against the mattress. With his other hand, he held her bottom high for his pounding. She felt his urgency and dark need as he slaked his lust upon her, as he tupped her wordlessly.

Without returning her declaration of love.

Pain and pleasure knifed her chest. Eyes stinging, she fought against her rising orgasm, but he shoved his hand around her hip, his knowing fingers searching out the heart of her desire. He rubbed the throbbing bud, and a humiliating climax broke. She came and came, and he groaned, his hips pummeling her bottom with even greater power. His fingers held her hips in a bruising grip as he filled her with his copious heat.

For long moments, neither of them moved. His harsh breaths filtered through the pounding in her ears. He withdrew, and the wet rush that leaked down her leg jolted her out of paralysis. She scurried off the bed, yanking the negligee he hadn't bothered to remove into place. Sitting on the edge of the mattress, his chest damp and heaving, his cock still hard and glistening, Knight looked at her—and the shield in his eyes chilled her to the core.

"I think...I think I'll sleep in my own room," she said through serrated breaths.

He'd never looked more foreboding, his expression starker.

"Perhaps that is a good idea," he said in a low voice.

She exited his room as quickly as she could without running. Once she reached the safety of her own bedchamber, she closed the door and locked it. Only then did she allow the shocked tears to fall.

33

"Francesca is doing tolerably well," Aunt Esther said. "Better than to be expected."

Severin's aunt was the master of understatement. They were at Princess Adelaide's glittering soiree the following evening, and Severin watched Fancy smile as she chatted with a ring of admirers. The Duchess of Knighton was a smashing success, and it was easy to see why.

Fancy looked captivating in an ivory silk gown that bared her shoulders and showed off her nipped-in waist. Embroidered flowers were scattered over the tulle overskirt of her gown and on the tiny puffed sleeves. To complete her transformation into a faerie queen, her hair had been fashioned into a lustrous coronet studded with golden pins shaped like bumblebees.

Yet it was more than Fancy's physical charms that drew admirers buzzing to her side. She radiated a genuine warmth that, evidently, even the jaded *ton* couldn't resist. Her beauty was tempered by the vulnerability in her doe-brown eyes; when she accepted an offer to dance, she always seemed surprised, as if she didn't expect or take her popularity for granted.

Severin watched on with pride, even as a vise of guilt clamped around his chest. He had behaved despicably toward her last night. He'd been in a dangerous mood since the Anna Smith business, which was why he'd avoided Fancy: he didn't want to be around her when he was not entirely in control of himself.

Yet when she'd opened the door last night, his good intentions had gone out the window. He hadn't been able to resist her sweet initiative, the feminine yearning in her eyes. No woman had ever given herself to him so freely. He'd taken advantage of her generosity, losing himself in her sweetness, in the marital heat that set his loins afire.

Then she had whispered words of love and he had...panicked. There was no other way to describe his reaction. The door had blown off the cage inside him: pain, fear, and need escaping in a dark charge. Caught in the mayhem, he had acted like a goddamned animal.

He'd fucked Fancy. There was no other word for it. No excuses for his conduct.

Although he knew he hadn't hurt her physically, he had done damage in other ways. He saw it in the way she had avoided his gaze since then. Even now she wouldn't look at him.

Shame and wordless terror twisted his gut.

"Knighton, what *is* the matter?" his aunt asked. "You do not seem yourself."

He wasn't himself. He didn't know who the bloody hell he was —and that was the problem. Fancy stirred the chaos inside him, and he was swamped by powerlessness, a feeling he'd hated since he was a boy.

Realizing that his aunt was awaiting a reply, he clipped out, "I'm fine."

"Fine?" She raised her brows. "One would think you would have more of a reaction to Francesca's success. She has wasted no effort, you know, and all to please you."

"I know," he said, his jaw clenching.

I know that I'm a damned bastard. That she deserves better than me.

"For heaven's sake, did the two of you have a row?"

He swung a surprised glance at his aunt. She wasn't the sort to pry into private matters. A trait they had in common.

"Why do you ask?" he said as calmly as he could.

"You are acting strangely, and Francesca has been giving you what is known amongst us ladies as *the cold shoulder*." Aunt Esther gave him a hard stare. "Don't look so surprised, Knighton. When Brambley was alive, he received his share."

Not knowing what to say, Severin kept his mouth shut.

"Hopefully your gift of the necklace improves the state of affairs," Aunt Esther said reprovingly. "Time may heal wounds, but jewelry accomplishes the task faster."

Severin wished he shared his aunt's confidence. The ruby necklace he'd given Fancy was a stunning piece to be sure, a string of rubies and diamonds that matched her ring. But he knew Fancy wasn't the sort of woman to be swayed by gifts. She would want an apology from him, which she undoubtedly deserved...but he didn't know what to say. Didn't understand why he had treated her so shabbily.

Besides, a woman who loved as wholeheartedly as Fancy deserved the same in return. Not some bauble, no matter how expensive, left on her dressing table by her cowardly fool of a husband.

"Good evening, Lady Brambley. Knighton."

Imogen's voice distracted him from his brooding. He turned, and she was standing there, in a pale blush gown that accentuated her fair fragility.

"You look well this evening, Lady Brambley," Imogen said in her impeccable way.

"As do you, Lady Cardiff." Aunt Esther waved her dark fan. "No husband this eve?"

Imogen's smile had a taut edge. "Cardiff had other plans, alas. He is in such demand."

"I see." Aunt Esther aimed another hard look at Severin.

"While a fashionable man does not live in his wife's pocket, I daresay a wise man doesn't tempt fate by leaving her to her own devices too long."

Severin translated her unsubtle message: *make amends to your own wife, you idiot.*

"Knighton, might I have a word with you?" Imogen asked.

Picking up on the urgency in her voice, Severin frowned. "What about?"

"It is a...private matter. It shan't take long."

It wasn't like Imogen to be desperate. Or indiscreet. The anxiety in her eyes was rare enough to elicit his concern.

He turned to Esther. "Aunt, will you excuse us?"

Aunt Esther closed her fan with a snap. "As you wish."

As he escorted Imogen away, he heard his aunt say beneath her breath, "But it is not me you need to worry about."

∽

All of Fancy's lessons, practice, and hard work had paid off. She was a success—a credit to the Knighton name, more than one of the lofty guests had commented. She had reached her goal and ought to be rejoicing.

She couldn't wait for the nightmare to be over.

For the first time that eve, she found herself alone. It was a welcome break; she felt as if her face might crack from all the smiling. Resting on a bench in an alcove partially blocked by a silk screen, she sipped a cup of lukewarm punch and tried not to look for Knight.

After his callous treatment of her last night, her feelings had veered between anger and despair. She was losing hope that things between them would ever change. Fool that she was, she had thought their lovemaking meant something...that the physical pleasures they shared were an expression of emotional desire as well.

Clearly, that was true only for her.

Humiliation scorched her cheeks. His reaction to her declaration of love expressed louder than words how he felt about her. He had used her, and what was worse, she'd found pleasure in it anyway because she loved him. She was forced to confront the truth: his heart might forever be beyond her reach.

And yet...she touched her fingertips to the ruby necklace. Finding it on her dressing table, she had debated whether to wear it. It had rankled her that Knight might think a piece of jewelry could substitute for an apology or explanation of why he'd treated her the way he had.

The necklace had, however, been accompanied by a note:

A small token of my regard. I know you will outshine these jewels tonight.

Your proud husband,
-K.

She knew Knight: he wasn't good at discussing his feelings, particularly those of a private nature. The note conveyed his affection, and the fact that he found her worthy of the magnificent necklace meant something. Once, his regard and approval might have been enough.

But not now. Not after the weeks of talking, teasing, and working together, the promise of what their relationship could be. Bleakly, Fancy knew that she needed to talk to Knight—to tell him that she could no longer accept the original terms of their marriage and to ask him outright if he could ever love her.

But what if he says no? What if he says he'll love Imogen and only Imogen forever?

"Why are you hiding back here?" an imperious voice demanded.

Fancy jumped up as Princess Adelaide glided into the alcove in a stately blue gown, her pale blue ostrich feathers adding to her vertical consequence.

With a curtsy, Fancy said, "I was, um, enjoying some punch, Your Highness."

Princess Adelaide waved her back to the bench and sat down beside her. "Well, what do you think of my salon?"

"It's lovely." Fancy summoned a smile. "I enjoyed the opera singer very much."

"I should hope so, given the cost of importing her from Venice." The princess snorted. "I am glad you are enjoying yourself. I can see that you have made changes since we last met,"—hawkish eyes swept over her—"and they are improvements. As I suspected, you have backbone, and that should get you far in Society."

Not long ago, Fancy would have been ecstatic to win the princess's approval. Now she wasn't certain it mattered. The reason she had wanted to be a lady was to win Knight's love; the irony of winning the battle but losing the war was almost too much to bear.

Fancy managed a wan smile. "Thank you, Your Highness."

"You have received the royal stamp of approval." The princess's dark brows inched toward her steel-grey hair. "One would think that should warrant some expression of happiness."

"I am happy…" To Fancy's horror, her voice wobbled.

"Goodness, gel. What is the matter?"

She bit her lip, trying to prevent herself from bursting into tears.

"Here, take this." Princess Adelaide passed her a handkerchief. "If anyone asks, we shall tell them you got something in your eye."

Fancy dabbed discreetly at her tears.

"Let me guess," the princess said. "Husband problems?"

"H-how did you know?"

"Because men are the source of most problems, my dear. And husbands are the worst of the lot." The princess folded her veined hands in her lap. "I may be old, but I remember being a newlywed. In those early days, my husband Franz and I fought like cats and dogs."

"But things improved with time?" Fancy asked hopefully.

"Only because Franz had the decency to depart this earth five years into the marriage."

"Oh. I'm, um, sorry."

"As he was in his mistress's bed at the time, I saw no reason to mourn him," Princess Adelaide said bluntly. "The marriage was not without its merits, however. Franz gave me Ruprecht, my son and the heir to the throne of Hessenstein."

"You must be very proud," Fancy said uncertainly.

"Of Ruprecht, yes. Of my marriage..." The princess shrugged. "I tell you this because life has its peaks and valleys, and I sense that you, Your Grace, are in a valley. Because of Knighton, I presume?"

"He and I had a disagreement," Fancy admitted.

"That is not surprising. Men are often disagreeable."

"Knight isn't." Fancy nibbled on her lip, not wanting to divulge too much. "We just, um, don't see eye to eye on a certain matter."

"Have you told him your feelings on said matter?"

Fancy squirmed beneath the princess's stare. "Not entirely."

"Then why are you sitting in an alcove talking to me?" Princess Adelaide scolded. "Go find your husband and talk to him."

"What if...what if I don't want to know how he feels?" Fancy said in a whisper.

"I did not take you for a wilting hothouse flower," the princess said. "In my country, we value hardiness and strength of will. The royal flower of Hessenstein is the alpine rose. It is not a rarefied species, but one that blooms year after year, in the harshest of climes. Your roots may be common, gel, but I sense your backbone is not."

Princess Adelaide's words bolstered Fancy's resolve. She had been hiding from the truth, and it wasn't getting her anywhere. One way or another, she had to find out what lay in Knight's heart...and whether there was any hope for their future.

She drew a breath. "Thank you, Your Highness."

"Run along and find your husband." Princess Adelaide waved her fingers in dismissal. "Last I saw him, he was headed to the south balcony."

∼

Fancy went to the balcony before she lost her nerve. It was off a quiet area of the ballroom, and she was glad for the privacy given the conversation she needed to have with Knight. The French doors were open, thick red velvet drapes covering the entryway. As she neared, she heard Knight's voice...and he was not alone. The hairs on her nape rose at the familiar bell-like tones.

Her heart hammering, she peered through the slit in the velvet panels.

Knight was standing at the far end of the balcony, and Imogen was with him. They were talking, too low for Fancy to hear what they were saying. Knight leaned closer, and the rest seemed to happen in slowed time: Imogen wound her arms around Knight's neck...and pressed her lips to his in a passionate kiss.

Knight went still. But he didn't push Imogen away.

Fancy stumbled backward from the curtain, her jagged breath scoring her throat. The destruction of her dreams felt like a physical thing: its shards slashed at her tender core, pain bleeding through her veins. She might have crumpled if her survival instincts hadn't kicked in. The grit and fortitude of a tinker's daughter came to her rescue.

I have my answer, she thought numbly. *Now I know what I need to do.*

34

As Severin walked the final blocks toward his home, it was nearing eleven in the morning. He had not slept, but he didn't feel tired. He felt as if he were awakening from a daze. Last night's events had made him see things clearly at last. The cloudless sky seemed a reflection of his own state of mind. The truth was obvious to him now: he was in love with his wife.

With Fancy, his beloved, his duchess.

It had taken Imogen's rash kiss to make him realize that he didn't want anyone but Fancy. The touch of Imogen's lips against his own—which he had for so long fooled himself into thinking he wanted—had felt wrong. He had felt nothing, in truth, but a sense of shock.

Snapping out of his paralysis, he had pushed Imogen away, yet he knew with stabbing guilt that the damage had been done. He would have one more apology to add to all the rest, and he could only hope that Fancy, with her generous heart, could forgive him that too. He would spend the rest of his life making it up to her... making her as happy as she made him.

For he *was* happy. Over the bloody moon when he was with Fancy...or even when he was just thinking about her, the memory of her smile lighting him up inside. Having never experienced such unfettered joy, he hadn't recognized it for what it was.

He had hated leaving Fancy at the soiree last night. But after he had repudiated Imogen's advances, she had broken down in tears, the awful facts pouring out of her. Her marriage to Cardiff wasn't merely unhappy, it was abusive. She'd lifted her sapphire necklace, showing Severin the bruises her brute of a husband had left on her throat, and tearfully asked for his help.

As a gentleman and her friend, he could not ignore her plight. Thus, he had sought out Fancy, who'd been about to leave with Aunt Esther. His aunt had informed him that his wife had a headache, but when he'd tried to ask Fancy about it, she had given him the infamous cold shoulder (a lady-like behavior he wished she hadn't mastered quite so well). As he couldn't very well discuss Imogen's abuse in public, he had told his wife and aunt that a pressing matter had come up, and he would meet them later at home.

Then he had attended to Imogen.

While Imogen had wanted Severin to be her champion, he had known with crystal clarity that it wasn't his role or, frankly, one that he desired. His heart and his protection were pledged to Fancy—even if, idiot that he was, he hadn't recognized it—and he would not betray his wife.

He could not leave Imogen in dire straits, however. He'd taken her to her father's house. Hammond hadn't been happy to see him, but he didn't give a damn. He'd given Imogen the support of a friend as she haltingly revealed the truth of Cardiff's cruelty. The shattering of Severin's illusions continued from there.

For the first time, he witnessed what lay beneath the cultivated façade of the Hammond family. Mrs. Hammond had blamed her husband for marrying Imogen off to a cad because he was too busy dallying with his whores to pay proper attention to their daughter. Mr. Hammond had retorted that if his wife hadn't been such an icicle in bed, he would not need to find pleasure elsewhere. Mrs. Hammond had shot back that he was a fortune hunter who'd married her for her dowry.

And on it had went. The pair shredded their canvas of perfection with malicious glee, hurling the strips of their discontent at one other. Finally, Severin had cut in to ask if anybody planned to help Imogen, who'd been sitting by quietly, her expression resigned. Luckily, Imogen's older brother Roger had arrived and said that he would talk to Cardiff—do more than talk, if necessary, to keep his sister safe. Seeing the resolve in Roger Hammond's eyes, Severin knew his time with the Hammonds was done.

Imogen had seen him to the door...and she had apologized.

"I don't know what came over me," she whispered. "I hope it will not ruin things between us."

Things between them were already ruined, Severin had realized. Had been the moment he'd seen their relationship for what it was: an illusion. He had mistaken his boyish idealization of Imogen for love. As a man, what he felt for her was gratitude for the years of friendship, for her kindness to him when he had had no one else.

"You have been a good friend to me," he said. "I wish you well."

And Imogen had given him that sad, beautiful smile he'd adored as a boy.

"You love her, don't you?" she asked.

"With everything that I am," he said simply.

"But we will still be friends, won't we?" She put a hand on his arm. "You will still be my knight?"

Seeing the desperation in Imogen's eyes, Severin had felt a tug of pity and fondness. The concern he would have for a friend. Yet he did not think her fantasy was doing her any favors—and, out of respect for Fancy, he could not let it stand.

"My protection belongs to my wife." Gently and firmly, he

removed Imogen's hand. "She will always come first. If you wish for us to remain friends, then you must honor that."

Imogen's eyes shimmered. "Then this is...goodbye?"

He nodded. "If your brother needs help dealing with Cardiff, he knows how to contact me. Take care, Imogen."

He had left and spent the early morning hours wandering through the streets. He passed the tenements where he and his *maman* had lived, the alleyways where she'd sacrificed herself for their survival, the gin palaces where she'd obliterated her sorrows and lost herself. He walked the streets that had birthed him, where he had bled while his mother had been torn away, where he had known loneliness and hunger and despair. When he emerged at his own house, he finally left all of it behind.

Or, rather, the past was a part of him, but it no longer drove him. He was no longer running like a terrified, powerless guttersnipe. Because, as a man, he'd found what he needed: Fate had bestowed a gift upon him, giving him the love of a lifetime.

He let himself in, walking past his startled butler.

"Is Her Grace up yet, Harvey?" he asked.

"No, Your Grace." The butler's gaze flicked to the poesy Severin had bought from a flower girl. "When Her Grace returned last night, she asked not to be disturbed."

Severin continued heading up the stairs. It had been a late night, and Fancy had looked tired when she left the soiree. His chest expanded with tenderness and pride as he thought of how entrancing she'd been last night. How she'd won over even a stickler like Princess Adelaide. His only regret was that he hadn't been a husband worthy of her...but that was going to change.

Now that he understood his own heart, he would tell Fancy everything, bare his past and his soul. He would beg her forgiveness. Give her anything and everything she desired if she would let him.

Reaching the next floor, he ran into Eleanor, Toby, and Aunt Esther.

Disapproval glinted in his aunt's eyes. "Are you just arriving home, Knighton?"

"I had business to attend to. Have you seen Fancy?" He tried but failed to keep the eagerness out of his voice.

"Francesca is still abed. She wasn't feeling well after the party." Aunt Esther sniffed. "Likely she overexerted herself doing her duty to this family."

Remorse constricted his chest. "I'll check in on her."

"Are the flowers for Fancy?" Toby beamed at him.

"Yes." And because his wife had helped him build a bridge to his kin, he thought to ask, "Do you think she will like the violets?"

"She will." Although Eleanor's tone was serious as usual, her new white frock with pink ribbons made her appear more her age. "All ladies like flowers…except me."

"You do not like flowers?" he asked.

"I prefer books. Flowers last a moment, books forever."

"I shall remember your advice the next time I get Fancy a gift," he said, amused.

"You don't have to worry," Toby reassured him. "Fancy isn't hard to please. She even liked the picture I drew of Bertrand, and I'm not a very good artist. I could only fit three of his four legs onto the paper."

Talking about Fancy, seeing the changes she had sown with her warmth and love, made Severin all the more impatient to get to her.

"Come along, children," his aunt said briskly "Your brother has matters to attend to."

"Thank you, Aunt Esther." Severin paused. "For everything you have done for this family."

Emotion flashed in her eyes, which she quickly covered up by herding his siblings along.

Finally, Severin was free to go to his wife. Arriving at her bedchamber, he felt as nervous as a bridegroom. Gripping the flowers in one hand, he knocked softly. He did it again, louder when there was no response.

When silence still greeted him, he wondered if he should leave her to rest. He should, probably, for as his aunt had said, his wife had exerted herself last night...but, hell, he couldn't wait.

Finding the door locked, he went into his own chamber. The knob to their private door turned in his hand and, heart thudding with anticipation, he entered his wife's room, still darkened from the drawn drapes. He headed toward her bed.

"*Chérie?*" he said softly, not wanting to startle her. "Are you awake?"

No reply. Arriving at the bed, he saw it was empty.

"Fancy?" he called, heading to her sitting room.

It, too, was unoccupied.

Brows drawn, he circled his gaze around the room...and then he saw it. On her escritoire, the ruby ring and necklace he'd given her sat atop a folded piece of paper. Dropping the flowers, he strode over, pushing aside the expensive paperweights to grab the note. A vise clamped around his heart when he saw that it was written in Fancy's painstaking hand and blotched...by her tears.

Knight,

Seeing you with Imogen, I know now that you cannot give me the marriage I want. The love and respect that I deserve. No matter how hard I try, I will never be her—and I should not have to be. There is only one solution, and I'm sorry for the pain it will cause the children. I will miss them. Please do not come after me.

Take care of yourself,
  Fancy

P.S. Please tell Toby to take good care of Bertrand.

Pain lashed Severin, his scar an agonizing burn. Once again, his world was torn apart, but this time *he* had caused the damage. Fancy had given him everything, and he had repaid her with callousness.

"Don't leave me, Fancy," he said in an anguished whisper.

But she *had* left him...because he deserved to be left.

Heat singed his eyes, and he closed them briefly, letting the pain and helplessness flood him. Letting the loss of his beloved permeate every fiber of his being. Everything he felt now and the grief of his past merged as one, and when he opened his eyes, his vision was burning but clear.

He had no idea where his wife had gone.

No idea where to begin looking.

But he would move heaven and earth to find her and win her back.

35

"Fancy, I be wanting a word with you."

"Yes, Da?" Fancy asked.

She paused in the act of making dough in the kitchen of the caravan. Her brothers had brought home a brace of plump pheasants that had "wandered" from a neighboring lord's estate, and she was getting rid of the evidence by making a big pie for supper.

Her father sat down at the table where she was working.

"'Ow long be you planning to 'ide from your 'usband, petal?" he asked.

The mention of Knight brought a piercing pain. In the week since she had found her way to Derbyshire, where her family always camped this time of year, she'd tried not to think about her husband at all, burying her sorrow in work. Her family knew, of course, why she'd come back. The afternoon she'd shown up, Da had taken one look at her...and opened his arms. She'd run into them, that safe haven that had protected her all her life, and wept.

Afterward, she had told her father the essential details about why she'd left Knight. He had not questioned her, just let her talk and sob and talk some more. When she was done, he'd patted her hand and told her to take her old bunk, and he hadn't mentioned Knight again.

Until now.

"I'm not hiding from him, Da." She attacked the dough with her rolling pin.

"You didn't tell 'im where you'd gone." Her father raised his brows. "'Ow's 'e supposed to find you in the wilds o' Derbyshire?"

"He is not supposed to find me." She grimly pushed the pin into the dough. "And you're assuming he'll bother to look."

"'E'll be looking for you."

"How do you know?"

"Was at your wedding, wasn't I?" Da snorted. "Saw the way the fellow was with you. Wasn't the manner o' a man who planned to let go o' 'is bride anytime soon."

Fancy's chest knotted as she thought of her wedding. How things had changed. Back then, she'd been full of hope for their future, even though he'd told her about Imogen. She couldn't even blame him, she thought with angry despair. He had never lied to her; she'd simply been a stupid fool for believing she could win his love.

"Careful, me Fancy, or you'll o'erwork the pastry."

Annoyed, she realized her father was right. She was overworking the dough.

Blooming hell, I should've made bread instead.

Blowing out a breath, she finished rolling out the pastry and fitted it over the pan of pheasant and vegetables.

"I don't know why you're taking Knight's side," she muttered. "I thought you didn't like him."

"I like the cove well enough. I just wasn't sure 'e was the 'usband for you." Da's bespectacled gaze was wry. "But you went and married the toff, and now you be a duchess with a 'ousehold depending on you."

Her heart ached as she thought of Toby, Eleanor, Jonas, and Cecily. She'd told her family about Knight's siblings and even his aunt. How far they'd come...how much she'd grown to care for them.

She stabbed holes in the crust. "They'll forget me in time."

"Ain't like you to sulk, me Fancy."

She frowned at her father. "I'm not sulking."

"You are, and I be understanding why. You 'ad your 'eart broken, and you need to lick your wounds. Which is why I've left it until now. But you can't 'ide forever."

Her throat thickened. "Are you saying...I can't stay?"

"I want you to be 'appy. If staying would make you so, then I'd be telling you to stay for as long as you like." Her father's smile was sad. "But it's plain to see that you ain't 'appy, me girl."

To her horror, she felt heat push behind her eyes. Her father was right: she wasn't happy. She was angry at Knight and pining for him at the same time. When she left him, she had taken only two mementoes, her wedding band and his button, both of which she wore on a string around her neck. Beneath her bodice, she felt their comforting weight.

"What am I supposed to do, Da?" She slumped into the chair beside him. "Knight loves another woman. A beautiful woman I can't hope to compete with. I'll never be the lady she is."

"Well, o' course you can't be 'er, and, more importantly, why would you want to be? You're *yourself*, Fancy, and if that ain't good enough for your duke, then 'e's got bacon for brains. But I don't take your fellow for a fool." Da gave her a keen look. "From what you've told me, the two o' you were rubbing along fine until you saw 'im with the other lady at that ball."

She nodded morosely.

"But you didn't actually talk to 'im about it, did you?"

"What was there to say, Da?" She clenched her hands together on the table. "I saw them...embracing."

"I've lived long enough not to always trust me own eyes," her father said sagely. "Even if it were a lover's tryst, running from it does no good."

His words stirred the memory of what Princess Adelaide had said about being a hardy bloom. After everything Fancy had endured in life, why had she balked at confronting Knight? Why had she fled instead of talking to him?

"You remind me o' your ma. Sweet as 'oney, me Annie, a dreamer and the most capable woman I e'er knew. Weren't anything she couldn't do if she put 'er mind to it, and being a loving wife and mama, she put 'er mind to looking after us. But for all that, she 'ad a flaw."

"She did?" To Fancy's mind, her mother had been perfect.

"She lacked confidence in 'erself. She never asked for what she wanted, always made do with what we 'ad and never once complained." Da's voice grew scratchy. "It was a part o' 'er charm, no doubt about it, but it also kept 'er from 'er 'eart's desires."

"You were what she wanted, Da," Fancy said softly. "She loved you."

"Aye, and what I wouldn't 'ave done to give 'er more." Da's eyes suddenly glittered. "Did you know your ma 'ated those ironstone dishes I bought 'er?"

Fancy blinked. "No, she didn't. She mended them again and again, so well that the cracks didn't show. We used those dishes for years."

"She fixed 'em because she knew I couldn't afford to buy more," Da said heavily. "But before she breathed 'er last breath, I asked 'er if there be anything she wanted to tell me, any last thing she would regret 'olding back. And she said to me, *Milton...I always 'ated those ugly dishes.*"

Awareness prickled through Fancy, her throat thickening.

"We both laughed and then we cried because our life together 'ad been so blessed that the worst thing about it was those damned dishes." Da took off his spectacles to briefly wipe his eyes. "But you see, petal, if I'd but known 'ow much me Annie longed for a bit o' real porcelain, I'd 'ave moved 'eaven and earth to get it for 'er. All she 'ad to do was ask."

"Oh, Da." Fancy reached over and grasped his hand.

"Me point being, don't sell yourself short. Don't be afraid to make demands o' your 'usband, especially when what you want be more important than dishes, more important than anything. I know you thought that by making yourself into a duchess, you would win 'is 'eart, but that ain't what you need to do, petal."

"Then what?" she asked achingly. "What am I supposed to do?"

"Believe in yourself, me Fancy. Trust that you're the woman your fellow needs. The truth is, you've always been a lady in 'ere,"—Da pressed his palm to his heart—"where it counts. If your duke don't see that, then 'e's the one who ain't deserving o' you."

～

Later that afternoon, still mulling over her da's words, Fancy went to help her brothers pick apples at a nearby orchard. Da had fixed up the farmer's pots and pans, and in exchange the farmer had said they could take as many of the last harvest fruit as they could carry.

Sam Taylor, whose family was camping nearby, decided to tag along.

Fancy was glad to see Sam again and especially glad that no tension lingered between them. She'd always thought of him as a brother, and it was a relief to have him acting that way again. The moment they arrived at the orchard, Sam and her brothers began pelting fallen fruit at each other. When she told them they had work to do, the nodcocks started aiming at *her*. To defend herself, she joined in, and by the end of it, they were all sticky and laughing like lunatics.

It felt good to laugh, she realized. To play in the sun and fresh air. She thought with a pang that Toby and Eleanor would love apple picking.

"Oi, Fancy," Sam called. "You want to 'elp me with this tree?"

He was standing at the end of the row, pointing at the tallest tree.

"The apples are the biggest, but they're 'igh up, and we ain't got a ladder," he said. "I'll 'oist you up, and you grab 'em."

She went over, craning her neck to look into the leafy branches. Clusters of red, plump fruit beckoned. Sam was right; these apples did look the best.

"Can you lift me that high?" she asked dubiously.

Sam grinned and held up an arm, flexing. "I'm strong as an ox."

"And dumb as one too," her brother Liam said with a snicker.

Before the lads could start another battle, Fancy said hastily, "All right, then. I'll climb on your shoulders, but you be sure to hold me steady, Sam Taylor."

"I'll treat you like me ma's finest china."

"Your ma doesn't have any china," Fancy pointed out.

Sam got down on one knee and gestured at her. "Stop arguing, will you, and climb up."

Taking off her shoes, she clambered onto Sam's shoulders. True to his word, he held her steady. Stretching upward, she was able to reach several ripe apples, dropping them into the burlap sack that he held.

"I can't reach the biggest ones." She gazed at the remote fruit, which seemed redder and larger than the rest. "I'll have to stand on your shoulders."

"I ain't sure that's a good idea—"

She managed to balance on her knees. "Quit complaining and hold still."

"'Ave a care..." Sam panted.

"Just hold steady another second."

With great concentration, she stood up, her stockinged toes curling on Sam's shoulders. He dropped the sack, his hands gripping her ankles for extra support.

"Almost there," she said.

Triumph surged through her as her fingertips touched the fruit...then Sam lost his balance, jerking forward. With a shriek, she tumbled through the air, bracing for impact, but strong arms caught her, holding her against a large, hard, and achingly familiar chest.

Breathless, stunned, she stared into her husband's eyes.

36

As Severin gazed into his beloved's face, a tide of relief and yearning crashed over him. After a week of desperate searching, he had found her. She was safe in his arms and everything he had ever wanted.

"Fancy." Her name left him in a hoarse whisper. Love and desire robbed him of thought, drove his lips toward hers—

She shoved at his chest, nearly causing him to drop her. He managed to hold on, settling her safely on her feet. The moment she had her balance, she struggled against his embrace, and he let her go. Not because he wanted to, but because he knew she had every right to push him away.

"What are you doing here?" she demanded.

With her eyes sparkling with anger and plaits disheveled, she had never looked more beautiful to him. He ached with love and remorse, with the primal need to drag her into his arms and hold her there forever.

"I am here for you," he said.

Her brothers and Sam Taylor gathered in a protective ring.

Taylor glared at him. "You want us to take care o' this bounder for you, Fancy?"

Severin curled his hands. How *dare* the bastard presume to protect her? Fancy was *his*—and he would be the one looking after her. Even if he had to fall to his knees and grovel for the privilege. Knowing that his wife would not appreciate him pummeling Taylor, Severin reined in his jealous fury.

"Fancy, may I please speak with you alone?" he asked tautly.

Her brother Liam crossed his arms. "We're not leaving her with you."

"Me sister travelled by 'erself for a week to get away from you," Oliver snarled. "What kind o' 'usband lets 'is wife do that?"

"Or makes 'er cry 'erself to sleep?" Tommy twisted the knife.

"Hush," Fancy said, her cheeks pink.

Self-recrimination roiling in his gut, Severin said in a low voice, "I know I've been a bastard, Fancy, and I have no excuse. But there are things I would like to tell you...things I've only just realized. Please will you give me a chance to explain?"

The doubt in Fancy's eyes punched him in the gut, and he had no one to blame but himself.

What if it is too late? What if she can't forgive me for not knowing my own heart?

He held his breath, awaiting her answer. Agonizing moments passed.

"All right," she said. "Follow me."

∽

Fancy led the way to the back of the orchard. Her emotions were tangled skeins, like yarn tossed in a basket. She didn't know where one feeling started and another ended, whether she was angry, irritated, or hopeful. She felt Knight's presence behind her, his pulsing masculine energy.

Why did he come after me? she thought. *Is it out of obligation...or something else?*

Arriving at the fence that marked the end of the grove, she

turned to face her husband. Sunshine filtered through the leafy canopy, light and shadow playing across his stark features. His grey eyes burned into hers with breath-disrupting intensity.

"How did you find me?" she managed.

"Bertrand."

She blinked.

"The damned donkey led me to your family's campground," Knight clarified. "It was Toby's idea. He said donkeys have an excellent memory and sense of direction and turns out he's right."

Exhaling, she asked, "Why did you come after me?"

"Because you are my wife, and I love you," he said steadily.

Shock percolated through her. How she had yearned to hear those words...yet now she couldn't believe them. Not after what she'd seen.

She lifted her chin. "You have never lied to me. There is no need to start now."

"I'm not lying." Squaring his shoulders, he said, "I understand why you might think so—"

"I *saw* you with Imogen," she said scathingly. "At Princess Adelaide's salon."

He didn't flinch at her accusation. "What did you think you saw?"

"I *know* what I saw. On the balcony, you were...kissing her," she said, her voice hitching.

The fact that he didn't deny it brought her anger from simmering to a full boil.

"Do you know what I have finally realized?" She didn't wait for him to answer. "I may not be a lady or a proper duchess *and I don't give a blooming farthing*. I am a tinker's daughter, and I'm proud of it. When I married you, I tried to fix myself up. To make myself into the duchess you wanted. But it didn't work, did it? I'm still Fancy Sheridan, a woman who can mend most things, but I can't mend your heart. I'm tired of trying and, what is more, *it isn't my job*. I deserve better than to be second best, the woman you settled for. I deserve better than a made-over marriage and my husband's hand-me-down heart. I want my faerie tale ending, and I won't settle for less!"

She hadn't meant to shout. But once uncorked, her bottled-up emotions burst from her.

"I know." By contrast, Knight's voice was soft and low. "All of that is true. You deserve better than me, sweeting, I have always known that. But make no mistake: I am not letting you go."

"Because of the scandal?" she asked bitterly. "No one will care. In fact, they'll think we're proper blue-bloods if we live separate lives. You and Imogen can carry on however you like, and I'll do the same—"

"The hell you will. And devil take Imogen." He took a step forward, his hands closing around her arms, his eyes smoldering into hers. "You're mine, Fancy."

"Let me go," she said.

"Never. You are the best thing that has happened to me, and I am *never* letting you go."

His ardent declaration, raw with emotion, startled her into silence.

"I have made so many mistakes with you," he said tightly. "Too many to count. But the one I will not make is losing you, the woman I love, who taught me what love *is*."

Her heart seemed to stop at his words.

"You don't love me." She forced the words through her cinched throat. "You love *her*...Imogen. You always have, and you always will."

"No." He shook his head with vehemence. "I don't love her."

"Don't lie to me," she cried. "I *saw* you kissing her."

"What you saw was Imogen taking me off guard. It's true, she sought me out that night at the soiree. She said she had something urgent she needed to talk about. I shouldn't have gone to the balcony with her, but she seemed desperate. Like she needed my help." Knight dragged a hand through his hair. "Once we were out there, she threw herself at me."

Pain lanced through Fancy. "So you *did* kiss her."

"Not on purpose. I didn't realize what she meant to do." His eyes were fierce yet imploring. "When she kissed me, I froze. Because I didn't expect it...and because I felt nothing. I ended the kiss an instant after."

"I don't know why you would when you've saved your kisses for her for so long."

"Because I've fallen in love with *you*," he said hoarsely.

"Oh, really?" She crossed her arms, unwilling to open herself up to more pain. "When did that magical moment happen?"

"Probably from the moment I laid eyes on you arguing with that damned donkey." At her look of disbelief, he amended, "I knew that I wanted you then. That I'd never felt such a strong physical attraction to a female before."

She huffed out a breath. "Lust isn't the same as love."

"It wasn't just lust I felt for you, but the lust *was* there. So much so that it blinded me to everything else I was feeling." He exhaled. "I think that was why I was confused."

"You were quite clear when you proposed. You love Imogen. You were willing to settle for me because you'd compromised me," she said flatly. "And because we're compatible between the sheets."

"I'm an idiot." Remorse thickened his voice, his gaze pleading. "Fancy, I had no idea what love *was* before I met you. When I met Imogen, I was fifteen. I thought I loved her, but it was the immature infatuation of a boy who saw only her beauty, the life of privilege she led, and wanted it for himself. I've come to realize some things. Truths I had kept buried because they were unsavory. I've never shared them with anyone, but I would like to with you, if you would give me the chance."

The roughness of his voice betrayed his agitation. It wasn't easy for him to say what he was saying. Despite her hurt, she felt herself softening toward him.

"I'm listening," she said.

"Thank you." He cleared his throat. "I now understand that I put Imogen on a pedestal, used her as motivation to lift myself out of poverty, the miserable conditions of my life. Everything around me was dark, filthy, and brutal. You know my *maman* was a seamstress but what I didn't tell you was that she was also...a whore."

Seeing the anguish in Knight's eyes, Fancy felt her anger begin to ebb. His large frame was braced as if he were confronting an army of demons, and she couldn't let him do it alone. Slowly, she reached out a hand to him, and he took it, gripping it like a lifeline.

"I was eight when I realized how she truly earned our keep. I thought we'd been surviving on the piecework she did. I never questioned why she went out at night, wearing paint, a tawdry dress." His voice had a serrated edge. "There were times she came back with bruises on her face, a horrible blank look in her eyes, and I would ask her why. And all she would say was that she'd had an accident."

"Oh, Knight." Fancy didn't know what else to say.

"When one of my friends enlightened me on my mama's true profession, I bloodied his nose then foolishly demanded to know the truth from her. Do you know what she said?"

"What?" Fancy asked softly.

"*Don't make the same mistake I did. Don't be blinded by desire,* she said. *When you find yourself a woman, treat her like a true gentleman, like a knight who would never forsake his lady.*" His throat worked above his cravat. "I didn't understand then that she was talking about my father who had abandoned her, stripped her of everything little by little. First her youthful dreams, then her hope, then finally even her physical dignity."

"Yet she never lost her strength," Fancy whispered.

"I beg your pardon?"

"Your mama endured so much, yet she kept fighting to survive. And she never lost hope in you, Knight: she believed that you could be the gentleman your father never was."

"I have never thought of it that way," he said gruffly. "I only knew that I had failed her. Failed to protect her, to provide for us so that she wouldn't have to suffer indignities. I tried to help. I turned to what most boys my age could do in the stews: pickpocketing, petty theft. But whenever I managed to bring home a loaf of bread, a stolen purse, my *maman*..." He swallowed. "She would look at me with such disappointment in her eyes. And I knew what she was thinking. Knew that she wished I could be more. Then I saved Imogen, and for the first time in my life, I felt like..."

"A hero?" Fancy said with understanding.

He nodded jerkily. "It was a powerful feeling, knowing that I could be more than a sticky-fingered guttersnipe. That I could rise above my origins. I wanted so badly to be a gentleman who would make my *maman* proud and who could win a well-bred lady's heart."

"You are a gentleman." Then, as much as it hurt her to say it, "And you have won Imogen's heart."

"Imogen doesn't love me, and I don't love her." He grasped her hands in a powerful grip. "I was infatuated with Imogen, idealized her, but I never *knew* her. And she never knew me."

Fancy furrowed her brow. "How could you not know each other after all these years?"

"Because she wanted a champion, I wanted to be a champion, and that was all we really had in common. We never talked about anything of substance," he said, his expression earnest. "Imogen has delicate sensibilities, and I never shared my problems, the darkness in my life, for fear of upsetting her. And she, in turn, was always a proper lady, never saying or doing anything impolite."

Heat prickled Fancy's cheeks as she thought of the things she and Knight had talked about. The impolite things they'd said *and* done in the heat of passion. Embarrassed, she tried to pull away but Knight held on.

"But you...you're *real*, Fancy," he said urgently. "A blood-and-flesh woman who isn't afraid of feelings or unpleasantness. Who isn't disgusted by the man I am beneath the polish and trappings of wealth."

"Why would I be disgusted by you?" she asked in a suffocated voice. "You are a man of honor, one who has survived on his own merits. You've made something of yourself, risen above the darkness that could have consumed you, and that isn't something to be ashamed of."

"I adore that you see the best in everyone, sweeting...even in me, when I don't deserve it." His eyes burned with desperate intensity. "Your warmth and generosity are unlike anything I've known. For so long, I had fooled myself into thinking love was something pure and unattainable. That is why I didn't recognize the gift you gave me: love, real love, the kind that not only survives darkness but grows stronger because of it. The kind that lasts forever and beyond. That is what I feel for you, Fancy—my duchess, my wife, the only woman I have truly loved."

Emotion clogged her throat. He was saying the things that had filled her dreams. She *wanted* to believe him...but she flashed to that scene on the balcony, the shattering anguish of seeing Imogen in his arms. How could she trust that he loved her, that he wasn't simply settling for the consolation prize?

She pulled away, and he let her, his gaze following her keenly.

"If that is the case, why did seeing Imogen at Maggie's ball affect you so?" When his brows knitted, she said, "After that night, you became distant. You didn't come to my bed, and then when I sought you out..." She bit her lip, humiliation throbbing like a deep-seated splinter. "I told you I loved you, and you... rebuffed me."

"I was a bastard." Self-condemnation hardened his voice.

"There is no excuse for how I treated you, and I cannot tell you how sorry I am. But you're wrong about one thing: it wasn't Imogen who triggered my mood—it was Anna Smith."

"But...why?" She tilted her head. "At that point, the danger was over. Shouldn't you have been happy or relieved at the very least?"

"I was relieved that the danger to you was over." Shadows deepened in his eyes. "But when I went to see Anna Smith, it brought back the memories of visiting my *maman*...in Bedlam."

At the revelation, Fancy stilled. London's infamous Bethlehem Hospital, commonly known as Bedlam, was an asylum for the insane.

"Your mother was ill?" Fancy said carefully.

"She didn't start off that way." His voice was gritty. "According to the mad-doctor, it was the gin that did it to her. My *maman*, she drank a lot. Not during my earliest years; I remember a time when her eyes and mind were clear. But when she started selling herself to support us, it changed her. She was a passionate woman, my mother, and doing something so contrary to her wishes and sense of dignity destroyed her. She had to find some way to numb herself...and blue ruin was her answer."

"Your poor mama," Fancy said achingly.

"She was a loving mother, but when she drank, she became a different person. I was twelve when she started hallucinating. Hearing and seeing things that were not there. When I tried to tell her it was just her imagination, she would grow distraught, and a few times she forgot who I was, thought I was trying to harm her. And she...she attacked me. One time, she chased me into the street with a knife. I should have gotten out of the way, but I wasn't fast enough. She stabbed me, left the scar near my heart."

Unable to bear the rawness of her husband's pain, Fancy went to him, wrapping her arms around his waist.

His arms circled her like iron bands. "She didn't mean to hurt me."

"Of course she didn't." Fancy held him with all her strength. "She was not herself."

"After that time, the authorities took her away. For years, I visited her in Bedlam, and seeing her suffering, how she was treated..." His voice was muffled against her hair. "There was nothing I could do to help her. I was glad when she died, glad that her torment was finally over. When I went to see Anna Smith, being in the asylum brought everything back."

Fancy stroked his back. "I understand."

Because now she did. Knight hadn't been brooding over Imogen; he had been reliving the horrors of his youth. She had the sudden insight that this was the root of his infatuation with Imogen: was it any wonder that he would seek a pure, untouchable love when the real love he'd experienced had been so full of darkness and pain?

He drew back to look at her but did not loosen his hold.

"I should not have made love to you that night," he said roughly. "In the mood that I was in, I should have stayed away. When you told me you loved me, I...panicked. And I don't even know why. Because I love you, Fancy, I do."

"I think I understand." She touched his jaw, his tension trembling through her. "Love hasn't been easy, has it? Maybe passion and lust felt safer."

She saw recognition fork through his eyes like lightning.

"I have come to realize that I made that vow to Imogen not for her sake, but my own," he said slowly. "Giving her that vow made me feel like I had left my past behind, and it shielded me from having to feel the darker side, the painful side of truly loving someone."

"You told me from the start that love was risky," she recalled.

"Yes, and you are worth any risk." The awe in his expression clogged her throat. "You have been my helpmate at home and at work. You've listened to me, supported me, made me feel that I am not alone. Hell, you've somehow patched things up with my family, a feat I didn't think was possible."

"I love your family," she said.

"Do you think you could love *me* again?" His tentativeness swelled her heart. "I swear to you that what I feel for Imogen is just friendship. Gratitude for the time when she was my only friend. And I swear also that I won't disrespect you or treat you shoddily in—or out—of bed again."

"It wasn't *all* bad," she admitted. "Just the part when you didn't tell me you loved me back."

"I love you, Fancy." He cupped her face in his hands as if she were the last flame guarding him against the darkness of the night. "So much that it terrifies me. Losing you would destroy me, but I'm going to love you anyway because I cannot stop. You are everything I've ever wanted, and the only one I'll want for the rest of my days."

Well, that *was* an improvement from the last time.

"I can't love you *again*...because I never stopped. I was afraid, too," she said candidly. "Afraid to ask for what I want, to believe that I deserve a husband like you. But I'm not settling for dishes I hate."

His brow furrowed. "What do dishes have to do with this?"

"I'll explain later. Just know that I'm no longer afraid of loving you."

He let out a shaky breath...and surprised her by getting down on one knee. Joy lifted her heart when he took out her ruby ring. He slid it onto her finger, saying huskily, "Fancy Sheridan Knight, will you be my love forever?"

"Yes." With a wobbly smile, she used her free hand to pull the string from beneath her bodice, showing him the objects she'd kept close to her heart, even when they'd been apart. "I've always been yours, Knight."

He rose, touching her dangling wedding band and the carved gold button beside it.

A notch between his brows, he said, "Is that one of my buttons?"

"I snipped it from your jacket. The one you lent me that day you found me fishing." Blushing, she confessed, "I thought that it was all I would ever have of you, and I've kept it close ever since."

"I am yours, Fancy. Heart, body, and soul," he said with a fervor that vanquished the last of her doubts. "May I have the honor of kissing my bride?"

Smiling tremulously, she tipped her head back in answer, and he brought his lips to hers. The first touch of their mouths was gentle, the fit tender perfection. The feel of her husband, the taste of him, was everything. What she had waited a lifetime for. He courted her with velvet-soft pressure, his lips brushing against hers with drugging sweetness.

In his kiss, she felt his love for her, his devotion and care. Their connection transcended the physical, even the emotional, touching a place that made her spirit sing. Her heart overflowing, she kissed him back with all the love she no longer had to hold back.

Their kiss caught fire, becoming a tangle of lips, tongues, and panted breaths. They kissed until she was clutching him for support, and he was holding them both steady, his chest heaving. She thought that she knew the power of their passion, yet with love as its tinder, their desire blazed to new heights. She saw her wonder reflected in Knight's gaze.

"Do you want to come back to the camping ground with me?" she whispered.

"I will go anywhere with you." Love illuminated his eyes, banishing the shadows and ghosts. "Wherever you are, my love, that is where I want to be."

37

Severin woke up in a sensual daze. It took him a moment to recognize what he was staring at: the ceiling of his carriage where he and Fancy had spent the night. Memories of their passionate reunion flitted through his sleep-clouded brain and evaporated in a haze of disorienting pleasure. He dipped his chin, and what he saw and felt ripped a groan from his chest.

He was lying on a velvet pallet on the floor of the cabin, and his naked duchess had made a place for herself between his thighs. Her delicate fingers circled the thick pole of his morning cockstand, her lips a hairsbreadth from the mushroomed tip.

"Good morning," she whispered against his erection.

"It bloody well is," he said raggedly.

A smile tucked into her cheeks, and she kissed him, butterfly touches up and down his turgid shaft. He wove his fingers into the thick silk of her tresses, enjoying the teasing caresses, arching his hips for more. As always, his wife knew what he needed, and he hissed out a breath when she took him inside her mouth, surrounding him with wet, sucking bliss.

Pleasure drilling down his spine, he watched Fancy's head bob upon his prick. The pretty, wanton picture she made and the sensations she bestowed upon him drove him mad with desire. He'd made love to her three times last night, yet he was nowhere near sated.

Then again, he had waited a lifetime for his beloved. Was it any surprise that he had so much need stored up for her? Yearning to possess her as completely as she possessed him pounded in his heart, his cock, his very soul.

His wife. His duchess. *His.*

With a growl of pure need, he sat up, reaching for her. He felt her surprise when he rolled her onto her back, reversing their positions so that he lay atop her, his head hovering over her pussy, his cock poised above her sweet mouth. His own mouth watered at the sight of her dewy pink cleft.

"Together, sweeting," he rasped.

He buried his face between her downy thighs, felt her jolt as he tongued her, from her pearl all the way to her hidden rosebud. God, but she was delicious. He ate her pussy with ravening hunger, and she drew on his prick with equal fervor. As he plunged his tongue into his duchess's cunny and his erection into her giving throat, he knew he'd found heaven.

Feeling her lips kiss his balls, he knew this trip through the pearly gates could be a short one. He wanted her to come first. Driving two fingers into her tight sheath, he pumped her while he licked and sucked on her love-knot. She gasped, the sound muffled by her mouthful of cock. Her passage convulsed around his fingers as her honey gushed against his tongue.

He shifted position, putting them face to face. Looking into his wife's peerless brown eyes, he thrust into her lush hole and growled, "I love you, Fancy."

Her eyes held him as securely as her body. "I love you, Knight."

He began to move, and she wrapped her legs around his hips, letting him in even deeper. He took her mouth in a hungry kiss as he pounded into her luxuriant heat, taking everything she offered, giving back the same. When she began to come again, he groaned, overwhelmed by his need and love for her. He blew inside his wife, pleasure turning him inside out as he gave every last drop of himself to her sweet keeping.

He collapsed on his back and cuddled her against his thundering heart.

"Knight?"

He looked into her sated eyes. "Hmm, love?"

"I didn't know life could be better than a faerie tale."

His heart full, he said, "It is going to get even better, I promise."

He kissed her again.

∼

At Knight's insistence, they stayed for three more days.

Fancy knew that her husband was a busy man, yet he was giving her time with her family because he knew how much they meant to her. He was also making an effort with Da and the boys. Although she had reassured her family that all was well—better than well—in her marriage, they'd understandably remained suspicious of Knight and his intentions.

He had taken it in stride, telling her that he deserved their hostility.

"I was a damned fool," he told her bluntly. "I deserve to take some licks. You won over my family; now let me win over yours. Don't fret, I'll work things out with them."

Bemused, she watched him "work things out" by helping her Da and brothers with their jobs. Without complaint, he, a duke, joined them in clearing trees and fixing fences for a neighboring farmer. He played kickball with her brothers and was so good at it that the boys fought to have him on their team. After supper, he sat on a log around the fire and smoked a pipe with Da. When

Fancy joined them, he pulled her onto his lap, holding her close while he and her father swapped stories.

Now that Knight had let her into his heart, he seemed less guarded in general. As they lay in their carriage at night, warm and lax from lovemaking, he told her more about his past...things, he confided, that he'd never told anyone. Hearing about his mama's slow descent into madness and his painful visits to Bedlam brought tears to Fancy's eyes.

But there were good stories, too. Memories of the French songs his *maman* had sung to him, the way she could set a table to look pretty, even if the flowers in the chipped vase had been discards from the market, the tablecloth an old patched bedsheet. As it turned out, his *maman* had been a good cook, and when she had the money, she would splurge and buy the ingredients to make his favorite almond cakes (Fancy made a mental note to try her hand at recreating the recipe). Fancy was more convinced than ever of his mother's strength and love. When she told him so, he gave a gruff nod and crushed her against him.

She also shared the story of her mother and the ironstone dishes, and the important lesson she had learned.

"For most of my life, I've made do with what has been given to me. I'm good at mending and patching things up, but rarely have I asked for what I wanted," she admitted. "Even though I knew that I loved you early on, I was afraid to tell you. To ask for your love in return. I should have stood up for my dreams instead of running away. So I am at fault as well."

"The fault is entirely mine for being an idiot. As to the rest, I *want* to know what you want," he said intently. "What you think and feel, your heart's desires. Everything that is in my power to give you, Fancy...it's yours. You need only ask."

The love blazing in his eyes warmed her. Emboldened her. Running her fingertips down the stacked muscles of his torso, she circled his cock. He instantly hardened in her grip.

"As a matter of fact, there *is* something I desire," she said, batting her lashes.

His lips curved in a slow, sensual smile. "Let us hope it is in my power to give it to you...again."

Which, of course, it was. Again *and* again.

Another evening, Knight told her about Imogen's abuse at the hands of her husband. Fancy's lingering resentment toward Imogen gave way to a swell of empathy.

"How dreadful," she said.

Knight nodded. "I think that was the real reason she approached me at the soiree. She needed someone to talk to, but she couldn't bring herself to voice her unhappiness and kissed me instead. When I set her aside, she broke down and showed me the bruises beneath her necklace."

Fancy's heart hurt for Imogen. She had always thought the lady looked fragile, on the verge of tears. She'd attributed that to Imogen's unrequited love for Knight, but maybe what the lady really wanted was protection from brutality that no woman should have to face.

"Poor Imogen," she said softly.

"That is why I couldn't leave her that night," Knight said. "No woman should suffer at the hands of her husband."

"Of course you couldn't abandon her," Fancy said. "No man of honor would."

The lines around his eyes eased. "At the same time, I didn't want to interfere where it was not my place. I convinced her to talk to her kin, and I accompanied her as a friend."

"How did it go?" Fancy asked.

"Her brother is handling the matter. If he needs help, he knows where to find me."

"I am glad Imogen is safe," she said sincerely.

"So am I." Knight cupped her jaw, his gaze fierce. "You are the only woman in my heart, the only one who has ever possessed me body and soul. You know that, don't you?"

"I do now," she whispered.

Because she finally did.

∽

On the day of departure, Fancy hugged her brothers and father goodbye. It wasn't too sad of a farewell since they had promised to spend winter in London with her and Knight.

"You take good care of me girl," Da said to Knight. "Keep an eye on 'er even if that business with the madwoman be over."

She'd told her family about Anna Smith. Knight had also spoken with Da, assuring the other that the woman was secure and would pose no further threat.

"I will, sir," Knight said gravely.

"You, me Fancy, be a good wife and 'elpmate, you 'ear?"

"Yes, Da." She kissed his cheek above his beard.

Da patted Bertrand on the neck. "And you, me sweet donkey, you were a good friend, bringing me Fancy's 'usband back to 'er. I can count on you to keep looking after the two o' them, can't I?"

Swishing his tail, Bertrand nodded and pulled his lips back in a toothy grin.

38

"Go to work," Fancy told her husband the morning after they returned to London.

"I would rather stay with you," he murmured into her ear. "I want to keep you in bed all day and pleasure you until you're hoarse from crying my name. Then I would start all over again."

Something, she knew from experience, that he was perfectly capable of doing.

"You're supposed to meet with Mr. Bodin today. And Jonas is chomping at the bit to see the new Jacquard device." She shivered when he licked her ear. "Stop that, or you'll be late."

"If I must." His exaggerated sigh made her giggle. "I'll save my wicked plans for you until tonight."

He gave her one last lingering kiss before heading out.

She spent the morning with Toby and Eleanor, catching up on Toby's breed choices for his puppy and discussing the latest cause Eleanor had adopted. At lunch, she chatted with Cecily and Aunt Esther about the gentlemen who'd come to call upon Cecily since Maggie's ball, all of whom Esther declared to be eligible *parti*. Afterward, while Esther and Cecily went to Madame Rousseau's, Fancy decided to stay home to write a long overdue letter to Bea.

Writing was still a laborious effort. Fancy was working out a crick in her neck, when Gemma came in with a pot of tea.

"Pardon, Your Grace, but you look like you could use a break," the maid said with a cheery smile. "Perhaps a quick stroll around the square? It's a lovely day."

"What a marvelous idea," Fancy agreed.

Gemma fetched her pelisse and parasol, and they headed out. The sunshine and crisp autumn air was a welcome change. They turned a corner onto a quiet street, Fancy so engrossed in chatting that she almost didn't notice the door of a parked carriage swinging open into their path. She yanked Gemma out of harm's way in the nick of time. Whirling to tell the offender to pay better mind to pedestrians, she found herself staring into sinister eyes, an instant before a handkerchief was shoved into her face.

A sweet scent filled her nostrils and lungs, choking off her shocked cry. She was pushed forward and landed with a hard thud on the carriage floor. The door slammed behind her. The world swayed, dissolving into darkness.

∼

Severin, Bodin, and Jonas were examining the new Jacquard loom that had been set up in a separate room of the manufactory. Severin was showing the other two how the punched cards suspended above the machine controlled the pattern of the weave when his secretary interrupted them.

"There are two gentlemen to see you, Your Grace," Potts said. "Misters Harry and Ambrose Kent."

Ambrose Kent, the investigator Severin had hired, must have information about Dr. Erlenmeyer.

With stirring unease, Severin wiped his hands on a cloth, saying to Bodin and Jonas, "You'll have to carry on without me."

"Take your time." Bodin's fascinated gaze was glued to the machine. "Plenty to keep us occupied 'ere."

Severin went to his office, greeting both his visitors. He'd had a previous meeting with Ambrose Kent to discuss his case, and seeing the Kent brothers together made the family resemblance obvious. Ambrose Kent was a tall, lanky man with silver at the temples and a distinguished air. His superbly tailored clothing proclaimed him a gentleman of means, yet the keenness of his amber gaze conveyed that he was no man of leisure.

"I presume you have news concerning Dr. Erlenmeyer?" Severin said after they were seated.

"Indeed. Compiling information on Dr. Erlenmeyer took longer than I expected." Ambrose Kent took out a leather-bound notebook, flipping it open to a page of notes. "It appears the doctor took some effort to cover up his past."

Severin's gut chilled. This was not a good sign.

"Eight years ago, Dr. Karl Erlenmeyer arrived in London as a graduate of the prestigious University of Vienna," Ambrose Kent said. "Having worked in several asylums in Austria, he secured a position at Bedlam and was there for approximately three years before he was let go."

"Why was he sacked?" Severin asked tersely.

"According to the attendants I interviewed, some of Dr. Erlenmeyer's treatments were less than humane." Kent's expression was grim. "His use of restraints, isolation, and extreme temperatures to 'drive out the madness' worsened the condition of some of his patients, including two who took their own lives while under his care."

"Christ," Harry Kent muttered.

The memory of his *maman*'s mistreatment chilled Severin's veins. "What happened next?"

"Erlenmeyer landed himself his present position as the head of Brookfield Asylum, where he's been for the last five years. When I tried to make inquiries into his current treatment techniques, the employees of the Asylum were tight-lipped as if they feared repercussions."

"What about Anna Smith?" Severin asked. "Did you find out anything about her?"

"On conditions of anonymity, one attendant confided to me that when Miss Smith was first brought in over a month ago, she was ranting that her real name wasn't Anna Smith but Rosamund Becker. The attendant said that she was clearly delusional, babbling about being the royal midwife."

Severin tensed. "A month ago? Erlenmeyer told me that Smith —or Becker—was a long-time patient. That this was not the only instance when she'd had delusions and attacked an innocent bystander."

"That is an odd discrepancy from the attendant's report," Ambrose Kent said, frowning.

"What I find equally odd," Harry mused, "is that a man with Erlenmeyer's history of inhumane and failed treatments was able to secure a position as the head of a private asylum."

"I was curious about that as well," his brother replied. "Thus, I did some digging into the financials behind Brookfield and discovered that most of the funding comes from a group of wealthy patrons. One of the patrons is Lord Snowden, whose wife happens to be a friend of my wife, Marianne. Marianne got me in to see Snowden, and he told me in private that he is no fan of Dr. Erlenmeyer...that, indeed, several of the patrons questioned the fellow's practices. But apparently Erlenmeyer has the backing of the most influential donor."

"Who is that?" Severin demanded.

"Princess Adelaide. She is the sister of the King of—"

"Hessenstein." Severin didn't like the coincidence of Princess Adelaide, who'd befriended Fancy, being involved in this tangled web. "Why would she back an Austrian mad-doctor?"

"Erlenmeyer is not Austrian by birth; he was born in the Principality of Hessenstein. It is apparently a custom of Hessenstein royalty to become patrons of commoners, a practice that has led to some scandal."

"Scandal?"

"Snowden mentioned that the reason Princess Adelaide resides in London is because she fell out of favor with her brother Ernst, the King of Hessenstein. King Ernst apparently broke royal protocol by falling in love with a commoner he was sponsoring. She was a dressmaker or something along those lines. Anyway, the king married the woman, against the wishes of his royal family—especially Princess Adelaide, who made her feelings known. He brought his new wife to London whilst she was carrying their first child, but something went wrong, and she and the child perished. Grief-stricken, King Ernst went back to Hessenstein, but Princess Adelaide stayed in London—some say because her brother forbade her return. Her son, Ruprecht, lives with the king as he is now the heir apparent to the throne."

With thundering dread, Severin asked, "How long ago did this happen?"

Kent consulted his notes. "Some twenty-three years ago… What is the matter, Your Grace?"

Panic had propelled Severin to his feet. "I think my wife may be the heir to the Hessenstein crown—which means she's in grave danger. I have to find her, and I need your help."

"Whatever you need," Harry said.

"I want eyes on Adelaide and Erlenmeyer straightaway. Find them and don't let either of them out of your sight. My men can go with you—"

"I've got it. And I'll get additional reinforcements." Harry gave a grim nod. "Go to Fancy."

Severin was already racing out the door.

39

Awakening from a nightmare, Fancy blinked groggily. Had she been sleepwalking? She didn't recognize the dimly lit room with it sagging ceiling and wilting wallpaper. The light was coming in from—she squinted—a boarded-up window. Footsteps sounded, and she whipped her head in that direction, a door opening...

"You are awake." Princess Adelaide entered. "That took longer than I anticipated."

Floorboards creaked as the princess, wearing a military-inspired dress, marched toward her.

"Your H-highness?" Fancy stammered. "What are you...wh-where am I?"

She tried to move; to her shock, she found that she was bound to a chair. Rope circled her arms and legs, securing her to the wooden frame. Her gaze flew to Princess Adelaide, who seated herself at a nearby table.

"You are my guest, Francesca," she said silkily. "Or should I say *Princess* Francesca."

Fancy stared at the princess's hooded black eyes. Was the

woman mad? Then the princess's words touched a nerve of memory. Anna Smith had said, *Your Highness...I must speak to you.*

"I don't understand." Fancy shook her head, willing herself to wake up from this terrible dream. "None of this makes sense."

"Since we are waiting for my final guest to arrive, I see no harm in elucidating you, my dear." Princess Adelaide fixed a predatory gaze upon her. "You are my niece. The daughter of my brother, King Ernst III of Hessenstein."

Shock saturated Fancy. "How is that possible?"

"Through betrayal." Adelaide shook her head, looking disappointed. "I had a perfect plan, and it was foiled by a mere servant."

"I don't understand—"

"If you shut up and listen, you will." Adelaide's eyes slitted, her tone dripping with venom.

She's mad...and she hates me. I shouldn't rile her up more.

Tamping down her fear, Fancy nodded, playing along.

"It all began when my brother was seduced by a woman named Louisa. It is a custom of the Royal House of Hessenstein to give promising commoners our patronage, and Ernst chose Louisa, an apprentice dressmaker, out of the pool that year. The stupid fool lost his head and fell in love with her," Adelaide said with disgust. "If he had just kept her as his mistress, then everything would have been fine, but he got it into his head that he wanted to marry her. Nothing I—or any of his court advisors—said could sway him. He was bound and determined to wed for love. Three hundred years of noble lineage destroyed because he had to wed that *nobody*. Mere months later, she was with child."

Despite the danger, Fancy's heart gave a small flutter at the romantic story.

"We were scheduled to visit London that summer," Adelaide went on. "The goal was to strengthen ties with our distant cousin, the King of England. But Louisa managed to ruin that important political mission with her miserable pregnancy. She was constantly ill, unable to make any official appearances, and my milksop of a brother insisted on remaining by her side instead of paying court to the king as was his duty. I was beside myself, watching the fortunes of my beloved country disintegrate because of that whore. I knew I had to do something."

Trepidation slithered through Fancy. "What did you do?"

"I obtained some herbs from the midwife and put them in Louisa's tea." Adelaide's mouth took on a crafty curve. "That night, Louisa went into premature labor and gave birth to a stillborn boy. I thought my mission was accomplished. Imagine my shock when, as she lay there, her life draining out of her, she delivered yet another babe. Worst of all, this tiny, fragile creature was *breathing*...and the only thing standing between my son and the throne of Hessenstein. In my country, female descendants can inherit the throne, and you would precede my son in the line of succession. I knew what I had to do.

"I instructed the midwife to get rid of you. She was supposed to smother you, dispose of your body as if you never existed. In the meantime, I consoled my brother over his dead son and his dead wife. Little did I know that the midwife betrayed me."

Fancy could barely speak through her horror. Adelaide showed no remorse as she spoke of her crimes, the blood stained upon her hands. Anger rose in a silent tide, clearing Fancy's head. Adelaide had murdered her mother and twin brother; she would not be a third victim. She had to buy time, keep Adelaide talking, for surely Knight would be searching for her by now.

"The midwife...was she Anna Smith?" Fancy asked calmly.

"Very good," Adelaide said. "Her real name is Rosamund Becker. She travelled with us from Hessenstein and was the one who gave me the herbs. I told her it was for one of my maids who'd found herself in an unfortunate way. When Rosamund realized that the herbs had found their way into the queen's tea, she was horrified. I told her that if she didn't do my bidding and get rid of the remaining twin, I would tell my brother that she was responsible for Louisa and his heir's death. I thought I had her under my thumb, especially since I believed she'd killed you too. Then I saw you that day at Madame Rousseau's and thought you were a ghost: that is how much you resemble Louisa, down to that wanton beauty mark above your lip."

Masking her fury, Fancy said, "You were certain that I was the babe you'd had murdered?"

"When you told me you were a foundling, I had no doubt. Just in case, I hunted down Rosamund. She had changed her name to Anna Smith and was living in this hovel on the outskirts of Camden Town. She broke down, confirming that she'd left you in a field. I would have killed her but my instincts told me to keep her alive. I realized that she might have other uses, particularly after your "accidental" death by bricks didn't work out as planned. Rosamund became a guest at the asylum run by Dr. Erlenmeyer, a protégé of mine, but then the wily bitch escaped. Dr. Erlenmeyer caught her just in time and put into play my final stratagem."

"You're going to blame her for my death," Fancy reasoned.

"You really are cleverer than you look." Adelaide's smile was as thin as a razor. "Your husband believes that Anna Smith has already tried to kill you once. How difficult will it be to convince him that she succeeded the second time?"

"Knight is going to find me," Fancy said fiercely. "Then you will pay."

"I don't think so, my dear. Dusk is falling, and Dr. Erlenmeyer will soon arrive with Rosamund. When your husband finds you, you will be dead in her old cottage, the pistol that killed you in her hand. He will find Anna Smith's crazed note, which will detail how she had completed her last mission: to assassinate you." Princess Adelaide's eyes glinted with terrifying satisfaction. "And since she, too, will be dead, the truth will die with her."

"You are sure Erlenmeyer is in there?" Severin said tightly.

Through a crack in the carriage curtains, he watched the back gates of Brookfield Asylum. Harry Kent had joined him in his carriage; Tessa Kent, Garrity, and Ransom were monitoring the other exits of the building.

"I'm certain," Kent said. "I went in there and asked for him."

"That didn't tip him off?"

"I had a convincing cover. Told him my father-in-law had bats in his belfry and I needed a place to put him. Erlenmeyer gave me a tour; he was quite proud of his treatment devices." Kent shuddered. "The bastard has a screw loose, that's for certain."

"Just as long as he has sufficient wits to lead me to Fancy," Severin said starkly.

His gut churned with fear, had been doing so since he'd discovered Fancy missing. According to her maid Gemma, she'd gone out for a walk alone and hadn't returned...which didn't make sense. Panic had swamped him, a certainty that something had befallen his wife.

Then he'd received the message from Kent, who had enlisted their other friends to help. Ransom and his wife Maggie had called upon Adelaide on the pretense of making a social call. The princess's butler had informed the duke and duchess that his mistress was not at home. During this distraction, one of Kent's men had gone in the back, verifying that the princess's carriage was indeed gone.

Severin had men combing the city now for Fancy and Princess Adelaide, his search abetted by Kent and Garrity's forces. Yet his instincts told him that his best chances of locating his wife now lay with Erlenmeyer. At first, he'd wanted to charge in and beat the truth out of the doctor, but Kent and Garrity had convinced him to bide his time and wait for Erlenmeyer to make a move. They'd reasoned that they had no solid proof of the doctor's complicity. If Erlenmeyer refused to talk—and his close relationship with Adelaide made that a high probability—then they would be wasting precious time with Fancy's life hanging in the balance.

Moreover, the waiting horse and wagon they had found tied up just beyond the back gates suggested that a journey would be made soon. Severin's knuckles cracked beneath their covering of dark leather. If that bastard Erlenmeyer didn't show himself within a few minutes, Severin was going to charge in and do whatever was necessary to make the man talk.

The back gate opened. The last rays of daylight revealed that it was Erlenmeyer. The doctor was pushing a patient in a wheeled chair: Anna Smith, her lolling head betraying her drugged state. Erlenmeyer heaved Smith into the back of the waiting wagon as if she were a sack of bricks, throwing a cover over her.

Then he climbed onto the driver's seat, and the wagon began to move.

Severin sent a man to alert the other teams.

"Follow him at a distance," Severin instructed his driver. "Don't let that wagon out of your sight."

∼

Adelaide left Fancy in the room, her voice carrying clearly from outside the door.

"If she makes any trouble, kill her."

A chilled droplet slid down Fancy's spine as she heard the affirmative replies of the princess's guards. One false move and she knew the men would not hesitate to snuff her out like a candle.

Which means...I cannot make a false move.

Her heart pounding in her ears, she pulled on her bonds. It was no use; her arms were tied to the arms of the chair and her torso was secured to the chair's back. If she tipped herself backward and landed hard enough, she might be able to crack the wood and break free...but the noise would alert the guards.

Think, Fancy. This is a problem like any other. How do you fix it?

What she needed was...a friend.

A tinker's friend.

She jiggled her leg—and her heart thumped with relief when she felt the reassuring bump of the tool against her right thigh. The width and layers of her skirts had hidden it from Princess Adelaide. She began wriggling her right leg. As she strained against the bonds, she realized that the tightness was around her ankle, over her half-boots. If she could just slip her foot out of the boot...

Gritting her teeth, she twisted her foot this way and that, and finally it popped free. Trying not to make noise, she lifted her freed leg, trying to get it to her bound right hand. She strained her hip to the side until she could grab hold of her skirts.

Almost there.

She inched her fingers closer and closer toward the hidden pocket. She got her hand into the pocket, but the tinker's friend was too deep inside. Sweating, she raised her leg upward as far as she could, felt the shifting gravity of the tool sliding down, down...

It hit her palm, and she closed her fingers around it.

Thank you, Da, for giving me a tinker's best friend.

She managed to open the knife, orienting the blade against her bonds. She shifted her hand back and forth, rubbing the rope against the sharp edge, sawing through the rough fibers. When the rope split, she grabbed the tool with her freed hand and dispensed with the rest of her restraints.

Her triumph was measured: she still had to escape her prison. She couldn't get past the guards shuffling outside the door. The only other way out was the boarded-up window.

Taking off her other boot, she carried her footwear with her to minimize any noise. A floorboard creaked, shooting her heart into her throat, but when no guard came charging in, she exhaled, continuing on. The distance to the window felt like a mile. Arriving, she examined the barrier to her escape.

Six boards were nailed into the windowpane, two nails on each side of the board. It would take a while to remove the nails...and even longer to do it quietly. What other choice did she have? Using her tinker's friend, she set to work prying the metal pegs free. The boards were thinner than she expected, the nails coming out easily. She popped them out one by one, catching them soundlessly in her sweaty palm.

When the last nail was out of the first board, she lowered it a fraction and peered out into the starlit darkness. It appeared that this was the back of the cottage and, luckily, she saw no guards. A dark shape loomed in the distance...a fence? Once she got out of the house, she would scale it and run for help.

Precious minutes passed as she removed two more boards. The opening she'd made was tight, but she could squeeze through if she shed her outer garments. With a silent apology to Amelie Rousseau, she ruthlessly cut off her clothes, layer after layer of fabric whispering to the ground. Clad in a corset, shift, and drawers, she put her boots back on and launched herself through the opening.

It was a tight fit, but survival was the ultimate motivator. Clenching her jaw, she ignored the harsh scrape of wood against her bare arms and pushed herself through, dropping to the ground on the other side. She got up, and an arm hooked her around the waist, pulling her back against a wall of muscle, a hand muffling her scream.

40

"Fancy, it's me."

Hearing Knight's voice, she felt relief pour through her. He turned her to face him, scanning her with fierce eyes.

"Are you all right, love?" His gaze dropped to her undergarments, ripped during her hasty exit out the window, and rage flared in those grey depths. "If they laid a finger on you—"

"They didn't," she said in hushed tones. "I took off my clothes so that I could fit through the window. No one hurt me. Well, except Adelaide. She drugged me and carted me off. How did you find me?"

Knight had taken off his jacket and was wrapping it around her shoulders. "Time for that later. For now, I want you to go with Garrity while I take care of Adelaide."

It was only then that Fancy noticed the group standing behind her husband. The shadowy figures included Mr. Garrity, Mr. Kent, Ransom, and a small army of guards.

She nodded at the men, then said anxiously to Knight, "Be careful. She has armed men."

He took out a pistol, holding it with lethal confidence. "I'll be right back. And Fancy?"

"Yes?"

His eyes blazed brighter than the stars. "I love you. More than anything."

"I love you," she whispered back, but he was already leading the charge, the others fanning out behind him.

"This way to the carriage, Your Grace," Mr. Garrity said.

Gabby's husband always looked dangerous, but with his pistol drawn and dark gaze pitiless, he looked more menacing than usual. In this instance, Fancy was glad for it. He, along with his own group of men, led her through the fence to a cluster of carriages. He assisted Fancy into one of them, and she was surprised to see her waiting friend.

"Tessa!" She hugged the petite lady before sitting beside her. "What are you doing here?"

"Aiding in your rescue, of course," Tessa said.

"Thank you," she replied tremulously.

"I couldn't let Harry have all the fun. Gabby and Maggie wanted to come too, but,"—Tessa wrinkled her nose—"their husbands aren't as modern as mine."

Garrity, still holding his firearm on the opposite bench, flicked a glance at the two women.

"Gabriella asked her old-fashioned husband to pass on a message, Your Grace," he said dryly. "She plans to pay you a visit tomorrow. Early."

"Do you think the men are all right?" Fancy fretted. "The princess's guards—"

"Are no match for the dukes and duchess of the underworld," Tessa said with reassuring conviction. "This is hardly our first battle. The men will be back before you know it—"

A blast cut her off, the carriage swaying.

Fear clutched Fancy's heart. "What was that?"

"One of Harry's toys," Tessa said blithely. "He's forever tinkering with explosives. I'm just glad he does it now at the laboratories of Great London National Railway rather than at our home."

"We're still rebuilding the last warehouse Kent destroyed," Garrity muttered.

Tessa looked at Fancy. "Why are you in your undergarments?"

Realizing that Knight's jacket was hanging open, Fancy hastily buttoned it up. "I had to escape out a window, and it was easier to do it without all the layers."

Tessa gave a sage nod. "I had to make a similar escape once—"

The door opened, revealing Knight and the other men. Fancy flew toward her husband, and he caught her, lifting her out of the carriage and crushing her against his chest.

"What happened?" she managed.

"We have Adelaide in custody." His arms still surrounding her, Knight looked into her eyes. "She will answer for her crimes, as will her accomplices Erlenmeyer and, I'm sorry to say, your maid Gemma. Then there is Anna Smith, whose real name is Rosamund Becker. She was—"

"My mama's midwife. Yes, I know," Fancy said. "Adelaide told me everything."

Knight studied her. "You do know what that means, don't you, love?"

Given the danger, Fancy hadn't fully contemplated the implications, but now she did.

"My father—my other one, that is—is still alive," she said in wonder. "I have more family."

"That too." Knight's lips twitched. "What I meant was that you are a princess and the heir to the Hessenstein throne. You always wanted a faerie tale ending, and I cannot think of a better one than that."

"I can." Smiling up at her husband, Fancy said, "The one you gave me."

Knight's eyes smoldered with emotion. "Tinker's daughter or king's daughter, I love you, Fancy. Now and forever."

He kissed her, and her heart sang with the sweetness of their happily ever after.

EPILOGUE

A FEW MONTHS LATER

"Knight," his wife gasped. "That's so *deep*."

Severin dug his fingers into her silky-smooth bottom as he drove his hips harder.

"You can take it, love," he grunted. "Keep playing with your pearl. I want to feel you come around my cock."

Fancy moaned, her fingers rubbing her love-knot as he plowed her pretty pink furrow from behind. Her hips were draped over a pillow, her cheek pressed against the mattress, her lips parted. She was wanton and real, everything he wanted, and she was his.

Sometimes he couldn't believe it. Sometimes he feared how much he loved her, how losing her would destroy his reason for living. Mostly, though, he just thanked the lucky stars that had given him his Fancy.

She closed her eyes, biting her lip, tell-tale signs that she was close. His duchess liked being tupped this way despite that one despicable time he'd used this position to avoid confronting his feelings. Now it was a regular pose in their bedchamber rotation, and he always made sure to end it the same way.

"Look at me, *chérie*," he panted.

Her lashes lifted, and she gifted him with her beautiful brown eyes. In them, he saw his own devotion reflected, and that was enough to put him over the edge. Luckily, she flew over too, and they came together, their gazes connected, shuddering in the throes of love.

Afterward, he cuddled her in the firelight.

"We should get some rest," he murmured. "We're leaving early in the morning."

Tomorrow they would be embarking on their journey to Hessenstein. Fancy had been corresponding with King Ernst, who desperately wanted to meet his daughter. His sister had confessed to her crimes and would spend the rest of her life in prison. King Ernst had struck her son from the line of succession, declaring his intention to officially recognize Fancy as the Crown Princess of Hessenstein.

"I don't know if I can sleep," Fancy admitted. "I'm too excited."

Severin stroked her hair. "About meeting your father?"

"That too." She tipped her head to look at him. "I asked the physician to come by this morning."

His fingers stilled, tangling in her silky tresses. "And?"

"I'm increasing." Her eyes shone with exuberance. "We are going to have a baby."

"Fancy, my love." He rolled her onto her back and ran an unsteady hand over her flat belly. "How are you feeling? Should you be going on a ship tomorrow? Christ, was I too rough—"

She took his face between her hands. "Knight, stop fretting. The physician said I am perfectly healthy and fine to travel. And marital activities will not hurt the babe."

He looked into Fancy's smiling face, and his chest clenched with joy. With the recognition of all she had given him. With the knowledge that, whatever the future held, their love would see them through.

He leaned down and kissed her with all that he felt.

After a while, his wife giggled. "I thought you were tired?"

"We can sleep on the ship," he decided and took her lips once more.

∼

THE PRINCIPALITY OF HESSENSTEIN, A FEW YEARS LATER

"Your Royal Majesty." Bea's lavender eyes sparkled as she curtsied. "May I congratulate you on your coronation?"

"Thank you for coming, Bea." Abandoning protocol, Fancy hugged her best friend. "I am just glad I made it through the ceremony."

They were in the castle's grand receiving room, and Fancy had just come from the coronation ceremony, which had taken the entire day. The Royal Abbey had been sweltering. If her husband hadn't had the foresight to have a flask of iced water on hand, she might have fainted in her fur-lined robes and jewel-studded crown. Somehow she had muddled through and managed to give a speech in Hessensteinish, her first as Queen Fancy I.

Her fears that she would not live up to her new responsibilities had been drowned out by the cheering crowds that lined the streets from the Abbey to the castle. It seemed Hessenstein's citizens welcomed having a queen with commoner's roots. The people also adored Knight, who had spearheaded technological advancements that brought new jobs and wealth to the principality. King Ernst had been so impressed by his son-in-law's work that he had made Knight a prince.

With a bittersweet pang, Fancy thought Ernst must be smiling proudly down at her from Heaven. Although they had lost so many years, she and her father had made the most of the ones they'd had. Ernst had lived to meet his three grandchildren, and he had spoiled them shamelessly.

Now Fancy had a small respite in this intimate reception with friends and family. Afterward, she and Knight would honor a three-hundred-year-old tradition and step out onto the castle's balcony to wave at their new subjects.

Fancy let out a squeal of unqueenlike delight when she saw Tessa, Gabby, and Maggie heading toward her and Bea. She hugged the women as she accepted their felicitations, touched but not surprised that they had made the long journey to her new home. That was what friends were for, after all. In the past few years, the five of them had celebrated countless milestones together, including the births of their children who were at present being corralled in the adjoining room by a team of palace nannies.

"Your gown is ravishing, Your Majesty," Gabby said. "The embroidery is ever so exquisite."

Made of white silk, Fancy's coronation dress was embroidered with hundreds of alpine roses, which weren't roses at all but a hardy species of rhododendron that grew in the mountains of Hessenstein. She ran her fingertips over one of the flowers, the center sewn with beads of pure gold, and thought of her mother Louisa, who she later discovered had stitched that first bloom on her christening gown.

"Thank you," she said, smiling. "And thank you for coming all this way."

"We wouldn't miss this for the world," Tessa said with a wink. "Coronations are important."

Tessa would know, for not long ago her grandfather had stepped down as King of the Underworld, and she had been chosen as its new ruler.

"Heavens, we have two queens amongst us," Maggie said with a laugh. "I do not know if I belong with such a rarefied group."

"You belong. We all do," Fancy said happily.

Looking around the room, she saw the people she loved, the motley bunch who meant the world to her. Her older brothers and their wives were helping their children to the buffet, her younger brothers helping themselves. Da was chatting with Aunt Esther, pausing to catch Fancy's youngest son, Louis, who had, as usual, escaped his nannies. Da swung Louis up on his shoulders, the little prince chortling with delight.

By the champagne fountain, Toby was impressing a Flemish princess with tricks he had taught his spaniel. Eleanor, who had bloomed into a pretty young lady, was ignoring a group of noblemen and trying to read the book she had hidden in her skirts. Cecily was *not* ignoring her beaux, of which she had many. Jonas stood with a group of prominent Hessenstein industrialists, expounding, no doubt, upon the technological innovations in which he had taken so much interest since Knight had put him in charge of the weaving business.

Speaking of Knight, where was he?

Fancy was scanning the room when her husband came toward her, a commanding, princely figure in formal court dress. He greeted the ladies, and even after the years of marriage, Fancy tingled when he put an arm around her waist and kissed her temple.

"I was just looking for you," she told him.

A smile glinted in his eyes. "I was preparing a surprise, sweeting."

"What surprise?"

"Come and you'll see."

Knight led her by the hand, her smiling friends following in tow. He took her to a covered easel placed next to the official royal portrait. Framed in gilt, the portrait on the wall showed their family in a perfect, majestic pose. While Fancy knew it was a beautiful work of art, she couldn't help but think it was a tad unrealistic.

She was sitting serenely, not a hair out of place. A clean, calm

Louis reposed upon her lap. She was flanked by her twins: Ernst Milton, the elder by ten minutes, was to her right, Madeleine Anne to her left. Ernst and Maddy looked like little saints, their grey eyes glowing with boundless goodwill. To Fancy's mind, the only one who looked true to life was Knight, who stood proudly and protectively behind her and their progeny.

A bell was rung, the guests gathering around. The children came in too, and the twins raced toward Fancy, who bent to receive their sweet kisses...and hear the grievances they each had about the other. Maddy and Ernst were the best of friends and most determined of rivals. Not to be left out, Louis raced into the mix, nearly toppling Fancy in his enthusiasm.

A look from Knight and the children settled for the time being.

"Dearest friends and family," Knight said in his deep voice. "Thank you for your presence at Her Majesty's special day and in our lives. I have a small gift to honor the occasion, which I think you will appreciate. Without further ado, I present the unofficial royal portrait."

He whipped the cover off the easel, revealing another painting.

Fancy burst out laughing, as did the rest of the room.

Done by the same artist, the glowing oils this time showed what had actually happened during the sitting. Fancy's crown sat a bit askew, her lips pursed as she tried to keep a wriggling, cake-smudged Louis upon her lap. Maddy and Ernst were facing off in an argument, their small fists at their hips. Knight stood behind them all, protective and rolling his eyes.

"What do you think of the portrait, *chérie?*" he asked when her giggles had subsided.

"I think it is perfect," she said, smiling.

"Did you see what I named it?"

He pointed to the inscription on the gilt frame, and her heart swelled with emotion.

Happily Ever After.

Yes, it was.

She lifted her lips, and her prince kissed her. The perfection of their love flowed through her. And she knew that all her dreams had come true.

AUTHOR'S NOTE

The Jacquard mechanism was patented by French weaver and merchant Joseph-Marie Jacquard in 1804[1]. This machine was built upon previous developments by inventor Jacques de Vaucanson and others. The significance of the Jacquard mechanism was that it allowed for the automation of pattern weaving. Punch cards, rather than a person, controlled the warp threads that dictated the weave of the fabric. As a result, patterns of increasing complexity could be manufactured more quickly and cheaply.

By the 1820's, Jacquard mechanisms were in use throughout Britain. Since my story is set in 1840, Knight would have been on the slower side to adopt the new technology, so I finessed it by saying that he was waiting for the best version of the device before making the switch. As a technology turtle myself, I can understand his cautious approach.

The punch cards used in the Jacquard looms might have brought to mind those used by computers not so long ago. This is no coincidence. Indeed, the Jacquard loom may be considered an ancestor of computer technology as it used a pattern of instructions to automate operations previously done by hand.

NOTES

AUTHOR'S NOTE

1. https://www.scienceandindustrymuseum.org.uk/objects-and-stories/jacquard-loom

ABOUT THE AUTHOR

USA Today & International Bestselling Author Grace Callaway writes hot and heart-melting historical romances. Her debut book, *Her Husband's Harlot*, was a Romance Writers of America Golden Heart® Finalist and a #1 Regency Bestseller, and her subsequent novels have topped national and international bestselling lists. She's the winner of the Daphne du Maurier Award for Excellence in Mystery/Suspense and the Passionate Plume Award for Historical Novel. Her books have also been shortlisted for numerous awards, including the National Reader's Choice Awards, the Maggie Award of Excellence, and the National Excellence in Romance Fiction Award.

Growing up on the Canadian prairies, Grace could often be found with her nose in a book—and not much has changed since. She set aside her favorite romance novels long enough to get her doctorate from the University of Michigan. A clinical psychologist, she lives with her family in Northern California, where their adventures include remodeling a ramshackle house, exploring the great outdoors, and sampling local artisanal goodies.

Keep up with my latest news!
Newsletter: gracecallaway.com/newsletter

- facebook.com/GraceCallawayBooks
- bookbub.com/authors/grace-callaway
- instagram.com/gracecallawaybooks
- amazon.com/author/gracecallaway

ACKNOWLEDGMENTS

This book helped me through some challenging times, and my fondest wish is that Fancy and Knight's story will bring that same sense of joy, hope, and renewed belief in happily ever after to my readers. Now, more than ever, we need to draw strength from love.

Thank you to my readers for supporting my journey. I appreciate you more than I can say. From one romance novel lover to another: never stop believing in happy endings. The world needs us.

Thank you to my editor Ronnie Nelson for always bringing out the best in my characters and in my writing. You have saved my bacon more than once. My appreciation always.

To my writing pals who kept me sane and inspired me through video conferencing and texting...girls, I couldn't have written this book without you. Hugs.

And to my family. We've been through some crazy times, but I am glad we are at this interminable house party together. Love you.

PAMUNKEY REGIONAL LIBRARY
PO BOX 119
HANOVER, VA 23069

JUL 2020

Made in the USA
Monee, IL
04 July 2020